PENGUIN BOOKS

# The Last Four Things

Paul Hoffman is the author of four other novels: *The Beating of His Wings* (2013); *The Left Hand of God* (2010); *The Golden Age of Censorship* (2007), a black comedy based on his experiences as a film censor; and *The Wisdom of Crocodiles* (2000), which predicted the collapse of the world financial system.

# The Last Four Things

PAUL HOFFMAN

PENGUIN BOOKS

## PENGUIN BOOKS

Published by the Penguin Group
Penguin Books Ltd, 80 Strand, London WC2R ORL, England
Penguin Group (USA), Inc., 375 Hudson Street, New York, New York 10014, USA
Penguin Group (Canada), 90 Eglinton Avenue East, Suite 700, Toronto, Ontario, Canada M4P 2Y3
(a division of Pearson Penguin Canada Inc.)
Penguin Ireland, 25 St Stephen's Green, Dublin 2, Ireland (a division of Penguin Books Ltd)
Penguin Group (Australia), 707 Collins Street, Melbourne, Victoria 3008, Australia
(a division of Pearson Australia Group Pty Ltd)
Penguin Books India Pvt Ltd, 11 Community Centre, Panchsheel Park, New Delhi – 110 017, India
Penguin Group (NZ), 67 Apollo Drive, Rosedale, Auckland 0632, New Zealand
(a division of Pearson New Zealand Ltd)
Penguin Books (South Africa) (Pty) Ltd, Block D, Rosebank Office Park,
181 Jan Smuts Avenue, Parktown North, Gauteng 2193, South Africa

Penguin Books Ltd, Registered Offices: 80 Strand, London WC2R ORL, England

www.penguin.com

First published by Michael Joseph 2011
Published in Penguin Books 2012
Re-issued in this edition 2014

002

Copyright © Paul Hoffman, 2011

Set in Garamond MT Std 12.5/13.35 pt
Typeset by Palimpsest Book Production Limited, Falkirk, Stirlingshire
Printed in Great Britain by Clays Ltd, St Ives plc

A CIP catalogue record for this book is available from the British Library

ISBN: 978-0-141-04239-8

www.greenpenguin.co.uk

For Richard Gollner

Give me a dozen healthy infants, well-formed, and my own specific world to bring them up in, and I'll guarantee to take any one at random and train him to become any type of specialist I might select – a doctor, lawyer, artist, merchant-chief and, yes, even into a beggar-man and thief, regardless of his talents, penchants, tendencies, abilities, vocations and race of his ancestors.

J. B. Watson, *Psychologies of 1925*

I fought like an angel.

Wilfred Owen

# Prologue

Imagine. A young assassin, no more than a boy really, is lying carefully hidden in the long green and black bulrushes that grow in great profusion along the rivers of the Vallombrosa. He has been waiting for a long time but he is a patient creature in his way and the thing he waits for is perhaps more precious to him than life. Beside him are a bow of yew and arrows tipped with black country steel capable of penetrating even the costliest armour if you're close enough. Not that there will be any need for that today because the young man is not waiting for some rascal deserving of his murder but only a water bird. The light thickens and the swan makes wing through the rooky wood, the cawing crows complaining bitterly at the unfairness of her beauty as she lands upon the water like the stroke of a painter's hand upon a canvas, direct and beautifully itself. She swims with all the elegance for which her kind is famous, though you will never have seen movement quite so graceful in such still and smoky air on such steeple grey water.

Then the arrow, sharp as hate, shears through the same air she blesses and misses her by several feet. And she's off, web strength along with her grace convey her whiteness back into the air and away to safety. The young man is standing now and watching the swan escape.

'I'll get you next time, you treacherous slut!' he shouts and throws down the bow, which alone of all the instruments of death (knife, sword, elbow, teeth) he has never been able to master and yet is the only one that can give him hope of restitution for his broken heart. But not even then. For though this is a dream, not even in his dreams can he hit a barn door from twenty yards. He wakes and broods for half an hour. Real life is careful of the sensitivities of desperadoes but even the greatest scourge, and Thomas Cale is certainly one of those, can be mocked with impunity in his nightmares. Then he goes back to sleep to dream again of the autumnal leaves that strewed the brooks in Vallombrosa, and the great white wings beating into swirls the early-morning mist.

'The Lay of Thomas Cale, Angel of Death' is the second worst poem ever to emerge from the Office for the Propagation of the Faith of the Hanged Redeemer. This institution subsequently became so famous for its skill in spinning the grossly untrue on behalf of the Redeemers that the phrase 'to tell a monk' passed into general usage.

### Book the Forty-Seventh: The Argument

Wake up! For sunrise in the spoon of night
Reveals the Left Hand
of the Lord of Might.
His name is Cale, his arm is strong
As the Angel of Death he does no wrong.
Searching for traitors who'll murder the Pope
Cale left the Sanctuary by means of a rope.
To protect the Pope he pretended to flee
The quiet and care of the Sanctuary
And Bosco his mentor he claimed to reject
And all for the sake of the Pope to protect.
In Memphis the city of Sodom and Vice

He rescued a princess, a maiden of ice.
With wiles and with lust his soul's ruin she sought
And when he said, 'No!' his assassins she bought.
Now long had her father conspired 'gainst the Pope
And attacked the Redeemers to further this hope
But in the great battle at Silbury Hill
With Princeps and Bosco, Cale gave them their fill.
The Empire of Memphis they wasted that day
Then Bosco and Cale they returned to the fray
The Antagonist heretics them for to slay.
For Pope and Redeemer let all of us pray!

It is a generally accepted wisdom that true events pass into history and are transformed according to the prejudices of the person recording them. History then turns slowly into legend, in which all facts are blurred despite the interest of the tellers, who will by now be many, various and contradictory. Finally, perhaps after thousands of years, all intentions, good or bad, all lies and all exactness merge into a myth of universal possibility in which anything might be true, anything false. It no longer matters, one way or the other. But the truth is that a great many things depart from the facts almost as soon as they happen and are converted into the great smog of myth almost before the sun has gone down on the events themselves. The doggerel above, for example, was written within two months of the incidents it so badly attempts to immortalize. Let us go then through this drivel verse by verse.

Thomas Cale had been brought to the grim Sanctuary of the Hanged Redeemer at the age of three or four (no one knew or cared which). As soon as he arrived the little boy was singled out by one of the priests of this most forbidding of religions, the Redeemer Bosco, mentioned three times in the poem not least because he was the man who caused it to be written. It should not be thought that this was inspired by anything so simple as human vanity or ambition.

The Redeemers were not only infamous for their harsh view of the sinful nature of mankind but even more for their willingness to enforce that view through military conquest led by their own priests, most of whom were brought up to fight rather than preach. The most intelligent and the most pious (a line more easily blurred among the Redeemers than elsewhere) were responsible for ensuring correct beliefs and the administration of the faith in all its many conquered and converted states. The rest were reserved for the armed wing of the One True Faith, the Militant, and were raised and frequently died (the lucky ones, went the joke) in numerous religious barracks, of which the largest was the Sanctuary. It was in the Sanctuary that Cale was chosen by Bosco as his personal acolyte – a form of favouritism only an inhumanly tough child could ever hope to survive. By the time he was fourteen (or fifteen) Cale was as cold and calculating a creature as you could ever have wished not to meet in a dark alley or anywhere else – and apparently animated by only two things: his utter loathing of Bosco and his indifference to everyone else. But Cale's general bad luck was about to change for the worse as he opened the wrong door at the wrong time and discovered the Lord of Discipline, Redeemer Picarbo, dissecting a young girl, still alive if only just, and about to do the same to another. Choosing self-preservation over compassion and horror, Cale shut the door quietly and left. However, in a moment of madness which he claimed forever to regret, the look in the eyes of the young woman about to be so cruelly disembowelled caused him to return and in the ensuing struggle kill a man perhaps tenth in line to the Pope himself. What you already have gathered of the Redeemers will make clear the fate Cale could expect: one that, you can be sure, involved a great deal of screaming.

If escape from the Sanctuary had been easy Cale would have already been long gone. While, as the twaddle of 'The Lay of Thomas Cale' claims, it did involve a rope there was no plot to murder the Pope – another invention of Bosco's to cover up the flight of an acolyte he had particular reason to want back, a reason that had nothing to do with whatever bizarre and revolting business Picarbo had been up to. What the poem does not mention is that Cale was accompanied by three others:

the girl he'd saved; Vague Henri, the only boy in the Sanctuary he remotely tolerated; and Kleist, who like everyone else regarded him with suspicion and dislike.

While Cale's intelligence, schooled by long training, meant that he evaded the Redeemers trying to recapture them, his habitual bad luck led to all four walking into a patrol of Materazzi cavalry out of the great city of Memphis, a place richer and more varied than any Paris or Babylon *or* Sodom, another one of the few references in the 'Lay' that has any echo of the truth about it. In Memphis the four came to the attention of its great Chancellor, Vipond, and his unreliable half-brother, IdrisPukke, who for reasons unclear to anyone, even to himself, took a shine to Cale and showed him something he had never experienced before, a little kindness.

But it would take a good deal more than a touch of decency to get round the back of Cale, whose suspicion and hostility quickly began to earn him the loathing of almost everyone he encountered, from the Materazzi clan's golden boy, Conn, to the exquisite Arbell Materazzi. Usually known as Swan-Neck (no coincidence that the murderous dream which begins our story has a swan as its object of hate), she was the daughter of the man who ruled a Materazzi empire so vast that it was one upon which the sun never set. Bosco, however, placed very great store by Cale's hostility and he had no intention of letting Cale misuse it where it was only likely to get him killed. It is of no surprise that for all her dislike of him, a person like Cale could not fail to fall in love with a distant beauty such as Arbell Materazzi. She continued to regard him as a thug even, or especially, after he saved her life during a pitilessly lethal act of violence (dismissed later by his enemies as no more than a form of pretentious swashbuckling). Kleist's complaint about Cale that wherever he went a funeral shortly followed came to be more widely understood, particularly by IdrisPukke, who had been witness to the murderously cold rescue of Arbell. However, the alien and the strange can be a strong brew for the young, hence the reference in the 'Lay' to the attempted seduction of Cale by the lovely Arbell. Except that there was no seduction, if seduction implies persuasion of the reluctant, and there was never any point at which the word 'No!', or anything like it, ever crossed his lips. She certainly never paid to have him assassinated – nor, as Kleist later joked when he eventually read the poem, would she have needed to, given there were so many people willing to do it for nothing.

Equally unreliable is the claim that Arbell's father had ever nursed the slightest intention of attacking the Redeemers. His entirely fictional aggression had been invented by Bosco with the sole intention of providing an excuse to his superiors to wage a war that was in fact designed for one purpose: to return Cale to the Sanctuary. The law of unintended consequences being what it is, Bosco's desperately disease-wasted army under the generalship of Redeemer Princeps found itself trapped by a Materazzi army ten times its size at Silbury Hill. The ensuing battle was watched by a horrified Cale (who for reasons too complicated to explain here had provided the plan of attack for both armies) as a mixture of bad luck, confusion, mud, folly and a lack of crowd control that caused one of the most lethal reversals of fortune in the history of warfare.

To his astonishment Bosco found himself the conqueror of Memphis and possessed of every prize the world could offer, except the one he wanted: Thomas Cale. But Bosco had long had a finger in Memphis's nastiest pie, one owned by the appalling wheeler-dealer, businessman and pimp, Kitty the Hare. Kitty knew that Cale had lost his abnormally inexperienced heart to the beautiful Arbell just as he also discovered in due course that her intense passion for this most peculiar boy was already beginning to burn itself out – strange fruit, as Kitty joked, for such a hothouse flower. All the better for Bosco, whose men had taken her prisoner. As soon as he arrived in Memphis, Bosco applied his talent for human nature – one far too advanced for a beautiful young princess, however intelligent – by convincingly threatening to lay waste to the city if she did not give up her lover, while also reassuring her, entirely sincerely as it happened, that he had no intention of harming him. So she betrayed Cale, if betrayal it was, but with what kind of conscience it would be hard to say. So it was that Cale gave himself up, at the additional price of the release of Vague Henri and Kleist, only to learn that he had been delivered up to the man he hated above all things by the woman he loved above all things. This then brings us to the last of the lying verses of the 'Lay of Thomas Cale', with our hero heading into the wilderness with two great hatreds blistering his heart: one for the woman he once loved and the other, more familiar, for the man who had just told him one more thing about himself that had his brain spinning in his head. Bosco told him to stop feeling sorry for himself because he was not a person at all, not someone who could be either loved or betrayed but, as the 'Lay' had assured us all along, no more than the Angel of Death. And it was now time to go seriously about his God's business.

From now on everything that follows is the truth.

There are taller mountains than Tiger Mountain, many far more dangerous to climb, those whose sheer heights and dreadful crevices make the soul shiver with their hostility to any living thing. But there are none more impressive, none more likely to raise the spirits, to inspire wonder at its solitary splendour. Its great cone shape grows up from the Thametic plain that surrounds most of it and flatly stretches into the distance so that from fifty miles away its majestic symmetry seems like the work of man. But no man ever lived, not the most egotistical, no Akhenaten or Ozymandias, who could build a giant peak like this. Closer, its inhuman vastness is revealed, a hundred thousand times as big as the great pyramid of Lincoln. It's not hard to see why it has been held by many different kinds of faith to be the one place on earth from which God will speak directly to mankind. It was at the top of Tiger Mountain that Moses received the tablets of stone on which the six hundred and thirteen commandments were written. It was here in exchange for victory over the Ammonites that Jephthah the Gileadite, with considerable reluctance it must be said, cut the throat of his only daughter upon an altar after he had promised to sacrifice to the Lord the first living thing that greeted him on his return home. Willingly she went and to the very last the miserable Jephthah hoped for a compassionate reprieve – a voice, an angelic messenger, the stern but merciful proof that it was just a test of faith. But Jephthah returned from Tiger Mountain on his own. It was here, on the Great Jut below the snowline, that the Devil himself, at the instigation of the Lord, showed the Hanged Redeemer all the world that lay below and offered to give it to him.

On the other hand the Montagnards, a tribe without much of a place for religion in their lives, and who had controlled Tiger Mountain for eighty-odd years, referred to it as the Great Testicle. The reason why was starting to occupy Cale as, along with the Lord Militant Bosco and thirty guards, he made his way up the lower reaches of the mountain.

To describe Cale's mood as foul would be to do that mood an injustice. There is no word in any language ever spoken to describe the hurly-burly in his heart, his loathing at the idea of his return to the Sanctuary and the bitterness of his anger at his betrayal by Arbell Materazzi, known to everyone as Swan-Neck, and about whose beauty and gracefulness as a result nothing more need be said – nothing about the suppleness of her long legs, the breath-catching span of her narrow waist, the curve of her breasts (they were not proud, her breasts, they were overweeningly arrogant). She was a swan in human form. In his mind Cale was endlessly imagining the wringing of this swan's neck and then miraculously reviving her and murdering her all over again – this time a violent snap, the next a slow strangling and then after that perhaps a cutting out and burning of her heart, followed by a good raking for it among the ashes to make doubly sure.

For two weeks since they had left Memphis he had not spoken once, not even to ask why they had changed direction in the middle of the Scablands and started travelling away from the Sanctuary. On balance Bosco thought it better to let his former acolyte stew. But he had underestimated Cale's talent for mute anger and finally decided to break their silence.

'We're going to Tiger Mountain,' volunteered Redeemer Bosco, softly and even with kindness. 'There's something I need to show you.'

It might be thought that someone whose heart was moithering with so much hatred for one person might not have enough intensity of feeling left over to loathe another in the same way. In part this was true, but Cale's heart, when it came to hatred, was made of stern and capacious stuff: his aversion to Bosco had merely been shifted further from the centre of the fire, in the clinker at the side as it were, to keep warm, for bringing back to the broil later. Nevertheless, despite his current preoccupation with hating, Cale could not help but be puzzled by the great change in Bosco's attitude towards him. Since he was a very small boy Bosco had driven him like a ship in a storm – relentless, merciless, pitiless, cruel, never slacking, never giving him a place to rest. Day after day, year after year he had scoured him black and blue, teaching and punishing, punishing and teaching until there seemed no difference between the two. Now there was only restraint, a great softness, almost something like tenderness. What was it? There was no answer to be had, even when he had the energy to spare from mind-murdering Arbell Materazzi (beating her to death with a stick, martyring her on a wheel, drowning her to applause in a high mountain lake). But despite the hammers beating out their cacophony in his soul, something in Cale was paying attention to the terrain through which they were moving, resulting in a moment of understanding, though not of amusement exactly – he was in too dark a place for that. Now he could see why landscape there were many small holes, the decayed entrances to the deposits of salt between thirty and a hundred feet below the surface. Despite his foul temper and silence Cale could not help but be distracted by the intriguing features of this sacred landscape. But while it lacked great crevices and dangerous crags, the going inevitably became tougher and soon they were forced to dismount and lead the horses up harsher and more awkward paths. Finally they did come to a narrow pass, with steep and rocky walls to either side.

Bosco ordered his men to make camp, though it was still early afternoon, and then turned to Cale and spoke to him directly for the second time.

'They'll stay here. We have to go on. There's something I need to show you. We should also get something straight. The only way back down this part of the mountain is through this pass. If you attempt to come back down on your own you know what will happen.'

With this gently spoken warning he set off up through the pass and Cale followed. They climbed for thirty minutes, Cale always staying about ten yards behind his former master until they reached a shelf about twenty feet deep. To one side there was a simply constructed but beautifully made stone altar.

'That was where Jephthah kept his oath to the Lord and sacrificed his only daughter.' His tone of voice was odd, not reverential at all.

'And I suppose,' replied Cale, 'that stain on the side

there is supposed to be her blood. She must have been filled with strong stuff – you can still see it a thousand years after it was spilled halfway up a mountain.'

'With God all things are possible.' They looked at each other for some time. 'No one knows where he killed her. This altar was built for the benefit of the faithful, some of whom are permitted to come here on Bad Friday – a painter comes the day after their visit and paints it again so that there's time for it to weather in for the following year.'

'So it's not true.'

'What is truth?' he said and did not wait for an answer.

After two hours they were only some five hundred yards from the snowline and into the last climb before they could talk to God himself. But it was just here that Bosco turned aside and began to walk around the mountain parallel with the snow. Here the thin air made the going harder for all that they were no longer climbing. Cale's head began to ache. As he followed Bosco around a small bluff he lost sight of him for a moment and when he made contact again almost knocked him over. Bosco had stopped and was looking with great intensity at a flat rock cantilevered out from the mountain like the abandoned first section of a bridge.

'This is the Great Jut where Satan tempted the Hanged Redeemer by offering him power over all the world.' He turned to look at Cale. 'I want you to come out there with me,' he said, pointing at the end of the Jut.

'You first.'

Bosco smiled. 'I'm putting my life as much in your hands as you are in mine.'

'Not really,' replied Cale, 'given there are thirty guards below us with spiteful thoughts on their mind.'

'Fair enough. But do you think I've gone to all this trouble to try and throw you off a mountain?'

'I don't care to think anything about you.'

In the past Bosco would have beaten Cale severely for speaking to him like this. And Cale would have let him. It was then that Cale realized something, though he could not have said what it was exactly, about just how great was the change that had come over both of them in only a few months.

'If I say no?'

'I can't make you and I won't try.'

'But you'll have me killed.'

'To be honest – no. But however great your hatred for me – something that gives me great pain – you must realize by now that you and I are bound together by unbreakable chains – I believe that's the expression you used to Arbell Materazzi when we left Memphis.'

Perhaps Bosco realized how very close he was to having his neck broken. If he did, he didn't show it. But there was anxiety there, the anxiety, incomprehensible to Cale, of someone who deeply wants to be believed, to be understood, and fears that they will not. 'Besides,' added Bosco, 'I have something to tell you about your parents.' With that he walked down the rough granite of the Great Jut. Cale watched him for a moment, shocked, as he was meant to be, by what Bosco had said. It is not easy to imagine the feelings of someone like Cale for whom the notion of mother and father was as notional as the sea to the landlocked. What would such a person feel in the moment they were told the ocean was just over the next hill? Cale walked out onto the Jut, a good deal more warily than Bosco – he was not afraid of heights but he did not love them. Besides, walking on the Jut proper it seemed a good deal more fragile than standing in front of it. As he came up behind Bosco his former master stepped aside as carelessly as if he were in the middle of the training field of the Sanctuary and gestured Cale up beside him, a few inches away from the dreadful spaceless fall below.

Cale looked out over the world feeling as if he was being held in the middle of the sky itself; heart pumping, eyes astonished, he could see around for miles with the vast blue sky above and the yellow earth beneath bending to meet it in an arc of shimmering purple haze. It seemed as if it was the entire world he was looking at and not just a crescent of fifty miles or so. Bosco said nothing for several minutes as Cale was battered by the vastness. Finally Cale turned to face him.

'So?'

'Firstly – your parents. I heard the rumours . . .' He

paused for a moment. '. . . the rumours from Memphis not long after your slaughter of Solomon Solomon.'

'He got what he deserved, which is more than can be said for the men you had me kill.' Of all the many unpleasant memories the two of them shared this was the worst. Convinced that Cale's murderous gifts were divinely inspired it had barely occurred to Bosco that being obliged to fight half a dozen experienced, if disgraced, soldiers to the death might have been deeply traumatic for a boy of twelve or thirteen, however skilled or callous.

'My heart was in my mouth for every second I thought you were in danger.' This was not quite the lie it seemed. At first he had been ecstatic at the murderous proof of the boy's talent for killing. It was of an excellence that only religious inspiration could explain. But after the sixth death Bosco realized that God might resent his desire for proof and punish his presumption by allowing Cale to be hurt. It was realizing his presumption that suddenly made Bosco afraid for Cale and caused him to put an end to the slaughter.

It was more astonishment than restraint that prevented Cale from throwing him off the Jut there and then. The man who had beaten him for every reason that malice could devise, and half as many times again for none at all, was professing concern for him all along in tones that would have penetrated the hardest heart. But Cale's heart was a good deal harder than that. If he

17

let Bosco live it was only because his curiosity was even greater than his hatred. And besides, there were thirty evil bastards still waiting for him below.

'Tell me about the rumours.'

'After you killed him it was bruited about that the Redeemers had taken you while you were a baby from a family related directly to the Doge of Memphis – that you are a Materazzi and not an inconsiderable one.' Can silence be stunned? You would believe it can had you been standing there on the Great Jut.

'Is it true?' Cale's voice was only a whisper despite himself. There was a brief pause.

'Absolutely not. Your parents were illiterate peasants of no importance in any way.'

'Did you kill them?'

'No. They sold you to us, and happily, for sixpence.'

Even Bosco was surprised by the bark of laughter that followed this.

'I thought you might have been disappointed – about the Materazzi I mean – but it pleases you to have been bought for sixpence?'

'Never you mind what pleases me. Why are we here?'

Bosco looked back over the great plain below.

'When God decided to make mankind he took a rib from his first great creation, the Angel Satan. And from Satan's rib he formed the first man out of the dust of the ground. Displeased that God had taken his rib while he was sleeping without consulting him, Satan rebelled against the Lord God and was thrown from heaven. But God took pity on mankind because he had been wrong to make him out of the rib of such a treacherous servant. And because it was God's error he sent many prophets to save mankind from his own nature, hoping to bring out all those good things from which he had been formed. Finally, and desperately, he sent his own son to save them.' Bosco turned slightly, his expression one of utter amazement, his eyes filling with tears. 'But they hanged him.'

Again he said nothing for two or three minutes. 'The Lord God brooded over this terrible wound for a thousand years, so loving a God is he. In all that time he turned over in his mind all that was good about men, all that was kind. But always he could hear and see the unbearable repartee between what was Godly and the poisonous error built into him by this loving, but terrible, mistake.'

Again there was a short silence as he stared out over the dizzying landscape below. When he spoke again his voice was even softer and more reasonable.

'The heart of a man is a small thing but it desires great matters. It is not big enough for a dog's dinner but the whole world is not big enough for it. Man spares nothing that lives; he kills to feed himself, he kills to clothe himself, he kills to adorn himself, he kills to attack, he kills to defend himself, he kills to instruct himself, he kills to amuse himself, he kills for the sake of killing. From the lamb he tears its guts and makes his harp resound; from the wolf his most deadly tooth to polish his pretty works of art; from the elephant his tusks to make a toy for his child.'

Bosco turned back to Cale, his eyes shining with all the love and hope of a doting parent desperate to be understood by the person they love most in the world.

'And who will exterminate him who exterminates all others? You. It is you who are charged with the slaughter of man. Of the whole earth, you will make a vast altar upon which all that is living must be sacrificed, without end, without measure, without pause, until the annihilation of all things, until evil is extinct, until the death of death.'

Bosco smiled at Cale, tolerant, genuinely understanding.

'Why would you do such a terrible thing? Because it is in your nature to do so. You are not a man, you are God's anger made flesh. There is enough of mankind in you to wish to be other than what you are. You want to love, you want to show kindness, you want to be merciful. But in your heart you know you are none of these things. That is why people hate you and why the more you try to love them the more they fear you. This is why the girl betrayed you and why you will always be betrayed as long as you live. You are a wolf pretending to himself that he is a lamb.

'Where else do you think you get your genius for

mayhem and death? You kill with as much ease as others breathe. You turn up in the greatest city in the world and despite all your good intentions it took you six months to leave it in ruins. You do not bring disaster, you *are* disaster. You are the Grimperson, the Angel of Death, and you'd better like it or lump it. But if you don't like it you'd better get used to wandering where everyone will despise you and everyone will try and kill you for no reason they'll ever know. Come with me and when your work is finished and everything that lives now is dead, you will come here and be taken up into heaven. It is the only way you'll ever have peace of mind. This is a promise.'

Within three hours the two of them had walked down to the Redeemers waiting for them and that night a respectful Bosco talked to a silent Cale late into the night.

'Do you know why God made you?' It was a quote instantly recognizable from the Catechism of the Hanged Redeemer. Cale's reply, cautious, was nevertheless by rote.

'He made us to know and love him.'

'Do you think God made him well?'

'Not in my experience,' said Cale, 'but I might just have been unlucky.'

'But your experience is a good deal broader in the last eight months. In fact I'd say it was uniquely so. Clearly God ordained your escape and all the extraordinary things that have happened to you precisely so you could answer the question. You've walked hand in hand with the great and the good of this world, been loved in all the ways possible by the most beautiful, done mighty services and been mightily betrayed for your trouble.'

All of this had the great advantage from Bosco's point of view of being more or less precisely what the young man himself believed to be the case: truth and self-pity formed a harmonious whole.

'I'd say,' continued Bosco, 'that you'd seen as much as anyone that man is a wolf to man.'

'Hypocrites,' replied Cale, 'I've come across a lot of them recently. I mean by that I understand now how many of them there are.'

'That's at my expense, I suppose,' said Bosco, apparently not insulted. 'If so, I'm afraid you must explain why.'

'How do you look at me with a straight face and clack on about treachery?'

'You've still lost me. Suppose I'd left you in the hands of the kind of people prepared to sell you for sixpence. Since the day you could walk you'd have been behind a plough staring at a horse's arse for fifteen hours a day – stupid, ignorant, probably dead by now – a kind of nothing.'

'God has been merciful. Besides, I thought I was special.'

'There are a great many people who are *born* special. As the Hanged Redeemer said, "Full many a flower is born to blush unseen and waste its sweetness on the desert air.'"

Cale laughed. 'A flower? I am, it's true, sweeter and more flowery than people give me credit for.'

'Then let me put it more clearly: you were born to wade through slaughter to the throne of God. Many are called, few are chosen. But I chose you and made you fit to be the agent of the promised end.'

'Do you have any idea how mad you sound?'

'Indeed I do. I have in moments of doubt considered the question of my sanity.' He smiled, an oddly fetching expression of self-awareness and mockery.

'And?'

'Then I consider what a piece of work is man. How defective in reason, how mean his facilities, how ugly in form and movement, in action how like a devil, in apprehension how like a cow. The beauty of the world? The paragon of animals? To me the quintessence of dust.' Bosco had seemed to lose himself but then looked intensely at Cale.

'You disagree?'

Cale did not reply.

'Leave your hatred of me to one side for a moment and consider your experience of the world. Do you disagree in your heart of hearts?'

There was another long pause.

'Tell me more.'

'This is not the first time the Lord has wiped away

mankind for its failures. It is not generally known that there was a kind of Man before Adam. God destroyed him in a great flood in which he drowned the whole world and started again.'

'Everything?'

'Everything. Even to the last blade of grass.'

'Sounds easy enough. Why not do the same again?'

'Too many people, not enough water. Too much grass.'

'Does the Pope believe any of this?'

'Not exactly,' replied Bosco, 'but whatever he looses on earth shall be loosed in heaven.'

'I don't get . . . Oh, I see.' Cale thought about what he thought he saw. 'You're going to kill the Pope and take his place.'

'If I didn't know better I'd say you were more devil than angel. Do you really think you can kill a Pope anointed by God and not immediately damn yourself?'

'I suppose not.'

They sat in silence, Bosco wanting Cale to ask for an explanation. Knowing this, despite his curiosity, Cale declined to give him the satisfaction.

'The Pope is not himself,' said Bosco.

'Who is he?' replied an astonished Cale. It was not an expression he'd heard before.

'No, I mean he's not well. He is an old man and he is suffering from a disease of the mind – a weakening, one that's slowly getting worse. He forgets.'

'I forget.'

'He forgets who he is.'

'If he's that bad he'll die soon.'

'He is that bad but people afflicted in this way often live for a long time – very long.' He looked at Cale, enjoying the feeling of, once again, being master to his pupil.

'What must I do?' asked Bosco. It was not a question but a prompt that Cale should demonstrate his good judgement.

'You must be there when he dies and become Pope.'

Bosco laughed. 'A little easier said than done.'

'You can laugh,' said Cale, 'but am I wrong?'

'No – let's look simply at complex things. That is, indeed, the end but what's the beginning? Even for the very clever it can be like breaking bones to stand back from something that's been in front of you all your life.'

'How powerful are you?' Cale asked after a long time.

'Excellent,' laughed Bosco. 'When you murdered Redeemer Picarbo you were kind enough to promote me from, let's say, tenth in line to the papacy to perhaps ninth.'

'You wouldn't have punished me?'

'Hard to say. Your actions at the time were inconvenient. My plans for you – for all of this – were years in the future. Tenth in line to the papacy is not in line to the papacy at all. Your vanishing and my coming for you advanced everything in a most peculiar and unexpected way. Memphis is fallen. I have much of the credit and what is not mine is yours. I am now fourth in line to the papacy. Alas' – he smiled – 'fourth in line is, in reality, little better than tenth or twentieth.'

'Who are first and second?'

'To the point!' mocked Bosco. 'Gant and Parsi.'

'Never heard of them.'

'Why would you? I was mistaken in thinking these things were premature when it comes to you.'

'So now you're going to tell me?'

'Now I am going to ask you to work it out.'

'Why not just tell me?'

'Because you will see it more clearly if you do so. And also because it will give me greater pleasure.'

Told by the devil who has tormented you all your life that he will let you guess his secrets, what intelligent boy, however deep his hatred, might not be curious?

'There was a book in the library with its own lock – the census. I managed to open others but not that.'

'You did manage to break it trying, though.'

'How big is the Redeemer empire?'

'It's not an empire, it is a commonwealth. The commonwealth has achieved enosis with forty-three countries and, according to the last census, has the chance to redeem one hundred million people.'

'How big is the world?'

'I have no real idea. Concerning the Indies and China we know little enough. But concerning the four quarters, not including Memphis, we are, perhaps, four times the size and many times wealthier than is generally held to be the case.'

'Why not including Memphis?'

'Memphis drew its clout from its military power. We conquered Memphis and destroyed the Materazzi but we did not conquer its empire: that merely collapsed. Each country in that empire has declared itself free and started squabbling with its neighbours about the same things it squabbled about before the Materazzi arrived. Taking Memphis has turned out to be a mixed blessing, and given time it may turn out not to be a blessing at all.'

'If the Redeemer empire is so much bigger an empire than everyone thinks . . .'

'Commonwealth,' interrupted Bosco.

'. . . than everyone thinks, why are you stuck in the fight with the Antagonists?'

'Good. Exactly so.' Bosco was clearly pleased with this question. 'The commonwealth of the Redeemers is not only large but bloated – full of contradictions. Some parts of the commonwealth are slack in their beliefs and so full of blasphemies they're hardly better than Antagonists. Many extract from us more in subsidies than they pay in taxes. Others are fanatical in their beliefs but always arguing with each other after this or that doctrinal point. There are numerous schisms threatening to become full-grown heresies like Antagonism.'

'If things are so bad why haven't the Antagonists defeated you?'

'Again, well done. They face the same problems. It is not lack of religion that's destroying mankind, it is mankind that is destroying religion. Such a creature is incompetent to aspire to the likeness of God. God tried but failed. He will try again.'

'I thought God was perfect,' said Cale.

'God is perfect.'

'Then why has he made such a mess of mankind?'

'Because he is perfectly generous. God is not some criminal who cheats in his own card game. He wishes to engage with us freely, out of choice. Not even God can make a circle square. God is lonely – he wants mankind to choose obedience, not be frightened into it. Do you understand what I'm saying?'

'I understand what you're saying, yes.'

'Neither I nor the God we both serve need you to agree. You are not a man and you are not a god, you are anger and disappointment made flesh. What you do is what you are. What you think is irrelevant.'

'And when it's over?'

'I have been told in my visions that you will be taken up and set aside in the Island of Avalon, a place flowing with milk and honey. You will stay there clothed in white samite until a time, if it comes, when God needs you again.'

After this Cale did not say anything for some time.

'Tell me about Chartres.'

'The Sanctuary is the military heart of the faith but that's why it's positioned here in the back of beyond – to curtail its shout. Although I have great power, any commander of the Sanctuary who approaches within forty miles of Chartres would be excommunicated by fiat of the Pope. I am permitted there only by his express permission – rarely forthcoming – and never with more than a dozen priests. Even then I haven't met with him alone since Gant and Parsi sealed him off from the world like a pea in a pod.'

'I don't know what that is.' A pause. 'Why don't they kill you?'

'Straight there as usual. They count me as a rival but one effectively neutralized because all my power is in the army and not in Chartres. Your running away, Cale, advanced matters too quickly.'

'Or you,' said Cale, 'have allowed them to drift.'

'Not so. Almost since the day you arrived here I have been recruiting three hundred military officers who have accepted that mankind cannot be cured and that you are its solution. They will be here soon. You will train these already considerable men and they will train three hundred more and so on. Within two years you will have prepared four thousand officers and I will be ready to move against Gant and Parsi. If I am successful we will be invited into Chartres to save the Pope.'

'And how will you do that?'

'That's not something you need to worry about.'

'But I *do* worry.'

'Then worry away.'

'What's samite?'

'Silk. Heavy white silk.'

It was not that Cale believed Bosco about Avalon, though Bosco was clearly sincere in his certainty of the existence of the place, but he was dubious at the picture of the pleasures that awaited him there.

'The last time I saw anyone wearing heavy white silk it was some archbishop giving a high mass in praise of God. Four hours was bad enough. In case you hadn't noticed, I'm not the praising type.'

'Why would you be? In Avalon you will be cared for by seventy-two creatures who are not exactly angels.'

'Meaning?'

'They are feminine spirits. Lesser than the rebel angels they made common cause with because they were resentful, as always, about their place in heaven. But seventy-two of them realized before God's final victory that they would lose even what they already had, and so, weeping tears, they persuaded God to show them mercy – against the advice of the Holy Mother, who saw them for the conniving slags they were. But a forgiving God sent them to Avalon in recognition of that repentance and as punishment for having wavered in their faith. They are waiting for you and to serve you in any way you desire.'

'Like the nuns in the convent.'

'That will be a matter for you – and so I assume not at all like the nuns in the convent.'

'And how do you know this?'

'It was revealed to me in the desert.'

According to the Janes the heart of a child can take forty-nine blows before it's damaged for ever and what's done can never be undone. Consider, then, the heart of Thomas Cale, sold for sixpence, fed on beatings, steeled to murder and then betrayed by the only living creature to show him love (a particularly hard one, that). Self-pity, while it should be accorded due respect, is the greatest of all acids to the human soul. Feeling sorry for yourself is a universal solvent of salvation. Imagine what poison was poured into Cale's breast that afternoon and night on Tiger Mountain. Consider the damage done and the power offered to make it right. It is not against reason, said the Englishman, to prefer the destruction of the world to a scratch on your finger – how much easier to understand the same price for the gash in your soul.

# 3

When Vague Henri, IdrisPukke and Kleist had decided on their careful pursuit of Bosco and his prize they had expected him to head straight for the safety of the Sanctuary, so the long detour taken by Bosco made them wary and suspicious. IdrisPukke only realized where they were going a few hours before Tiger Mountain appeared on the horizon. He was surprised that the news seemed to amaze the two boys.

'This is the Holiest site in the Good Book,' said Vague Henri.

'I didn't think you believed in all that any more,' replied IdrisPukke.

'Who said we do?' For the last few days Kleist had been even touchier than usual.

'It's not that,' said Vague Henri, 'but we've heard about this place all our lives. God spoke to Prester John on that mountain. Jephthah sacrificed his only daughter to the Lord there.'

'What?'

The two patiently explained the story, so often repeated to them it no longer seemed a real event with real people

– a none-too-sharp knife and a twelve-year-old girl willingly bent over a curved rock.

'Good grief,' said IdrisPukke when they'd finished.

'And it was where Satan tempted the Hanged Redeemer with power over the whole world. I got a hefty thrashing for pointing out that Satan must've been a bit of a dunce.'

'And why's that?'

'What's the point of tempting someone with something they don't want?'

The unexpectedness of Bosco's diversion meant that they had little water and no food for two days. But Kleist had shot a fox and they were waiting with sore stomachs for it to cook.

'Do you think it's ready?'

'Better wait,' said Kleist. 'You don't want to be eating undercooked fox.'

IdrisPukke didn't want to be eating fox, undercooked or otherwise. When it was ready Kleist cut it (carving a fox into three equal parts was no mean feat), complete equality of shares being ensured by the law of the acolytes that whoever divided what they were about to eat had to take the smallest portion, an insight into human nature that had it been extended to a great many grander matters would have transformed the history of the world. IdrisPukke was still looking down at the fair third of the crisply done animal on his plate while the other two were on the point of finishing, though a good half-hour of bone and marrow sucking would follow.

'What's it like?' said IdrisPukke.

'Good,' said Vague Henri.

'I mean what's it taste like?'

Vague Henri looked up, thoughtfully, trying to be exact in his comparison. 'A bit like dog.'

Eating it, it was food after all, IdrisPukke was reminded of pork cooked in axle-grease, if axle-grease tasted anything like it smelt. When, with a full and queasy stomach, he fell asleep, he dreamt all night, as it seemed to him, of teapots pulsating in the night sky. When he woke up with the sky beginning to barely lighten, it was to the sound of Vague Henri cursing in a foul temper.

'What's the matter?'

Vague Henri picked up a rock and hurled it at the ground in a great fury.

'It's that shit-bag Kleist. He's run away, the treacherous bastard.'

'You're sure he hasn't just gone to relieve himself or to be on his own?'

'Do I look like an idiot?' replied Vague Henri. 'He's taken all his stuff.' He continued pouring execrations on Kleist's head for a good five minutes until, picking up the same rock and throwing it down with a last burst of temper, he sat down and boiled in silence.

After leaving him in silence for a few minutes, IdrisPukke asked him why he was so angry. Vague Henri looked back at him, indignant as well as bewildered.

'He left us in the lurch.'

'How so?'

'It's . . .' He was unable to put an exact finger on why. '. . . obvious.'

'Well, perhaps. But why shouldn't he leave us in the lurch?'

'Because he was supposed to be my friend – and friends don't leave their friends in the lurch.'

'But Cale isn't his friend. I heard him say so any number of times. I don't remember Cale having a good word for him either.'

'Cale saved his life.'

'He saved Cale's life at Silbury Hill – and more than once.'

Vague Henri gasped in irritation.

'What about me? He was supposed to be my friend.'

'Did you ask him if he wanted to come with us?'

'He didn't say anything when we started.'

'Well, he's said something now.'

'Why couldn't he say it to my face?'

'I suppose he was ashamed.'

'There you are then.'

'There you are nothing. Granted that judged by the highest standards of saintliness he should have explained his reasoning to you personally and in full. You claim to be his friend – has Kleist ever implied any aspirations to saintliness?'

Vague Henri looked away as if he might find someone ready to support his case. He said nothing for some time and then laughed – a sound partly humorous, partly disappointed.

'No.'

Unable to resist moralizing, IdrisPukke continued complacently. 'It's pointless to blame someone for being themselves and looking to their own interests. Whose interests would they look to? Yours? Kleist knows what's waiting for him if he's caught again. Why should he risk such a hideous death for someone he doesn't even like?'

'What about me?'

'Why should he risk such a hideous death for someone he *does* like? You must think awfully well of yourself.'

This time Vague Henri laughed without the disappointment. 'So why have you come then? The Redeemers won't be any kinder to you than to me.'

'Simple,' said IdrisPukke. 'I have allowed affection to get the better of my good judgement.' He could not resist the opportunity to expand on another one of his pet notions. 'That's why it's much better not to have friends if you have the strength of character to do without them. In the end friends always turn into a nuisance of one kind or another. But if you must have them let them alone and accept that you must allow everyone the right to exist in accordance with the character he has, whatever it turns out to be.'

They struck camp in silence and had carried on the same way for a good while when Vague Henri asked his companion a surprising question.

'IdrisPukke, do you believe in God?'

There was no pause to consider his answer. 'There's little enough goodness or love in me, or the world in general, to go about wasting it on imaginary beings.'

# 4

It is well enough known that the heart is encased in a tube and that sufficient distress causes it to fall down the tube, generally called the bunghole, or spiracle, which ends in the pit of the stomach. At the bottom of the bunghole, or spiracle, is a trap-door – made of gristle – called the springum. In the past, when bitter disappointment struck a man or woman and was too much to bear the springum would burst open and the heart would fall through it and give those who had suffered too much pain a merciful and quick release by stopping the heart instantly. Now there is so much pain in the world that hardly anyone could bear it and live. And so ever-protecting nature has caused the springum to fuse to the spiracle so that it can no longer open and now suffering, however terrible, must simply be endured. This was just as well for Cale as the first sight of the Sanctuary rose out of the early-morning mist as grim as a punishment. All the way along the last part of the journey a childish hope had emerged from somewhere in his soul that when he saw the Sanctuary first it might have been utterly destroyed by fire or brimstone. It was not. It sat squat on the horizon, unalterable in its concrete watchfulness, and waiting for his return, as solid in its presence as if it had grown into the flat-topped mountain on which it was built that itself looked like an enormous back tooth implanted in the desert. It was not made to delight, to intimidate, to glorify, or boast. It looked like its function: constructed to keep some people out no matter what and to keep others in no matter what. And yet you could not easily describe it: it was blank walls, it was prisons, it was places of grim worship, it was brownness. It was a particular idea of what it meant to be human made out of concrete.

All the way up the narrow road that corkscrewed up the side of the vast tabletop hill Cale's heart battered against the gristly door of his springum as it clutched at oblivion – but oblivion would not come. The great gates opened and then the great gates shut. And that was that. All the daring, the courage, the intelligence, the luck, the death, the love, the beauty and the joy, the slaughter and treachery had brought him back to the exact point where he had started not even a year before. It was the canonical hour of None and so everyone was in the dozen churches praying – the acolytes for forgiveness of their sins, the Redeemers for the forgiveness of the acolytes' sins.

Had he been less miserable, Cale might have noticed that he was helped down from his horse not even by a common Redeemer but by the Prelate of the Horse himself and with extraordinary deference. Bosco, making do for the dismount with an Ostler of the vulgar kind, walked forward and gestured him towards a door that Cale had barely noticed in all his years at the Sanctuary, because it was forbidden for an acolyte to go anywhere near it. It was opened for him by the Prelate of Horses and he led the way not as his superior but, as it were, as a guide. They walked on in the brown gloom that was the common feature of the Sanctuary everywhere, but even in the depths of misery Cale began to be aware of the oddness of having lived in a place all his life and then in a moment being shown there were vast areas of that place he had no idea existed. Brown it still was, but different. There were doors! There were doors everywhere. They stopped at one. It was opened and he was gestured inside, but this time no one went ahead of him and only Bosco followed. The chamber was large and furnished with brown furniture and lots of it. And it was disturbingly familiar. It was the same layout as the room in which he had killed Redeemer Picarbo. It even had a bedroom. This was a place only for the powerful.

'It will be necessary for you to stay here for two days, perhaps three. There are preparations, I am sure you understand. Your food will be brought to you and anything you need, just knock on the door and your . . .' He wasn't quite sure of the correct word. '. . .your guardian will arrange for it to be brought to you.' Bosco nodded, almost a bow, and left, closing the door behind him. Cale stared after him, astonished not just by the notion that he had a guardian, but more by the idea that he could ask for what he wanted. What could possibly be in the Sanctuary that anyone would want? As it turned out, Cale's justified assumption that there was indeed nothing turned out to be entirely wrong.

Meanwhile, Bosco had a great many pressing problems to deal with. In the eyes of Cale, Vague Henri and Kleist, Bosco appeared to be a figure of absolute authority among the Redeemers. This was far from the case. It might have been true concerning acolytes and even many senior Redeemers. His writ might now run in the Sanctuary but, however important it was, the centre of power for the faith lay with Pope Bento XVI in the holy city of Chartres. For twenty years a formidable bastion of power and orthodoxy, he had spent those two decades rolling back the changes of the previous hundred years in search of a renewed purity for the One True Faith. However, for some time he had been prey to that great affliction of age, Mens Vermis, first as a great tendency to forget, then to wander, then to wander and not return except for brief flashes of a few hours where his old grasp seemed to return in its entirety. From where, who knows? In the three years during which the Vermis had ruined his mind many cabals and juntos, cliques and coteries, had emerged preparing for the moment when death might release him from his duties. The two most important of these were the Redeemers Triumphant, run by Redeemer Cardinal Gant – responsible for religious

big lie,' he was fond of saying to Redeemer Gil, the nearest Bosco had to a confidant, 'is more easily believed than a small one and a simple one more readily than anything too complicated.' He had therefore commissioned Redeemer Eugen Hadamowski, his propaganda Burgrave, to write a book, the *Protocols of the Moderators of Antagonism*, outlining the details of such a plot. They had then, after careful searching, found the body of a Redeemer who shared all the most exaggerated features generally held to be typical of an Antagonist: he had green teeth (a lucky symptom of the disease from which he had died), thick lips, a large nose and black curly hair. They had thrown his body into the sea just off the Isle of Martyrs, where they knew the current would carry it, and let the general willingness to believe in such conspiracies do the rest. The *Protocols* did not, however, confine themselves just to the details of the ghastly plot itself, but also expressed fear that an unusually brave and holy Redeemer spy was out and about and that through great risk and holy cunning had infiltrated the Antagonist plotters to try to save the Pope. More cunningly it claimed that an Antagonist fifth column had converted an undisclosed number of Redeemers to their heresy and that many of these apostates had worked their way to important posts in both Gant's Redeemers Triumphant and Parsi's Office of the Holy See, where they fed vital secrets to their masters and awaited the opportunity offered by any moments of weakness in the faithful. The *Protocols* also reluctantly conceded that despite all their efforts little headway had been made against the religious purity of Bosco's Redeemers in the Sanctuary.

Bosco's belief that the *Protocols* could be as crude as a four-year-old's painting of the Hanged Redeemer as long as the faithful were convinced by their origins turned out to be more true than he could have reasonably hoped. The body's apparently one-in-a-million chance arrival from the sea was proof that there was no conspiracy. So natural did it seem that the question of its fakery never arose. The Office of the Holy See and the Redeemers Triumphant were reduced to arguing that while the threat was clearly real, the Antagonists were mistaken about the heretics in their ranks. Nevertheless there were mighty purges. Torture as such was forbidden to be used on Redeemers but the Office of Interrogators had no need of racks and branding. A few nights without sleep, followed by ducking in water, soon had entirely innocent men – innocent of heresy at any rate – confessing to collusion and apostasy and trafficking with devils all followed by the naming of names. Bosco watched with considerable satisfaction as a great number of his enemies were burnt at the stake by a great many of his other enemies. The authority he gained as a result of his own rule at the Sanctuary being accused by the *Protocols* of being a model of resistance to Antagonism gave him a renewed influence sufficient to launch the attack on the Materazzi with its utterly unexpected and magnificent consequences. He was now very much in the ascendant over Parsi and Gant and he had proved to his followers, beyond any shadow of a scruple or doubt, that God had blessed his daring and dangerous plan and that Cale was indeed God's instrument. Work, and very serious work, remained to be done. Neither Gant nor Parsi were to be underestimated and realizing the threat from Bosco they had joined together to oppose him. The Antagonist purge had eventually been brought to an end by their concerted efforts and they were on the move against Bosco and at any price.

That night Bosco lay on his bed, brooding over the many plans he had set in motion to destroy his rivals and bring about the end of the world. Exhilaration and worry kept him awake. What, after all, could shock the soul so intensely as the decision to bring everything to an end – the terrible vertigo of commitment to the ultimate solution of evil itself? His wariness was more ordinary but not less important. Bosco was not foolish enough to countenance grand ideas without knowing he needed the wit and competence to carry them out and, of course, the luck. Then there was the wariness and exhilaration he felt about Cale. Everything he had ever hoped for from this boy had come true and more than that. And yet he was puzzled that God had given everything his vision had promised and pressed down into the barrel yet there were still traces of something inadequate about him: pointless anger and resentment not turned into a proper righteousness. He comforted himself before he fell asleep that he had not intended Cale to be made manifest to the world for another ten years at least. If it hadn't been for that lunatic Picarbo and his ghastly experiments, things would have been very different. Soon after a short fulmination he stopped indulging his bad temper and comforted himself with one of his oldest dictums, 'a plan is a baby in a cradle – it bears little resemblance to the man'.

Early the next morning he waited in the Square of Martyrs' Blood, expectant and impatient, for one of his most carefully laid plans to reach its maturity. The great gates creaked open and three hundred Redeemers marched into the Sanctuary. It would be hard to describe them as the cream of the military wing of the priest-hood because cream would give entirely the wrong sense of something smooth and richly soft. They were as forbidding a collection as perhaps had ever stood together in one place – only great care and patience over nearly ten years had won them to Bosco's cause, it being no easy thing to bend the inflexible and reason with the fanatical. Hardest of all had been to preserve the flickers of daring and imaginative violence that brought them to his attention in the first place. These were Redeemers who had shown a talent for unlikely innovation, along with their more conventional talent for cruelty, brutality and the willingness to obey. They would be Cale's most direct servants. Cale would train them, each of them in turn train one hundred others and each of them again one hundred more. Now that he had Cale and the men in front of him he had the origins of the end of everything.

Bosco might still lack his rivals' power base in Chartres but he had a great variety of followers of different kinds, many unknown to one another. Some were fanatical in their devotion, true believers in his plan to change the world for ever, most had no idea of his final intentions but regarded him as more zealous in matters of faith than Parsi and Gant. Others were more lukewarm still: he was someone powerful who might yet become more powerful. Probably he would be eclipsed by the Pope's death, peace be upon him, but you never knew. Through this ugly rainbow of alliances he had spread the word about Cale by revealing the heroism of his part in saving the Pope from the malice not only of the Antagonists but from the expansionism of the now ruined Materazzi. Unofficial pamphlets were written telling disapprovingly but salaciously of the temptations and dangers Cale had faced. Their portrait of Memphis was crude but by no means untrue: the availability of flesh, its cunning politicians, and beautiful but corrupting women's wiles. But while some Redeemers might have enjoyed the horrors that they read about most of them were not hypocrites: they were genuinely revolted by what they read. It may surprise you that men such as these could feel love, but be unsurprised. They did. Cale had saved the Pope they loved.

The vast expansion of acolyte numbers over the last few years as Bosco built up his control of the military future of the Redeemers meant that, vast as the Sanctuary was, there was little in the way of accommodation for the three hundred of his new elite. Redeemers in general might not expect much in the way of life's pleasures but a room of their own when not on active service, however small, was a matter of great significance in lives generally full of privation. The many cells in the House of Special Purpose had been built when space was less of a luxury and Bosco had decided to clear out those who had been languishing there for any length of time. Over the last few weeks large numbers of executions had been carried out to create the space needed for the new arrivals. As with all enclosed institutions, those inside the Sanctuary were terrible gossips and as such relentlessly nosy. There was bound to be talk about the arrival of these imposing-looking officers but, in hindsight, Bosco felt he ought to have spent time on a convincing explanation for their presence. At the time he relied on the considerable intelligence of the highly experienced Chief Jailer to carry out his orders to treat the men well and put them in the north wing of the prison now cleared of inmates by means of the recent spate of murders. Bosco arranged for the excellent feeding of the three hundred men and explained that the wing would be locked to keep out the curious. They knew they were a chosen elect and that secrecy was vital to their own survival, so there were no objections.

Then Bosco spent several hours explaining his intentions to a mostly silent Cale.

'Whose authority are they under?'

'Yours.'

'And whose authority am I under?'

'You are under no authority – certainly not mine, if that's what you meant. You are God's resentment made flesh. You only imagine that you are a man and that the will of another man can ever matter to you. Deviate from your nature and you will destroy yourself. That's why Arbell Swan-Neck betrayed you and her father also betrayed you – even when you had saved the life of his daughter and recalled his only son to life just as much as if you had brought him back from the dead. People are not for you – you are not for people. Do what you're here for and you'll return to your father in heaven. If you try to be something you can never be then you are due more pain and misery than any creature that ever lived.'

'Give me Memphis.'

'Why?'

'Why do you think?'

'Oh,' said Bosco, smiling. 'So that you can tear it down brick by brick and sow salt into its foundations.'

'Something like that.'

'By all means. That's what you're for after all. But I do not have the authority and therefore you don't have it either. We must have an army. Sleeping in the House of Special Purpose is the means to get one. Even then I will need to be Pontiff before you can get up to mischief on that scale. As you have now discovered, nothing you can do for a man or woman will make them love you. Except for me, Thomas, I love you.'

And with that he stood up and left.

That night a nervous Redeemer Bergeron, Deputy Chief Jailer, arrived with a list of the names of the three hundred Bosco had asked for to check against his records and to guard against infiltrators. The new list confirmed there were, in fact, only two hundred and ninety-nine. The missing Redeemer would have to be accounted for in case he'd had second thoughts or been arrested. It turned out some time later that he had died of smallpox on his way to join the others. The jailer was nervous because he was new to dealing with the fearsome Bosco. His boss, the Chief Jailer, had been imprisoned himself only the day before on charges of Impious Malateste, an offence serious enough to have him arrested but not to inform Bosco about. The Chief Jailer had chosen his deputy now in charge precisely because his limited intelligence would lessen any threat to his own position. The deputy returned an hour after Bosco had read the list of names. Bosco did not look up when he entered, merely pushed the list in his direction.

He nervously picked it up without looking and got out of Bosco's intimidating presence as quickly as possible.

Outside, the jailer's heart was beating like a girl's who had just had her first kiss. He tried to calm himself and, taking the list to a taper burning weakly on the wall, examined it carefully. When he finished, his eyes were bulging with fear and uncertainty. Uneasy lies the head that wears the crown. He was too afraid to ask for clarification from Bosco and too proud to consult his predecessor. He was right to think that he would have looked foolish and inept in the eyes of both. His promotion, after all, was yet to be confirmed. 'Whatever you are,' he had once overheard, 'be decisive.' This not very good advice, misunderstood in any case, had been lurking at the back of Redeemer Jailer Bergeron's mind for many years awaiting the opportunity to betray him. At last its opportunity had come. How many of us are any different? How many of our worst or finest hours are rooted in some minor piece of nonsense that was stuck in our souls like a weed into a rocky cliff and flourished there against the odds? It forces its roots into a crack, the crack is widened, a sudden storm, the water invades the crack, the water freezes in the winter night and opens up the split. A stranger passes, his horse stumbles on the loosened rock and horse and rider are ejected into the dreadful chasm of the scarp. So Bergeron hurried to the cell of Petar Brzica and knocked with absolute conviction on his door.

'Yes?'

'The people on this list in the north wing are to be executed.'

Brzica was not especially surprised given that so many prisoners from the north wing of the House had been put to death recently. He examined the list, calculating roughly what sort of task it was. 'I thought,' he said, more to make conversation than anything, 'the executions were finished for now.'

'Obviously not,' came the bad-tempered reply. 'Perhaps you'd like to go and see the Lord Redeemer Bosco and ask him yourself what he thinks he's up to.'

'Not my job,' replied Brzica. 'Ours is not to reason why. When?'

'Now.'

'Now?'

'I've just come from Redeemer Bosco's presence.'

This was compelling.

'What's the rush?'

'That's nothing to concern you. All you need to worry about is how quickly you can start and finish.'

'How many exactly?'

'Two hundred and ninety-nine.'

Brzica considered, his lips moving in silent calculation.

'I can start in two hours.'

'How soon can you start if you get your finger out?'

Again Brzica considered.

'Two hours.'

Bergeron sighed.

'Then how long?'

'Once the rotunda gets going we can do one every two minutes. With breaks – eleven hours.'

'And without breaks?'

'Eleven hours.'

'Very well,' said Bergeron, in a tone that suggested he had concluded his negotiation successfully. 'The rotunda in two hours.'

Brzica was in fact working in the rotunda in less than an hour with his four assistants or topping coves. He had taken a look at his victims carefully. They were a tough-looking bunch. If they caught a sniff of what was happening there would be trouble. At the moment it was clear they were unaware – though not blissfully so. Not even men as ginty-looking as this could be so care-free in the face of death and the everlasting torment that waited. One thing bothered him a great deal. 'Why,' he said to the Redeemer on guard, 'aren't they locked in their cells? Why's there no one but you to watch them?'

His reply was convincing. 'No idea.'

If the guard was uncommunicative it was not just because he genuinely knew nothing, but also because no one wanted to talk to Brzica. Even the most thug-gish Redeemers looked down on, indeed despised, him in the way executioners have always been despised. Nobody liked him but he didn't care, or at least that was what he told himself. In fact he was sensitive about the way he was regarded. He liked being feared. He liked being seen as deadly and mysterious. He was aggrieved, however, by the disdain. It was uncalled for. It was unjust. He held himself aloof but his feelings were hurt by this lack of respect.

He suffered in silence, not out of choice but because no one wanted to talk to him. Not even his assistants, two of whom had recently, and much to his irritation, tried to get themselves reassigned to ministering to lepers in Mogadishu. They would get theirs in due course for this disloyalty, but tonight required unity and harmonious skill.

Problems still remained and he decided to walk along the ambulacrum to clear his head. Should they be bound first? No. The advantage of tied hands and hobbled legs needed to be offset against the clear worry this would give that something unpleasant was up. These were not the kind of men to go quietly and given the fact that for some reason they had been left with the doors to their cells open, a riot could easily result. It was better, he decided as he loped up the ambo, to keep them innocent and do it all so quickly they wouldn't catch on until they were halfway to the next life. It required more deftness and a surer touch but then these he had in abundance.

'Good night, Redeemer.' It was Bosco walking past, mulling over Cale.

'Good . . .'

But Bosco was already gone.

The Rotunda had been designed by Brzica's predecessor – a Fancy Dan, in Brzica's opinion – and had been constructed, in his professional opinion, more elaborately than was necessary. Keep it simple was his motto. He had replaced the Rotunda's three-room system for mass executions – one about to be killed, one in the next room being prepared and the third the victim in waiting – and replaced it with something that relied more on the cooperation of the victim under the impression that something else was happening. The victim was told he was to have a brief introduction to the Prior of the Sanctuary. When he entered through the thick and soundproof door he would see the Prior kneeling to pray with his back to him and facing a Holy icon of the Hanged Redeemer. He and his two guards would kneel side by side, the latter a little closer perhaps than one would expect. The Prior would then stand up and turn around, the victim would look up, Brzica in his leather apron would grab his hair, the two guards hold his arms and then Brzica would draw the knife embedded in his glove across his throat. Already dying and in shock, he would be dropped onto the false floor in front of him, this would be lowered by the guards, the dead or dying man would be pushed down the chute to be pulled away by the Redeemers in the room below, who would wash the false floor quickly and carefully and then the floor would be pushed and raised back into place. A quick check for signs of the struggle and then the guards would be up and leaving the room by a door further along the corridor. Outside the next victim would be patiently waiting with his two guards. He would see dimly in the shadows what he thought was his predecessor leaving through the exit door. Then the whole procedure would begin again.

This went on throughout the night with only a single interruption. One of the victims, more alert than all the rest, sensed something was not quite right. As a tired hand grasped his hair and another his left hand he instinctively jerked free. Slipping and sliding and screaming as all four of his murderers grappled and tried to pin him down, screaming and fighting till they bundled him into the shaft, stamped on his hand, beat him about the head and finally pushed him through to be finished off by the Redeemers in the chambers below. Not even the thickest door could prevent the sound of such a dreadful struggle reaching the ears of the man waiting in the corridor outside. Brzica went out himself and stabbed the frightened Redeemer where he stood before he could raise a fuss. Other than that, everything passed as it should.

The next morning at eleven, Redeemer Jailer Bergeron inspected the pile of lightly washed bodies laid out in the Rotunda Aftorium, waiting to be removed to Ginky's Field under the cover of night. It was a sobering but impressive sight. Half an hour later he was standing in front of a slightly impatient Bosco, who was trying to work out the boring but complicated documents involving an argument over the delivery of a large consignment of spoiled cheese.

'What is it?' said Bosco, not looking up.

'The executions have been carried out as you ordered, Redeemer.'

Bosco looked up having lost, to his irritation, his train of thought over the claim and counter-claim concerning responsibility for the rotten cheese.

'What?'

A terrible dread flushed through Bergeron as if he had been hit by a winter spate.

'The execution of the prisoners in the House of Special Purpose.'

Bergeron's voice was whisper thin. He took out the order sheet with the names and pointed to the last page. 'There's the cross you put at the end to confirm it.'

Bosco took the paper from him without fuss. A horrible quiet settled over him. He looked at it for a moment. His precious gauleiters gone, every one.

'The cross at the bottom,' he said softly, 'was to show that I'd read it.'

'Ah.'

'Ah, indeed.'

'I . . .'

'Please don't say anything. You've brought me a disaster this morning. Take me to see them.'

*

In his room Cale was looking pointlessly out of the window, his mind hundreds of miles away. Behind him there was the clatter of an acolyte laying out his second meal of the day. If nothing else, eating, now that his food came from the nuns as it did for the other Redeemers, was one pleasure he still felt. Of a sort. The acolyte dropped one of the covers on the floor and it bounced noisily and rolled over near his feet. The nearness of the acolyte's scrabble to pick it up made him look at the boy's face for the first time. The boy, though he was at least Cale's age, picked up the cover and looked back, but uncertainly.

'I don't know you,' said Cale.

'They brought me here ten days ago from Stuttgart.' Cale had read about Stuttgart only a few days before in an almanac Bosco had given him that set out in the driest detail every armed and walled Redeemer citadel with a population above five thousand. It was five hundred pages long and there were ten volumes. According to Bosco, the Redeemer commonwealth was fragile. What was clear from even what he had read in the alamanac was that it was vast, bigger by far than he had ever imagined.

'Why?' asked Cale.

'Don't know.'

'What's your name?'

'Model.'

Cale went over to the table and sat down. There were scrambled eggs, toast, chicken legs, sausages, mushrooms and porridge. He started to help himself.

'You're Cale, aren't you?'

Cale ignored him. 'They say you saved the Pope himself from nasty Antagonists.'

Cale looked back at him for a moment then went back to eating. Model stared at him. He was hungry because acolytes were always hungry, just as for most of the year they were cold. But it did not occur to him that the food on the table, some of which he did not even recognize, might be shared with him. It was like a beautiful woman to an ugly man – he could appreciate the beauty but could not expect at all to participate in it. But, distracted as he was, Cale could not eat this well in front of another acolyte.

'Sit down.'

'I couldn't.'

'Yes, you could. Sit.'

Model sat and Cale put a dish of fried potatoes in front of him. But there was, of course, a problem. Cale picked up the dish of fried potatoes and emptied all but one on his own plate. Flushed with desire and longing, Model's face fell.

'Look,' said Cale. 'You eat too much of this stuff and you'll be yawning your guts up in five minutes. Believe me. What did you eat in Stuttgart?'

'Porridge and bunge.'

'Bunge?'

'Sort of fat and nuts and stuff.'

'We call it dead men's feet.'

'Oh,' said Model.

Cale removed the skin from a small piece of chicken and scraped away the delicious jelly that clung juicily to the underside. Then a smaller helping of just the white of an egg and a larger dollop of porridge but just a little bit, not too much.

'See how that goes down.'

Well was the answer, ecstatically wonderfully in a heavenly way it went down well. Not even in the depths of his anger and fury could Cale fail to take pleasure in the delight of Model as he ate the fried potato, the white of the egg, the porridge slipping down his parched and hungry throat as if it had come from the gardens of paradise, where it was said that there were lemonade springs and the rocks were made of candy.

When Model finished he sat back and stared again at Cale.

'Thank you.'

'You're welcome. Now go and lie down for five minutes and turn your face to the wall so you aren't looking at me while I finish. You might feel a bit strange.'

Model did as he was told and Cale finished his breakfast without giving him another thought. As he finished there was a knock at the door.

'Go away,' he said, signalling the alarmed Model to get up. There was another knock. He waited. 'Come in.' It was Bosco.

Ten minutes later the two of them stood alone in the

Aftorium looking silently at the two hundred and ninety-nine dead bodies, all that remained of Bosco's ten years of planning for the means to bring the world to an end.

'I wanted to show you this because there should be no secrets between us. I don't want you to learn from my mistake because I did not make a mistake. I wish that I had, because then I could learn from it. But this error, shall we call it, is simply what it is. An event. There was a plan, a carefully arrived at and exactingly thought-out plan. What you need to learn here is that there is nothing to learn. That there are foolish men and that there are inexperienced men and that there are misunderstandings. This is the nature of things. You understand?'

'Yes.'

'I will consider an alternative.'

But for all his acceptance of the terrible carnage done to his years of irreplaceable planning (Bergeron had been replaced but to his astonished thankfulness not disembowelled or even punished) Bosco was white with shock.

'Consider them for an hour. Then leave.'

'I don't need an hour,' said Cale.

'I think . . .'

'I don't need an hour.'

Bosco moved his head, just a slight move. He turned to leave and Cale followed up the winding steps known as the Stairway to Heaven going up and, for reasons lost in time, Yummity's Steps going down. They moved slowly up past the Rotunda, Bosco's knees not being what they once were, and up into the Bourse, the hall that led off into the various departments of the House of Special Purpose.

Towards the back of the Bourse a man, a Redeemer, stripped of his robes, was being led towards an open courtyard. He was wailing quietly, a drizzly sobbing like a tired and unhappy child. Cale watched as the three attending Redeemers ushered him forward. Cale watched them as if he might be a buzzard or one of the more thoughtful Falconidae.

'Stop them.'

'Pity is nothing of . . .'

'Stop them and tell them to take him back to his cell.'

Bosco walked over to the execution party as they stalled, trying to push the prisoner through the door-way and out into the bright sunshine of the courtyard.

'Hold on a moment.'

Ten minutes later Cale, followed by a wary Bosco, was walking silently through the cells where the Purgators, those whose sins of blasphemy, heresy, offences against the Holy Ghost and a long list of others, were kept while they waited for their fate to be decided, usually a very simple and uniform fate. Cale walked up and down carefully looking over the waiting prisoners – the terrified, the despairing, the bewildered, the fanatical and the clearly mad.

'How many?'

'Two hundred and fifty-six,' said the jailer.

'What's in there?' said Cale, nodding towards a locked door. The jailer looked at Bosco and then back at Cale. Was this the promised Grimperson? He didn't look like much.

'Behind that door we keep those condemned to an Act of Faith.'

Cale looked at the jailer.

'Unlock the door and go away.'

'Do as you're told,' said Bosco.

He did so, face red with resentment. Cale pushed the door and it swung open easily. There were ten cells, five on each side of the corridor. Eight were Redeemers whose crimes required a public execution to encourage and support the morale of the witnessing faithful. Of the other two, one was a man, clearly not a priest because he had a beard and was dressed in civvies. The other was a woman.

'The Maid of Blackbird Leys,' said Bosco, when they returned to his rooms. 'She has been prophesying blasphemies concerning the Hanged Redeemer.'

'What sort of blasphemies?'

'How can I repeat them?' said Bosco. 'They're blasphemies.'

'How was she charged then, at her trial?'

'The case was heard *in camera*. Only a single judge was present when she repeated her claims and condemned herself.'

'But the judge knows.'

'Unfortunately, may peace be upon him, the judge died of a stroke immediately afterwards, clearly brought on by the Maid's heresy.'

'Bad luck.'

'Luck had nothing to do with it. He has gone to a better place – or at least a place from which no traveller returns, nor anything the traveller might have learnt before his departure. It's all in the paperwork.'

'And I can read it?'

'You are not a person to be tainted, you are the anger of God made flesh. It doesn't matter what you read, what you hear, you are the sea-green incorruptible.'

Cale thought about this for a few moments.

'And the beardy man?'

'Guido Hooke.'

'Yes?'

'He is a natural philosopher who claims that the moon is not perfectly round.'

'But it is round,' said Cale. 'All you need to do is look at it. If you're going to kill people for being stupid you're going to need a lot more executioners.'

Bosco smiled.

'Guido Hooke is very far from stupid, although he is eccentric. And he is right about the moon.'

There was a snort of dismissal from Cale.

'Anyone can see on any unclouded night that the moon is round.'

'That is an illusion created by the moon's distance from the earth. Consider Tiger Mountain – from a distance its slopes seem smooth as butter, close to it's as wrinkled as an old man's sack.'

'How do you know? About the moon, I mean.'

'I'll show you tonight if you wish.'

'If Hooke is right, why is he going to die for telling the truth?'

'It's a matter of authority. The Pope has ruled that the moon is precisely round – an expression of the perfect creation of God. Guido Hooke has contradicted him.'

'But you say he's right.'

'What does that matter? He's contradicted the rock on which the One True Faith is built: the right to the last word. If he is allowed to do so, consider where it will end: the death of authority. Without authority there is no church, without the church no salvation.' He smiled. 'Hooke speaks for the lower truth, the Pope for a higher one.'

'But you don't believe in salvation.'

'Which is why I must become Pope so that what is true and what I believe become the same thing. Why are you so interested in the Purgators?'

# 5

Kleist was singing wildly, happily off-key.

'The buzzing of the trees and the cigarette bees
The soda water fountains
Where the bluebell rings
And the lemonade sings
On the big rock candy mountain
In the big rock candy mountain
The priests all quack like ducks
There's a five-cent whore at every door
At dinner there is always more
And never was heard a discouraging word
In the big rock candy mountain.'

He reached down, casual like, to check the knife sheathed in a pocket of the horse's saddle and went on bawling not with much respect for tunefulness.

'There's a lake of stew and whisky too
You can paddle all around it in a big canoe
In the big rock –'

Then he was off, pulling the knife with him and running for a patch of blackberry briars. He leapt into the middle, his speed and weight carrying him, thorns scraping his skin red as he went. But the tangle of shoots was thicker than he'd realized and the older suckers in the middle were tough and thick-barbed and his headlong flight was painfully brought to a halt.

Powerful hands grabbed him by the heels and dragged him backwards out of the briars. They had to tug hard and it gave Kleist a couple of seconds to decide. He dropped the knife in the briars and then he was free and being dragged into the open.

Other hands grabbed his wrists as he kicked and wriggled. Once he was held fast he knew there was no point and stopped struggling.

One man stood in front of him, his precise features hidden by the sun in Kleist's eyes.

'We're going to search you, so don't move. Any weapons?'

'No.'

Two hands, swiftly and cleanly, skilfully frisked him.

'Good. If you had lied to us it would have been the last thing you ever did. Get him up.'

Kleist was pulled roughly into a sitting position and all five men, knives and short swords pulled, let him go in disciplined order. These people knew what they were doing.

'What's your name?'

'Thomas Cale.'

'What are you up to out here on your own?'

'I was heading for Post Moresby.' A hefty blow landed on the side of his head.

'Say "Lord Dunbar" when you speak to Lord Dunbar.'

'All right. How was I supposed to know?'

Another blow to teach him not to be lippy.

'What would you do there?' said Lord Dunbar.

Kleist looked at him – he was scruffy, dirty and badly dressed in an ugly-looking tartan. He didn't look like any lord Kleist had ever seen.

'I want to get on a boat and get as far away from here as I can.'

'Why?'

'The Redeemers killed my family in the massacre on Mount Nugent. When they took Memphis I knew it was time to go away where I'd never see one of them ever again.' This was half true as far as it went.

'Where did you get the horse?'

'It's mine.'

Another blow to the head.

'I found it. I think it was a stray from the battle at Silbury Hill.'

'I heard about that.'

'Perhaps the Redeemers would pay cash for him,' said Handsome Johnny.

'Perhaps they'll string you up when you try,' said Kleist, getting another clip on the ear.

'Lord Dunbar!'

'Lord Dunbar, all right.'

'Handsome Johnny,' said Dunbar. 'Search his horse.' Dunbar squatted down beside him.

'What are these Redeemers after?'

'I don't know. All I know is they're a bunch of murdering bastards, Lord Dunbar, and the best thing to do is get away from them.'

'The Materazzi haven't been able to catch us in twenty years,' said Lord Dunbar. 'It doesn't much matter to us who's trying to hunt us down.'

Handsome Johnny came back and laid an armful of Kleist's possessions on the ground. There was a good haul. Kleist had made sure that however basic the purpose of anything he took from Memphis, it was all of the highest quality: the swords of Portuguese steel, inlaid with ivory at the handle, a blanket of cashmere wool, and so on, then the money – eighty dollars in a silk purse. This cheered the five men considerably. For all Dunbar's boasting, the pickings were pretty scant if their clothes and ragged state were anything to go by.

'All right,' said Kleist. 'You've got everything I own. It's a pretty good drag. Just let me go.'

Another blow.

'Lord Dunbar.'

'We should shallow the cheeky little sod.'

Kleist didn't like the sound of that.

'Let me take him back there,' said Handsome Johnny. 'I'll save any trouble.'

Lord Dunbar glared at him.

'I know what beastliness you want to do before that, Handsome Johnny,' he shouted. He looked back at Kleist. 'Get up.' Kleist got to his feet. 'Give us your jacket.' Kleist took off his short coat, one he'd stolen off a hook in Vipond's attendance room, soft leather and simply but beautifully cut.

'You've been lying to me and I like that in a man,' said Dunbar, admiring the jacket and mourning the fact that it was too small. 'But you're right about fair dos.' He pointed to a roughish path. 'That'll take you in the general direction out of the woods. After that you're on your own. Now bugger off!'

Kleist didn't need to be told twice. He passed by Handsome Johnny, who watched him go with resentful lasciviousness and vanished into the woods with nothing but half the clothes he'd been wearing five minutes before.

'You can't replace three hundred men carefully chosen for their great qualities and bound to you with hoops of steel with those degenerates in the House of Special Purpose.'

'How else are we going to replace them? Do we have ten years?'

Bosco was not so green that he was unaware this was the first time Cale had spoken of them both in this way,

71

and that he was being charmed. Still, that he was making an effort to be deceptive was encouraging.

'No, we don't.'

'Are there any records?'

'Oh, each Redeemer has a tally codex. Everything about him is recorded there.'

'Do you have one?'

'Of course.'

'I'd like to read it.'

'This idea won't work.'

'It *might* not work. They're standing on the edge of death followed by eternal hell where devils every day will disembowel them with a spade or swallow them alive and shit them out for all eternity. Save them from a fate like that – those are the hoops of steel that'll bind them to me.'

'These are deviants. The very boilings of moth and rust.'

'If they don't come up to snuff, I'll return them for execution. These are trained men abandoned by everyone. At least give me their tallies.' Cale smiled, the first time in a long time. 'I don't even believe you disagree.'

'Very well. We'll both read the tallies. Then we'll see.'

'Tell me about Guido Hooke.'

There was a knock at the door which opened immediately followed by a Redeemer who nodded obsequiously to Bosco and dumped a large file in a box, marked 'INTRO'. He nodded again and left.

'Hooke,' said Bosco, 'is a nuisance to me and of no real concern to you.'

'I want to know about him.'

'Why?'

'A hunch. Besides, I thought I was to know everything.'

'Everything? You see that file Notil just bought in. That's just a day's paperwork – a slack day. Stick to what you're good at.'

'Tell me.'

'Very well. Hooke is a know-all who thinks he can understand the world by the book of arithmetic. He is a great inventor of engines. He is brilliant in the way of the best of such people but he has stuck his gonk once too often into things that he had much better not have done. I've left him alone because I admire his mind, and for ten years. But his declarations about the moon contradicted the Pope, I warned him to leave and suggested the Hanse might be willing to employ him. While I was in Memphis he went to Fray Bentos to take ship but was caught by Gant's men in a hoteli waiting to embark.'

'Why didn't they take him to Stuttgart?'

'Because in Stuttgart he wouldn't be my responsibility. Now I must either make an Act of Faith of him or be seen to defy the ruling of the Pope.'

'But you said the Pope was wrong.'

'You are being deliberately slow.'

'What kind of engines?'

'Blasphemous engines.'

'Why?'

'A machine for flying – if God had meant us to fly he would have given us wings. A wagon cased in iron – if God had meant us to have armour we would have been born with scales. And for all I know, or care, a machine for extracting sunlight from cucumbers. Most of the drawings he's made are fantasies. His idea for a hopio-copter that flies is twaddle. It doesn't look as if it could move along the ground, let alone fly through the air. But I have made use of his water gate in the east canal.'

'If God had intended there to be water gates wouldn't he have made water flow upwards?' Bosco would not rise to the bait.

'If you want to know about him, read his tally. He's a dead man, whether you do or don't.'

Kleist had been forced to hang around until the next day before Lord Dunbar and his men left and he could collect the knife he'd dropped in the bramble bush. He thought carefully about what to do next. He was not interested in revenge, not being the indulgent type – it was dangerous and Kleist did not believe in risk. On the other hand he was in the middle of some bumhole wilderness with no horse, no chattels, no money and few clothes. All in all he decided he had to follow them but he wondered repeatedly over the next three days if he hadn't made a mistake. He was cold and hungry. He was used to that, but though the surroundings were green enough he came across no standing water. Weakness from lack of water could take you quickly and once he lost touch with Dunbar he was finished. He had one break: he found some bamboo – spindly but good enough. Probably. He cut himself a section five feet long and a dozen thin poles and hurried to catch up. Following for the rest of the day he found a small puddle of green and brown water and decided to risk it. He'd tasted worse but not often. Dunbar and his men stopped an hour before darkness and Kleist had to work quickly in the fading light. The bamboo was still green, which made it easy to cut it into thin lashings to twist and use for a bow string. Then he split the bamboo down the middle into three staves, each one shorter than the last. By the time it was dark he'd bound one stave on the other with the lashings like the leaf spring of a cart. He slept little and badly when he did. The next day he began work as soon as it was light, following as they moved off, and finished the bow as they stopped for a couple of hours at midday. He would have liked to recurve the ends for more power but there wasn't time – it was a complicated process. The sun came out and tormented him with thirst but while it desiccated him it did the same to the bow, drying it fully and binding everything archer-tight. There was flint enough lying around and it took only ten minutes to make an arrowhead.

A maggoty crow provided the feathers for the fletch,

looked like a large bush at the edge of the camp. In a few seconds he was urinating at the edge of the camp and shouting orders for them to strike it. Arrow into bow, string pulled, the huge power of his right arm and shoulder and back tensed and a deep breath and then loose. A scream from Dunbar as the arrow took him in the left hip. Three-second pause – the other four stared. 'What?' called one.

Another arrow hit Handsome Johnny in the mouth and he fell back waving his arms. A third raced off, slipping and sliding in terror to the cover of the trees. An arrow, pulled badly, hit him in the foot and he hopped the last few yards, shouting in pain, and vanished into the trees. Another unscathed raced out of the camp in the other direction. The fifth man in the almost centre of the camp did not move. Kleist took aim, the bow creaking with the bend and let loose into the middle of his chest. A dreadful gasp of anguish. He bowed another arrow and drew it back, carefully and quickly making his way into the camp, moving the point back and forth over the points of threat. Handsome Johnny wasn't going to be any trouble. The man kneeling with his head bowed was still groaning but there was now a strange whistling sound alternating with each indrawn breath. No one could fake that noise. He wasn't going to be any trouble either. He just wished the sound would stop. Dunbar, lying on his side, was a dreadful white colour, lips bloodless.

'I should,' said Dunbar, softly, 'have killed you when I had the chance.'

'You should have left me alone when you had the chance.'

'Fair enough.'

'Any weapons?'

'Why should I tell you?'

'Fair enough.' Nervous, Kleist kept watching the trees. This was too risky.

'This could take hours. Finish me.'

'So I should, but it's easier said than done.'

'Why? You did for those two without much problem.'

'Yeah, but I was angry then.'

'When all's said, I let you go. Finish it.'

'Your men will be back. Let them do it.'

'Not for hours. Maybe not at all.'

'Well I don't want to, see.'

'You'd best be . . .'

There was a loud 'THWACK!' as Kleist loosed the bow almost point blank into Dunbar's chest. His eyes widened and he breathed out for what seemed like minutes but was only a few seconds. Fortunately for both of them that was that.

Behind him the man on his knees still groaned and whistled. Kleist dropped to his knees and heaved. But there was nothing in his stomach to come out. It was not easy to keep on retching and keep an eye on the trees. He dropped the bow – he needed his hands free to search his new possessions and claim his old. He stood up slowly and screamed.

Standing five yards away was a girl. She looked at him wide-eyed and then threw herself into his arms and burst into tears.

'Thank you! Thank you!' she sobbed, hugging him as if he were a lost parent, her hands clutching him with desperate relief and gratitude. She kissed him full on the lips, then pushed herself into his chest, her hands squeezing his upper back as if she would never let him go. 'You were so brave, so brave.' She stepped back to examine him, eyes brimming with admiration.

It would not have taken a talented student of human nature to have read Kleist's not only astonished look but also the deep shiftiness of his expression as she looked adoringly at him. He watched the understanding that he had not arrived to rescue her move over her face like a fast sunrise. The admiration washed out and her eyes began to become wet with tears. It was not often that Kleist felt mean-spirited.

She stepped back rather more than the emotion of her discovery warranted and produced the knife she had lifted from Kleist's belt while she was so gratefully hugging him.

The look of astonishment and anger on Kleist's face was so comic in its effect, the girl burst into laughter.

His face went red with anger, which only made her

laugh harder. Then he stepped forward, knocked the knife out of her hand and punched her in the face. She went down like a sack of coal and fetched her head a nasty blow. He picked up the knife, keeping his eyes on her, then gave a quick scan of the trees. Things were getting out of control. Her expression now was one of shock and pain at her bloody nose. She sat up.

'Laughing on the other side of your face now.'

She said nothing as he backed away and started examining the bundles around the camp for his own stuff and anything else portable. The man on his knees was still moaning and his punctured lung still whistling.

The girl started crying again. Kleist carried on searching. In what must have been Lord Dunbar's pack he found his money. Otherwise the pickings were scant. Their lives as robbers can't have been up to much. And they only had three horses, including the one they stole from Kleist. The girl's crying became louder and more uncontrollable. Along with the groan and whistle of the kneeling man, it was getting on Kleist's nerves. But more than that.

*The tears of a woman are an alcahest to the soul of man, Redeemer Fraser had once said to him. A tearful bitch can dissolve all a man's good judgement in its liquid gerrymandering.*

At the time this warning had seemed of dubious relevance, given that he had no memory of ever having seen a woman. His experience in Memphis, though it had very much expanded his experience of women in some ways, was not helpful when it came to tears, the whores of Kitty Town not being given much to weeping.

'Shut up,' he said.

She reduced the sound to a grizzling and the occasional heavy sob.

'What the hell were you doing with these desperadoes?'

She could not answer at first, trying to bring herself under control with wet gasps of emotion.

'They kidnapped me,' she said, which was not true or not entirely true, 'and they all raped me.' His time in Memphis had made Kleist familiar with the term. He had heard a number of puzzling amusing stories about rape and had caused even more laughter by asking for an explanation. He was shocked by the answer and did not approve. She was clearly a liar but she looked as distraught as even Kleist would have expected. But then a few minutes ago she'd been laughing at him.

'If you're telling the truth, I'm sorry.'

'Let me have one of the horses.'

'That would mean you could keep up with me. I don't think so.'

'You'll have the best horse – the others are just kick-bags.'

This was true enough.

'I could sell them in the next town. Why should I give one to you when you're a thief? Or worse.'

'They're both branded. They'll hang you for a horse thief if you try to sell them.'

'Well, you look as if you'd know,' he said, tying his newly filled bag onto his horse saddle.

'Please. Two of them are still out there.'

'One of them isn't going to be following anyone for quite some time.'

'But the other one could.'

'All right. Just shut up. But you go in that direction,' he said, pointing to the west. 'If I see you again, I'll cut your bloody head off.' With that he mounted his horse and set off, leaving the girl sitting on the forest floor, next to the kneeling man, still wheezing and whistling. If his actions in leaving the young woman in the clearing were ignoble, they were in the light of the appalling consequences of his only other experience of rescuing young women in distress at least understandable.

'Do you think he's right?' asked Gil.

'What do you think?' said Bosco.

'I think he's wrong,' replied Gil, 'I think the Purgators are where they deserve to be. Their fate is their character. If God has not been able to change their hearts not even someone who is the anger of God made flesh can change them, blessing be upon him.'

'We must hope, Redeemer, that you are wrong. Cale is full of surprises.'

'Now I know why I never loved him.'

They both laughed.

'Should I continue?' said Gil. 'With the plan to invest Bose Ikard?' Bose Ikard was the Burgrave of Switzerland, notionally second only to the notorious King Zog of that country, but a very close second. With the Materazzi empire having collapsed Bose Ikard was now the most powerful of all the rainmakers in the four quarters. He had made, in Bosco and Gil's eyes, the mistake of allowing a remnant of the Materazzi to take refuge in Spanish Leeds, something they rightly regarded as hostile to their interests. What they did not realize was that Bose Ikard took the same view and only a screaming fit by King Zog had forced his hand to allow the Materazzi to take refuge in Spanish Leeds. The Redeemer Diplomatic Service was not adept at either diplomacy or the gathering of intelligence and Bosco had limited access to its findings, which in any case did not include the fact that Bose Ikard had done everything possible to encourage the Materazzi to go away. Beyond simply allowing them to stay he offered no help and no money, a lack of assistance he hoped would effectively starve them into moving on somewhere else where they would no longer be his problem. Understandably he did not want their presence to give the Redeemers an opportunity to cause trouble. However, Bosco knew nothing of this reluctance and could only infer Ikard's attitudes from his apparently hospitable treatment of the Materazzi. He'd thought it might be a good idea to have him killed to mark Zog's card and to discourage anyone else who might be thinking of harbouring the Materrazi or anyone else the Redeemers had taken a dislike to.

'No. We must delay his death until . . . for several months at any rate – until we have some idea whether Cale can turn the Purgators.'

'It's risky to delay.'

'It's risky not to. We are midstream in a spate. It's dangerous to go forwards, it's dangerous to go back. Meanwhile I mean to spread Cale's name and reputation. I want you to take him to Duffer's Drift.'

'Because?'

'Because he will solve the problem.'

'You seem very sure.'

'Take him and see. Clearly you have less faith in the power of God's exasperation than you ought.'

'*Mea culpa*, Redeemer.'

Bosco sniffed, now out of sorts at Gil's lack of zeal.

'What about Hooke?'

'Reluctant as I am to have my hand forced by Gant, we must avoid provocation until Cale succeeds or fails. If Hooke is to die we must make a show of it, and we must swallow the humiliation like it or not by broadcasting it wide. Invite persons of note.'

There was a knock on the door and Cale was shown in. He was told he was to be sent south with Gil to deal with the Folk. He didn't argue or even ask any questions.

'I want him. Hooke, I mean,' said Cale.

'Why?'

'Because I've read his tally and seen his drawings. Some may be what you say but his machine for storming walls looks right – maybe even the giant crossbow. There are good ideas everywhere. You said his water gate was a fine piece of work.'

'He has offended the Pope.'

'You intend to kill the Pope.'

'Not so. But if I did I wouldn't offend him first.'

'Hooke's engines could help you not to worry about offending him.'

Bosco sighed and walked over to the window. 'There are many irons in the fire and unlimited kettles boiling over them. I have to balance conflicting needs.'

'My needs come first.'

'You are the resentment of God – not God Almighty himself. There's a considerable difference, as you'll learn if you push your luck too far.' He laughed at Cale's expression. 'My dear, this is not a threat. If you fail, I fail with you.'

'I used to think you were so powerful no one could stand against you.'

'Well, you were wrong. We stand on the edge of a gnat's wing, you and I. Let me say this. If you succeed at Duffer's Drift then I can use the power this will give both of us to delay Hooke's execution. I don't have the power to stop it and that's that. Set him to work while you're away. Succeed at Duffer's Drift with your Purgators and who knows? It's in your hands.'

It took Cale, along with Redeemer Gil and two others, six days to reach the Drift. They had made more than seventy miles each day, changing ponies at horse stations placed at twenty-mile intervals until the last eighty miles, where Antagonist outriders were causing too much trouble for anything permanent. When they arrived, Cale was exhausted, his shoulder was killing him and his finger hurt like hell itself, as bad almost as the day Solomon Solomon had cut it away in the Red Opera.

'Get some sleep, sir,' said Gil as Cale was shown to a tent made from blue sacking. Cale never slept easily but two minutes served when he hit the hideously uncomfortable cot laid for him. Gil woke him with a cup of foul-tasting liquid eight hours later. It occurred to Cale as he drank that he must now be as soft as lard compared to only a few months earlier. Then he would have thought this muck was bearable.

'This,' he said to Gil, who was watching him thoughtfully, 'is bloody horrible.'

Gil looked genuinely disconcerted. 'I'm sorry.' He took the mug and tasted it to see what was wrong. 'It tastes all right to me.' They looked at each other – a pointless exchange. 'Go and have a look around the camp. Get the measure. There'll be something here to eat when we come back.'

'Can't wait.'

The veldt of the Transvaal is a wide-open prairie four hundred miles to the south-west of the Sanctuary. The people there, who call themselves the Folk, farm and hunt across its great spaces and are recent converts to Antagonism. For that reason and because they are an odd bunch by any standards, their beliefs are rigid and intense. They have two ranks: the ordinary Folkhusbands and a leader, the Folk Maister, now nearly always a Predikant, or pastor, who never has authority over more than a thousand souls. Not having been of the Redeemer faith before their conversion and having had little to do with it, their loathing and hatred of their monkish assailants were intense to the point of insanity. It was said, an exaggeration of course, that the Folk were born onto a saddle and with a bow in their hands. The trench warfare of the Eastern Front was useless as a model for fighting such people in such terrain. The Folk did not fight in armies but in commandos of between a hundred and four hundred men – but often less and sometimes more. If they were attacked they just retreated into the endless veldt. A trench system against such methods was like trying to kill a fly with an axe.

It had become the Redeemers' forgotten war. Most of their troops were bogged down in the great attrition of the Eastern Front. But even if there had been more in the way of Redeemer soldiers there was no obvious way of using superiority of numbers against such a fluid and skilled group fighting on ground they knew and loved. In addition, the Redeemers used cavalry rarely and were not very good when they did. In a straight fight it was true a force of Redeemers would annihilate even a vastly superior number of the Folk. But they never gave them a straight fight.

Because the war on the veldt was regarded by the Pope and his close advisors as of minor importance, Bosco and Princeps had been allowed greater freedom to decide on new tactics, something always considered with suspicion on the Eastern front. Even before Bosco and Princeps had been drawn to attack the Materazzi by Bosco's desperate need to recapture Cale, they had changed the conduct of the war against the Folk in dramatic fashion. A string of thirty forward forts had been established. They were not forts in any normal sense with solid walls and defined defensive barriers, but, so it was intended, fluid defensive positions to guard all the most important strategic points in the veldt. Behind them would be eight much larger conventional forts from which each of the forward positions could be reinforced when they inevitably came under attack. It was the most original plan in Redeemer military history. Unfortunately the problem with all great plans is that they must be put into practice. Lacking the presence of Princeps, now moved to the more pressing assault on the Materazzi, the execution of the new tactics by his clueless replacement created a terrible crisis. Instead of large numbers of Redeemers standing in trenches defending territory the Folk had no intention of attacking, they had now ventured out into territory where none of their hideous military virtues were of any help and all of their weaknesses could be punishingly exploited. The result was a change from a war that was going nowhere to one that was coming close to collapsing into defeat. The advance forts were relentlessly attacked and taken over by the Folk with heavy casualties for the Redeemers and few for their assailants. When they attempted to retake the forts the Redeemers again took heavy losses. But the Folk always knew when to make their retreat quickly so that their casualties were light. A few weeks later, having attacked the forts furthest away towards the Drakensberg, they would be back and the whole bloody process would start again. Bloody, that is, almost solely for the Redeemers. Duffer's Drift had won its lamentable name because it was the most important of the advanced forts and had been lost to the Folk so often.

Imagine a great U formed by a river bend. The land inside the U is twenty feet lower than the land outside it, except towards the back, which is dominated by a low hill. Past this hill runs the all-important road that crosses the river and straight out the other side, cutting the U into two equal halves. A few hundred yards down this road is a large tabletop hill. The twenty-foot difference between the north and south bank meant that for eighty miles in either direction no wagon could make its way up the near vertical sides except for on this one road at the Drift. The entire field of defence was barely two thousand yards wide. Cale's problem was as easy to set out as it was difficult to solve. There were perhaps fifty of these choke points on the veldt and not enough troops to hold them by conventional means. To cut down the movement of the Folk and their ability to resupply from the sea, nearly all the points had to be held nearly all the time. At the moment they were taking them at will, holding them while supplies passed through and then vanishing whenever the Redeemers showed up, and taking various other similar forts up and down the front line.

Cale spent nearly eight hours walking the U.

'What do you think?' said Gil, anxious to hear the answer of the great prodigy.

'Tricky,' was all he got in addition to a request to talk to survivors of the last attack. There were only two, this not being a taking prisoners kind of war. Nevertheless, Cale spent all evening talking to them.

'How many are here now?' he asked Gil.

'Two thousand.'

'How many can you keep here?'

'Not more than two hundred. There aren't the troops or supplies for them if there were.'

'Send away eighteen hundred.'

Gil was too intelligent to ask why. There had to be few enough defenders or there would be no attack.

'So what are you going to do?'

'Nothing,' said Cale, 'except leave.'

Cale was simply being annoying but he kept Gil swinging on his rope, following in the rear of the eighteen hundred as they retreated and doing nothing about the defence of the Drift. Having travelled some five miles with the withdrawal, Cale turned his horse to one side and the fuming Gil was forced, along with the two guards, to come with him. Soon Cale turned back towards the camp and a small rise some eight hundred yards to the rear of the Drift. It was probably not high enough nor close enough to attract Folk scouts when there were better, nearer lookouts they would visit first. Cale dismounted and gestured to the others to do the same. Then he started for the top of the rise and ended up crawling the last few yards. Gil, relief softening his fury, came up behind him.

'Do you want something?' asked Cale, hostile.

'I'm just doing as Redeemer Bosco would tell me, sir.'

This was true enough so there wasn't much point arguing, although this didn't stop him thinking about it. He took what looked like a leather bottle without a top from his knapsack and two glass circles and fitting them in either end of the topless leather bottle he pulled two straps around the middle and tightened them so they were held fast. It was the telescope with which Bosco had shown him the imperfect moon and the identical twin of the one he had stolen from Redeemer Picarbo and which had been filched in turn by one or other of the soldiers who'd captured him in the Scablands. It seemed like half a lifetime ago.

The more awkward and taciturn Cale was with Gil, the more the Redeemer's earlier bad temper at being treated as if he were of no importance seemed gradually to change. His initial confusion about Cale's change of status from expendable acolyte to manifestation of the wrath of God was a leap even for the most obedient of Redeemers. But the greater the contempt or indifference with which Cale treated him, the more Gil found himself able to let his decade-long familiarity change into awe and trust. He had a natural desire to worship and for all his intelligence it was as if the black intensity and seemingly total indifference that had come to dominate Cale in the last eight months was exerting its magic over a man very much sensitive to magic. Cale sensed the change, the respect, admiration and the fear that was more than physical – something he knew Gil barely felt. What surprised him more was that he could feel the growing adoration working on him like the air he and Vague Henri used to blow into the soft animal skins that held the holy water in the sacristy so that they could bounce them up and down on the floor in blasphemous delight. To walk past a group of men and feel them diminish themselves at the sight of you – this was something.

Through the rest of the day Cale barely spoke between

spying out the landscape and drawing maps of the field of battle in the dust, then scrapping, re-drawing and scrapping again. Throughout he tried to keep the intensely curious Gil from seeing or understanding what he could see of the diagrams he was drawing of trenches, heights, lines of sight and so on. This was not so much from any need he felt to keep things secret as a desire to annoy Gil. But, though frustrated, Gil only seemed the more impressed. In time, Cale began to enjoy the feeling of gawping admiration so much that he started making up marks and signs just to amuse himself by making his diagram insanely and meaninglessly complex in a way that clearly left Gil drowning in wonder.

Just before dark Cale backed down the hill and Gil followed. He started to arrange the rota for guard duty and was dividing by four when he realized something. Instead, and without facing a murmur of protest, he divided the night watch into three. His insolence, and he could feel it, increased their awe of him still further. Deeply satisfied with his deviousness, he went back to the top of the rise and made himself as comfortable as possible before falling asleep and dreaming of Arbell Swan-Neck. Impossibly beautiful, she managed to keep eluding him as he tried to follow her in the corridors of the Palazzo as if he were a nuisance she must politely – but not too politely – deal with and not a once-adored lover. In his dreams of her often he was robbed of his anger and violence, stripped down to a humiliated supplicant who could not accept that he was now graciously despised while he preposterously hoped that if he could only get her to stay still and talk to him she would certainly be able to explain that her apparent betrayal had all been a terrible mistake. And it would be all right. He would be happy again. But always she turned away as if his presence was utterly unwelcome. He woke up just before dawn, miserable and burning with shame and anger at his weakness.

He ate and drank silently and then, Gil by his side, waited to watch the Drift emerge slowly in the light of dawn. The trenches now filled with archers in the centre of the U were built at angles so that bolts and arrows could not be aimed down a straight line. The problem, now clearer than ever, was that the red earth thrown up by the digging was a stark contrast with the yellow grass of the veldt, marking the ground as plain as a target painted with circles. From this distance the fifty or so archer men-at-arms hidden in the bend of the river with its cracks and crevices seemed well hidden, not easy to spot even with his bioscope. An hour later with the sun well up, Gil pulled at his arm and pointed to a dust cloud coming from the north by the side of the tabletop mountain in front of the Drift. The dust cloud gradually revealed a large body of Folk, mounted soldiers pulling four wagons behind them and heading for the Drift. At first it seemed as if they were going to ride straight on through its middle, a manoeuvre of such suicidal stupidity that only the events at Silbury Hill made him suspect for a moment that the commando approaching might actually do so.

They halted about four hundred yards away. There was a pause of about ten minutes and then the commando split into two – one part to the east along the river, the other to the west. A small number of men with the covered wagons moved back behind the table mountain and Cale was unable to track them though he was anxious to do so. There was something odd about the wagons – they were covered but a peculiar shape. The Redeemers in the Drift would have to wait for the attack. Nearly an hour passed then Gil again pulled his sleeve. 'Look, sir, on the shoulder of that butte.' He was pointing at a flattish section down from the top of the table mountain. Taking the line, Cale examined the wagons now several hundred feet above the Drift and saw the three of them being stripped, though fuzzily, the glasses being not so good at such a distance. What he could make out consisted of frames and ropes but these were not structures he recognized beyond their being some sort of catapult. He passed the glasses to Gil who said he thought they looked like ballistas, a contraption much used for a while by the Antagonists on the Eastern Front.

'Never heard of it,' said Cale.

'It's just a glorified crossbow, but much bigger. They used it for a while about nine months ago but it was only any use against hill defences and there aren't many of them on the Eastern Front. I can't see the point of them here.'

They didn't have to wait long for the first surprise. After five minutes of manic activity the ballistas had been set up – but instead of pointing the ten-foot-long bows at the trenches in the Drift, the three were clearly fixed pointing almost straight up into the air. When they fired, the powerful bows lashed the enormous bolts upwards but at a slight angle. An unpleasant nerve-jangling scream went up.

'They fix a wheezer around the shaft – makes them wail. Gets on your tits.'

The whining bolts shot upwards and then curved in a sharp arc and smacked heavily into the yellow stub grass around the trenches as if straight down from the clouds directly above. For the next twenty minutes the ballistas were fired repeatedly to get their range until almost two in three of the bolts were landing in the trenches. A few screams made it clear that some of the huge bolts had found a target – but though this was nastily unfamiliar, Cale couldn't see it was going to be decisive.

There was another hiatus and then the iron 'TWANG!' of the ballistas starting up again with the oddness of the difference in sight and sound – the giant bolts were almost in mid-flight before the metallic noise of the release rippled over Cale and Gil on the distant rise. But this time there was something even odder about the sound – it was deeper – and the arc of the bolt as it hit the top of its natural curve and began to fall to earth. The shaft, even without using the 'scope, was clearly much thicker and Cale scrabbled with the bioscope to catch sight of the bolt as it moved. Just as he fastened on to it, the thick shaft started to fall apart in mid-air and a dozen much thinner bolts gently separated from the main shaft and slowly formed a loose group before hitting the trenches as a loose pack – there was a beat and then the screaming of half a dozen men. Then another thick bolt was released and another. From time to time one of them failed to unravel but mostly the nine bolts fired every minute landed on the Redeemers in the trenches as one hundred and eight bolts every sixty seconds. The hideous screaming of the dead and dying was continuous now. Gil's face set with a stoic pallor. Through the glasses he could see the surviving Redeemers desperately digging to get themselves deeper but it was as much use as digging to get out of the rain. Realizing this, the survivors started scrambling out of the trenches and running away. They were allowed to go about fifty yards before a sea of bolts and arrows from either side of the great U took them like a boy taking a stick to weeds. Some twenty Redeemers surrendered. From all around the U, the soldiers of the Folk emerged from behind bushes and the great termite hills. There must have been a hundred and sixty men within a hundred yards. As a handful of the Folk came to take the surrender and Cale was wondering whether the Redeemers were going to get

Redeemers, whose remains had been shovelled into a shallow pit about five hundred yards away. He then explained why they'd been so easily defeated. He asked for questions. There were a few. He asked for answers. There were a few of those too. None of them, it was clear to Cale, would have resulted in a different outcome, though a couple would certainly have held back the Folk for longer.

'You've got two hours to agree a plan. Then two hundred of you'll stay here and see if you can hold out for the three days it'll take to reinforce.'

'How will you choose, sir?'

'Prayer,' said Cale. On his way back to his tent Cale had time to consider the cheapness of his remark. Redeemers or not, two hundred men were going to die.

Which is exactly what they did. Cale listened to the new tactic for defence, decided to order a few changes because he wanted to see their manoeuvres in practical operation and then chose the men to carry it out by lot rather than any blasphemous play with devotion. He added one name himself, that of a centenar he had recognized during the initial conflab as a Redeemer who had once beaten him on the arse with a rope as thick as a man's wrist for talking during a training session. Possibly the Redeemer might have lived had it not been for the fact that it had not even been Cale doing the talking but Dominic Savio, who had been whispering to Vague

Henri that he might, indeed probably would, die that very night and be shat out by a devil for all eternity.

For a second time Cale withdrew along with Gil to the scrubby rise about half a mile away from Duffer's Drift. Again the wait, two days this time, which Cale passed occasionally tormenting Gil in any trivial way he could think of – hinting at lascivious experiences in Kitty Town, which, being in the early stages of love, he had not visited along with Kleist and the guilty but fascinated Vague Henri. 'You could get a beezle,' said Cale to Redeemer Gil, 'for a dollar or less. And,' he added, 'a bumscraper for two.'

He had made up the names of these perversions and therefore thought they did not exist. He was wrong about this. In Kitty Town even a depravity no one had ever thought of could be found if you had the money.

Most of the rest of the time he slept, ate most of the food allotted to Gil and the two guards, and made notes and imagined over and over the attack that had happened on Duffer's Drift and the ones that might happen. And also he thought about Swan-Neck and the next meeting, where she would throw herself into his arms, weeping with loss while the dying Bosco with his last gasp would admit her betrayal had been an evil trick. Then he would be ashamed of his absurd delusion and imagine slowly wringing that beautiful neck without pity or remorse as she choked and gargled under his merciless hand-grip. After these often lengthy daydreams he would feel ashamed and a little bit mad. But this did not stop him from revisiting them on many occasions to commit, as the Holy Redeemer Clementine called it, the sin of pursuing evil thoughts. Cale found himself pursuing evil thoughts on an ever more demented and epic scale than even Clementine could possibly have imagined. 'It is as well for the world,' IdrisPukke had said once to Cale, 'that the very wicked are generally as pusillanimous about turning their thoughts into deeds as anyone else.'

When Cale had looked down from the Great Jut on Tiger Mountain, he had felt an uneasy joy and delightful unpleasantness and now on the rise above Duffer's Drift he felt the same uneasiness and unpleasantness and the same delight and joy. There's nothing like an itch, after all, you can finally scratch.

The centenars under a millenar had agreed that while deepening the trenches was of no use, the strength of the soil would allow them to dig a shelf at the bottom of the trench so that each man could escape from the rain of projectiles coming from the ballistas. To cover the main trench at the centre of the U more trenches were built outside it to the left and right. The plan to cut and burn every bush outside the U for four hundred yards was prevented by Cale because he would only let two hundred men do the work and not the eighteen hundred that were available. 'You won't have more than two hundred men in future so what's the point in having them now?'

# 6

'You're my hero.'

Kleist and the girl were sitting in front of a partly dead and hollowed-out oak that held a fire in such a way that it looked like a hearth.

'I'm not your hero.'

'Yes, you are,' taunted the girl. 'You saved me.'

'I didn't save you. You just happened to be in the bushes when I took back my stuff. I didn't even know you were there.'

'Your heart knew,' teased the girl.

'Think what you like,' said Kleist. 'Tomorrow you go where you were going and I'll go somewhere else as far away from you as possible.'

'My people believe,' said the girl, chattering as happily as a starling, 'that when you save someone's life, you're responsible for them for ever.' This claim was as outrageous a lie as she had ever told and contrary to everything the Klephts believed when it came to matters of obligation.

'Where's the sense in that?' said an exasperated Kleist. 'It should be the other way around.'

'All right. Now I'm responsible for you.'

'Firstly,' said Kleist, 'I don't give a toss what your people believe and secondly I don't want you to be responsible for me – I want you to go away.'

The girl laughed.

'You don't mean that. Tell me your name.'

'I don't have a name. I'm nameless.'

'Everybody has a name.'

'Not me.'

'Shall I tell you my name?'

'No.'

'I knew you were going to say that.'

'Then why did you ask?'

'Because I *looove*,' she said, lengthening the sound of the word, 'to hear the sound of your voice.' And she laughed again. It took perhaps two hours for Kleist to be completely done for.

Two days later Cale and Gil watched as the Folk accepted, clearly after some argument and with a lot more caution, the surrender of the six surviving Redeemers. They were tied up and loaded in a wagon and ten minutes later had vanished beyond the tabletop mountain.

'How many more times?' said a morose Gil.

Cale did not answer but walked down off the rise, mounted his horse and started back to the not entirely reliably named Fort Bastion. Five days after their arrival there, the four of them were back in the Sanctuary and facing a bad-tempered Bosco.

'I told you to stay in the veldt until you'd sorted the problem out.'

'I *have* sorted it out.'

Cale had the pleasure of surprising Bosco into silence, not something in all their long association he had been able to do before.

'Explain.'

Cale did so. When he'd finished Bosco looked dubious, not because Cale had been unconvincing but because his claims looked too good to be true. Bosco was being offered a way out of what was becoming a terrible trap with its origins in the ludicrous events that had caused the execution of his two hundred and ninety-nine carefully chosen vanguard. When someone offered you a way out of the teeth of your greatest problem that was not the time, in Bosco's experience, to worry about the price, or even whether it was a delusion made plausible by desire. People believe what they want to believe. It was perhaps, thought Bosco, the most beautifully true of all the great truisms. He had little choice but to accept, even if it did coincide exactly with what he most needed.

'While you were away I had the Purgators put on parade and had one of their members executed in front of them. It was an arduous death. And I mean arduous to watch. When you tell them what you want from them they will have had a very recent reminder of what will happen if they fail to come up to the mark.'

'Not all the Purgators are suitable. There are about thirty who're too mad or stupid to be of any use. But I'm not an executioner. I want them sent to the Bastille at Marshalsea.'

'What makes you so sure they'd be better off?'

'That's as might be. I told you I'm not an executioner.'

'Very well. But you have no right to discredit the mystery of Petar Brzica.'

He should have known better, but cocky because he had managed to get one over on Bosco concerning the veldt he could not stop himself.

'Mystery? That butcher.'

'How many times do you have to be told about letting others know what you're thinking,' said Bosco, wearily. 'However, *listen*. God has spoken. And it must follow that what he has spoken is the truth. The One True Faith is not intolerant because it is some pompous schoolmaster terrified of contradiction, it is intolerant because the Truth is intolerant by virtue of the fact that it *is* true. It is not intolerant to refuse to allow a teacher to state that two and two is five or three. Such a person would be stopped in all societies at all times. How much less should we be prepared to tolerate a lie that prevents a man from being saved for all eternity. So it is clear as two and two make four that there can be no tolerance for all our sakes of anything that deviates from God's truth. The Pope is the source of all faith on earth and he must form a great partnership with the hangman to enforce the only love that truly exists: the narrowest, hardest and most inflexible dogma.'

'Brzica serves nothing but a desire for blood.'

'Not so. Not fair. Like any other Redeemer he could have chosen to prepare acolytes for the defence of the faith. He could have learnt to sermonize on the love God bears all of mankind, poor as mankind is, poor as all his works are: his vision corrupt, his tastes disgusting, his body a vile traitor, everything about him humdrum and banal. Instead Brzica has chosen the most arduous vocation of them all: the torture and killing of his own kind. No one will eat with him, no one will pass the time of day or pray next to him. In the midst of this desolation of fear and loathing he must consign himself not to the ordinary pleasures of the human voice but the groans of the dying only. He arrives in the courtyard of the Act of Faith in front of an assembly of his fellows who see him only with dread. A heretic or blasphemer is tossed to him – he seizes him, stretches him, ties him to a wooden bar and lifts his arms. There is a horrible silence save only for the sound of bones cracking and the shrieks of the victim. He unties him. He stretches him out on the ground and drags a sharpened hook through his body from chest to pubic bone and pulls his entrails out before the screaming eyes, the mouth open like a furnace.'

'And you wonder why no one wants to sit next to him?'

'I don't wonder at all. And yet for all that hatred he is all greatness, all power. Remove the executioner from the world and in an instant order yields to chaos; kindness and fellowship and good works are defenceless before the wicked opportunism of the malicious and the cruel, the apostate and blasphemer who would rob each man of an eternal life of bliss. Tell me he is not a hero and a saint.'

They stared at each other for a moment.

'I want Hooke.'

'I explained that will not be possible.'

'You must make it possible. The Folk have new weapons. They didn't get them from under a stone. I need Hooke.'

'Everything is vulnerable. To defy the Pontiff on this would be the excuse they need to send the Congregation of the Office for the Propagation of the Faith.'

'Gant is the Pertius of the Congregation, is that right?'

'The Peritus,' corrected Bosco. 'A pertius is the piece of skin left over after a circumcision.'

'Oh.'

'Your point?'

'Will Gant come with the Congregation?'

'Nothing would keep him from the chance to take control of the Sanctuary.'

'Could he have you made an Act of Faith?'

'The wish is father to that thought, my dear. The

answer is no. But I could be removed from the Carme-lengo and all my power would go with it.'

'If I succeed on the veldt, will that be enough to stop them?'

'No. The failures there are wounding to our pride and a delight to the Antagonist in the East, but the Folk are a nuisance even to them. Where you have one Folk Antagonist you have a fanatic. Where you have two, you have a schism. Even if they defeat us on the veldt and we withdraw, they'll soon start squabbling amongst themselves.'

Cale said nothing for a moment. 'There's no prob-lem,' he said, finally.

'How so?'

'Give them what they want, Hooke's death, and then they'll have no excuse for coming here.'

'I take it,' said Bosco, after a moment, 'you don't mean what you appear to mean.'

'No. I want Hooke and I mean to have him.'

Outside Model, who had been assigned to him as messenger boy, was anxiously waiting, having heard Bosco's slightly raised voice speaking without apparent reply for so long. Was Cale in trouble? When his boss came outside he didn't speak for a few minutes but shook his head as if he were trying to clear a thick fog out from between his ears.

'Can I get you something, boss?'

Cale looked at him.

'Yes. Go and get me another breakfast then take it back to my room and eat it for me.'

'My name is Thomas Cale and I hold you in the palm of my hand.'

As he stood in front of some two hundred abject Purgators under a number of cloudy layers of many kinds of mixed emotions (take anger, self-pity, fear, despair, grief, more anger, hate, loss, love and so on) he was enjoying the curious pleasure of standing in front of so many Redeemers who, despite the joyful pomposity of his proclamations, actually were in the palm of his hand. Who could blame him? Who would not enjoy the idea of moulding them as if they were new-born babies? All this power and not even the slightest worry about being fair or generous or kind. In ecclesiastical law they were already dead – it was just that the actual deed of execution (a matter of minor technical importance) had not been carried out. He could do whatever he wanted to them. He felt not a licence for revenge but a great opportunity to satisfy his curiosity. What if you could do anything you wanted and it would be all right?

'I am going to tell you to do a great many things you've never done before. If you disobey, you'll be punished. If you disobey silently, you'll be punished. If you complain, you'll be punished. If you fail, you'll be punished. If I feel like it, you'll be punished. But there will be one thing and one thing only for which there will be no punishment. If you fail to learn to think for yourselves you will be returned to this square for immediate execution of sentence.'

Then he started to walk out of the square. He noticed one of the Purgators just at the edge of his eye and recognized him as Redeemer Avery Humboldt, someone he knew of old. The expression on his face was one of utter disdain, contempt and loathing. As he passed Humboldt, Cale lashed out with all his great power to the Redeemer's head. He went down as if his strings had been cut and, without more than the slightest break in his stride, Cale walked on and out of the square. In fact, Cale had been quite wrong about the expression on Humboldt's face. It was not one of disdain or contempt or loathing. The apparently dismissive sneer was simply due to damage to the nerves on the left side of his face which had caused it to droop and which resulted from a beating he had taken from two of the guards who had overheard and taken exception to his opinion that the Maid of Blackbird Leys was a well-meaning woman and should not be subject to the horrors of an Act of Faith. On the other hand, Cale's error certainly made a point not lost on the remaining Purgators.

It was a peculiarity of the Redeemers that while they believed any number of fantastical notions they had little or no imagination. And this was true even of so intelligent a man as Bosco. Quite capable of believing seven impossible things before breakfast, so long as they involved miracles, bizarre divine punishments, the preserved gallstones or foreskins of martyrs, he was puzzled by Cale's elaborate plan for removing Guido Hooke from prison.

'I can just send in some guards and remove him.'

'But what happens when there's an investigation by the Office for the Propagation of the Faith and they find out that before he mysteriously died he was in perfect health and was for no good reason removed from his cell against all protocol and convention?'

Bosco, being a passionate and conventional believer in his youth, had come late to lying. Now he invented plausible lies, sure enough, but the things he said were not deeply interrogated because by the time he started deceiving his fellow Redeemers he was very powerful. He had suspicious enemies but there was only so much pressure they could bring to bear, only a short rope on which to hang awkward questions. Cale, Vague Henri and Kleist on the other hand had been deceiving, cheating and lying to people who could subject them to anything they liked if they had the slightest suspicion of any wrong doing, wrong thinking or wrong feeling. A guilty look was evidence of sin, just as an expression of innocence was a proof of the disgusting sin of pride. The result was that they all, perpetual liars, had learnt to be untruthful in the same way that they had learnt to walk – unsteady at first but quickly so fluent they did not even have to think about it. A powerless liar has to know what they're doing in order not to be found out. A lie had to be alive and be so like the truth that the one hundred errors that bad liars make to give themselves away even to the stupid are never given air to breathe. Number one in this respect was that you never break any routine – once you discover even a small change in the way things are always done, even the dimmest interrogator starts to smell a rat.

'Only sickness will make your taking Hooke out of a condemned cell look right. If it comes to an ecclesiastical review where you must answer, you have to have a story. Work it through in your head so it's as real as something that happened – more real. Send a doctor you can trust – is there one?'

'There is.'

'Get him to take Giant Scabious – it'll make him sweat and go red in the face. The doctor can find it growing behind the Great Statue of the Hanged Redeemer.'

Bosco was offended. He had allowed Cale to take to his bed on three occasions with such symptoms.

'What do you expect,' taunted Cale, 'from the wrath of the Lord? By the next day all the guards will be worrying it's jail fever. Then you can remove him for a good reason and you won't have done anything out of the ordinary. You used to tell me that was a sin.'

'Clearly I failed. As I hoped to do, remember that. God plants his great messengers in many places. Mostly they go mad for lack of a guide to tell them who they are and what they have to do.'

That night the weekly check for signs of jail fever was made a day ahead of schedule. Guido Hooke was given a tincture of Scabious and took it without demur. Why suspect the Redeemers of poisoning him when they had such public and unpleasant plans for his death. By the next day he had the required fever, sweats and blisters. If they were not the symptoms of the much dreaded jail fever – dreaded because it could so easily spread to the wider community of Redeemers – they were still alarming enough to ensure the doctor was recalled by jailers who would never have the wit or courage to lie to the Office for the Propagation of the Faith. Part one of the lie was firmly embedded in the truth. Much fuss was made of taking Hooke from his cell and through the Purgators in order to provide as many witnesses to his obvious sickness as possible. His face was distinctive because of his moustache-less and abundant ginger beard. It gave him a hideous aspect but he had been told twenty years before by a malicious young woman that she found it especially suited him and he had for ever after continued to devote much time to maintaining it. Now ranting and delirious because the apothecary had tripled the dose in error, Hooke was taken to an isolated room where those suffering from jail fever were left to die without food or water. For once this was the kindest solution the

Redeemers could offer. It was better to die reasonably quickly from a high fever exacerbated by lack of water than linger on into the hideous last stages of the disease. Within a few minutes, Cale arrived followed shortly after by Bosco and Gil who watched him trying to go about his deceptive business with some difficulty, given Hooke's raving state. Cale cut the ginger beard as close to the skin as possible, leaving him with a pile of red hair that was both impressive and repellent.

'Give it eyes and a tail and it'd look like a ginger rat.'

Gil and Bosco then left but were back ten minutes later with a dead body of an age and weight similar to Hooke's. Cale had certainly requested the body and in doing so suggested it come from the morgue. Whether the cadaver had truly and conveniently done so he did not ask – and Gil and Bosco did not tell.

Cale had already stripped Hooke of his clothes and then did the same to the corpse. He then dressed the dead man in Hooke's clothes and wrapped a large bandage, as was the custom for the dead, around his head and under his chin. He then stuffed the hair from the pile inside the bandage to give the impression that Hooke's beard was squashed beneath. Bosco sniffed. If it was an ingenious idea it was not quite so impressive in execution.

'It's just a first go,' said Cale. 'Give me an hour and it'll look a lot better. Besides – people see what they expect to see. When we burn him tomorrow we'll keep the Redeemers well back.'

'It's an after-death execution,' said Gil. 'The Father-hood will expect to see Brzica.'

'Brzica's not a problem.'

With that Bosco signalled Gil to help Hooke to his feet.

'Give us a kiss, gorgeous,' said the delirious Hooke.

'Where are you taking him?'

'God,' said Bosco, 'fashioned hell for the inquisitive.'

'Just a little one,' said Hooke, and with that they dragged him out of the room and Cale went back to re-arranging the fur inside the dead man's face bandage.

Within twenty minutes Hooke was being settled in a new room, separated from the rest of the Sanctuary by two walls and being attended to by a fat nun in a wimple.

In the room with the dead man, Cale began to arrange the appearance of the ginger beard that now looked almost orange against the dead white of the man's face. He sang softly to himself as he worked.

'Nobody likes us – we don't care

Nobody likes us – we don't care

Nobody likes us – we don't care

Nobody likes us – we don't care.'

'Tell the jailers that there is an alert about the Purgators and they must prepare them to be moved. Lock the place up with them inside for twenty-four hours. The Purgators and jailers are the only people who ever saw Hooke close up. Bring everyone to the post-mortem execution but keep them well back in case they catch the jail fever. Then get the burning over quickly.'

'Why not burn him on the QT?' said Gil. 'It's too risky doing it in front of so many.'

'No, Cale is right. People will see what they expect to see. The Office for the Propagation of the Faith will expect us to make a show of the execution of such a notorious heretic. We'll give them what they want.'

*Too clever by half, both of them*, thought Gil. He regretted his disobedience and pride almost at once. There would be hours of praying, at least ten minutes ablating. Perhaps half an hour defuscalating. Why couldn't he have bitten his tongue? Then he remembered he would have to do that as well.

'Thank you, Redeemer,' said Bosco, dismissing Gil. When he had left, Bosco looked at Cale, his expression mocking and expectant.

'You want to ask me something?'

'Yes. What was Picarbo doing cutting up that girl?'

'Ah. Extraordinary.' He unlocked a small cupboard at the side of his desk, took out a bound folder and handed it over.

'There are a great many pages in his room. It would take months, I'd say, to read them all. But this was his testament of sorts. Apparently.'

'So you knew nothing about it?'

'Me? No.'

'How was that possible?'

'You think I'm lying to you?' He seemed surprised. 'Clearly I have in the past been willing to keep the truth from you, sir.' The title was genuinely respectful yet also genuinely mocking. 'But I don't recall ever lying directly to you. I suppose I would have if it had been necessary. But I'm not lying now.'

'He kept *women*. He kept them in rooms big enough for a small palace. How is that possible?'

'All Redeemers must still seem alike to you. All are all-powerful. But only with acolytes, not with each other. There are many divisions and hierarchies. Lines there are that cannot be crossed. Picarbo ruled these areas. No arbitrary king had more power. It was not done to ask questions of one another. To have the power to control knowledge of something in a world where everyone knows everything in common, this is the most jealously guarded power a Redeemer can have. Like a bunch of keys, it is a sign of worthiness before God.'

'Others must have known.'

'Indeed they did. Twelve of them knew and had read the document here.'

'What happened to them?'

'Now you're being provocative.'

'The nuns?'

'A Redeemer can always be replaced; someone who can cook and iron a vestment in a way acceptable to God cannot. Besides they knew nothing about Picarbo's intentions. It is a matter of considerable debate, theologically speaking, whether women have souls or not. I'm inclined to think not. In which case they are not entirely responsible for themselves.'

'And the girls?'

'Ah yes. The answer is that there is no answer. Because the sisters have always been sealed off, it's been surprisingly easy to keep these young people a secret. Picarbo clearly found it so. I've things to deal with. Take your time.'

And with that he left and Cale started to read the manifesto that had changed his life and beggared an empire.

# 7

It was dawn and the twites were singing raucously in the trees. The beautiful arias and choruses they sang before the sun went down were now replaced with an appalling racket that sounded like men with out-of-tune whistles having a fist-fight in the branches of the trees.

Despite the noise, the girl, Daisy, was sleeping deeply in his arms. Kleist had slept in the same room with hundreds of boys and they looked to him even uglier when they were asleep than when they were not. She looked beautiful, something that was not quite the case when she was awake. A deeply pleasant feeling swept through him as he looked at her, like the feeling in his chest after a large swig of brandy or gin.

He was both in awe and mistrustful of women. Who is not? But until recently even ignorance could not have described his lack of understanding, which is to say he had none. Now his experience was significant in parts but both partial and peculiar. His hostility to Riba, the girl whose rescue by Cale was the inadvertent cause of all his woes, was based on the numerous occasions when, through no fault of hers, she had nearly got him killed; his second source of experience was of the aristocratic beauties of Memphis, who regarded all men, and especially him, as beneath contempt; and finally the whores of Kitty Town, whose misery or coldness had eventually put him off going there at all.

Overwhelmed by the clash of sudden tenderness with the violence of his upbringing, he furiously decided that he would hunt down the remaining two members of Lord Dunbar's gang and kill them horribly. To his surprise and mortification – he had more or less expected her to swoon with love and adoration when he explained his noble quest – she gasped with irritation and told him not to be so foolish.

'Will it change anything?'

'No,' he said, reluctantly. 'But I'd feel better.'

'So would I,' she said, smiling. 'But fighting is risky. You never know what could happen. Risking your life to kill scum like that really, really, really isn't worth it. One day we'll come across them maybe, drunk, and when they fall asleep we'll stab them in the back.' She laughed and he stared at her, bewildered. If this had not happened to her he would have agreed entirely. He fell even more in love. Truth be told he would have liked a few days' respite to get used to these new ways of feeling but Daisy was not a patient girl. Lightning moved slowly compared to her and she was on top of him and devouring every inch before he really knew what to do. As the great convulsion shook her body he thought she was dying of some sort of stroke. Nothing like this had happened during his miserable sorties to Kitty Town. When she lay back exhausted she was somewhat startled to have to explain to the deeply worried Kleist what had happened. It was a lot to take in, even or especially for such a very hard young man. He looked so surprised and thoughtful that she confused him even more by bursting into tears.

With enormous care he lifted the sleeping girl from his, now numb, left arm and made them both breakfast. Hungry, he ate his immediately and waited for her to wake up. He was so impatient to talk to her that he even tried giving her a push. But this was clearly a girl who knew how to sleep. He was so frustrated by this, and a little resentful that she could snore through something so momentous, he ate her breakfast as well.

'Where's mine?' she said, softly, as he was finishing up by licking the plate.

'I'll make it for you now,' he said, all irritation vanishing with her smile. The water was already boiling and in twenty minutes she was wolfing down the beans and rice they'd taken from Lord Dunbar.

'What were you doing out here on your own?'

'Just going for a wander.'

'Out here?'

'There's not much point in wandering somewhere you've been before.'

'You're too young.'

'I'm older than you.'

'I can look after myself.'

'So can I.' They looked at each other awkwardly. 'Usually. I was careless and got caught. It was my fault.'

This made him indignant.

'How could it be your fault what they did?'

'I didn't say that. But if you try and steal a horse from bastards and ruffians you know what to expect. Besides,' she said, 'they didn't kill you and I'm grateful for that.'

At this he hardly knew what to say. She smiled. 'So maybe I won't stab them in the back.'

'Where do you come from?'

'The Quantocks.'

'Never heard of it.'

'They're about three days from here. I want to go home now. Come with me.'

'All right.'

He replied without a pause. He regretted it instantly, but only because it was such an alien thing for him to do. He felt as if he had become inhabited by another person and one who might do or say something very stupid.

'Do you have a family?'

'Of course,' she said, and then regretted it. 'Sorry.'

'No need to say sorry. Your family shouldn't let you go wandering off.'

'Why not?'

'It's too dangerous.'

'You're the one who wants to go off on a killing bender.'

'I wanted to avenge your honour,' he said.

She laughed. 'The Klephts, that's my clan. They don't really believe in things like that. We're very curious but not very honourable.'

'You're making a fool of me.'

'No, I'm not – really not. Respect and integrity and honesty – we don't believe in all that. All the tribes around us do, they're always getting into fights about their honour this and honour that. They kill themselves over honour and they kill their wives and daughters over it too. If I was a Deccan they'd strangle me if they'd found out I'd been raped.' She stuck two fingers in the air. 'That's what I think of honour.' She could see this had shocked Kleist, though startled would have been more like it. She laughed. 'And they're as stupid and lacking in curiosity as a cow. "Curiosity killed the cat" – that's their favourite saying. My uncle Adam canoed down the Rhine for five days because he heard there was a whore in Firenze with unusually shaped genitals. I myself am famous because I taught a chicken to walk backwards.'

'Why would you do that?'

She laughed, delighted. 'Because the Klephts have a saying as well: "You can't teach a chicken to walk backwards."'

# 8

## The Manifesto of Redeemer Picarbo

It is clear and it requires no great arguments that our fore-fathers were in error. This is no easy thing to say concerning famous men deserving praise. But to err is human and God has given us reason to struggle to make the best of our nature. Woman was given to us in the first to be a friend but she was no companion to us as was required. No – not even from the beginning. Would a friend and companion tempt a man to his own destruction, to listen to Satan, to eat the one thing – the one thing, for God's sake, the *one* and only thing forbidden to man and woman? Such generosity, so small a burden, to bear in exchange for happiness and joy. All of it was lost because women are never satisfied but are always in the ears of men and wanting whatever they cannot have. It is no wonder that even the misguided Janes who will refuse to represent the world in images have a sign for the devil that has its origins in a picture of a woman's tongue, and for temptation as a man's ear. Women then from the first cor-rupted the friendship God had ordained between men and women. The friendship that grows from reason has seen that reason inflamed by women's desire. Desire has made that friendship go mad. Men and women should live as man and wife in harmony and companionship and yet again and again we see men spurred always on by women into loving their own wives immoderately. A proper love takes reason as its guide and will not allow itself to be swept away in impetuous desire. And so the reasonable and sane is corrupted by women who want, greatest of all depravities, to be loved as if they were adulterers. All men commit adultery with their own wives and cannot help but do so because women will not be loved reasonably and in proportion. Love for women is their whole existence and they cannot in their nature bear what is moderate or rational. The soul of men alone, history has proved, struggles to free itself of desire as it rises to the divine. No woman will allow this escape by men. It is she and not God who must be the centre of everything. By my investigations and experiments I have discovered women inflame the reason not only by their parts and their fondling but by a secret liquid that flows from their gallbladders.

As we have many times done with sheep and pigs, breeding this one for better meat, the other for finer wool, I have by diverse means schooled such women as I have confined here in all that is voluptuous and concerned only with physical sensation regarding the pleasure of beauty, of the delicacy of the skin and the hair and all the ways in which the organs of immediate sensation can be puffed up and exaggerated. They have been taught since very young all the business of delighting men so that (even more than ordinary women) they think of nothing else but giving pleasure to men so that men in turn find pleasure and solace only in their company and not in the pursuit of God. By these means I have greatly stimulated their wombs to exude this uterine milk to such an intensity and strength that it, strangled and thickened by its own excess, has glutinated to become as solid as amber or pitch (which in being the stuff of hell is most apt). By my arts and inspired by God and the Hanged Redeemer, I have found out and removed these resins and revealed that they have the power, reduced to a powder and mixed with holy chrism, to supply any man with the original goodness of the friendship of women that they so quickly and destructively took from men and from themselves. With this prepared mixture, which I have called Redeemer's Oil, not only men may resist women as it eases away their lust, but even Redeemers who have been lost to madness and dreadful fits may be restored to happiness and good fellowship and be reclaimed from the destruction of penis fury and the sorrow at the loss of women that afflicts so many.

The door opened and Bosco returned.

'Finished?'

'Not yet.'

'Show me.'

Cale pointed to the last sentence he had read, old habits dying hard. It was done before he could stop himself.

'Well,' said Bosco, awkward himself at this reminder of their past. 'You can read the rest later. Your opinion?'

'Too much penis fury.'

Bosco smiled.

'Indeed so. He was as much possessed by women in his way as any fornicator. If you think what you've read is mad, the rest of it goes on to lay out his plans for a special farm in which his creatures would be raised to produce this resin in sufficient amounts to calm the world. But if it hadn't been for this you would never have left the Sanctuary and the Materazzi empire would still be the greatest power in the four quarters. Odd, isn't it, how things work out?'

'What will you do with the girls?'

'I don't know. They can stay where there are.'

'A trap for someone.'

'Exactly. Would you care to meet them?'

It was fair to say that Cale was astonished.

'A trap for me?'

'There are many traps laid for you but none of my making. I am your good servant.'

'Yes. I mean, yes I do want to see them.'

'I'll arrange it when you return from the veldt. Picarbo may have been a lunatic but his handiwork is most interesting.'

A week later Cale was standing on the low hill at Duffer's Drift, surrounded by the Purgators – suspicious, hopeful, wary, resentful – and Guido Hooke. Cale had thought there might be a fight to retake the Drift, particularly if the Folk holding it had realized that there were only two hundred and thirty Redeemers come to do so. As it turned out, by the time they arrived the Folk had simply vanished into the prairie.

'Look around you,' shouted Cale. 'If you are stupid you'll die here. If you're clever you'll die here. If you use all the great skills you've learnt, you'll die here. Let me tell you this: unless you become like little children, you will die here.'

'Speak up!' shouted a Redeemer at the back. Cale looked at Gil and with two guards he moved behind the Redeemer who'd spoken out and gestured him forward. He stepped to the front with a hard-man swagger and stood in front of Cale, staring at him with eyes the colour of the leavings in a mug of beer.

'What did you say?' asked Cale.

'I said speak –'

Cale stepped into the man, crashing his forehead into his face. The Redeemer went down instantly, clutching his broken nose. Cale stepped back onto the flat boulder he had been speaking from.

'If you have bad hearing – you will die here.'

He told them to turn around and outlined the various ways the Drift had been defended – pointing to this trench system here, another there, how this hill had been reinforced, that field of fire covered to prevent an attack.

'The one thing they have in common,' he said, when he'd finished laying out the battlefield, 'is that everyone who planned them and everyone who carried out those plans is now dead. You will be placed in cohorts of fifteen. You will elect a cohort leader and a deputy and a sergeant. You will unlearn together or you'll die. You have one day to walk this place and each cohort will come up with a plan to keep you alive for the three days it will take for reinforcements to arrive. I don't need to threaten you that, if you fail, I'll have you returned to the Sanctuary for your immediate Act of Faith because the Folk will take care of you on that score. Back here an hour before sunset.'

Cale had hoped that by his pointing out why the previous defences had failed, by showing them the lie of the land, not in maps but rock by trench, by keeping everything particular and down to earth, the Purgators would realize that their salvation lay in one place. But it became clear to Cale, as the cohorts produced one doomed-to-fail plan after another, that while fear could do almost anything, you could not frighten anyone into thinking for themselves.

The next day Cale assembled the Purgators down by the river crossing. He took out an egg and laid it on the flat top of a large rock.

'If any one of you can balance this egg on its narrow end you get the safest job in the battalion – taking messages to the rear. As soon as the Folk come into sight you'll be on your way.'

For the next few minutes there were about twenty

efforts before the Purgators were certain it could not be done, even if they were also sure Cale had some trick up his sleeve. Which, of course, he did. When they'd given up he stepped to the rock, picked up the egg and tapped it gently against the rock, breaking it slightly and leaving it stood on one end.

'You didn't say we could break it.'

'I didn't say anything. You decided the rules, not me.' He pointed at the ford. 'The crossing here is in a bad place from a defender's view. I want you to work out how to move it.'

'It can't be done.'

'You're sure?'

'How can it be?'

'You're right. It can't. So why do all of your plans to defend it put you in trenches so close you could fight them off with your bare hands? If you had a bow that could fire ten miles, that's how far away you could be. If you can walk the battlefield but even if you can't – think like a child. Imagine yourself into every real place in every real way. Put yourself in the mind of your enemy and then walk the battlefield in fact or in your head. Make your mind a model of the real world – with a horse and then in a trench. Put everything to the test of what's real. You don't have time to learn from your mistakes.'

He took them to the trenches where most of the Redeemers had died in the last attack.

'Where's the front?'

By now the Purgators were beginning to catch on.

'There's no point in hiding. Make your mistakes now when there's only me to answer to.'

One of the men pointed to the Drift forward of the trench.

'Wrong. There is no front here. The direction of attack is to the side, the rear and facing you. Here it's front all around. What ground should you take?'

'The high ground.'

This came out of the Purgators as naturally as the response to a priest in morning mass. At the familiarity there was a buzz, almost like amusement at the memory of something in common, of no longer being outcast.

'Wrong again. The ground you take is the best ground. Usually, but not here, it's the high ground. I'm telling you that if you do what's usually right, you'll usually end up dead.' He pointed at the U-shaped bend in the river.

On either side of the bank it was as ragged as if it had been cut into repeatedly by a giant axe.

'Use the land around you. Those cuts in the bank can be deepened and prepared, but look at it – most of the work has been done for you. This is the best cover for twenty miles.'

'Hold on, sir,' said one of the Purgators. 'You said we needn't be next to the ford as no one can steal it. This plan puts us right on top of it.'

'If it wasn't for the fact that I used up the last fresh egg I'd have given it to you. I changed my mind because I didn't want to think about giving up the high ground. Just like the rest of you.' He pointed out into the scrub beyond the U of the river. 'The ford could be defended from there well enough – but on balance the ravines on the bank are better. At least you better hope so. Besides, remember there is no front or rear in this place. I'm going to put some of you on the high ground. If the Folk try to get in between us, they'll be trapped from both sides.' He looked around the group. 'Are any of you Sodality Marksmen?' Mostly Redeemer archers were used in massed ranks and great accuracy was not required but where it was needed the specially trained Sodality Marksmen were used. There were six. He told them to collect food and water for three days and while they were doing this set most of the Purgators to digging into the ravines on either side of the bank to improve on what nature had offered them. Thirty of the others were set to digging trenches.

'Make sure you cut a space big enough inside the bottom of the trench to hide from arrows coming at you from directly above.' He gave Gil some further instructions and then set off, running to the tabletop mountain in front of the U with the six marksmen.

As the Redeemers dug they talked. Friends of the priest Cale had dropped for pretending he couldn't hear were muttering.

'A few months ago and anyone of us could have dis-embowelled the little shitehawk for even thinking of touching one of us.'

'He better not try it on me or . . .'

'Or what?' said another. 'The days when we could do anything to anyone have gone. He's annointed by God, you can hear it in his voice and what he says.'

'And the way he said it.'

'He's an acolyte gone cocky. I've seen it before – one of them claims he's seen a vision of the Holy Mother and suddenly they're all over him until he's found out for the little liar he is.'

There was a mumble of agreement all around. Aco-lytes claiming to have seen visions of this or that saint prophesying one thing or another and causing general excitement until they were, unless particularly skilled, caught out and made an example of were not uncom-mon.

'Well,' said another, 'you better hope you're wrong because he's all that stands between us and a blunt knife. I want to believe in him and I do. You *can* hear it in his voice. Everything he said makes sense once he explained – the fact that he's just a boy makes it true. Only God could have put knowledge like that into a child's head.'

'Shut your gob and get on with your digging,' said Gil as he passed by. To him they were Purgators but the mixture of awe and doubt about Cale was clattering about in his brain just the same.

Within two hours Cale was back, this time alone and putting in place the notions he had conceived while looking down on the site from the top of the mountain. One of the marksmen, a veteran of the Eastern Front, had come up with an idea of his own he'd seen at Swineburg during the Advent offensive. He was promoted on the spot by a delighted Cale to the position of Bum-Bailey – a deadly insult in Memphis, but important-sounding to the other Redeemers. On his way down the mountain he felt that what had seemed like a good joke at the time was in fact childish and, worse, might come back to haunt him. What was done was done but he stayed away from that kind of thing in the future.

When he got back to the Drift he ordered up the twenty best riders and then told them to take off their cassocks. Having collected a bale's worth of prairie grass from the scrub he had the cassocks filled with the grass and then impaled the scarecrowish results on twenty staves driven into the bottom of the old trench in which so many Redeemers had died in the previous attack. Once you were thirty yards away or more you couldn't tell the difference. It was unlikely that the Folk would catch on that Redeemers had no reason to fight with their cowls over their heads.

'What do you want the riders for?' asked a suspicious Redeemer Gil. Cale considered avoiding a straight answer but there was no reason to.

'I need protecting when I watch you from up on the

hill back there,' he said, nodding to the rise half a mile away from which they'd watched the previous two massacres.

'What about leading your men?'

'I'm not here to save people, isn't that right? That's what you believe, isn't it?'

Gil stared at him.

'Yes.'

'I remember you saying once that a man in command has to make two choices – lead from the front always or only sometimes. Yes?'

'Yes.'

'Well, try never. Who am I, Redeemer?'

They just stared at each other at first.

'You are The Left Hand of God.'

'And why am I here?'

Gil did not reply.

'Is there anything here,' continued Cale, 'you don't understand?'

'No, sir.'

Hooke walked over to them having spent several minutes examining a curiously coloured boulder.

'I think there is brimstone in these rocks.'

'Get on your horse. We're leaving.'

Thirty minutes later Cale with Hooke only next to him was looking down on his handiwork from the familiar rise. He was pleased with himself. Except for the dozen or so men he had sent out to place rocks and boulders to give the archers ranges at fifty-yard intervals, he could see no one – even though he knew where to look.

It was two hours after first light the next morning that Hooke spotted a cloud of dust away to the north. Cale ordered a blunt arrow to be fired into the centre of the Drift to warn the Purgators that the Folk were coming. Within the hour Cale could see scouts coming in clumps of two, sometimes three, in a ragged line that extended over a front of a thousand yards or so on either side of a small group of ten heading for the Drift. As they approached the crossing and saw nothing, the land dipped inwards herding the inner groups together. Cale felt an intense thrill gripping him along the back of the neck, pleasant and unpleasant at the same time. By now a group of fifteen scouts had carelessly bunched together about a hundred and fifty yards from the nearest line of about seventy Redeemer archers. Then they stopped, clearly spooked by something.

'Shit!' said Cale. They had started to turn and split up when a silent arc of arrows rose into the air in a majestic curve and in less than two seconds rained in on the scouts taking all but one of them off their horses. The survivor raced off to the south followed by another flight of thirty or so arrows. Cale gasped with irritation. The arrows were a waste for just one man even if they could take a single target moving away at the rate the terrified scout was going. Clearly Gil had the same idea.

His shout to hold fire drifted lazily up towards the rise. Gil had the sense to realize that there would be no more surprises and no more tightly packed groups of fifteen to make an easy target.

Thirty minutes later a thick mortar arrow shot up almost vertically into the air from the shoulder just a hundred feet or so below the tabletop mountain. It landed about ten yards from the trenches manned by the Redeemer cassocks stuffed with prairie grass. By the third shot the mortars had got their range and a barrage of arrows and their twelve equally murderous bolts scoured the trenches for another hour. The idea of the fake defenders had been that of the sniper on the tabletop mountain, for which he'd been rewarded by the insulting promotion. It had been successful, and out of all proportion. Not only had they wasted an enormous number of mortar arrows but it was clear the Folk still hadn't caught on and were clearly convinced, though for good reason, that the Redeemers were following the same dismal chain of tactics they had shown at Duffer's Drift and elsewhere on the veldt. A large body of them were crawling up the south side of the hill in order to take the high ground and fire down at the men in the riverbank who had killed so many of the Folk in the first volley. While this was happening, Cale spotted two groups of perhaps a hundred men each galloping away to the east and west. Cale's guess was that they were heading for the river some distance away on either side.

The black night, instead of being something surrounding you, seemed to fill the inside of your head, all sense of being inside or out slowly being lost unless a cloud passed away from the thin moon and illuminated a distant tree or the side of the table mountain. Then the black space your senses told you was only inches away now revealed itself as miles in the distance and not even where it should be. A dead white tree on the prairies – just caught in the light of the moon – seemed to Cale to be stranded above him in mid-air when in fact he knew it to be on the flat almost a mile away. With even the most basic senses being all higgledy-piggledy it was a bad experience to be waiting in the coal-black night for someone with murder in their heart to come and get you. In the dark and even for those with good nerves the veldt at night became an implacable enemy waiting, mocking, for you to make the first move. A wild dog or night deer trotting along became twice its size and its speed like three ordinary living things. The sound of a hedgehog snuffling about became as loud as a lion grumbling before a leap. What if the creeping crawling thing making that scraping sound just outside your trench had a deadly bite or sting? The night was an unpleasant alchemist for ordinary things – it made a bush into the man who was waiting to kill you if you even breathed too loud. Still, it would be worse if you were doing the getting. Imagine trying to move in this. And, of course, with no way of checking, time vanished.

Two hours passed which might have been four or five minutes. Odd thoughts began tormenting you. What if tonight the sun went down and didn't come up. Something you would never have bothered thinking about, on a night like this seemed possible. 'Never shall sun that morrow see', a phrase he had heard Lord Vipond quoting from somewhere, kept coming back to him. 'Never shall sun that morrow see.'

Then at once there was a flare of light from what looked like a point way up in the clouds. Then another. It was Gil lighting up the river bed with fire arrows – one after the other, beautifully cupped by the shape of the river. After the seventh or eighth Cale heard screams and shouts. The arrows had caught the Folk trapped on either side by the steep riverbank. You could not see the volleys of unlit arrows rasping in on the attacking Folk, but there was little cover for them and no chance of rushing the Purgators because Cale had placed a deep line of staked thorn trees across the river and several more lines of sharpened stakes.

It didn't, or didn't seem to, last for long even though there was one pause before a second attack. This was much briefer than the first. Then nothing until the first lightening of a beautiful rose-red dawn.

The sun came up after this gentle start like a clap of thunder and by seven o'clock it was already too hot. Down in the riverbank, the far side he could see at any rate, the dead and dying numbered thirty-three. Perhaps half as many again were obscured by the near bank. The men were trying to crawl back down the river bed but not quickly. One was so badly injured he was crawling, equally slowly, towards the Purgators he wanted to escape from.

One of the retreating wounded was beginning to make progress and an arrow from the Purgators lashed out fast as a heron and struck the wounded man.

'About time they showed some mercy,' said Guido Hooke, gravely. 'No one should have to die so slowly in sun like this.' Cale laughed. 'Did I say something to amuse you, Mr Cale?'

'If they put the poor bastard out of his misery, it was by accident. They'll be wounding him again to try and encourage his friends to do something heroic.'

'Scum.' Hooke looked at Cale, trying to read him. 'You think me weak?'

Cale considered this carefully for a moment.

'No. I think it's surprising.'

'That someone should have some feeling for a suffering human being?'

'That you would expect anything else from the Redeemers.'

'You can still disapprove of something you expect.'

'Why bother? Will it make any difference?'

'You must have been brought up very careless.'

'I was.'

'Why so cynical?'

'I don't know what that means.'

'Cynicism is –'

'I don't care what it means either.'

Miffed at this rebuke, Hooke didn't reply. After a few minutes it was Cale who spoke.

'A friend of mine used to say it was a waste of time blaming people for their nature.'

'I was right.'

'About what?'

'About being brought up careless.'

Cale refused to take offence and just smiled. 'I wish IdrisPukke had brought me up. I'd be more to your taste, Mr Hooke, than I am now.'

At that there was another arrow flash and another wounded man struck.

'It's not foolish to wish for a life better than this.'

But Cale had had enough and did not reply. Then he noticed a dozen or so Folk crawling towards the hill at the back of the U and beginning to move up the slope, then another ten and another. The centenar in the firing trench at the top was being more patient in letting them come close to his position than made sense.

'Come on,' he said under his breath. Then a volley of arrows and what looked like half a dozen hits. But now more of the Folk were crawling and, stooped low, even running over a hump on the hill and it became clear that it was only when moving over this hump that the attackers had to suffer the arrows from the trenches.

When he had decided on the defence of the hill the slope below had seemed devoid of any cover for the entire climb and so making it almost impossible to mount a successful attack. Now it was clear that he had missed something. Once they got two thirds up the hill the Folk attackers were able to move into a shallow dip that protected them from arrows and allowed them to gather on the slope high enough to make a rushed attack. It was impossible that he had missed something so obvious.

Endless were the times it had been driven into him about the moment of holy revelation, the vision on the road or on top of a mountain that made the scales fall from the eyes. There was nothing divine about what struck Cale on top of the rise over Duffer's Drift but it was a vision of the truth all the same. He could not afford to fail here.

His most desperate desire since he could remember thinking at all about anything was to be left alone. But now as he watched the Folk creeping towards the top of the hill he could see the failure of his greatest hope. If they took the hill they would be able to take the Drift. They would kill the Purgators and with them Cale's ability to deliver to Bosco the power to keep him safe. But at the price of never being left alone. He could run away now but there were only Redeemers behind and Antagonists in front. He was five hundred miles away from what? Nothing like safety. To be alone anywhere in this world was to be isolated and vulnerable. Any peace and any quiet came at the pleasure of someone else. There was no corner, no crack, however small, where he could creep away from the world and please himself. The roof had to be earned, the food bought. He had to fight and keep fighting and if he stopped fighting he would drown. Wake up. March or die. March or die.

In Memphis he had made enemies as easily as breathing because he was stupid and made mistakes. The only people he knew and understood were Redeemers. Here he had some chance because he was one of them and he had a place. Everywhere else he was a child with a talent for being angry. He was as bound to the Purgators about to be annihilated in the Drift as much as if he loved and believed in every one of them. There was no choice and never had been. All this, realized in a fraction of the time it took to tell, flooded over him in a great deluge as if he had been standing below a great collapsing dam. And even as everything, heart and soul, cried out against it, he was on his feet and racing down the rise to the twenty Purgators waiting by their horses, ignorant of the disaster unfolding just out of sight.

Desperate to attack but needing to explain his plan, Cale started drawing the Drift in the dust and giving instructions as he did so.

'Understand?'

They nodded.

'Then you,' he said, 'repeat it back to me.' The Purgators hesitated but returned a fair account of what Cale had told them. Cale repeated it again and mounted them.

'Succeed and you'll be as good as saints to Redeemer Bosco.' Longing to be cast out himself, it had taken the dreadful vision on the rise to see that belonging was more to these men than life itself. He thought he had offered them escape from hideous death but it was more than that. If he had been an angel sent to pardon them and set them free in the world they would have been lost, wanderers without place or meaning. Their freedom would have been the freedom of a ghost.

As they rode in good order to the top of the rise watched by the bemused Hooke, Cale could feel the power of brotherhood and loyalty sweeping through them even in the teeth of their own death. Then they swept over the rise and were slowly raising their speed in line with Cale, faster towards the hill as the Folk were preparing their final rush towards the top, thoughts bent on the struggle ahead and no one thinking of the rear until the Purgators were only fifty yards behind and racing towards them. Now seen, the Purgators screamed for Saint this and Martyr that and then the slaughter began.

The horse charge of the Purgators flowed into the dip and pulled to a halt – they were trained as mounted infantry not cavalry – dismounting in a hurried scramble hurled him at the other man who staggered backwards only to be stabbed by an arriving Purgator, struck through the liver and an instant death. Lucky for him – few die quick that die in battle. No time for thanks as Cale finished the broken-footed Arnoldi – he flung out both his hands and cried out 'No!' Much good it did him, Cale's blow severing his spinal cord that runs from haunch to neck. Then the next man rushed to Cale and his inevitable death. Juanie De Beer, who fought to the last at Bullbaiter's Lane and earned the name De Beer the Bitterender, took a blow from Cale just above the genitals. He fell for all his courage, writhing in the sand in agony. Cale screamed at the Purgators behind him to close the gap. The Folk held back for a moment. Startled by the gross belligerence of the boy in front of them, they'd stopped to gawp like peasants open-mouthed as some great bishop passed. He seemed to need no one, so dreadful and so natural the spleen he brought to bear on everyone who challenged him. Startled by his shouts, the Purgators rushed to surround him as the attacks began again. Cale stepped back, leery now, once again aware of the danger he was in from the short spears in ones and twos incurving their way into the body of monks behind him, no sound like it even among the shouts and screams, no bolt or arrow makes the horse-slap muffled thud of a javelin stopped in a moment by flesh and blood. He stepped forward to avoid the spears, using the Purgators ahead of him as a protective wall. But now the dip in the slope that had protected the Folk was not enough to shield them from the archers on the top of the hill. They had to stand to fight off the surge from the side but that left them exposed. Penned in and squeezed by Cale's wall of men, the thirty-yard gap to the top that had promised them victory now made them easy prey for the archers.

It was Predikant Viljoen, sermonizer of Enkeldoorn, who realized that their only chance was to break through the Redeemer wall and become so mixed in the fight that the archers on the hill would be forced to stop. Hell was Viljoen's great passion – his sermons would raise the hackles of his congregation like the quills upon a fretful porcupine. Now he was handing out hell himself in spades. The Predikant was half as big again as any of the other Folk and had a face like an ample plate, fringed with a beard. Like all the Folk he carried a small shovel, used on the veldt for everything from digging holes to slaughtering animals. It was light, the shaft of bamboo, the blade a square of steel sharpened on three sides with only the top left blunt. The grindstoned edges of the shovel that he swung sliced shoulder, hip and knee.

It was with the spade the Predikant burst through the wall of Purgators, shouting for his flock to follow, lashing with skill and holy madness from side to side. He took the top off the head of one Redeemer as if it were a Memphis lady's breakfast egg. A mercifully instant death, it appalled the Redeemers to either side, courage grasped the javelin and raised it over his shoulder, took two steps and threw. Nothing you've seen was ever so graceful, power and balance combined to perfection. No bite from a snake was struck with such instinct. The spear took the pastor just above the groin. Splitting his bladder and smashing his pelvis it emerged from his buttock. Crying with anguish he fell to the ground, the blood and the urine pouring into the sand, like wine and like water, the steam of it rising. Cale remembered it always. Now he was shouting and urging them forwards and two of the Folk who'd seen that their pastor had died at the hands of the boy who was roaring came for him, instantly pumped up with vengeance. But only one made it – the other was taken by Purgators, their courage returning. The second man struck – the blow would have cut Cale in half had it landed. But colder and colder Cale watched his opponent like a man who was playing at fighting with children – the blows were just clumsy, ungainly and awkward. But the arrows came close now – one nearly took him and broke his attention and the moment of focus fled for a moment. The clang and clatter, the yelping and shouting brought him to earth and the gracefulness left him. The man saw him waver and gaining in confidence moved to kick at him. The blow swept past Cale, who kicked at his standing foot, grabbed at his waist and then pulled him downwards onto the sand. How long was the second as Cale took his time and bending him backwards reached for his knife. They struggled so, quietly grunting sonably regarded as a terrible mistake, the Folk Maister ordered his troops to cross the river from in front of the hill and attack the Drift from inside the U. Once the centenar recalled his troops and Cale established a new defence lower down, the attacking Folk found that they were playing to another Redeemer strength. Flights of bolts and arrows from the hill they thought they'd won now took them from the rear and from high above where they could easily be picked out. The few who took refuge in the trenches along with the fake Redeemers did not survive for long. Fighting in trenches was the third Redeemer strength. The Folk were shown as much mercy as they were accustomed to offering themselves. None.

With such heavy losses and shocked by the peculiar way in which the Redeemers had fought, the Folk withdrew and attempted to use the mortars on the shoulder of the tabletop mountain to cover their retreat. This was when the Redeemer snipers Cale had left on the tabletop itself finally came into play. From what was now complete safety, the archers picked off half the Folk artillerymen before they realized that they could neither defend themselves nor remove the mortars. Abandoning them, they fled to join what remained of the escaping Folk.

Cale had made every judgement that day correctly, except for the one that would have made his brilliance and courage completely unnecessary. It was a lesson of sorts but of what kind he was unsure – never make a mistake, perhaps. He walked up to the top of the hill, where Gil was waiting for him. Cheers and *God bless you*s came everywhere from men he despised but had now been forced to risk his life to save and who depended utterly on him, as, he now realized, he did on them.

Gil bowed only slightly but in such a way that Cale could sense some even deeper change towards him.

'You have won golden opinions. Men, even degenerate men, find it hard not to love someone who has saved them twice.'

'Well, we were very nearly even.' Cale got down into the trench and looked back down the hill. He'd chosen the site from horseback some seven feet off the ground and from where he had a clear sight down its entire length. But at ground level it was obvious that there was a bulge in the middle of the field of fire which meant that until you were twenty yards away there was easily enough cover to attack the trench, protected from bolt and arrow. He was amazed at his own stupidity. How was it possible, when he had been so right about everything else, to be so witless about this?

'They deserve an apology,' he said to Gil, and for all his loathing of the Purgators he meant it.

'Keep your mouth shut!' said Gil, firmly, and then, worried, added an apologetic 'sir'.

'They can see my mistake.'

'They can see you set up the battlefield to keep them alive and you came to their rescue when things went bad. It's been a long time since this lot were victorious in anything. They won. They're yours. You made a mistake and you put it right. What else can a general do?'

'I don't remember you being so forgiving on the Martyr's training field.'

'Train hard, fight easy.'

'So, all that was just for my benefit?'

'You're alive and you won so I'd say it was.'

'I've sent out scouts to make sure the Folk don't double back. You'll need to talk to them.'

'No. You talk.'

'No, sir.'

And so it was that ten minutes later Cale stood on a rock in the centre of the U and tried to keep the hatred and resentment of them out of his voice. But they didn't need much. He had risked his life for them and they were back from the dead.

By now, Hooke had walked down from the rise and had listened to the celebrations of the Redeemers and the reluctance of the boy they were begging to adore, all of their longings invested in what to them was the blank slate of Thomas Cale. Finished and in a bad temper Cale told Hooke to inspect the mortars now being brought in from the mountain and give him a report within an hour. Hooke bobbed his head, mocking.

'I shouldn't worry about having to be faithful to people you hate. There are many different kinds of loyalty, Mr Cale,' he said. 'There's the loyalty, for example, that the pig farmer owes to the pig.' And while Cale was silenced by that he turned off down the hill to inspect the waiting mortars.

An hour later Hooke was giving his report. He was holding a large bolt about three feet long in his hand. Around the barrel of the bolt twelve smaller darts had been lashed carefully side by side.

'The lashings are made of ordinary twine, woven with rubber. You know what rubber is?'

'No.'

'I'm not surprised. Condamine tried to demonstrate it to the Pope at Avignon but the Archbishop tried to arrest him for witchcraft because it repelled water unnaturally.'

'What's that got to do with the lashings?'

'Nothing. But rubber also stretches.' He pulled a length of the twine and it expanded, not by much but enough to make it clear that he was right.

'When it's fired from the mortar, a line of cat gut attached to the bolt with wax loosens the rubber twine and it unravels, from what I could see, in about five seconds. The twelve darts simply fall away and follow the main bolt to the earth. There's more to it, I'd say, but that's the basic principle.'

'Can you copy it?'

'I don't see a problem.'

'Then do it.'

'Except one.'

'Yes?'

'Not a question of engineering, a question of theology. The Pope does not care for rubber. There has been no infallible pontifical ban *Urbe et Orbe* concerning rubber as such but there is great suspicion concerning flexible substances as not being natural. The attempt to arrest Condamine means that in common ecclesiastical law the use of rubber may be prima facie evidence for the practice of witchcraft.'

'Are you sure?'

'I am sure that the position is unclear and I am sure that I wouldn't want to take the risk. You, however, are better placed. Perhaps Bosco will make some sort of temporary ruling. Although I believe he and Cardinal Parsi are opposed.'

Cale sighed. 'How do you know so much?'

'How do you know so little?'

'If you're so well informed, Mr Hooke, how is it you needed me to get you out of prison?'

'Touché, Mr Cale. Nevertheless there are more ways than one to skin a cat.'

'Yes?'

'I have been working on an engine close to my heart.'

'I thought it was engines that got you put in the House of Special Purpose.'

'Yes.'

'So if you're prepared to risk blasphemy, what's the problem about witchcraft?'

'Because I am ready to die for this engine but I am not ready to die for rubber string. If I'm going to risk death I want something in return.'

'Something in return? Bosco told me the prescribed punishment for building blasphemous engines was to have all your skin removed while you were still alive and then dip you in a barrel of vinegar.'

'The mere adding of years to life is not living.'

'I'll try to remember that. But *you* remember this: I own your very teeth, Mr Hooke.'

'I am not ungrateful.'

'Does that mean you're grateful?'

'It's human nature to work in your own interests, no matter how indebted you are to others.'

'So what does this engine do?'

'As such it can do nothing. It is an engine I am making in the pursuit of natural philosophy. I wish to uncover the nature of things. But before you berate me, this natural speculation has at least one practical use that spins from pure enquiry. Will you listen?'

'Do you have friends, Mr Hooke?'

'None that are powerful enough.'

'If I think you're trying to take me for a fool I will discard you.'

'Fair enough, Mr Cale.'

Cale smiled and gestured for him to sit down. He did so but also bent to draw a circle in the dust.

'Imagine this circle only two hundred feet in diameter

and consisting of a fully enclosed pipe made of hardened brass. It is my belief that all matter is comprised of a single particle, an atom as I have named it, from which all things – earth, air, fire and water – are composed and made different solely by the various ways that nature has combined these atoms. But it follows, if my idea is correct, that only great power can undo the work of nature. I must find a way to make the purest substance on earth and form two balls of that substance and drive them at each other from opposite ends of the circular pipe and with such energy that when they collide they will smash each other into the atoms that alone make up their fabric and the fabric of all things.'

'How do you know atoms exist if you need this to prove it?'

'Ah,' said Hooke. 'You are not merely a general of precocious gifts. You are a most intelligent boy.'

'That friend I told you about, he told me that when it comes to flattery you should lay it on with a trowel. Perhaps you know him?'

'Just because it's flattery doesn't mean it is untrue, Mr Cale.'

'Go on.'

'I have arrived at the existence of atoms by mathematical speculations.' Cale looked at him. 'I can see you are unimpressed. Nevertheless, I have faith *and* numbers in my favour. But even if I'm wrong it doesn't matter. The problem I face and have yet to solve is how to bring the two balls of pure substance together with such force that they split the glue of nature. It was the search for a means to propel a heavy object at many times the speed of an arrow that brought me into the House of Special Purpose and so close to a squalid death from which, I freely admit, you alone saved me.'

'Enough.'

'I had spent nearly two years experimenting on a written formula for an explosive powder from China. I had only a smidgen of the powder, nearly all of which I was forced to use to satisfy myself that it would work. But the formula was crude – the ingredients and a few clues as to the way they might be combined poor stuff. I tried and failed many times but in the few months before I was arrested I had some success. A powder that made great flashes and smoke and light but with little in the way of force. But it frightened my assistants. They blabbed into some big ears. The Redeemers came back and found the powder and, well, one or two other things not easy to explain to men of that sort.'

'Such as?'

'A cadaver. Nothing untoward – it was brought from the executioner. I considered dissecting the dead to be a grey area – religiously speaking.'

'They didn't?'

'It turns out that in religious terms the notion of grey areas is something of a grey area.'

'So what's your point?'

'If I can have your protection in the business of developing the Chinese powder and money too, our hands can wash each other.'

'How?'

'If I can fire two balls of a pure substance at one another I can also fire a ball of iron at a man. Think of what such an engine would do. A man carrying such a device, even if he could only use it once, must wound or kill an enemy – or more than one. Think of the terror. He could discard it and fight on like any normal soldier but having killed or wounded the equivalent number of his opponents in the first moments of battle.'

'You're nowhere near making such a thing.'

'I could be. Give me the space and the means.'

'And how would I know whether you were giving me the run-around?'

'I know my obligation,' Hooke replied, offended. 'But you can see that to achieve my life's work I must be able to fire a solid object from a metal tube. The search for knowledge and the discovery of a great weapon are virtually one and the same. War is the father of everything. Besides, if you become a great general my life is protected. Correct?'

'As long as you don't take me for an idiot. You might take advantage of my ignorance of these things once but I'll catch you out if you try and play on me – then you'll be bobbing up and down like an onion in a vinegar jar. Understand?'

'Your threats are not necessary.'

'I think they are. Did you watch me fighting on the hill today?'

'Yes.'

'And I didn't have any strong feelings about these men one way or the other. What are the Folk to me? Yet they're dead, all the same, gone as if they'd never existed. I'll think about it. Now, I'm tired.'

# 9

By now Kleist had spent nearly a month living with the Klephts in the Quantocks. It had taken some time to persuade him that he would be safe there. Although he'd never heard of the Klephts or the Quantocks he had come across the bad-tempered and touchy tribesmen, the Musselmen, who inhabited the Quantocks' lower foothills. He had seen them once in Memphis and had been told to stay away from them and particularly the few women they brought down to repair the carpets of the very rich and draw up designs for new ones. 'Go near one of their women and they'll kill you whatever the cost to them. And savages that they are they'll kill the women, too, just in case.'

Alarmingly, Daisy had agreed that this was true and even more generous than it should be.

'Musselmen are fanatics, loopy, wicked and bad. They hate their women and treat them like dogs but their religion curses them because, for all their fear that they are liars and sluts, their God has ordained that the wives and daughters contain all the men's honour in a bowl inside their livers and that once it's defiled then the only way they can get it back is to kill the woman and start again. Can you believe it? Even if the woman has been raped they strangle the poor bitch. Disgusting.'

'The Klephts aren't like that?' asked a worried Kleist.

'God, no.'

'Why?'

''Cos we're not mad for one thing and because we came to the Quantocks and kicked them out a thousand years ago.'

'So you're like the Materazzi – not much in the way of being religious?'

'Oh no – we're very religious.'

This was a blow.

'How?' he asked, heart sinking.

Her description of her faith, despite her protestations as to its importance, didn't really seem to amount to much that he could pin down. It seemed to restrain them very little so far as he could make out. It was strong on the distinctions between eating clean and unclean animals of a kind it seemed to Kleist no one would want to eat anyway. It was strictly forbidden to eat bats, for example, or anything that crawled or wriggled. Eating spiders meant you were unclean for a fortnight and should Kleist be tempted, which he was not, to go back to his former butchery skills the consequences would involve an exile of six months. Their notion of God seemed very distant. The Klephts talked of him as if he were a rich uncle who was benign enough but had lost day-to-day interest in their side of the family. For himself he could not shake his guilt at having deserted Vague Henri and, to a much lesser extent, IdrisPukke. All reason told him that he had every right not to risk his life so hideously for other people who had not even asked him if he agreed to go along. On the other hand he realized that if he really felt so clearly about the rightness of his position he wouldn't have left them like a thief in the night. About Cale he did not feel guilty at all.

'What about you and me? You know?'

'I'm not a cow,' she said. 'My father doesn't own me. He is a civilized person who will thank you for helping me.'

So it proved. But despite his welcome Kleist was uneasy because he couldn't bend his mind to understand the Klepht way of thinking about the world. It was not just that he understood the Redeemer mentality because he'd lived among them for so long; he felt he had a pretty good handle on the Materazzi even after only a few weeks. And Memphis was full of races and types from all over the world. But none of his meetings with remarkable races in Memphis had left him with a vague sense of missing something that he felt all the time in the Quantocks. The Quantocks were a conundrum in limestone, riddled with spatey gorges, rocky unclimbable juts and chasms. Everywhere secret recesses punctured the high cliffs providing a hideaway or a place to gather for an attack. From here the Klephts disrupted trade by sacking, snatching, grabbing, nabbing, dispossessing, confiscating and generally depriving passers-by of everything but the clothes they stood up in – and not always those either. Their energetic approach to larceny became so notorious that amongst the dwellers round about (which other than the aggravating Musselmen was the only label the Klephts could be bothered to attach to the rich and ancient cultures they robbed) anyone who stole was known as a klephtomaniac. From time to time the other hill tribes would decide the rapacity and general nuisance level of the Klephts was no longer to be tolerated and they would band together for a punitive expedition into the mazy and innaccessible middle of the Quantocks.

It was no more than three weeks after Daisy had brought him into the heart of the Quantocks that Kleist had his first taste of their, to him, unique way of waging war. He had no intention of volunteering his services, and had been furious with Daisy about her boasting concerning his epic brutality to Dunbar and his men. His principle since Memphis was to keep his mouth shut about everything he possessed in terms of goods and services that might be useful to others and he told her to do the same in future.

'Why?' she said, astonished.

'Because I don't want them trying to stick me in the Vanguard to see if I'll play Barnaby the Berserker.'

'You worry too much.'

'That's why I'm still alive.'

'No one's going to ask you to do anything. It's got nothing to do with you.'

'Just remember that.'

Four days later at the specific invitation of Daisy's father he found himself sitting on top of a great limestone crop with (he had checked) plenty of rear avenues of escape, Daisy beside him, elated but not nervous. They were looking down into a valley about eight hundred feet across where the Klephts had built a rough wall. There were about five hundred Klephts in position, wandering up and down, talking, laughing and acting as if they didn't have a care in the world. At the other end of the valley there was a Musselman force of about a thousand. They waited for half an hour and then advanced in close order, spears and silvered shields shining in the sun. At two hundred yards they stopped, at which point the Klephts started to pay them some serious attention, which took the form of shouting endless and colourful abuse about the Musselmen's sexual practices with animals, the ugliness of their mothers, and the sluttishness of their wives and daughters. It was these last two that seemed to drive the Musselmen into an almost hysterical fury. Some, indeed, were so overcome with grief at this abuse to their honour that they burst into tears and knelt down and began throwing dirt over their heads. It settled into a routine. From one side of the defensive wall in the valley a dozen Klephts would call out a name: 'FATIMA!' and another dozen would shout back: 'DOES IT BEHIND THE PIGSTY!' And then again: 'AIDA!', to the chorus of: 'LIKES THEM THREE AT A TIME!' But the biggest reaction was provoked by what seemed to Kleist like the least offensive of them all: 'NASRULA!' To which a lone voice of unusual clarity shouted back: 'HAS A MOLE UPON HER INNER THIGH!' This instantly struck a nerve with one of the Musselmen, who screamed in fury at the precise nature of the description of his hapless wife and instantly started to run suicidally towards the Klepht front line. Fortunately in his hysterical haste he tripped over a stone and before he could get back to his feet half a dozen of his friends and relatives grabbed him and dragged him noisily protesting back to their front line.

General order took a good ten minutes to restore. Still laughing, Kleist turned to Daisy.

'You don't think it could be a mistake – twisting their ropes like that?'

She shrugged but wouldn't say any more. But now the attack began, the Musselmen advancing in good order, impressively disciplined as if they knew their business. To Kleist it looked like something bloody was coming. Still the insults poured on like the arrows at Silbury Hill. And then the final furious screaming charge. At this, the Klephts launched a not very impressive and completely inaccurate flight of arrows, turned and ran away. Daisy leapt up and down, clapping her hands in delight as the Klephts raced back into the endless winding defiles at the rear of the valley. The rough stone wall delayed the Musselmen by a minute, laden as it was with traps on the far side – sharp slivers of bamboo hidden in pits that could slice through a foot, poisonous snakes in the crevices of the walls and thousands of spiders poured over the walls just before the Klephts ran away. None of them were poisonous but spiders were unclean for the Musselmen even to touch let alone eat. By the time they had regrouped and started after the Klephts, most were well out of sight, except for the young blades who stayed back at the top of the defiles to shout even more insults. They didn't hang about for long as some of the furious Musselmen chased after them but, met by a lashing of rocks from the limestone cliffs that fitted into the defiles like fingers, they soon realized a chase was both fruitless and likely to be lethal.

'Come on,' said Daisy, and pulled him back from the cliff and, via a circuitous route in case they were spotted by any Musselman scouts, took him back to the village. For the rest of the afternoon the Klephts from the great unbattle drifted in, delighted with themselves and boasting of their lack of feats of daring, the complete absence of any brave deeds, and their total success in not even standing to the first man let alone the last.

Several days of celebration followed in which many

war stories, endlessly exaggerated in the telling, were told of the cunning with which the teller caused havoc to his particular enemy without sustaining any personal risk to himself or demonstrating the slightest bravery. Each one of them competed in fabricating outrageous claims concerning the ways in which, from the complete safety of an unbridgeable chasm or the top of an unclimbable cliff, they had tricked outrageously stupid Musselmen into revealing the names of their female loved ones so that a wife's, sister's or mother's sexual purity could be defamed in ever more inventively grotesque ways. As Kleist listened in delight it became clear that to the Klephts the ultimate victory over an enemy was not to defeat him man-to-man in a heroic struggle of arms, but to cause, without risk to oneself, the absurd opponent to drop dead of a spontaneous heart attack or stroke, caused entirely by his gullibility regarding the honour of his women relatives and the ingenuity of the lies of his Klepht opponent. But however amused, Kleist was also somewhat shocked. The fact is that while the military philosophy of the Klephts appealed to him precisely because it was against everything he had been taught by the Redeemers in terms of pain, blood, self-sacrifice and duty, it also clashed for exactly the same reason: it was against everything he had been taught by the Redeemers.

Daisy's village, Soho, was surrounded by a path shaded with specially planted olives where every evening Klephts would walk in pairs and talk about all and everything under the sun. Kleist was in much demand as a talking partner because of the Klephts' immense curiosity about everything in general and about the Redeemers in particular, whose practices and beliefs they found completely incomprehensible and therefore utterly fascinating. They assumed that every tale of brutality, every ghastly story of heaven and hell, every detail of the faith that Kleist recounted was merely an outrageous and entertaining lie. There was nothing he could do to persuade them that there were people who really believed and acted as the Redeemers believed and acted. 'VIRGIN BIRTH? HAR! HAR! HAR! WALKING ON WATER? HE! HE! HE! BACK FROM THE DEAD? HO! HO! HO! THE LAST FOUR THINGS? TEE! HEE! HEE!' A few days after the fight against the Musselmen, this time it was Kleist busy asking questions of Daisy's father – a good-humoured old villain who had taken an immense, if not to be relied on, liking to him.

'Look, Suveri, I've got nothing against running away but we were taught it's the quickest way to get yourself killed.'

'I'm alive, aren't I? How many funerals can you see being prepared?'

'You wouldn't get away with that stuff in many places. Anywhere a horse could go they'd ride you down. Infantry, too, if they were good enough.'

'But we didn't fight in many places, we fought here.'

'But what if you had to?'

'We don't.'

'You raid.'

'And sometimes we get killed – but we take what we've stolen into these mountains – and if we have to stop to fight a pitched battle, well, we just dump whatever we've filched and leg it back here.'

'What if they trap you before you get here?'

'I suppose you fight and get out or you don't and you die.'

'You can't win a war without standing and fighting – that's just a fact.'

'True enough, I suppose. But we don't fight wars. We just steal and rob. It's none of my business if the Redeemers want to die for God or the Materazzi for glory. It wouldn't suit us, that kind of thing, but it takes all sorts to make a world.' He laughed and gestured at the limestone landscape around them with its endless crags and chasms and canyons. 'Deserts make fanatics, everyone knows that. But a place like this breeds a noble cowardice. We know how to let other people be.'

'You steal from other people all the time.'

'Other than that. Nobody's perfect.'

Over the next three months Cale and Gil expanded the campaign against the Folk by splitting the Purgators into groups of ten, each in charge of two hundred ordinary Redeemers.

There were more defeats in the early part of the campaign than victories but the vicious nature of the fighting had the advantage of killing off those who were unable or unwilling to grasp the new tactics. To his surprise most of the Purgators survived and even flourished. It was, supposed Cale, because they had broken with a life of complete obedience already – that was why they were Purgators in the first place. Something in him refused to accept that something else was just as important – their adoration of Cale. Gil saw it and regarded their faith in him as yet further evidence of his peculiar divinity. Cale was not holy, of course, not to be revered as a saint or prophet. He was not, so far as Gil understood Bosco, a person in the sense that even the most apostate Antagonist was a person. He was, in a sense, not really alive. He was the incarnation of a divine emotion. He was, perhaps, becoming an angel, pure in the way that emotions given absolute expression are pure. Everything else about him was in the process of being burnt away. He had to be human in order to be born and grow up. But that was not required any more and Gil could see Cale the boy disappearing in front of him. There were occasional flashes of what you might call a person: he would laugh at something ridiculous that happened in the camp or you could see his tongue sticking out the way you saw in a small boy when he was lost in concentration on some task – but less and less. No wonder then that the Purgators were drawn to him

'So,' said Hooke. 'You have a stalemate. No victories for them and none for us beyond holding these forts.'

'Not at all,' said Cale. 'I mean to go on the offensive very soon.'

'How? You don't have the troops.'

'No, but I'll soon have the services of two great generals.'

'Greater than you?' mocked Hooke. 'How could that be? Who are these paragons?'

'General December and General January,' said Cale.

While Cale was working to cut off the lifeblood of the Folk, Bosco was engaged in slowing the attempt by his enemies at the Pontificate to do the same to him. Instead of violence they used theology, and their means of putting a foot on his windpipe involved the commissioning of a conference instead of a blockade.

The theological question involved concerned oil and water. Only an omnipotent God could save a creature like man, so vicious, low and debased was his nature. Yet it was a tenet of central faith that the Hanged Redeemer was both man and God. How could this be possible? Until recently the problem had been dealt with by ignoring it but Redeemer Restorious, Bishop of Arden, had stirred things up by preaching the theory of Holy Emulsion. The Hanged Redeemer's two natures were like, he claimed, oil mixed with water and stirred together. For a time during his life on earth, the mixture looked to the observer like a single fluid of one kind, but over time that liquid would separate into clearly definable oil and water again. It could be mixed but was always separate. 'Nonsense!' replied Bishop Redeemer Cyril of Salem. 'The nature of the Hanged Redeemer was like water and wine – they are separate until they are mixed and become inseparable in a form that *no* power could reverse.'

Despite the bitterness of this disagreement neither Parsi nor Gant had the slightest interest in indulging the rancour of a pair of squabbling clerics until, during a brief period of lucidity, Pope Bento expressed a desire to resolve the issue. The reason why was lost in the fog that descended on his brain the following day, but Gant and Parsi had been given the authority to establish a conference to decide the matter wherever they saw fit. They saw fit to hold it in the Sanctuary because wherever such a commission was being held temporarily became subject to the presiding authorities – which in this case were Gant and Parsi. They would have the right to go anywhere in the Sanctuary and talk to anyone. You will understand now how very important in so many ways the issue of emulsification had become. Unfortunately for Bosco the deadly blow of the death of the three hundred had meant that even so great a tactician became subject to Swinedoll's Law of Momentum: if you are not moving forwards you are moving backwards. He could now only retreat as slowly as possible. He had influence in Chartres but it was fragile, built over the years from many favours and with unreliable allies not easy to keep an eye on from the Sanctuary. Those favours were now being used up, and while the unreliable allies did not desert him they would not risk exerting themselves on his behalf until it was clearer how the struggle for power between Bosco and the two cardinals would work itself out. Gant and Parsi's plan to hold the conference in the Sanctuary and do so within the month suddenly became unblocked in the Apostolic Camera and moved ahead without any serious opposition. This was all bad news for Bosco. His counter was to use up most of his remaining store of favours. A committee was set up in Chartres duly packed with those who for whatever reason either owed Bosco or were committed secretly to his belief in a reformed Redeemership. A mission to the veldt was dispatched and duly confirmed Cale's great success. Gant and Parsi made an attempt to prevent it but failed. One reason was that the Redeemers required a victory to repair the morale of the faithful much tested during the long stalemate on the Eastern Front, morale that had been further damaged by rumours that the Antagonists had discovered a silver mine in Argentum so large that they could hire an entire army of Laconic mercenaries. The second reason was that while theology and politics were all very well, there was nothing like the defeat of an enemy to raise the spirits. And if the enemy poor; unofficial rumours of miracles were started, stories of Redeemer soldiers of dreadful piety meeting him and then having visions of St Redeemer Jerome, blood pouring from his severed hands, and of St Redeemer Finlay, who had been wrapped in a blanket steeped in pitch and then set fire to like a match.

Unaware of this consider Cale's astonishment as, by way of a slower and more populous route ordered by Bosco, he made his journey back to the Sanctuary from the veldt. He found that even in the back of beyond there were people by the road bowing and calling to him for a blessing, some of whom had walked for days on the rumour of his passing by. In the towns and villages subject to the cruelty and destruction of punitive raids by the Folk, men and women wept with thankfulness and burst into hymnal songs of sacrifice and martyrdom.

'Faith of our fathers, living still. In spite of dungeon, fire and sword!'

The hairs on his neck spiked unpleasantly to hear that particular hymn again.

Even in places far removed from the raids of the Folk, statues of the saints were paraded, holy gibbets that had not seen the light outside a church for a dozen generations were raised in the noonday sun. To Gil's scandal and alarm the blind and scrofulous were dragged forward to touch the hem of Cale's cassock or even the hair of his horse so that he might intercede with heaven for their sake.

By the time they were on the winding road up to the Sanctuary, Gil hardly knew what to think. Even the apparently affectless Cale looked as if something peculiar was going on in his brain, more than just his loathing of the sight of the Sanctuary walls.

Halfway up the massive rock on which the Sanctuary was built, their column was joined by the Officer of Mortification. It was his task, one he performed with enormous satisfaction, to remind a victorious returning Redeemer that all human achievement was utterly futile. All the way up the second half of the mountain and through the great gates and into the Courtyard of Repentance, the Officer of Mortification whispered in Cale's ear: 'Remember man that thou art dust and unto dust thou shalt return. Remember man that thou art dust and unto dust thou shalt return . . .' At the twentieth time of saying Cale turned his head towards him and whispered back: 'Shut your gob.'

The Officer was so astonished at this he did indeed stay silent all the way until they were in the courtyard where the great phalanx of the six orders of the Knights of St Redeemer Barnabus waited for Cale's return and the Officer felt safe enough to continue, this time shouting aloud for the benefit of the faithful.

'Remember man that thou art dust and unto dust thou shalt return.' And then 'STOP!'

Cale did so. 'Turn to me.' Again he did as he was asked. In his left hand the Officer of Mortification held a whitish linen bag. He reached inside and took a pinch of the contents, the mixed ashes of the twenty-four martyrs of the great burning at Aachen and raising them to Cale's forehead drew the simplified shape of a gallows like an upside-down L.

> 'Death, Judgement, Heaven and Hell
> The last four things on which we dwell
> Mortification, death and sin
> These are the clothes that we lie in.'

Cale looked around the great square for once ablaze with the High and Holyday colours of the Redeemers in the multilayered ordered blocks of the Sodalities to which each one of them belonged. There were the Bon Secours in vestments red and gold, Lazarites in white with their gurning Servitors, Knights of the Curia ululating the charm and beauty of the One True Faith, the Necrotic Asphyxiates with hempen ropes around their necks, rubbed raw. There were the Scarlatti in crimson bowler hats, the Quinzième in green and black braces, faces covered by a hood that towered to a point, hands rolling in perpetuity the fifteen beads of sorrow one by one. Opposite on their knees were Batteni with the cincture of abstinence around their waist, knotted with the seven nodes of denial of the flesh and wearing dried pigeon peas inside their socks. There were Fromondi with knittles singing a hallelujah from the throat, the

Peccavi lamenting the loss of the many and the finding of the few. Then Bosco began to walk along their ranks with a reedy aspergill in hand, shaking over them the waters of affliction and the oils of grief. At every tenth Redeemer he stopped and offered them salt to represent the bitter taste of sin and they accepted the rebuke with tears. Then he placed a five-fold scapular around their necks, yoke of the Redeemer, burden of the Lord, while behind him a thurifer swung his thurible incensing the faithful in their penitential gorgeousness.

And then the singing began in earnest, the bass notes of the Alimenteri so deep the hearing of them seemed to begin somewhere in the stomach, shaking the bowels like some great underwater tow. Then softly the lighter tones of the cantabile that merged and clashed and merged again as if they were different songs. Then the high notes of the juveniles, pure as ice, freezing the hairs along Cale's spine, the sound rising to heaven with a pitch so terrible it made him want to scream. Then it slowly began to end, first the high pitch of the young boys, then the middle tones and then the gradual diminishing of the bass rolling away like a storm passing out to sea.

It was beautiful beyond imagining. And yet he hated it.

When he had first come to the Sanctuary he had been uncomprehendingly impressed by the extraordinary sights and sounds of a major holyday – a vast but vague pageant of noise and colour to such a small boy. As he grew older the holydays began to clarify into the hideous boredom of the ceremonies and the power of the music. Those with a talent practised for hours every day out of hearing – Cale himself had been tested for the quality of his voice and dismissed with the observation that he sounded like a cat having its throat cut with a rusty saw. Unkind but not untrue. So four times a year he heard the choir and the orchestra perform and grew to love it and hate it in equal measure. How could the dead souls of the Redeemers produce anything to move him so?

Then the procession into the great basilica and the Mass for the Dead, not for the legions of those killed in the cause of the faith but for the souls of those unsaved who had died before hearing the word of the Hanged Redeemer. In sorrow and mourning all the statues of martyrs, the sister of the Hanged Redeemer and all the thousand holy gibbets in the Sanctuary, large and small, had been covered in purple silk and would remain so for another forty days until at the exact same second the pins that held them closed were pulled away and the purple cloth would shimmer to reveal the beautiful smiles, the tortured limbs, the wounds and weeping sores of holy suffering.

If the beauty of the Agnus Dei in the courtyard had shaken him, Cale had two hours of utter dreariness in the basilica to calm himself. Without the great music to endow them with its command, the reds and blacks and golds of high hats and curiously shaped vestments, the burning incense and the waving hands in elaborate blessings were reassuringly dull and ridiculous, soothing to his fury at the insulting loveliness of the sound of the three great choirs of the Sanctuary. The stupidity and ugliness of the Prayer of Self-Loathing was especially dreary balm to his resentment:

'Less than the dust beneath my feet
Less than the weed that grows beside my door
Less than the rust that stains the careless sword
Less than the need thou, Lord, has of me
Even less am I.'

So it was with a queasy mixture of anger at the beauty of the singing and the numbing boredom of the Mass for the Dead that Cale finally made it back to his set of rooms. What with the aching journey all he wanted to do was lie down and go to sleep, but Bosco wasn't finished.

'You've done well. But I need you to tell me: do the Purgators have it in them to succeed?'

'I'm tired.'

'Briefly. We can talk in detail later.'

'Probably.' He instantly regretted giving Bosco the satisfaction. 'Possibly.'

'Time is tight, Cale. We must win or die.'

'Later.'

'I had not intended to take Memphis. It's only that I hold the old Marshall and most of his family that prevents their empire taking up arms against us.' This was no longer true but Bosco thought it best not to unsettle Cale with the fact of their escape. Besides, his knowledge of what had happened subsequently was patchy. He did not know, for example, that old Materazzi was already dead from pneumonia. 'We cannot take on the Materazzi Empire and the Antagonists.'

'Shouldn't you have thought of that?'

'I thought of nothing else. Your escape made it impossible to do otherwise. Now if you hadn't gone blundering into Picarbo's room everything would have been different.'

'You sent me in there.'

'So I did. But you're beginning yourself to realize that almost everything that happens for good or bad has its origin in a blunder.'

Cale laughed.

'Yours?'

'No.'

'I want to sleep.'

'Very well. But for the avoidance of doubt – you and I are bound together with unbreakable chains. There is nowhere you can go but by my side. As you've seen after your frolic in Memphis it's in your nature to cause every man's hand to turn against you except through this course now, here, with me. Tell me you understand this.'

Cale looked at him for some time and then nodded, as reluctant as you like. Bosco nodded back.

'Sleep well. God bless.'

As soon as he had gone there was a knock on the door and Acolyte Model came in. Cale was surprised by how pleased he was to see him.

'Sir.'

'You look well.' And he did. It was not just the extra food that Cale had demanded Model be given but the quality of it. His face had filled out – he was not fat or anything like it but he no longer had that gaunt expression attendant on eating barely enough and doing hours of heavy exercise. His skin glowed even, instead of being patchy and dull. A decent meal a couple of times a day was, as Cale had come to realize, one of the greatest gifts that life could offer. It would be smart to use this on the Purgators.

'Are you well, sir?'

'Yes.'

'We are all excited by your great success.'

'We?'

'The acolytes.'

Cale noticed that there was something awkward and hesitant now about him.

'What is it?'

'Sir?'

'Spit it out.'

'I've been sharing the food around with my oppos, sir.'

'You're in trouble?'

186

'It's not that. But one of them is on water duty in Clink Number Two.' He looked even more hesitant. 'One of the Antagonist spies there waiting the drop, he says he's a friend of yours.'

Cale was as puzzled as he was shocked. No wonder Model was so uneasy. Passing around information of this kind was like holding poison and no chalice.

'I don't know anyone like that but I won't say anything. Did he give a name?'

'He wouldn't say but he gave my oppo a message for you.' He took a scrap of paper out of an illegal pocket and handed it to Cale. It was clumsily sealed with God knows what. He opened it. There were two words written on a scrap clearly torn from an old hymn book.

'VAGUE HENRI'.

# 10

'Has he been tortured?'

'Apparently not,' said Bosco.

'Did you know he was here?'

'You must be mistaking me for a middle-ranking official in the Carceral Pelago. Why would *I* know he was here?'

'I want him released.'

It took Cale by surprise when Bosco replied calmly, 'Very well.' Bosco smiled. 'You expected me to refuse?'

'Yes.'

'Why? He clearly came here to be reunited with you. And we both know you have no intention of going anywhere.'

Realizing he was being mocked Cale changed the subject.

'Why wasn't he tortured?'

'A good question if I may say so. An administrative error. There's been an outbreak of jail fever in Clink Number Four so overcrowding in the rest. Pressure of numbers and work and a man guilty of Gomorrah was accidentally given the same number as your faithful friend.'

'They seem to make a lot of mistakes in the prisons here.'

'They do, though, don't they? Perhaps it was God's will.'

'I'd like to see him now.'

'I'll send Redeemer Gil. He knows him. Will that satisfy you?'

It was not that Bosco expected thanks but it amused him to make Cale feel awkward. 'You don't mind,' said Bosco, 'if I ask how you knew he was here?'

Cale turned back to look at him.

'No.'

'Well?'

'No. I don't mind if you ask.'

'How one gets used to change. Cheeking me would once have got you a thrashing.'

'Yes?'

'I mean nothing by it. Your acolyte seems very fond of you.'

'I don't have an acolyte.'

'But you do. In all ways. I understand how things have changed between you and me but I wonder if you have. I fear that perhaps, not so deep down, you might still just be an angry little boy.'

'I thought that's all I was supposed to be?'

'Righteous anger is something very different from bad temper. I just thought I might point that out. Vague Henri will be with you within the hour.'

'I want to go into the convent.'

'Very well.'

'You're being indulgent.'

'That worries you?'

'It's meant to, isn't it?'

'Only because I take some pleasure in confounding your expectations of me. You don't quite seem to have grasped, if I may say so, how things are.'

'I can do what I want, is that it?'

'You know very well what the answer to that is. But you'd do well to think more carefully about what's permitted to you and what isn't.'

'I'm just a bad-tempered boy.'

'For both our sakes I hope that's not true. The keys to the convent will be brought to you. You may do as you wish there.' As he placed his hand upon the door handle, Bosco turned back. It had always been a habit of Bosco's, this – to leave what was really on his mind to the last moment as if it were an afterthought.

'What do you know about the Laconics?'

'Soldiers for hire. Expensive.' He thought for a moment as if trying to remember. Only his years of deadpan insolence stopped him from smiling at this unexpected opportunity to mock his former master. 'Chrononhotonthologos,' he added thoughtfully. Bosco looked at him realizing he was being dared.

'It is not a term I'm familiar with,' he said, refusing to take the bait.

'It means a swashbuckler, a desperado.'

'Really. Anything else?'

'No.'

'There has been a rumour that the Antagonists have discovered a silver mine in Argentum. It's no longer a rumour. Not quite as sure but probable is that they will use this find to pay for a large army of Laconics to fight against us.'

'I thought they never fought for hire more than three hundred at a time.'

'And I thought you didn't know anything about them.' An impudent silence followed. 'I'm going to send you a brief concerning them. As your life may depend on it I'm sure I don't have to ask you to read it carefully.' He'd had enough of Cale and left without saying anything more.

With Bosco gone Cale considered what he felt. Alarm and delight in equal measure. Delight at the shock of seeing Vague Henri, alarm at the depth of that delight. His anger at Arbell Materazzi had swamped the dreadful loneliness that her absence caused him. But it had also hidden the loss he felt for his friend. Until that moment he had believed that he could take or leave Vague Henri though he'd got used to having him around. Now he was alarmed at the realization at how much he'd missed him. The excitement at the idea of his return was unbearable. He was a soul made out of great dams connected by great canals and constructed with great locks. But there's nothing built that doesn't leach or seep.

And what had happened to Kleist? Dead probably, he thought.

of his fascination. Because she was leaning back and kneeling astride him her thighs were tensed slightly, stretched over the bone and revealing the powerful muscles. They were not like the long and slender legs of the Materazzi girls he'd been able to glimpse as they insolently strode into a great ball sometimes with dresses slashed to the upper thigh revealing that elegant smoothness you could never be allowed to possess. If the harlots in Kitty Town were less coltishly refined and more various in size and shape, plump Mukie girls, the tiny but cheerful Gascons with enormous brown eyes, still none of them had the great muscularity of Daisy's thighs, oddly out of proportion to the rest of her, like those of an unusually strong young man. And then the hair and folded skin between her legs, the source of so much wonder and astonishment. Unimaginable until a few months ago except that he had assumed that the inhabitants of the mythical Devil's Playground would have had something familiar like a pair of balls and a cock but more pointy and ferocious befitting something so infernal. The reality of something so hidden and so soft still made him catch his breath with shame and joy. What an idea? What a thing? Then her belly with just a barely perceptible belt of fat. Then the roundness of the breasts and the harder brown and pink, the strong neck, the wide lips tinged with that waxy red stuff that she almost always liked to wear. Then the happy, smiling eyes and the long hair.

'Do you notice anything different about me?' she said. 'If you've finished gawping.'

He opened his eyes fully.

'You don't like me to look at you?'

'I love it. But you don't have to hide.'

'I wasn't hiding,' he said, irritable and ashamed.

'Don't be angry. You can look at me any time you like. Anyway you haven't answered my question. Well?'

Obviously there was something that he ought to have seen but hadn't.

'I don't know,' he said, after looking her up and down. 'Tell me.'

'You've no idea?'

He noticed that her tone and expression had changed. She was not annoyed with him for having failed to appreciate a braiding in her hair or a more elaborately decorated middle fingernail. She was naked after all. What could possibly be different?

'I'm pregnant.'

He stared at her as if he didn't understand. Which in fact he didn't.

'I don't know what that means.' She stared back at him in equal bewilderment; this was going to be more difficult or at least much stranger than she had thought.

'I'm going to have a baby.'

Although his expression changed to one of astonishment, it didn't seem to Daisy to suggest any greater understanding.

'But how?' he said, appalled.

'What do you mean?'

'How can you be having a baby?'

'You don't know how babies are made?'

'No.'

'They didn't tell you at that Sanctuary of yours?'

'I never even saw a woman until this year. No. No I don't know anything. What are you talking about?'

'You didn't think to ask?'

'About babies? Why would I?'

'How did you think they got here?'

'I don't know. Why would I think anything about babies?'

'I don't believe this.'

'Why would I lie to you?'

She looked at him, bewildered and bothered.

'No, I don't mean you're lying. I just can't believe you had no idea about . . .'

'Well, I don't.'

They looked at each other, Kleist white with horror, Daisy pale with confusion. There was a brief silence.

'So tell me why you're having a baby,' he said.

'Because of you.'

'Me? I don't know anything about babies.'

'You gave me a baby.'

'How could I?'

She realized slowly just how unfathomably deep his ignorance was. She sat down, lost.

'When your penis is inside me and you have the conniptions. That's how you make babies.'

'My God! Why didn't you tell me?'

'I didn't know you didn't know.'

'I don't know anything.'

This was not an unreasonable claim. Before he went to Memphis he knew nothing much except about religion, which he hated and feared, and killing, which he was good at but also feared because he feared to be killed back. In Memphis knowledge about all sorts of things had been poured over him and like the great dry sponge of ignorance he was he had soaked up enormous quantities of stuff. Sadly he had yet to put it all in order and make the kinds of connections which even a very stupid fifteen- or sixteen-year-old might have made long before. In some respects he wasn't much more than a baby himself.

'What are we going to do?' he said hopelessly.

'You've already done it,' she replied, unfair and bad-tempered.

'You knew about this. It's your fault.'

'Mine?'

'Yes. Your father will kill me.'

'No, he won't.'

'Thank God. Are you sure?'

'Only,' she said, 'if you don't marry me.'

'Marry you?'

'Now you're going to pretend you've never heard of marriage.'

'That's ridiculous.'

'It's no more ridiculous than not knowing how babies get made.'

This was too much to hear.

'People get married in front of you. They talk about it. Nobody ever talked about babies and how to get them.'

'Well,' she said, miserably, 'now you know.'

Daisy's father was neither as pleased as she expected nor as murderously angry as Kleist feared. Her father was well disposed towards him because he had saved both his daughter's life, probably true, and her honour, definitely not true. But this had happened elsewhere and they only had Daisy's word that her description of events concerning her rescue was to be relied on. But even if they had taken her account of his physical courage and martial skill at face value the problem was that the Klephts did not particularly value these qualities. As a result, beyond their willingness to accept a stranger who had done a great kindness to one of their own, he had no significant status among the Klephts. Daisy was the daughter of a man of considerable wealth and importance based upon a talent for theft much admired even amongst a people whose name was a byword for larceny. Kleist's offer, set on by Daisy, to be involved in Klepht raids after the revelations about the pregnancy only added to the problem. It was made so lightly and with such a clear belief that stealing on the scale practised by the Klephts was obviously not difficult that he caused offence, especially among those who had been sympathetic to his situation until his enforced clumsy proposal. This so undermined his request for permission to marry Daisy that she accused him of doing it deliberately. He had now offended everyone but especially the girl he now realized that he loved very much. Once over his astonishment at the means and fact of becoming a father, he became astonished all over again at how wonderful an idea it seemed. Babies as far as he could see from those around him were lovely and beautiful and, mostly, happy. Given that they were whisked away as babies usually are when they became a noisy nuisance and that he merely observed them at their best through a thick veil of total ignorance, his optimism was, perhaps, forgivable, however unjustified. But there were also many buried feelings growing in the depths of his tough young soul. Fatherhood, an unthought-of impossibility, now seemed like a wonderful adventure. However, his clumsiness concerning the offer to accompany the Klephts on one of their raids seemed to have tied the feet of his own happiness. Something drastic was called for. First he offered everything he owned to Daisy's father, namely everything he had looted from Memphis and then stolen back from Lord Dunbar's gang. This managed to please him and to mollify Daisy. Next he proposed a demonstration of just how very useful his brutally won skills as an archer could be and in such a

were morose and some greatly grief-stricken at being reminded of such a calamity. Kleist had constructed twenty pretty roughly man-shaped dummies and Daisy and her friends had strapped them to the horses that had been so reluctantly provided. Kleist stood behind a chest-high wall he had built and disguised with branches just where the massacre had taken place. Five hundred yards away the bored horses looked on, unenthusiastically feeding on the spindly grass. Then, twenty or so girls herded the reluctant animals into a rough line facing the distant Kleist and each one drew back a leather whip and, at Daisy's shout, lashed down heavily on the flanks of the horses. That changed their attitude and they squealed and reared and with the girls screaming behind them set off at a terrified charge, the straw men on their backs bouncing and waving about on top of them. Just to make his point, Kleist had stripped to the waist to show off to the best his strange but impressive upper body, muscles like knots in thick rope and of someone twenty years older. He let off one shot. All watched as it arched upwards faster and in a far greater arc than anything they had seen before. It took the straw man he had been aiming at straight in the chest and came out the other side. It was impressive but still too far away to completely stun the natives with its excellence. He waited till they got closer, pushing his luck to make a show of it. Then in the ninety seconds it took the terrified horses to make it to his hide he loosed off an astonishing quick succession of arrows, missing only with two by the time they stampeded past.

The Klephts were impressed, but wary.

'There were a hundred of them on the day.'

'I could have taken out thirty long before they got here. No one will take those kinds of losses. Besides, I wouldn't do it like this. I'd have been picking them off for hours or even days before they got here. From six hundred yards I can make five shots out of ten – eight if you count the horses.'

There were a few more objections but his case was made. Besides, what did they have to lose but a pleasant stranger who was, all said and done, nothing to them.

## 12

When Vague Henri arrived he had to be helped in by two Redeemers.

'Lay him on the bed and leave.'

Cale walked over to him and knelt down by the bed. Vague Henri's nose and lower lip, thickened by a hefty beating, were bleeding.

'Look at the state of you. What in God's name are you doing here, you bloody idiot?'

'Pleased to see you as well.'

'Let's start with what you're doing here.'

'I was hanging around the Voynich Oasis waiting on a caravan bringing back black earth for the gardens. I followed them here and tried to hitch on the end but someone recognized me. Besides, they count everyone in and out these days.'

'You should have thought of that.'

'I should have but I didn't.'

'You should have thought of that and stayed away.'

'Well, I'm here now.'

'Pure luck. You came this close,' Cale pinched his thumb and forefinger together, 'to being slotted by

Brzica and dumped in Ginky's Field. And I'd never have known anything about it.'

'All's well that ends well.' But Vague Henri was looking increasingly green. Cale's bad temper diminished slightly. 'I am pleased to see you.'

'How about a kiss?'

'I'm not that pleased.'

They both smiled.

'How about something to eat?' said Vague Henri.

'It's ordered.'

As if he'd been listening outside, Model knocked on the door and entered with a tray of food for two.

'The same again,' said Cale.

'There's a limit, sir, they won't take my word for so much.'

Cale wrote a note threatening the kitchen with Bosco's wrath and as Vague Henri sat down to eat he demanded that Cale give his story first.

It was more than two hours and well into Vague Henri's second tray before Cale had finished.

'So Bosco really is as mad as a sack of cats,' said Vague Henri.

'Luckily for you and me.'

'So what are you going to do?'

'Stay here,' said Cale. 'See it through.'

'Meaning?'

'I'm the observed of all observers – where would I

go? There's no Memphis any more. There's no Materazzi. Except for Antagonists who'd drop me on sight. Who else, even if I could get there, which I can't, would be stupid enough not to hand me over? Without Bosco I'm done for. And now St Vague Henri of the goody-two-shoes, so are you. Bosco owns us from snout to tail more than he ever did.'

Vague Henri sat for a while.

'You're right,' he said, at last.

'Tell me something I didn't know.'

They drank beer and smoked in dismal silence for a while.

'Now you,' said Cale.

Vague Henri started with his decision to follow Cale after his departure from Memphis.

'Kleist wasn't keen.'

'I can imagine. I'm astonished he went at all.'

'Don't be too astonished. After a week he ran away.'

'Which is exactly what I'd have done if Bosco had taken you instead of me.'

'No, you wouldn't.'

'Yes, I would.'

'Anyway. IdrisPukke and me we lost you near Tiger Mountain – the approaches are a bit rocky for tracking. Not my strong point anyway. IdrisPukke tried to persuade me to go with him to take the ferry out of Whitstable. I miss him. I made it to Voynich and that's pretty much it.'

'You were a long time in Voynich.'

'It's a nice place that. I wish I was back.'

And that was that for explanations. Cale had kept things short despite talking for two hours, partly because he had no taste for war stories but partly because he had seen the look in Vague Henri's eyes when he had told him about Bosco's belief that he was the agent of the death of mankind. He was not sure what it meant, that look, not belief and not fear or anything he could put his finger on – or wanted to put his finger on. So he played it down after that, the wrath of God stuff, even as he failed to cover up what bothered him about Vague Henri's reaction. It was not that Vague Henri thought it might be partly true that rankled but that on the contrary he regarded the idea as laughable. Something inside was drawn to the idea of his own magnificence and did not care to be mocked.

Vague Henri on his part had not just played down the truth, he had directly lied, although when he began telling his story he had not intended to do so. In six months they had both changed. And the question in both their minds was by how much.

The next day when Vague Henri was brought to his room things between them were both good-natured and awkward. But Cale wanted to show that while he had made terms with the man and religion they both hated, he had done so in a way very different from the past. He took Vague Henri to the convent, though without telling him where they were going. Then he got his first surprise

– Cale produced a key! And it was, Cale let him see, one key among several keys. It was as shocking as if Cale had got down on his knees and started to celebrate mass or had produced a bishop's mitre and stuck it on his head. But while Cale was thinking that it demonstrated that he was now in power in the Sanctuary, for Vague Henri it was a worrying sign. Perhaps Cale had taken a bribe the way Perkin Warbeck had taken a gallon of sweet sherry and a dozen sheep to betray the Hanged Redeemer. It was not possible and yet the last year had taught him that anything was possible.

Cale opened the door and they were inside the first layer of walls that protected the convent. They walked on for ten yards to a second door with no fewer than three locks which required three separate keys. Inside the convent proper the harsh green pitch of the floor changed to limestone, softened by carpets, and there were candles every few yards throwing the soft warm light of beeswax and not tallow from cows and pigs. They approached another door and Cale opened it, without keys (an unlocked door?) and, throwing it wide, gestured Vague Henri inside.

There was a great gasp and a ripple of excitement, long repressed as if his arrival was the very summit of anticipation. Around the walls in each corner were nuns, benign and smiling, and seated in the room as squirmingly impatient as a group of children awaiting the arrival of a birthday cake were twelve girls from perhaps thirteen to perhaps eighteen – pink girls, brown girls, black girls, ones with perfect olive skin, ones with complexions white as ghosts. They almost groaned with pleasure as the two young men came in the room, there was even a stifled squeal followed by a reproving cluck of the tongue from the nun behind and a cautionary hand on the shoulder.

'Good morning, ladies,' said a smiling Cale.

'Good morning, Mr Cale,' they echoed back as one.

'Let me introduce you to my oldest and my greatest friend. This is the great Vague Henri that I told you of – legend of Memphis, hero of the Battle of Silbury Hill.' Vague Henri smiled the smile of a man wound up. The girls burst into applause only slowly calmed by Cale's raised palms.

'Now,' he said. 'Now listen all of you. Who would like to take special care of Vague Henri?'

A dozen hands shot in the air.

'ME! ME! ME! ME! ME! ME! ME! ME!'

Vague Henri seemed to go pale and blush with delight at one and the same time.

'Patience! Patience! Girls! Behave!' said the Mother Inferior. 'What will Vague Henri think of us?'

'I think I could answer that,' whispered Cale into Vague Henri's ear. Vague Henri looked at him and Cale realized he'd been teased enough.

'Mother Inferior, would you choose two and send for us when the room is ready?' The Mother Inferior bowed politely and Cale pulled Vague Henri by the arm towards a door, opened it, again without a key, and they were in a sitting room. He gestured Vague Henri over to a large sofa that was more like a bed than a place to sit.

'Do you want a drink?'

'No.'

'There's beer or wine.'

'Beer.'

Cale pulled the linen off a jug, poured a glass and handed it to him.

'What do you expect me to do with them?' he said after taking a long swig.

'What you want to do with them.'

'They're slaves – slavery is wrong.'

'For what it's worth, which isn't anything at all, they've all been freed in law. They're as free as you or me used to be.'

'You still haven't said what you expect me to do.'

'Why would I expect you to do anything? If you've got a guilty conscience it's because you're pursuing evil thoughts.'

'I'm not in the mood for jokes.'

'All right.'

It was an apology.

'Look. You're in a state worse than China. All these girls have ever been brought up to do is look after men.'

'Why?'

'It'll keep.'

'No. I want to know. Riba told me everything she knew. But I want to know why.'

'They can make you better here, look after you like you've never imagined being looked after, better than the most spoiled-brat Materazzi mademoiselle you could imagine.'

'Why?'

'Have it your own way. I'll tell you over lunch. You just lie back on the bed and we'll eat.' In a few minutes nuns with trays knocked and entered and began laying out the food on the huge sofa next to Henri. There was beef with German custard, a blancmange of signal crab with sugar lumps, fried chicken and a plate heaped high with the crispiest pork crackling dripping soft fat and foot-long doozle-dogs with tomato ketchup and yellow mustard sauce. There was caviar from Nigeria and champagne from the Ukraine. And then rosewater jellies mixed with curds to finish off.

While they ate, Cale took Vague Henri through the details of Picarbo's manifesto.

When he'd finished asking questions Vague Henri was silent for a minute and then shook his head as if trying to shake something off.

'And I thought Bosco was completely nafi. How can you be that mad and live?'

They both giggled, back to sharing their past again.

'And the girls don't know anything about this?' said Vague Henri.

'They think that we've been sent here to choose them as wives and that we really do have white horses and silver armour. No, really. They're clever enough but they don't know anything. All they've ever been taught is that men are like angels – brave and courageous and kind and noble and strong. Only now and then some men might get very angry because a devil makes them but that even if they hit them they have to be kind and say sorry and be nice and then the devil in them will go away and everything will be all right again.'

'You didn't try telling them the truth?'

'I don't know how. I thought you might have some ideas but you just listen to them and let them make you better first. You've never heard anything like the drivel they come out with. But they believe it – every word.'

'I'm not going to do anything to them.'

'They won't mind.'

'How do you know?'

'Do what you want or don't want. If they're willing, why not? You could be dead in a few weeks and so could they if Bosco makes up his mind what to do with them. Live, eat and be happy for tomorrow we die – isn't that what IdrisPukke said?'

'Just because IdrisPukke said it doesn't make it true.'

'Have it your own way.'

So it was that Vague Henri was taken to the wet and dry room.

# 13

Windowless and lit by beeswax candles so that it did not smell or feel like the inside of an oven, the wet and dry room in the convent of the Sanctuary was lined with red cedar from Lebanon and on the floor with menge from no one knew where but prized for its resistance to water and soap. In the middle of the room were two wooden squares that looked like oiled butcher's blocks. A curious Vague Henri, full of anticipation and worry, was led into the room by the two chosen girls. One introduced herself as Annunziata and the other as Judith.

'What are your surnames?'

'We only have one name,' said Judith.

'Are you,' enquired a hopeful Annunziata, 'feeling ill-tempered?'

'No.'

'Not at all?'

'I don't understand.'

'It would,' said Judith, 'be a help to us if you were to shout at us.'

'And slam those doors to the cupboards.'

'Why?'

'We'd like to practise calming you down.'

'Why?'

'Men shout a lot, don't they?'

Bewildered by what they wanted from him, Vague Henri had to concede that in his experience this was indeed true.

'We asked Mr Cale to shout at us but he said it wasn't a good idea.'

'Probably that's true.'

'Will you? Oh please!'

They were so sweetly beseeching that awkward as he felt, Vague Henri thought it would be churlish to say no. Five minutes later he was sitting in the corner of the room weeping as if his heart would break while the girls, pale and bewildered themselves now, stared down at him, shaken by the storm of fury that had erupted from the sweet young man, sobbing uncontrollably in front of them.

After ten minutes the agony began to pass and the girls helped Vague Henri to his feet.

'Sorry,' he kept saying. 'Sorry.'

'There, there,' replied Judith.

'Yes,' added Annunziata, 'there, there.'

They led him over to one of the large blocks of wood, after stripping him of his shirt and trousers and socks. He vaguely resisted when they started to remove his loincloth but 'We have to wash you,' they said as if it was as immutable as the laws of God. He was too tired to resist. The girls sighed at the ancient scars and the new cuts and bruises from the beatings in Clink Number Two and asked him so gently how he had come by them that he almost started crying again.

'I slipped on a bar of soap,' he said, and laughed and so was able to control himself. Seeing he was unwilling to tell them, the girls left him and went and fetched hot water and soap which they knew he had not slipped on because it was clear he had not seen soap for some time. Judith poured a bucket of hot water over him in a careful flow from head to foot and Annunziata began to work up a great frothy blanket of suds, so very careful not to press too hard on his cuts and bruises. Over the next hour they squeezed and rubbed and eased his aching body so gently and with such skill that he fell asleep and when they finished he did not wake even when they dried him carefully, like a baby, in every crease and fold and dusted him with fine talcum from the chalk farms of Meribah and scented him with oil of apricots. They covered him in towels and left him to sleep. He did not wake up until late in the evening when the girls returned, took him to the dining room and fed him all over again and questioned him about his life outside. There wasn't any point he thought in telling them anything unpleasant; nor did he want to. So he told them about his life in Memphis as they gasped in amazement and delighted in every word about its dreaming spires, its frantic markets and its golden youth – its great men, its snow queen

# 14

'Only God and those girls could love you for yourself,' said Cale to Vague Henri after two weeks of being handed from one set of girls to the next as if he were a wonderful prize. 'The poor things just don't know any better.'

'All the more reason to enjoy it while it lasts.'

And there was no arguing with that. One night one of the girls who had drunk more wine that she was capable of holding had blabbed to Vague Henri that he was by far the girls' favourite of the two boys. Obviously delighted, Vague Henri had demanded to be told more and, despite the scolding of her partner, the loquacious girl had happily spilled all the pearls. 'Your friend is always either sad or angry,' she complained. 'Nothing we do really delights him, not like you. He can be such hard work. You know what we call him, some of us?'

'Can't you keep your big mouth shut for once,' scolded her friend.

'Shut up, you! We call him – we call him Vinegar Tom.'

'You mustn't be too hard on him,' said Vague Henri,

a little maudlin because he too had taken too much wine. 'He has a broken heart.'

'Really?' said the girl and fell asleep. But the other girl, Vincenza, was a clever thing and, as was her smart practice, having hardly touched a drop questioned the loose-tongued Vague Henri and got the whole story out of him.

'A bad girl,' said Vincenza. 'What a wicked thing to do.'

'I used to like her,' said a now sad Vague Henri. 'Kleist never did.'

'I think your friend Kleist was right not to like her.'

'I don't think Kleist liked anybody.'

Unknown of course to Vague Henri this, if it ever had been true, was certainly no longer the case. Kleist was now happily, not to say ecstatically, married, not that among the Klephts this was particularly complicated. It was a simple, even cursory, affair without the weeks of pointless feasting and ruinous expense, as Daisy's father complacently pointed out, of even the humblest Musselman wedding. 'What a performance! What on earth for?'

In fact the Klephts were always anxious to pick up news of Musselman weddings in the hope that those they couldn't rob on their way to the ceremony they could rob on the way back. And it was during a particularly epic one of these even more fabulous than usual marriage celebrations that Kleist first went to work on behalf of his new relatives.

Realizing that large numbers of men would be away in one place for the duration, the Klephts launched a raid on Musselman territory and given the considerable nature of the opportunity they put more men into the raiding party than it was their usual habit to risk. Though carefully calculated, it turned out to be unwise. The Musselmen had spread the rumours of the great marriage solely as bait for the Klephts and having drawn them in had sprung the trap and surrounded them in the Bakah Valley, also with considerable skill and great cunning. Suveri had led a breakout from the valley at night and tried to lead the bulk of those who had survived the first day back to the mountains. It was a long way and a difficult one and he would certainly have died along with his seventy men if it had not been for Kleist. For the next three days the two hundred and fifty Musselmen, who had tried to follow with every intention of massacring them, were picked off by a sixteen- or possibly fifteen-year-old boy they never even saw. By the end of the third day Kleist had killed so many of them he had become sick of the slaughter and, much to his new father-in-law's annoyance, just shot their horses from under them. But when the screams of the animals also became too much to bear he just fired warning shots. With such terrible losses and all their attempts to find their tormentor a failure, the Musselmen reluctantly turned back, taking their dead with them and leaving the victory to Kleist, who returned to the mountains both

# 15

There is a children's rhyme about the Laconics to which the guttersnipes of Memphis used to skip and sing.

> The Ephors of Laconia
> Like skeletons but bonier
> Their soup is black and so's their wit
> They throw their babies in a pit
> ONE! TWO! THREE! FOUR!
> They kill their slaves and just for fun
> They go and kill another one
> They carry coffins on their heads
> And sleep in them instead of beds
> FIVE! SIX! SEVEN! EIGHT!
> They whip their children with a stick
> They beat them black and blue with it
> And if they wince or make a sound
> They treat them to another round
> NINE! TEN! ELEVEN! TWELVE!

There is a forbidden final verse not to be sung in the presence of adults or snitches.

Their children aren't for fighting just
They use them for their wicked lust
It's dreadful what they do to them
They stick it up their B! U! M!

While most of this verse is whispered, the final three letters are to be shouted as loud as possible.

Cale lay down to read the brief Bosco had sent him full of the cocky disdain common to the excellent when it came to those who were rumoured to be better. This soon became simple fascination at the peculiar details of what he was reading.

Admirers of the Laconic spirit and way of life (or Laconiaphiloidiods in the ancient Attic tongue) would regard the doggerel above as nothing more than street-urchin slander. But with the exception of the lines about coffins – which seems to be an entirely childish invention – the accusations in the song have strong backing from those less smitten than the Laconiaphiloidiods with this most strange of all societies. The Laconics, whose country resembled a barracks more than a nation, regarded themselves 'the most free of all the peoples of the earth' because they were dominated by no one and produced nothing of any kind whatsoever. They were a state where there was only one skill with which they were solely preoccupied: warfare. Healthy boys born into the Laconic peoples belonged to the state and at the age of five were taken away from their families – if such a thing could be really said to exist – and trained to do one thing, 'kill or die', until they reached the age of sixty something; it must be said, they rarely did. If they were not born healthy they were, as the gutter song rightly claimed, thrown into a chasm know as the Deposits. If the Laconics had written poetry, which they didn't, little of it would have been about the pleasures or pains of old age. They paid for this single-minded pursuit of violence in two ways. At any one time up to a third of their number, which never exceeded more than thirteen thousand, were engaged in mercenary activities for which they were famously well paid. The bulk of the Laconic state was financed by the existence of the Helots. The term 'slave' is insufficient to describe the subjugation and bondage of these miserable peoples, which is what they were. Unlike the slaves in the Materazzi Empire and elsewhere, the Helots were not a mix of races captured here and there and sold on from owner to owner. They were conquered nations, subordinated in their entirety and who now farmed what had once been their own land and made goods for trade that were owned entirely by the Laconic state. The Laconics brought their children up in barracks to fear nothing but one thing and that was their Helots. Vastly outnumbered by these state serfs who surrounded them in huge numbers, their continued subjugation of the slaves slowly became as one thing with their obsession with war. The Helots made the Laconics' single aim in life possible but were also the greatest threat to that life. Suppression of the Helots who had once been the means to wage war endlessly had now become the reason why it was now indispensable they do so. The vicious dog with razor teeth became obsessed with biting its own tail.

The Laconics were ruled by five Ephors elected from the small number who survived past their sixtieth birthday. The song's reference to their alleged boniness is not borne out by any known historical fact. It is often said by those who detested the Laconics, and there were many, that the famous Laconic humour was humour at the expense of others, especially the physically disabled, whom they despised. This was not always true if the famous story about the Ephor Aristades is true. Once every five years all Laconic males were permitted to vote for the execution of any Ephor who had generally displeased them by his foolishness or pride, or indeed for whatever reason, the sentence only to be carried out if the votes against exceeded one thousand. Knowing that the number of votes for his death was rapidly approaching that number, the Ephor Aristades was asked by an illiterate citizen from the sticks, who had never clapped eyes on him, to write the name, if he would be so kind, of 'that bastard Aristades' on a clay tablet used for voting. It was considered greatly to his credit as a wit that he cheerfully obliged. He is said to have survived by only two votes. There was little else to laugh about for a child born into the Laconian state. The joke in Memphis was that the children thrown into the Deposits were the lucky ones. Once assigned to a barracks the food was as bad as that given to Redeemer acolytes but there was much less of it. This meanness was intended to make them ingenious in having to steal in order to stay alive. If caught they were severely punished, not for immorality but for showing a lack of skill in the execution of their larceny. There is a story that a ten-year-old having stolen a pet fox belonging to the Ephor Chalon with the intention of eating it found himself called into a parade before he could wring its neck and hide it. It is claimed that rather than reveal its presence and demonstrate his failure amongst his fellows, he allowed the fox to eat his entrails and dropped down dead without uttering a sound. Those who found this tale completely implausible before they encountered the Laconics were never quite as sure once they had done so.

The infamous black soup mentioned in the song was made of pig's blood and vinegar. A Duena diplomat, a hired negotiator in the way that mercenaries are hired soldiers, having once tasted this concoction said to the Laconics who had given it to him that it was so revolting it explained why they were so willing to die. As such wits are prone to do, he repeated much the same joke about the Materazzi and their infamously difficult-to-please wives. The difference between the Materazzi and the Laconians was that the latter thought the joke extremely funny. Another oddity about this black soup, and a revealing one, is that while its taste can hardly have been better than the rancid fat and nuts of dead men's feet – Cale, Kleist and Vague Henri never thought of this revolting slab with anything other than a shudder – it was well known that the Laconics regarded black soup as wonderfully toothsome and that even exiles pined for it in their absence as for nothing else.

If their sense of humour softens your opinion of the Laconics and you find it preferable to the fanaticism and cruelty of the Redeemers, or the arrogance and snobbery of the Materrazi, we now come to the darkest and most revolting of all the practices conceived by perhaps the strangest people in the history of all the world. Whereas all right-thinking people regard sexual intercourse between adult males and young boys as a crime calling out to the heavens for vengeance and punish those who commit such actions by death (the more horrible the better), in Laconia this perversion was not only tolerated but legally enforced. The older man who did not choose a twelve-year-old to use in this way would be heavily fined for failing to set a good example in manly virtue.

How such a disgusting, peculiar hurdy-gurdy came about I cannot say. They are also reported to have had an unusually high valuation of mothers, allowing these to express insulting opinions to every rank of man and even permitting them to inherit property – a custom which, it is said, gives much offence to their neighbours and for which they are much more often criticized than for the disgusting practice of compulsory pederasty.

All of this information had been given to Cale by Bosco in an embargoed testament which he had been told to keep strictly to himself. But one section of the document clearly included long before most of the other information in the testament particularly caught Cale's attention, and was one he wanted to discuss with Vague Henri. It concerned the claim made by an exiled Laconian soldier who was reliably questioned in the document itself about the existence of the Krypteia – a small and particularly secret service made up of what he called 'anti-soldiers'. Selected from the most ruthless and cruel young Laconians, they were encouraged to develop qualities of originality and independence of thought and actions otherwise discouraged in those who were expected to fight in massed ranks without thought of personal survival.

'I wonder,' said Cale to Vague Henri, 'if that's where Bosco got the idea for me?'

'And I wonder,' said Vague Henri to Cale, 'if your head gets any bigger whether or not you'll be able to fit through the door. Besides even if you're right – just be grateful it was the only idea he took from them.'

Cale's face wrinkled with pruny disgust. 'Good God,' he said.

## 16

'I want to talk to the Maid of Blackbird Leys.' This was a demand from Cale that expected a refusal and it was a reminder to Bosco that the destructive soul of his God made flesh was also an adolescent. There was satisfaction to be had from refusing to conform to Cale's expectations.

'Of course.'

There was a gratifying silence in response.

'Now.'

'As you wish.' Bosco reached over to a pile of a dozen parchments already imprinted with his seal and began writing.

'I want to see her on my own.'

'I have no desire to see the Maid of Blackbird Leys again I can assure you.' More satisfaction.

Bosco made it clear that it would take at least an hour and a half to be cleared through the four levels of security that protected the ten occupants of the inner cells of the House of Special Purpose. He had to wait for fifty minutes at the last level because a messenger had to be sent back to Bosco to return with a letter of confirmation to confirm the letter Cale had brought with him. Forty of those fifty minutes were taken up by Bosco's third pleasure of the evening as he let the messenger hang about outside his office.

Eventually the messenger returned and the keyholder let Cale first through one great door and then through to the Maid's cell.

She had been lying down but sat up straight as the cell door opened, afraid as she had every right to be at such an unusual event.

'Go away,' Cale said. The keyholder tried to argue. 'I won't tell you a second time.'

'I'll have to lock you in.'

'When I call you back.' Cale paused to make his meaning clear. 'Don't.'

The keyholder knew exactly what this apparently mysterious warning meant because keeping Cale waiting when he called to be let out was exactly what he was intending to do.

In a terrible suppressed temper the keyholder locked the door and Cale put the candle he was holding on the table, no chair, that was the only other item of furniture in the cell. The girl, scrawny from dreadful food and too little of it, stared at him with huge brown eyes. They seemed bigger than they probably were because her hair had been shaved off – party because of lice, partly because of malice.

'I've just come to talk to you. There's nothing to be afraid of. Not from me.'

'From someone else?'

'You're in the House of Special Purpose in the Sanctuary – of course from someone else.'

'Who are you?'

'My name is Thomas Cale.'

'I've never heard of you.'

'I can see that you have.'

'Unless you're the Thomas Cale sent by God to kill all his enemies.' Cale did not say anything. 'God,' she said, a rebuke, 'is a mother to his children.'

'I never had a mother,' replied Cale. 'Is that a good thing?'

'*Homo hominis lupus*. Is that what you are, Thomas, a wolf to man?'

'It would be fair to say,' he replied thoughtfully, 'that I've done my share of wolfy things. But just because rumours have reached you about me even in here doesn't mean they're true. You should hear what they say about *you*.'

'What do you want?' she said.

This was a good question because he was not sure. Certainly he was curious about how a woman had managed to anger the Redeemers in so many different ways. But the truth was he had asked Bosco for this visit more to annoy him than to satisfy his own curiosity. He had expected him to say no.

From his pockets – he could now have as many pockets as he liked – he began producing food: a pastie, half a small loaf of bread divided in two for convenience, a large slice of cheese, an apple and some gurr cake, and a bottle of milk. Her eyes, which already seemed to fill her tiny face, grew even wider.

'I hope it's not too rich.'

'Rich?'

'For your stomach.'

'I'm not some bog trotter who never had a pie before or lived on rutabagas all my life. I'm a Reeve's daughter. I can read. I know Latin.'

'Is that what it was? Isn't that the sin of pride?'

'Being able to read?'

'I meant looking down on the poor – it's not their fault they never had a pie or some gurr cakes. I never had them much myself until recent times. That's why I'm taking offence.'

By now he was smiling and she took her rebuke well.

'May I?' she said, looking with a great covetous yearning at the food.

'Please.' She began eating but her intention not to stuff herself was lost in the sheer wonder of the pastie.

'The food is sickening enough outside this place – it must be beyond belief in this shithole.'

'Mnugh bwaarh gnuff,' she agreed and kept on eating. He watched with alarm as the cheese – at least a pound in weight – started to follow the pastie. With some difficulty he took what was left of the cheese out of her fingers and put it on the table. 'You'll be sick. Give it a chance to go down.' He held her by the shoulders and pushed her down onto the bed, giving her a moment or two to recover the equanimity of a Reeve's daughter – whatever a Reeve was. It was as if the very soul of the food, the milk, the cheese, the anticipation of the honey in the pastry, was breathing new life into her. He waited for almost a minute and it was as if she was a near-dead thing restored to life – she seemed to have grown, her eyes no longer straining against her skull. They began to fill with tears.

'You're not the angel of death, you're the angel of life.'

He did not know what to say to this and so said nothing.

'How can I help you?' she asked for all the world like the Reeve's daughter in her father's parlour brought out to impress the visitors with her piety and learning.

'I knew all about the placards you wrote and put on the church doors. That you got other people to do the same. I want to know why.'

She might have looked like a dead thing but she was not a fool.

'Will they use this against me in court?'

'You've had all the hearings you're ever going to have.' He felt sorry for the brutality of what he'd said but it was out before he could stop himself. 'I'm sorry.'

'Don't mention it,' she said, barely audible. 'Do you know when they'll kill me?'

This unnerved him. He felt shifty and responsible.

'No. I don't know. I don't think it'll be soon. From what I know they'll take you to Chartres first.'

'Then I'll see the sky again?'

This unnerved him even more.

'Yes. For sure. It's a hundred miles.'

There was a long silence.

'You want to know why?' she said at last.

'Yes.' Though now he didn't want to know anything more about her at all.

'About two years ago I sneaked into the sacristy at the church when the priest was away. I'm a very Nosy Parker – everyone says so.'

He nodded in the gloom but he did not know what a Nosy Parker was. 'In the reservatory which he was supposed to keep locked I found a strong box he was supposed to lock as well. Inside were the Hanged Redeemer's four books of good news. These were the words of the Hanged Redeemer as he spoke them himself to his disciples. Have you read the good news?'

'No'

'Have you talked to anyone who has?'

He laughed at such a barmy idea. 'Of course not. What was a parish priest doing with the four books of the Redeemer? Only the Cardinals are supposed to read them and then only once in case they defile them with human understanding. There aren't more than fifty of them and I can't see them sharing with a priest from the parish of Bumhole-in-the-Dale. No offence.'

She did seem, if not offended, then certainly startled.

'It was a copy. I'm sure it was the parish priest's hand-writing – he wasn't a proper scribe but his script was careful.'

'So it was done from memory.' It was clear what he thought of this and it wasn't much.

'Don't you care what it said?' she asked, clearly aston-ished.

'No.'

She would not be put off.

'It said that we should love our neighbour as we love ourselves, do to others as we would be done by, that if someone strikes us on the left cheek we should turn the right one.'

'Arse or face?'

'It's true!'

'How do you know?'

'It was written in the book itself.'

'In some nutter Redeemer's handwriting. They burn a dozen a year in the courtyard two hundred yards from here – madmen who've had the word of God revealed to them in a vision. The only difference is that your mopus had the sense at least to try and keep his gibber-ish locked away.'

'It was the truth. I know it.'

'That's what they all say – what else?'

'Peace and good will to all men,' she said.

Cale laughed as if this were the most delightfully

funny thing he had ever heard. 'Pull the other one,' he said, 'it's got bells on. "Obey and suffer . . . Give in and take your kicking", that's more the Redeemer style.'

She looked at him, eyes as wide, thought Cale, as that weird creature in the zoo at Memphis, the one with the index finger half the size of its body.

'Those who hurt children are to be punished. It will be better for them if they had a millstone tied around their neck and be cast into the sea.'

Oddly enough he did not seem to find this so amusing and said nothing for some time. She sat on the edge of the bed looking frail and scrawny and he thought about what was going to happen to her and he felt bad about laughing at the things that had brought her here to this dreadful place.

'I'll do what I can to get some food to you.' It was all the comfort he could imagine. She looked at him and it made him feel horribly old and bad, very bad.

'Can you help me to get away?'

'No. I wish I could but I can't.'

Once outside the House of Special Purpose it was to find that winter had arrived at last and in the great square of the Sanctuary the new-fallen snow lay round about, deep and crisp and even. The choughs coughed in the leafless trees as Cale crunched past and the nail-toothed hunting dogs barked at the cold as if it were a burglar or escapee. Nothing could give the drably monumental buildings of the Sanctuary charm, but covered in snow and lit by the only fitfully clouded moon it had that night a frigid beauty to it – as long as you didn't have to live there.

Later he asked Bosco if he could send the Maid food.

'I can't allow that.'

'You won't.'

'No. I can't. You've never heard that phrase: "A lion at home, a spaniel in the world?"'

'No.'

'Well, now you have.'

'What's a spaniel?'

'A dog notorious for its willingness to please. I can explain your presence in her cell – but only once. When it became known – and it would in a matter of days – that I had allowed her to eat more than necessary to keep her alive for the executioner I would be instantly revealed as a heretic. As I would be. Her sins against the Redeemer faith cannot be weighed.'

'I gave her a promise.'

'Then more fool you.'

'And her sins cannot be weighed because she read the copy of the sayings of the Hanged Redeemer and talked about them?'

'Yes.'

'You burnt the book she found I suppose.'

'It seemed best.'

'And?'

'And what?' His taunting of Cale almost involved a kind of gaiety.

'This book of sayings of the Hanged Redeemer. What was it?'

A thoughtful, still-teasing grimace from Bosco.

'It was a book of sayings of the Hanged Redeemer.'

A silence.

'You're mocking me.'

'Yes. But it was still a copy of the sayings of the Hanged Redeemer.'

'A good copy.'

'Good enough – a few errors but he was an intelligent man with an excellent memory.'

'Was?'

'Now you're being deliberately slow.'

'So why was it so sinful what she did?'

Bosco laughed. 'As you said yourself: the word of God is easily soiled by human understanding. That's terribly good, by the way. Would you object if I used it in a sermon?'

'You were listening?'

'Did you ever suspect otherwise?'

Cale did not reply for a moment. 'I don't know what it means, not really. It's just something I heard a friend of mine say in Memphis. He was joking.'

Bosco was a little disappointed. He had felt rather proud of Cale when he'd heard him say it. It had been, after all, just right. Perhaps the fact that he could not keep his promise to the girl had taken the wind out of his great vanity for a minute. And why not explain, after all?

'Even for those Redeemers who do not realize that God has decided to begin again, what we would agree on is that when it comes to men and to women there is no end to their garboils and quarrels over everything. There is no statement direct from the mouth of God, no matter how plain and easy to understand, that will not have them cutting each other's throats over what it truly means. As for me: to publish the word of God to mankind is casting pearls before swine. Either way, what the Maid of Blackbird Leys has done is unforgivable.'

But later that night the snow brought more than an unaccustomed allure to the Sanctuary – it had also driven Redeemer General Guy Van Owen to take refuge there. He had been waiting outside the great gates for ten minutes and was in a foul mood because the guards had refused to let him in. Van Owen had intended to return to his command on the Golan Heights that protected the Eastern Front, a journey that normally meant avoiding the Sanctuary and Bosco by twenty miles. But the snow had made the way impassable and unprepared in his rush to return in such extreme weather he was obliged to take shelter where he could or die. He also hated Bosco because thirty years earlier he thought he had seen him smile dismissively during a sermon he had given on Holy Emulsion. In fact Bosco had merely been bored and was thinking of the hot chocolate that would follow Van Owen's sermon – a rare treat special to that particular holyday because the saint in question had been boiled alive in sugar.

Finally Bosco turned up in one of the towers that guarded the great gate.

'Who are you and what do you want?'

'You know damn well who I am,' shouted back Van Owen.

'I only know who you told the Colour Chaplain you were. If you think that's enough to get you and a hundred men inside the Sanctuary uninspected and in the middle of the night . . .' He did not finish his sentence.

Van Owen swore and shouted at his lighterman to raise his lantern up so that he could remove his hood and show himself.

'Satisfied?'

'Get the lighterman to go along the ranks. I want to see the men with you.'

'Buggeration!' He turned to the lighterman. 'Do as he says.' It took another ten minutes for Bosco to be satisfied. It was certainly the case that he would have done this even had Van Owen been an ally but he had to admit that the delay gave him a mean-spirited pleasure. Eventually Bosco was persuaded and disappeared from Van Owen's view. He was made to wait, increasingly furious and uncertain, for another two minutes and then the gates slowly swung open – but only partly so that the men and horses were obliged to come in slowly one by one.

Van Owen came in first, looking for a row with Bosco.

'Where is he?' he shouted at the Colour Chaplain.

'The Lord Redeemer has gone to bed, Redeemer. He'll send for you after mass tomorrow morning. I'll show you to your room. Your men are to sleep in the main hall which will be locked.'

Fuming, Van Owen was led across the pristine snow unwatched by his men, who were only interested in stabling the horses and getting out of the cold. But one person was observing him carefully from a high window. When he had made his bad-tempered way into the main building Cale lit a beeswax candle, went to the library, unlocked the door with a key he had stolen from Bosco and searched carefully in the stacks for the file on Van Owen and a much thinner testament, 'Tactics of the Laconic Mercenary'. Then he sat down at Bosco's desk in Bosco's padded chair and began to read.

'I must be back in Golan as soon as possible.'

'What's your hurry, Redeemer?'

'Tell your acolyte to leave if you would.'

'My acolyte?' Bosco looked bemused. 'Oh, this is not my acolyte. This is Thomas Cale.'

Van Owen looked at Cale, his expression a mix of

the reluctantly impressed and the dismissive. Cale stared back, blank as you like.

'If you wish him to stay,' said Van Owen, 'by all means.'

'I do.'

'Now as time is so short . . .' Van Owen paused but only so that he could deliver his news momentously. 'There are eight thousand Laconic mercenaries in the pay of the Antagonists marching through the Machair towards the Golan Heights.'

'And you're to take command of their defence.' It was a statement rather than a question.

'No,' said Van Owen, clearly delighted at least to have something over Bosco. 'That is not my intention. The Golan is to be the base for a forward defence of the Heights. I am determined not to allow these creatures to inspire the fear and alarm they are accustomed to. A Redeemer army has nothing to fear of any soldier, particularly not these frightful sodomites. I have eight thousand of my own men waiting on the Golan and by tomorrow they will be joined by another ten thousand.'

'You have nothing to fear but you intend to outnumber them more than two to one?'

Van Owen smiled, feeling that he had surprised Bosco with his daring.

'You are not the only one, Bosco, who believes in new tactics. But I intend to be bold without taking unnecessary risks.'

'Yes,' said Bosco, as if conceding something. 'It is bold.'

There was a satisfied but silent acknowledgement from Van Owen. Cale spoke for the first time.

'It's mad attacking them on the Machair.'

'You know it well do you, little boy?'

'I know that it's mostly flat – and flat is flat wherever you are. It couldn't be better ground for the Laconics to fight on. Attack them there and they'll think all their birthdays have come at once.' The phrase about birthdays was one he'd heard often in Memphis and liked the way it sounded. As he realized when he said it aloud in Bosco's rooms it had less of a ring to it when used to someone who didn't have a birthday. You will remember that a Redeemer had the right to kill an acolyte who did something sufficiently unexpected. Who knows what might have happened if Van Owen had been less astonished at being talked to in such a way or had brought a weapon with him.

Bosco reached across the table and fetched Cale an enormous blow to the face. This time it was Cale's turn to be stunned by shock into inaction.

'You must forgive him,' said Bosco calmly to Van Owen. 'I have indulged him in the interests of his talents for the glory of our Redeemer and he has grown big-headed and insolent. If you will excuse us you will have every assistance and I will punish him. I am deeply sorry.'

Such humility from his enemy was almost as surprising

as the rudeness of Cale, and Van Owen found himself nodding idiotically and then outside in the corridor as Bosco showed him to the door and closed it behind him.

The Redeemer General turned barely breathing to look at Cale. It was not a pleasant sight. The boy had gone white with fury, an expression Bosco had never seen before not just on Cale but on anyone.

'There is a knife in the drawer just on the left,' said Bosco. 'But before you kill me, which I know you can do, just hear me out.'

Cale did not reply or even change his expression but neither did he move.

'You were about to say something that could have changed the world. Never,' he said, softly but shaking slightly, 'never interrupt your enemy when he's making a mistake.'

Cale still did not move – but slowly a sort of colour, a kind of inhuman reddish tinge began to return to his face.

'I'm going to sit down,' said Bosco. 'Over here. Then when I've finished you can decide whether or not to kill me.' For the first time since he had turned back from the door he looked away from Cale and sat down on a wooden bench against the wall. Cale's eyes lost the yellowy wild-dog look as something human began to seep back into them.

Bosco let out a deep breath and began talking again.

\*

It was twenty-four hours before Cale turned up in the convent to tell Vague Henri what had happened.

'I came this close,' said Cale, holding his thumb and forefinger almost together, 'to killing him.'

'Why didn't you?'

'My guardian angel, my guardian angel stopped me.'

Vague Henri laughed.

'Did he give you a name? Because I'd like to thank him, that guardian angel of yours. He saved my neck.'

'Don't be too pleased because there's bad news too.'

'What?'

'Bosco made a bargain with Van Owen to take me and the Purgators with him.'

'Why?'

'As observers. He told him that me and the Purgators however successful in the veldt had a lot to learn from a soldier like Van Owen. That and a bribe.'

'A bribe?' Vague Henri was wide-eyed at this. Perhaps there's a point beyond which the human heart contains so much loathing it cannot be added to. That was certainly what it seemed like to Vague Henri when he thought about the Redeemers. But he was shocked almost by the idea of one of them accepting a bribe.

'Bosco offered him,' said Cale, 'the preserved foot of St Barnabus. Van Owen has a personal devotion to St Barnabus. You know that stuff that the cats in Memphis go off their tracks for – he was just like that.' Cale could not bring himself to tell Vague Henri that he also had to apologize to Van Owen. It was necessary but heart-scalding.

*You must eat it up, Bosco had said. You will shortly watch him fail and that will make up for it.*

*Are you sure he'll fail?*

*No.*

'What's the bad news?' said Vague Henri.

'You're going to come with me.'

'Me? Why?'

'Because I asked for you.'

'What the bloody hell did you do that for?'

'Because I need you with me.'

'No you don't.'

'You should think better of yourself.'

'There's nothing wrong with the way I think about myself.'

'I need someone to listen to my ideas. Who else can I talk to?'

'I don't want to go.'

'I'll bet you don't. I'll bet you'd rather stay here getting your end away with a shoal of beezles who think the sun shines out of your backside – but you can't. Time to wake up.'

'All right!' shouted Vague Henri. 'All right! All right! All right!' He breathed out like a bad-tempered horse and swore. 'When?'

'Tomorrow as he purposes.'

'Why is Bosco letting me go?'

'Because he thinks we won't, either of us, leave the girls in the lurch.'

'And will we?'

'I don't know. What do you think?'

Vague Henri did not reply directly.

'At least it explains why he let us enjoy the sins of the flesh.'

'It explains why he let you enjoy them. He let me in there because you can't corrupt the Wrath of God.'

'And is that what you are?'

'What do you think?'

'You keep asking me that.'

'Because I want to know. I value your opinion – I told you.' There was a pause. 'Talking of which, what do you think about taking my acolyte, Model, into the convent before we go?'

'Why?'

'It would be a kindness. Who knows what will happen to us? He might never get a chance to see a woman.'

Vague Henri looked at him, furious now.

'They're not animals in the Memphis Zoo. They don't belong to you so you can lend them out to your pals.'

'All right, keep you hair on. I don't remember you objecting when it was your turn.'

'They're not *turns.*'

'Have it your own way. Good God! It was just an idea.'

Vague Henri did not reply.

The next day, two hours into the journey to the Golan Heights, Vague Henri was cold, miserable and deeply, deeply missing the lovely girls he'd left behind, nearly all of them in tears except for his favourite Vincenza who kissed him on both cheeks and then lightly on the lips. He shivered, and not from the cold, as he remembered what she had whispered in his ears between these soft kisses. She, wisest of the girls by far, was signalling him out as hers.

'Come back to me and I'll show you something you've never seen before.'

He missed them horribly and who can blame him. If there was a heaven how could it be better than life in the convent? Other, of course, than not being surrounded by hell. And that was the problem of problems – he was, he knew, willing to go through hell to get back to them but he was not able to. There was only one person with the skill required, the menace and the violence and the rage.

It was another six days before they made it to the Golan. The Golan is a great ridge about forty miles long and the same distance from the Pope's formal palace in the holy city of Chartres whose right flank it protected. The right side of the Golan led to the eastern Macmurdos, mountains impassable to any army before they descended two hundred miles later into a pass, Buford's Gap, disputed by both the Laconics and the neutral Swiss. This was the one weakness in the natural defences of the Redeemers on the east of the Golan. If the Laconics did agree to join the Antagonists this gap was the place through which they would attack. To the left of the Golan, Chartres and the vast Redeemer territories behind it were protected by the Fronts – a line of trenches sometimes ten deep and stretching the five hundred miles to the next natural defence: the Weddell Sea. Time out of mind the Antagonists had been pinned behind these great defences, natural and manmade. Only the fortune in silver discovered at Argentum would be enough to persuade the Laconics to put an entire army in the field because it was their policy never to hire out more than three hundred soldiers at once to protect their greatest resource from disaster. They also had to be bribed to risk war with the Swiss over ownership of Buford's Gap, otherwise a place of no great strategic importance to either side.

It was no summer progress for the Laconics to the Golan. Normally a place of mild winters which made a campaign at such an unusual time worth contemplating if the money was right, a cold coming they had of it, just the worst winter in living memory. The ways deep, the weather sharp, the days bitter, the nights unbearable, Bosco reassured Van Owen his delay at the Sanctuary would not matter because however bad the weather was on Shotover Scarp it would be worse for the Laconics trying to make their way across the Machair. On the rare occasions when it snowed there the winds moving over its wide and open spaces allowed the formation of huge drifts. The Laconics could take more adversity than any man but they could not fly so they were stuck where they were with their black soup and miserable Helots who died of the cold by the dozen.

Once they arrived on the Golan, Cale and Vague Henri were run ragged by Van Owen, who put them to every unpleasant or pointless detail he could find for them, not difficult when moving around in the freezing winds was a torture even in performance of the simplest task. Van Owen kept the Purgators in the worst and coldest quarters and supplied them as poorly as he was able.

'Who are those people?' he asked Cale of the aloof Purgators. 'I don't like the look of them. There's something not right here.'

Despite the fact that he knew that Bosco was right and that giving anything away to someone who wished you ill was the mark of childishness, he simply could not stop himself.

'Out of the crooked timber of humanity, Redeemer, no straight thing was ever made.' It was perhaps the most famous saying of St Barnabus, he of the preserved foot. And the especial devotion of Van Owen.

'Are you trying to be funny?'

'No, Redeemer.'

'So I ask you again. Who are these people?'

Another famous saying of St Barnabus was: a truth

that's told with bad intent beats all the lies you can invent. Cale knew this because he had looked up a Life of the saint in the library the night before they had left the Sanctuary. He was impressed by the saying about the truth because he thought St Barnabus had well said something he had learnt himself about telling lies when he was still only a small boy.

'They are men who have transgressed but are atoning by especial bravery for their errors. More I have sworn on the foot of St Barnabus not to say.'

Had Van Owen been used to being cheeked by acolytes he might more easily have realized he was being mocked. It was an error too far, thought Cale, and even as he said it he despised his own stupidity. God knows what might have happened if Van Owen had been familiar with the drollery of cocky young boys. Van Owen was not sure what he thought about the unlikeable boy in front of him (other than that he did not like him). Boy saints were not unknown although he himself had never met one. Usually they were saints because they had died proving their holiness and were therefore not able to become a nuisance. There had not been a boy warrior particularly recognized as chosen by God for three hundred years – St Johan – and he had conveniently died of smallpox a few years after he had defeated the Cenci at St Albans. A chosen boy who had lovely visions of the Redeemer's mother and a way with incomprehensible prophecies that might be usefully interpreted by wiser heads was one thing – a tergiversating sheep in wolf's clothing was something else again, particulary one who was in Bosco's pocket. The problem for Van Owen was that he was more than a self-serving, ambitious sly-boots (which he most definitely was); he was also a pious believer in the Hanged Redeemer. What if the odious twerp in front of him was not just some swashbuckling Mohawk with a talent for butchery but was blessed by God? Making a mistake in this matter was about more than politics; it might involve his immortal soul.

The unusually extreme weather that had brought the snow changed as quickly as it arrived. The knife-cold winds from the north were replaced by the usual warmer winds from the east that brought with them a thaw which melted the snow in less than three days. The earth of the Machair was light and peaty and the vugs and follicles of the catchiform rocks on which it lies drained the meltwater as easily as if it were an unplugged bath in one of the palazzos in Memphis.

Busy now with his preparations, Van Owen had no time to think about Cale and as soon as Cale could he dragged Vague Henri with him in search of extra food for the Purgators.

'Let them starve,' said Vague Henri. 'Let them freeze. I hope they catch the hog cholera so their spines bend over sideways and their rotting left ear falls into their right-hand pocket.'

'Pull yourself together, Vague Henri. Sooner or later your life and, more to the point, my life are going to depend on them.'

It was on one of these useless tasks, the unnecessary guard duty to a wagon train bringing fuel from the Sluff coalfields some ten miles to the south of the Golan, that a singular event took place. Forced on their return to take a byway back to the Golan because of a small avalanche that had closed the main road, they found themselves skirting the dreary smelting sheds that relied on the coal-fields for the heat in the manufacture of iron and the much rarer steel, so expensive and difficult to make that it was rarely used by the Redeemers. As they came over a low hill both saw the great pile beneath at almost the same moment. They reined their horses and stared down at the great stack beneath them, silent, shocked, horrified. Thrown together in a huge heap, wind-whipped and only partly covered in snow, was the armour of the Materazzi from the great disaster at Silbury Hill. From a distance it looked like a vast pile of shells from some human-shaped creature of the sea, empty and discarded like the crab and lobster shells scooped out and abandoned beside the seafood stalls of Memphis Bay. Within five minutes they were at the gates of the storage dump where two old men were standing at a brazier keeping themselves warm while they watched half a dozen men loading a wagon with bits and pieces from the great mound of armour in front of them.

'What's going on?'

The oldest man looked at him wondering whether the boy Redeemer was worth being insolent to. He took a middle line.

'These are the barbicans from that victory over the Mazzi. Where are they now in all their pride?' Then he added piously, 'Come to dust.'

'Where are they taking them?'

'To be melted down. Over there. In the great smelter. Nowt workin' now though. Not 'nuff coal, d'ysee, with this weather the way it is.'

The men at the wagon were working quickly, not out of zeal but to try and keep warm. One of them was singing as he worked, a blasphemous mixture of one of the Redeemers' most revered hymns and a pub song about Barnacle Bill.

'OOOOH Death and Judgement and Heaven and Hell
Are the last four things on which we dwell
I'd rather dwell on Marie the whore
And what she does with a cucumbore!'

The others, frozen, carried on clearly not listening, pulling apart the armour section by section, cutting the leather straps where they'd not rotted then throwing the lighter bits and pieces onto the wagon – gauntlets clanged, casques and back plates clattered, armlets and cubiteries pinged and set up a clank and a racket as they rattled over each other as they filled the wagon up. One of the men noticed Cale and Vague Henri. 'Shut up, Cob!' The singer stopped instantly, his good humour replaced magically by alert hostility.

Cale stood and watched Vague Henri walk over to the pile.

'It's a dollar if you want to look, pal,' said one of the men.

'Shut your gob,' said Vague Henri pleasantly.

'You'se not allowed here.'

'And now it'll be two dollars,' said the singer.

'Don't worry,' said Vague Henri. 'I'll give you what you deserve.'

Cale walked over to the men and gave them a dollar wordless. What had put such a bend in Vague Henri?

'We agreed on two.'

'Don't push your luck.'

He turned his back on the men who seemed to agree that indeed pushing their luck was not a good idea. Cale watched as Vague Henri walked among the strewn armour along the bottom of the great pile and bent down to pick up a half-crushed helmet. It had an enamel badge above the nosepiece just slightly bigger than a man's thumb – a red and black chequerboard and three blue stars.

'This is Carmella Materazzi's coat of arms.' He nodded over to another helmet exactly the same – but even under the grime one that was clearly pretty new. 'And that must be his son's. I'd heard they were both killed but no one knew for sure. Kleist stole the kid's wallet then got ten dollars when he gave it back and said he'd found it in the Sally Gardens.' He placed the first helmet carefully on the ground and walked right to the edge of the pile and placed a foot high up as if he were going to climb. With a great heave he pulled out another helmet, this one with a filthily bedraggled plume, raggedy, all colour drained by exposure to the hard winter. 'I thought I recognized it. This,' he said, holding the helmet out to Cale, 'belonged to that shit-bag Lascelles. He clipped me on the ear once for getting in his way.'

'Well, that'll teach him.'

Vague Henri laughed. 'You're right. Henri's curse on everyone who does me a bad turn. Let's hope he suffered.' He opened and shut the visor the way he had seen the puppeteers in the Memphis market do. 'Where are your jibes now, mate?'

He looked around the great heap. When all was said and done, Memphis had been a great joy for him. 'Seems a pity,' he said, at last, 'not to make some use of this. God there's a fortune here.'

The men carefully pretending not to listen could not contain themselves at this.

'How much, mister?'

'Ten thousand dollars? Fifteen?'

'You lie.'

Both Cale and Vague Henri laughed aloud at this.

255

'Sorry, mister. But that's not possible.'

'Suit yourself. But look at the state of it. Besides there's hardly anyone left alive could wear this stuff. It takes years to learn to move in their integuments. Much good it did them anyway. Armour always comes with a price,' replied Cale.

'Still,' said Vague Henri, 'it's mad to let it all be melted down.'

'Why? It'll be dark in three hours. We better go.'

As they walked away one of the men called out after them.

'Where would we take it, mister? Just tell us and we'll remember you in our prayers.'

In the great storeroom of Vittles of the Blessed Honoratus on the back slopes of the Golan, Cale ordered two sides of beef with a requisition stolen from Van Owen's battle quarters and with his quartermaster's forged signature.

'What if he works out it was you?'

'With any luck he'll be dead before he does.'

'What if he wins – or even if he lives?'

'I don't think he can do it – stop them, I mean.'

'That's what we thought at Silbury Hill.'

As you can imagine, it is no easy thing to bring two carcasses into a camp and not call attention to yourselves – but there was so much of the hive about the place and they had waited till near dark and gone around the long way that the food, along with the rutabagas for all, was delivered safely and received by the Purgators with awestruck gratitude. It was roasting and boiling in a minute. Cale had also taken a leaf out of Bosco's book and put a cutting he had made from the wooden foundations of Van Owen's battle quarters into a small brass box he had found on a body in the veldt and liked the look of. He claimed to the fuelbrother that it was a sliver of the true gallows on which the Hanged Redeemer had been sacrificed. In exchange he got fourteen sacks of coal and a fletch of wood. Cale and Vague Henri watched the blissful Purgators eat and warm themselves in front of the fires as if they were spoiled children.

'Does your heart good,' said Cale, smiling. But the trouble was that Vague Henri couldn't help himself, despite everything in his heart screaming the opposite. The trouble was it did do his heart good to see men whose brothers in faith had bullied and harassed him all his life. Now as they took such deep pleasure in being warm and well fed, warmth and food that he had provided and for which they were so pathetically grateful, he started to feel some connection with them as if a line were being drawn between them binding them together. He did not want this. 'How can I feel sorry for them?' he whispered to Cale miserably as the great but badly made hut in which they sat hummed with light and pleasure and deep content that only warm feet and a full stomach can provide. Cale looked at him.

'Careful with your tears – you might drown.'

The next morning both of them were ready to leave before dawn. As the sky began to lighten they were on their mounts and away from the Golan camp, now beginning to stretch like a great dog as the final day of preparations got cracking.

Used to seeing the two going in and out and with Cale much admired by reputation for his victories on the veldt, the guards nodded them through and out onto the heights leading down to the flat Machair. The sound of bells calling the Redeemers to mass began, the pi-dogs barking as the two of them picked their way downwards. In half an hour they were moving quickly but watchfully over the easy riding plain. Here and there were stubborn areas of snow but smaller and fewer as they moved away from the heights.

'Still,' said Vague Henri, as they stopped for a few minutes to rest the horses, 'I don't care how hard the Laconics are. Even if it's warm enough now, six nights out in the open in cold like that – bound to put a crimp in your swagger.'

'I suppose,' replied Cale. With the horses rested they remounted and walked them on slowly. If they came across Laconic cavalry doing some scouting themselves they wanted the animals to be rested. What Cale wanted to get a sense of was the terrain, how the melt had affected the ground, if there were choke points to defend or attack. Muddy ground, only to be expected, would be a disadvantage and perhaps a big one for the Laconics who, whatever their other skills, always tried to close on their enemies and use their ability to fight in powerful blocks ten deep and overpower their opponents with their strength, ferocity and unique ability to move these blocks around as if they were dancers in a troupe rather than soldiers.

'They do a lot of dancing, so it says in the testaments.'

'When they're not taking it up the chuff.'

'You never know, according to the testaments they have these sorts of ceremonies – I mean in public – where they do all that Gomorrah business in a ritual like on holydays.'

'You liar!'

'I'm not saying it's true, I'm just telling you what it said.'

'Better not get caught then.'

'Better not. Anyway, you'll be all right.'

'How do you mean?'

'You're too ugly.'

'That's not what the girls at the Sanctuary say.'

'What's that, then?'

'They say I'm gorgeous, absolutely gorgeous.'

Laughing they rode on in silence for nearly ten minutes.

'Do you see him?'

'Yes. He's not exactly taking much trouble to stay hid.'

For several minutes a horseman had been tracking them from a couple of hundred yards away having emerged from behind a rise, a shallow one, but high enough to have hidden him if he'd wanted not to be seen.

There was a loud click! as Vague Henri started to ratchet back the light crossbow that had been hanging from his saddle in such a way that the rider could not see that he was arming himself.

'Let's turn back.'

Cale nodded and they began easing the horses around. The rider stopped for a moment and then began to follow.

'If he gets any closer to you, reload time – send one past him.'

'Why don't I just put one in him?'

'What for? Just warn him off.'

Vague Henri raised the bow, steadied and fired a warning. The horse kicked as the bolt shot past, closer than Vague Henri had intended. But, after all, he was on a horse himself and out of practice. The two boys stopped and watched.

'I say,' shouted the Laconic scout. 'Would you mind if I had a word?'

Cale stopped and turned his horse as Vague Henri finished reloading.

'You set?' he said.

'What are you doing? This isn't the time for a little chat.'

'I don't agree. We might not get another chance.'

'Come forward!' shouted Cale. 'And keep your hands where we can see them. My friend here didn't miss the last time and he won't miss this time either.'

'My word of honour,' shouted the rider, laughing.

'Do Sodomites have any honour?' asked Vague Henri.

'Why are you asking me?'

'Come forward. Slowly,' shouted Cale. 'Try anything and you'll be laughing on the other side of your face.'

The rider moved forwards as he was told until he was about ten yards away.

'That'll do.'

The rider stopped. 'Lovely morning,' he said. 'Makes you glad to be alive.'

'Which you won't be,' said Vague Henri, 'if you've got any little friends planning to join us. I can put one in you and we can be back to our patrol before you hit the ground.'

'There's no need for all that, my dear,' said the young man, clean-shaven and with elaborately beaded hair.

'What do you want?' said Cale.

'I thought we might talk.'

'About?'

'You're Redeemers, aren't you?'

'Might be. What's it to you?'

'Forgive me for saying so but aren't you a bit young to be out and about when there's going to be so much blood and screaming.'

'I thought Laconics were supposed to be brief of speech,' said Cale.

'They are, that's true, usually. But it would be a sad world, wouldn't it, if we were all the same?'

'Are you Krypteia?'

The man's eyelashes flicked and he moved his head to one side. He smiled.

'Might be. You're very well informed, if I may say so.'

Cale took a quick look behind and to either side to check what might be about and knowing that Vague Henri had his mark fixed on the man's chest.

'Does your friend with the crossbow have a steady nerve?'

'I can't say that he does, to be honest,' replied Cale. 'So I'd stay still if I were you. I asked you already – what do you want?'

'I just thought we might have a chat.'

'Is that what they're calling it now?' asked Vague Henri.

'I'm not sure I understand you,' replied the young man although he clearly knew mockery when he heard it.

'I wouldn't distract him, if I were you,' said Cale, 'not while he's got that thing pointed at your chest.' The young man looked at Cale, amused and not at all nervous.

'Your name, young man?'

'You first.'

'Robert Fanshawe.' He dropped his head, all the while keeping his eyes on Vague Henri. 'Yours to the lowest pit of hell.'

'Dominic Savio,' said Cale, his return nod unnoticeable to all but an eagle blessed with particularly sharp sight. 'And that's where you're going if you do anything my friend here doesn't like. I'm always going on at him about his jumpiness, by the way.'

'Pleased to meet you, Dominic Savio.'

'The pleasure's all yours.'

But then something odd, a flicker of something in Fanshawe's eyes. Cale's horse, restless for some reason, had begun drifting to one side. He took one more step.

'Steady!' But Cale was no great horseman and the horse moved anyway. The hoof seemed to sink impossibly into the heather mix of sedge and wild grass and then the ground itself rose up as if it were some creature looking for its prey. Screaming with terror and off balance the horse reared up throwing Cale with a hefty thud back onto the ground, winding him so badly he just lay on his back groaning. Then a blur of movement as a man rolled out from under the sedge and grabbed the stunned Cale, turned him over on top of himself as a shield and had a knife at his throat.

'Easy! Easy!' shouted Fanshawe at Vague Henri, who, startled as much by the event as the speed of it, had not fired. This was as well: had he done so it would have certainly killed Fanshawe but also Cale.

'Easy! Easy!' said Fanshawe again. 'We can all live through this. Let me explain.'

Vague Henri, shaking, said, 'Go on.'

'I'd just left my man here under that,' he looked over at the six-by-four sheet of cloth covered in sedge and grass stitched to the surface, 'when I saw you heading straight for him. Thought I'd track you to make sure you went by – but you got too close. By then I'd realized you weren't old enough to be soldiers. Thought I'd lead you away. Wrong again, eh?' He smiled, hoping to calm Vague Henri down. He looked, thought Fanshawe, a dangerous combination: jumpy but knew what he was doing.

'We can all walk away from this,' repeated Fanshawe. 'Just lower the crossbow and my friend here will let Dominic go.'

'You first,' said Cale. 'I told you.'

'I'll cut this little boy's throat and then come for you!' said the man holding Cale.

'Let's all calm down. Now I'm going to ask my chum here to bring Dominic to his feet and then we can go from there. All right?'

Vague Henri nodded.

'Going to count to three. One, two, three.'

With that the man holding Cale pulled him upwards till they were both standing – the knife at his throat never giving a smidgeon or a jot.

'Jolly good,' said Fanshawe. 'We're all getting along famously.'

'Now what?' said Vague Henri.

'Tricky, I admit. What if we . . .' With that Cale raised his right foot, scraped it down the shin of the man holding him while driving his elbow into his ribs and grabbing the man's wrist and twisting with all his strength. The man's shout was smothered by the air leaving his lungs. Whippet quick, Cale squirmed away, cracked his elbow again to the forearm of the man and had the knife from his fingers. To Cale's astonishment the man could still move. He blocked the blow Cale struck with the knife and lashing out with his fist caught Cale on the side of his head. With a cry of pain, Cale stepped back to give himself room for another blow. As he lashed at his chest the man dodged once, twice and then kicked out at Cale's left shin, knocking one foot off the ground so that he fell to one knee. Another hefty blow from the man, which had it landed would have smashed every tooth in Cale's head, but he dodged back, his knuckles taking him at the lowest point of his chin and glancing away. Cale was on both feet now as his opponent overbalanced at the missed strike and scrambled away. They stood, Cale with the knife and the advantage, staring at each other and waiting for a chance to strike.

'Stop! We can stop here! Tell him!' shouted Fanshawe to Vague Henri. 'We can all go free. Nobody needs to die here.'

'It's all one to me,' said the man, glaring at Cale.

'Not me, it isn't,' shouted Fanshawe. 'Do as you're bloody well told and back away. Do it or by God I'll come over and help him.'

Trained to obedience even more than to slaughter, slowly the man eased back step by step as wary as you like.

'Congratulations. Every one of us. Get up behind me, Mawson.' He looked over at Vague Henri. 'May I, dear boy?'

'I'm not your dear boy.'

Fanshawe reached for the reins and eased his horse over to Mawson, who was still looking at Cale as if he were wondering whether to eat his heart first or his liver.

'Get on behind me, Mawson.'

'My knife,' said Mawson. Fanshawe sighed and looked at Cale with a weary what-can-you-do-with-them look.

Cale stood back then raised the knife and threw it with considerable force some forty yards in the direction he wanted them to take.

'I'm obliged,' said Fanshawe. Without an order Mawson, the blank expression of a much-experienced killer now absent, picked up his sedge blanket and leapt up behind Fanshawe as easily and gracefully as if he had pulled out a chair to sit down to his dinner. He looked much younger now.

'Till we meet again, boys,' said Fanshawe. With that he turned his horse and, pausing only to let Mawson pick up his knife, they were soon five hundred yards away and behind the rise he had emerged from only ten minutes before.

'I don't think,' said Vague Henri, 'I'm cut out for this stuff.'

'You were absolutely gorgeous,' said Cale. With that he went off to get his horse and they beat it back to the Golan as quickly as possible.

Fanshawe and Mawson, however, were not much further away than when the boys had seen them disappear behind the rise. They had found a small gulley and having spread the grass and sedge blanket beneath them were indulging themselves energetically in Laconic beastliness.

It was the night before the Battle of Eight Martyrs, so called because over the last six hundred years this number of Redeemers had given their lives for the faith in or around what was to be the battlefield. It was by no means a matter of luck that there should be a place of conflict already consecrated by the blood of martyrs. So hated were the Redeemers by their many adversaries that over hundreds of years there remained few places where one or more of them had not been hanged, decapitated, broken, dismembered, strangled, garrotted or crucified. There was an embarrassment of riches for the Redeemers when it came to naming battlefields after martyred saints. Indeed there was barely a village fist-fight that could not have been named after one.

Cale had not been asked to attend the final instructions for battle but neither had he been excluded. Lurking behind Van Owen's battle shack with Vague Henri and waiting for a group to form at the door so he could slip inside unnoticed, Cale whispered to Vague Henri, 'What have I got to do?'

'Keep your big mouth shut.'

'Right.'

Then five or six Redeemer subalts arrived and Cale followed them in, close behind, and moved to the darkest and most densely packed corner of the large room, which in any case was only well-lit where the large plan of the battle hung from the wall.

To Cale's great disappointment Van Owen outlined nothing spectacularly stupid in the way of tactics. Neither was there anything interesting beyond the use of much heavier armour for the front rank of the Redeemers who would take the initial brunt of contact with the Laconics. Cale had to admit that given the little that Van Owen knew about Laconic field tactics – he did not, of course, have access to the testaments in Bosco's library – it was hard to criticize any of his decisions. His only slight satisfaction was to sneer at the small size of Van Owen's reserves. Given the two-to-one advantage, he thought Van Owen should have kept back a much bigger share of his army to give him the option to deal with anything unexpected.

'On the other hand,' said Vague Henri, after Cale had

slipped out unobserved in the general rush to leave and prepare for the next day, 'suppose he weakens his first attack by not using his better numbers. Keeping too big a reserve is like dividing your forces. I'm not sure I'd do much different in his place.'

'Nobody asked you.'

'You did as it happens.'

'Well, now I'm sorry and I'll pray to God for forgiveness.'

'Do you? Still pray, I mean.'

Cale did not reply.

'Well?'

'Yes, I still pray.' There was a pause. 'I pray for deliverance from evil and having to look at your ugly face all day long.'

'Me? I'm gorgeous. You said so yourself.'

When they got back to the Purgators' hut there was a message from one of Van Owen's adjutants: Cale and his men were to observe the battle if they wished but were instructed to stay away from either the command centre or the battlefield. On no account were they to intervene in any way whatsoever.

This was excellent news. Cale's one fear was that Van Owen would include him in something dangerous out of spite. It was clear that in the event of victory or defeat he did not want to risk Cale making a further name for himself. Cale wrote back repeating the order and went cheerfully to sleep.

He gave most of the Purgators a lie-in the next day, something by which they were always delighted, but left at dawn with Vague Henri and ten men. At the opening of the gates the small band moved through the army as it stirred itself for the day's action. They made their way around in front of the Field of Eight Martyrs mostly ignored by men with too much else on their mind and rode away to the north and to a small bluff with a good sight of the battlefield they had marked out before the encounter with Fanshawe. Cale had his men check their surrounds for Laconic outposts put in place since they were last there and confirmed for himself two routes of escape in case things went wrong. Then they climbed the bluff and waited in silence for the day to begin. Already the Laconics were loosely gathered at their end of the plain, though not in any disciplined formation but like a crowd at an unusually large county fair watching as the Redeemers deployed.

First of all came the Black Cordelias, seven thousand strong, armour covered in purple and the black from which they got their name. Even from a couple of miles away on the bluff the wind brought snatches of a hymn. The boys, laughing, began mockingly to sing along.

> 'Remember man as you pass by
> As you are now, so once was I
> As I am now, so you must be
> Prepare for death and follow me

Today me, tomorrow you
I am dust and you are too
Hideous the truth of Death
Dreadful is the final breath.'

The two boys grew nearly hysterical with joy – observing their enemies, whatever the outcome, going to their deaths and they watching safe and sound. Vague Henri remembered a song the quads in Arbell Swan-Neck's palazzo used to sing. It took a moment to get the tune back and he had forgotten the first few lines.

'Oh! Death where is thy sting-a-ling-a-ling
Oh! Grave thy victoreee?
The bells of hell go ting-a-ling-a-ling
For you but not for meee!'

The wind must have changed slightly as the hymns faded in and out of hearing but impressively dominating their formation was the giant censer the size of a cathedral bell the Black Cordelias always took into battle as it swung back and forth, incense blooming upwards in a great pillar of smoke.

Still the Laconics drifted about in front of their camp like a crowd watching a vaguely interesting pageant. Now the fourth army of the Golan, known as the Hierophants, with its five Sodalities, ten thousand in all: the slaves of the Immaculate Heart, the Poor Simons of

Perpetual Adoration, the Norbetines, the forbidding Oblates of Abasement and then, grimmest of all, the Brotherhood of Mercy. For the next hour the Redeemer army deployed: cloth of gold, ensigns of red, banners of purple, the petioles of the confessors, the pink fronds of the medical friars not allowed to touch the dying until they called out the unctions in extremis. All of it now to the sound of bagpipes loud enough to defy the everchanging wind and which Van Owen, watching from the promontory sticking out of the Golan, would signal once the battle started and the hymns stopped to act as his voice, each Sodality having its own particular sound and its own instructions to advance, turn or retreat.

Now when the Redeemers were half drawn up in line to attack, the Laconic soldiers began to move but still with the same lack of intensity with which they previously seemed to watch. But within less than three minutes they formed into a loose series of ragged squares as if from nowhere. But then it was as if they had lost interest again, the groups remained clear enough but still without the precise and martial discipline of formal rank and file. Now they watched again as the Redeemer second army finished its own formation – a continuing line of Black Cordelias to the front and the others formed behind six deep, the most lightly armoured and most mobile to the rear. In a tight group half a mile back stood a thousand reserves. Then with a trumpet blast the six pipers cut short their skirling music, the sound drifting in the wind like the last breath of a great and wounded animal.

For a minute there was nearly silence, only the odd shout of a sergeant or the snort of a horse from the five hundred cavalry behind the right flank of the Redeemers.

In front of the Laconics there was movement as eight men with two flags each ran out and to each side in front of their still loosely grouped army.

Once they had dispersed they raised the flags and began to signal. Like a lazy horse midstream convulsed by the touch of a shocking eel, the army of Laconics flexed to life – six flabby squares hardened to edges sharp as a builder's float. A flash again of flags and then they began to march towards the Redeemers, nearly a mile below; perfect in step and rhyme like any dance troupe or crew of mimes.

Then again the flags. The six squares stopped as one. A beat and then the flags again. A shout, one voice, eight thousand men. Then a great clash of sword on shields, the inward face then quickly turned to their enemies. A vast great flash of colour, yellow and red. Each line headed in turn to left and right so each square became a line spreading across the field, moving from thirty deep to ten. Another wave of the flags and with another shout, another turning in and out of the shields, the six lines moved together into a wall a thousand yards across and six men deep. From Van Owen's watch on the Golan Heights the trumpets bellowed and a cry went up from every priest.

'DEATH! JUDGEMENT! HEAVEN! HELL!
THE LAST FOUR THINGS
ON WHICH WE DWELL!'

Even from the safety of their bluff and wrapped in the neutral malice that Cale and Vague Henri bore both sides an unpleasant thrill of fear ran from the nape of their necks and down their spines. Vague Henri defied the power of this hideous prayer by singing softly to Cale under his breath:

'I'd rather dwell on Marie the whore
And what she does with a cucumbore!'

The great army of the Redeemers lurched forward like a bull freeing itself at last from a riverbank of mud. Then astonishment from Cale and Vague Henri. The Laconic mercenaries began to run towards their enemy as if desperate and overjoyed to die. This was no jog or trot but a burst of speed that must be fatal to the order and power of their massy wall that relied on thousands acting together as a single will.

As the two great armies spread towards each other like a stain the small animals of the Machair were squeezed into the space between. First and only to escape are the pheasants, stupid almost to the last, they flap and cackle into the air just as the Laconic line is about to trample them. The hares now run for the cover they will never find darting backwards and forwards between the Laconic rush and the dead still patience of the Redeemers. The fox that was hunting them also makes a run for it, first one way then the other, terrified, and then is swallowed up, engulfed like the animals outside the ark in Noah's flood.

This sudden Laconic rush threw the centenars of the Redeemer archers on the left and right. Already the sudden burst of speed down the slight incline to the Redeemer line had caught them out. Seconds of delay made their confusion worse – the steady advance was all they had ever seen. By the time the centenars had heard the order for the release from a furious Van Owen, the chance for two flights of arrows had been lost. Then they recovered, shot, and the two boys watched as the dreadful sharps poured through the air towards the charging men in red. But speed like this had brought the Laconics through the arc so that only those in the rear were hit and many arrows fell uselessly behind.

Now so close the Redeemer archers were forced to shoot flat onto the advancing Laconics and straight into the protection of their shields. Another shock: the mercenaries had themselves hired men to do their fighting for them. Poor archers themselves and having disdained for too long the effeminacy of fighting at a distance, they had brought four hundred hired archers from Little Italy lagging just behind the Laconics on the right, who had taken the brunt of the arrows that had missed the bulk of advancing Laconics. A hundred and fifty were already dead, the others stalled – but now as the Redeemer archers were let loose to fire at will the Italians were ignored and now given time to set themselves up, they poured their fire at the Redeemer archers in their turn.

Havoc. Not expecting archers and little used to taking what they were used to handing out, the Redeemer bowmen were thrown into confusion by a lashing of arrows that landed almost one for one into their massed ranks. The centenars and sergeants shouting above the screams of the wounded and the dying. 'HEAD DOWN! HEAD DOWN! HEAD DOWN! HEAD DOWN!' 'Take care!' cries out another. 'Look out! OVER THERE! OVER THERE!' One Redeemer takes an arrow in the chest but it's the living man next to him who flinches like a horse that's felt an unexpected lash. Men duck and bend away at nothing – others just stand and take an arrow in the stomach or the face as if they had been taken completely by surprise. The archers who had so devastated the Materazzi cavalry less than a year before were reduced to lookers-on as the Laconics, barely touched by their arrows, slammed as if with a stepping punch into the ranks of the Black Cordelias.

force onto the helmets of the men in front of them. Helmets designed to take only a blow or cut were split apart by the force of something like a hammer and a spike. The terrible injuries inflicted with each crushing stroke trembled the lines of the Black Cordelias. Then the final twist of the bezel as the dreadful practised grace of the Laconics came into play. To the Laconic right, packed with the strongest men in any case, the middle line of Laconics at the rear – once they knew the line in the centre would not give – shifted their weight and made it stronger still. While the Redeemer centre and the Redeemer right moved slowly back as the Black Cordelias fell to the curved blades and were replaced by weaker or even less well-armoured men, there was a crushing collapse on their left as the curved swords, the strongest Laconics, and the swift and sudden reinforcement became too much. 'IS THAT IT? WHAT? WAIT! STAND THERE! STAND THERE!' The confusion and the collapse and the shouts – most on either side had no idea if they were about to win or die.

Amid the rumbling noise, the screams, the orders, the trumpets blaring instructions and the dead and dying, the Laconic right broke their opponents – those that could do so ran, those that could not were killed and only their bodies slippery with blood and excrement and soil made awkward the turning advance of the Laconics. The mercenaries overbalanced on the bodies underneath their feet, the flabby leadenness of the dead, the clutching hands of the dying and the still noisily wounded, some of them still fighting able to stab at the stumbling mercenaries being pushed from behind and suddenly disordered and vulnerable. Many more Laconics died in that decisive but messy turn than in all their previous ten years of fighting. But once it was done, the battle but not the killing was through. Van Owen watched on from his hill in hopeless horror, unable to do anything but send his thin reserves to die in delaying what could not be stopped. Now as the Redeemers in the centre and the right fought on, the Laconics attacked them from the side and simply but bloodily rolled them up like a carpet at a picnic's end. Those that did not run died.

For the second battle in a row, Vague Henri and Cale ended up watching a massacre. The Purgators around them had been yelling their encouragement, and became so loud Vague Henri swore at them to keep it down. He was about to point out to them that they were cheering on men who would have applauded at their executions, who regarded them as the living dead, men without souls. It was Cale who realized what he was going to say because he was thinking the same but put a hand on Vague Henri's arm to shut him up. This time, unlike the fiasco at Silbury Hill, Cale had the sense not to become involved and long before the terrible end he had withdrawn. But unlike the Redeemers that day, he had a stroke of luck.

Of Cale and Vague Henri and their squad of Purgators, some were in tears, others calling out the prayers for the dead and the dying.

'Death, Judgement, Heaven, Hell,' called out Purgator Giltrap, once the Prayer Sponsor of Meynouth before he was convicted of three of the nine offences against reason. To which, mindful of Vague Henri's rebuke, the others replied softly: 'The last four things on which we dwell.'

Chins on their chests, the two boys leading at the front were able to hide their unbecoming smirks.

As they returned towards the Golan, Cale protected the column by moving in a roundabout way along the Machair Fingers, called so because, long, low and thin, their stubby ends were held to point to the way around the heights. The Laconics were no better cavalrymen than they were archers but they had reserves, not used that day, of fast mounted soldiers and before they left the bluff, Cale had seen them in the distance slowly making their way around the far side of Van Owen's outlook. Cale moved back to the Golan slowly, wary in case he stumbled over the Laconic mounted troops. Along the fingers to either side and just below the crest of these hills he had scouts on donkeys, sure-footed on the uneven sides, keeping an eye out for anything that might threaten them. One of them, just before the fingers' stubby end, signalled Cale to join him at the top. When he made his way up on foot along with Vague Henri, the scout pointed to a troop of Redeemers about twenty strong leaving and heading towards the Golan.

'Is it Van Owen?' said Vague Henri, as Cale looked through his spyglass.

'Must be.' He handed the glasses to Vague Henri. 'Look over there.'

Vague Henri searched in the direction Cale was pointing. About thirty mounted Laconics were chasing down Van Owen's guard, who were, so it looked from their easy pace, unaware they were about to be attacked.

'Don't fancy Van Owen's chances,' said Vague Henri. 'What I saw of his guards were old men, preachers and a couple of orthodoxers.'

Cale took the glasses back and watched as the Laconic horsemen closed. Even so hammers were working in his brain. Even without glasses, Vague Henri could see clearly enough. In five minutes the Laconics had closed to about two hundred and fifty yards before Van Owen's rear guards saw them. Vague Henri watched as they moved at once from a slow gallop to a full one and all but five or six guards around what must have been Van Owen fell back to put a line of horsemen between him and the advancing Laconics. But if the Laconics were no cavalrymen they were still the better horsemen and with the better horses. It was clear the Redeemers would soon be caught and showing some sense at least the guards made for a small hill, little more than a glorified pimple on the landscape. Dismounting, Van Owen's guards took up a circular position around their general and waited. Cale handed Vague Henri the glasses. Now he could see the Laconics dismount no more than thirty yards from Van Owen and move in quick formation up the slight rise. And then the fight began.

Cale started to move back down the finger. Vague Henri grabbed his arm.

'What do you think you're doing?'

'Me? I'm going to save Van Owen. You stay here.'

'Why?'

'All right. Come with me.'

'I'm not going to help that shit-bag. Why are you?'

'Watch and wonder, Sonny Jim.'

'You're a nutter.'

'We'll see.' And with that he was off down the hill like some mountain goat.

Vague Henri waited on top of the finger along with the donkey scout and watched as Cale and his Purgators moved out into the plain and to the fight on what they came later to call Pillock Hill half a mile ahead.

As Cale and the Purgators quickly advanced, Vague Henri realized that Cale had not been as peculiarly impulsive as he'd at first seemed. As long as he was quick he'd catch the Laconics from the rear. Squeezed between the lines of Redeemers their inevitable victory would become almost certain defeat. Besides, he wouldn't risk an attack directly. Vague Henri was always arguing that crossbowmen could more easily replace archers because bowmen took years to train. The cross-bow delivered the same and sometimes better results in only a few months. So it went as Cale dismounted his Purgators seventy yards away from the top of Pillock Hill and stood behind his men, some way back in fact, and started instructing them to shoot the Laconics down with their crossbows. Later that day one of the Purgators told Vague Henri one of them questioned the order because of the danger to Van Owen's guard. Cale had punched him so hard that, as the Purgator described it, 'his nose burst like a Bicester plum'.

Whatever the danger to the eminent guard of honour on Pillock Hill, the effect on the Laconics was devastating. Within a minute half a dozen of the red-cloaked mercenaries had fallen. They had no choice but to break off and attack Cale and his Purgators. But with the guard of honour behind they seemed to be swapping one inevitable kind of defeat for another. They charged down the hill, a fearsome enough sight even from Vague Henri's distance, and were into the Purgators with only a further three casualties. What followed was a terrible fight and hideously close run. It should not have been but Van Owen's guard of honour, instead of following down Pillock Hill and giving the Laconics the impossible task of fighting front and rear, simply stood and watched their rescuers fall into a desperate struggle for their lives. Despite their smaller numbers, now two to one, the Laconics were armoured – though than two feet and kicked out at the next man's vulnerable knee-joint. The man's scream of agony as the joint snapped was cut short by a kick to the side of his head as he fell. Cale grabbed the two desperately pressed Purgators he had saved and began trying to roll the Laconics up from the side, pulling each Purgator he could rescue around him to form an outflanking wall. At the other end of the line things were going badly for the unarmoured Purgators, who in any case could not match the strength or skill of their better-disciplined opponents. But Cale, furious at Van Owen's treachery, was a whirlwind of animosity and bile. Without intending to he inspired his men, his courage as they thought, even his love for them, showing in his monstrous and ugly skill. Something in the focus of his talent for killing seemed to oppress even the Laconics for whom violent death was, in all essentials, the point of being alive. His every action so lacking in grace or elegance, in everything except a brutal conviction in each stab or blow that you and you only would fail, that anything you brought to this fight was futile, seemed to cause even the Laconics to lose heart as they were enfolded from the left. They did not show it, merciless as they were to themselves as well as to others, but in the minutes before their deaths they had time to understand that they were sure to lose. Seven became three, three became one, and then it was over. Then the usual monstrosity: the wounded crying out, the numb, the delighted, the cruel finishing of the Laconics still alive. One of the Laconics was only lightly wounded in the leg and the two Purgators were both leery of any danger – a hidden dagger perhaps – and enjoying taunting him as he shuffled backwards away from their jabs. 'Antagonist bag of shit!' Not accurate but the worst thing they could think of. 'Atheist malefactor!' This was nearer the truth of the Laconics, if misapplied, but it was an odd fact that most Redeemers had no idea that the Antagonists were a splinter of their own religion and believed most of the things that they did. The edge of one of the swords caught the Laconic soldier on the hand cutting deep into the palm and his cry of pain caught Cale's attention. He raged over towards the two Purgators and pushed them irritably out of the way. The eyes of the Laconic soldier, already terrified, widened as he saw Cale standing over him – he crouched with his arms outspread waiting, the blow arriving in an instant, down through the collarbone and sheering into his heart. A horrible cough which lasted seconds and then unconsciousness and death. A kinder end than for many over the next few hours who were left to die in agony from their wounds or who were slowly finished off by the cruel or the clumsy. All that horror was still to come for thousands on the battlefield. It is always better sometimes, had said IdrisPukke to Vague Henri once when they were eating fish and chips on a sandy beach on the Gulf of Memphis, to reserve the right to look away.

It was then that Vague Henri arrived, the donkey scout still three hundred yards behind. He looked at the dead men around him.

'I never saw anything like it,' he said to the surviving Purgators, eight of them. Cale stared at him knowing exactly what he meant and that it was not a compliment.

'Strip a pair of them of armour and weapons and quickly.' Within a couple of minutes they were gone, taking their dead with them.

Despite Cale having come even closer to death than at Silbury, things turned out all right in the end. He learnt a lesson, although as he later said to Vague Henri, 'I still don't know what it was,' and he lived. But the day hadn't finished with him by any means.

Although the sedge and heathers of the battlefield of Eight Martyrs were robust enough, a fair stretch of them had been churned up and the mud underneath exposed and dragged over. Despite the freezing weather of only a week before, the warm winds from the sea that had melted the snow had grown even warmer. That afternoon it was unseasonably hot, and it brought new life where there was only hideous death. Midge eggs lay buried under the warmth of the sedge and several inches into the mud. Exposed by the battle, heated by the sun, they hatched in their millions and in only an hour they formed a whirling single column the size of the battlefield and rising to over a thousand yards above.

The nearly three thousand Redeemers who survived the carnage and escaped in a ragged mass towards the foot of the Golan looked back and saw something in the air that few of them had seen before – a cloud in the sky moving and shifting like no mist or fog but like something alive. Which, after all, was what it was – now like a weasel on its hinds, now like a camel, now to those who'd seen one very like a whale. But to most, exhausted, shamed, afraid and terrorized it looked like the Hanged Redeemer shaking his head in rage at the dreadful loss and blasphemy of the Laconic victory. And then finally the wind and the causeless flight of the insects changed and the grief-stricken visage of the saviour became for a moment the stern and watchful face of an implacable boy. Or so it later seemed certainly to many – even, after a few days, to a growing number who had not been there at all.

Within hours the survivors were beginning to stream back into the Golan and rumour began to spread like butter on miraculous bread: news of the promised end, that Jews had been swarming to Chartres to convert, that the four dwarf horsemen of the Apocalypse had ridden through the streets of Ware, on Gravelly Hill a red dragon appeared standing over a woman clothed in the sun, and at Whitstable a beast from the land forced the people in the town to worship a beast from the sea. In New Brighton an angel appeared carrying the Wrath of God in a bowl. Once these reports became common knowledge, out of the horror of this hideous defeat came a strange exuberance. The story swept the Golan that an acolyte, a boy, had defeated a hundred soldiers of the enemy with the jaw bone of an ass and had rescued Redeemer Van Owen from the Antagonist traitors who had betrayed his army to their enemies.

While this last rumour was not entirely untrue, neither was it entirely accidental. Bosco's fellow travellers in the Golan, along with those who knew and who believed, found that their garbled version of the numbers and events on Pillock Hill had fallen on desperately willing ears. Events at last conspired with them. The Laconics, instead of advancing either to try and take the Heights or even go around and take the entrenched Redeemer line from the rear, to the astonishment of all stayed exactly where they were. Within hours every Redeemer on the Golan knew beyond certainty that the Laconics had halted because the vision of the Hanged Redeemer and his manifested Wrath had stilled them with the fear of God.

It was neither midges nor God that caused the Laconics to pull back into the camp they had already occupied for a week before the fight but a terrible nagging and habitual fear. It has been wisely said that if you put all your eggs in one basket you'll end up spending all your time watching the basket. It's an even more worrying prospect if the eggs in that one basket are unusually rare. This was the heart of the problem for the Laconics. Their capacity to work together like dancers in the chaos and horror of the battlefield was created out of a lifetime of brutal care and violent solicitude. Each one of them cost a fortune in time and money and the treasure needed to buy that time was earned by slaves. These slaves were not brought from the four quarters of the earth, their families and all their other ties destroyed in the process, but by the bondage of entire peoples living with them cheek by jowl – the slaves many, the Laconics few. There was barely a Laconic warrior who was afraid of death but not one who wasn't fearful of the men and women that he owned. At the Battle of Eight Martyrs the Laconics killed fourteen Redeemers for every one of them that died. And yet they were traumatized by this loss. The effort that had gone into the grave with those eleven hundred men was such that they could never entirely be replaced even within a generation, the Laconics being so few and their training so long and hard.

In the light of such a successful catastrophe the Ephors of Laconia must have their say on what to do and this was why they stopped, when had they advanced around the Golan Heights and taken the Redeemer trenches from the rear this great war might have counted its end in months or even weeks.

The Ephors ordered their troops before the Golan to dig themselves in and then made an offer to their Helot slaves: if they would pick among themselves three thousand of their strongest, most courageous and their brightest men then all who fought with the Laconics in the Golan would be freed on their return, and given two hundred dollars and a strip of land. The Helots seized upon this unprecedented chance of freedom and prosperity and three thousand of their finest turned up at the appointed time and place unarmed and were immediately massacred by the Laconics where they stood. And so reassured that they had both terrorized the Helots that remained and killed the strongest who had the will to free themselves, the Ephors took the additional money offered by the Antagonists and decided to advance once more. But planning and delivering a massacre takes time, as did extorting more money from the Antagonists, and it was nearly three weeks before the Laconic army was on the move again and during that time Bosco had excelled himself.

Within less than two days he had news of the defeat and in another two he'd taken advantage of the paralysis that had descended on the Holy See and was in Chartres insisting he be allowed an audience with the Pope, all the while having sent go-betweens to his secret fraternity of believers, and his most persuasive envoys to fellow travellers who, though in a panic and a funk, also watched to see what in this calamity they might profitably do.

However desperate the need for salvation from the Laconics it did not follow that everyone was equally willing to believe in Cale. Bosco's enemies were in something of a bind. On the one hand they were as appalled by the defeat to the Laconics as any Redeemer would be and equally horrified by its likely consequences. And just because they were treacherous, scheming and self-interested did not mean they lacked genuine religious zeal. What if he was indeed the Grimperson, long if vaguely promised in a roundabout and ambiguous fashion? Some doubted if the Grimperson was a prophecy at all but was a mistranslation of the original and badly damaged text and could have meant not a deadly destroyer of the Redeemers' enemies who might, or might not, bring about the end of all things, but a kind of holy cake of seventy raisins and nuts that would be provided by the Lord to bring an end to hunger should famine ever last longer than a year. The debate as to whether the prophecy concerned a dark destroyer or a substantial cake was largely unimportant considering that the Redeemer faith unquestionably faced annihilation.

At first Bosco's astonishing request that Cale be put in charge of the Eighth Army of the Wras was rejected out of hand. A more cautious and plausible decision was made by the Pope in a brief moment of clarity to order Redeemer General Princeps, conqueror of the Materazzi and already in Chartres, to take command. However, at Bosco's instruction Princeps claimed to be at death's door with a fish bone stuck in his throat. He wrote a letter, not for the first time, making it clear he had only followed Cale's plan in his victory over the Materazzi and called for the Pontiff in all humility to confirm the young man at the head of the Eighth Army. To convince unbelievers in his illness, of whom they were many, Princeps asked for the prayer for the dying to be said for him by the Pope himself. This was a blasphemy he had been unwilling to undertake other than at Bosco's insistence on the grounds that unrequested their enemies would be certain to smell a rat.

It would be hard to exaggerate the blow this struck to Gant and Parsi. They regarded Princeps as if not their last hope then certainly their best.

'We must act at once or we will be lost. Give it to the boy,' moaned Parsi.

'I'll be damned if I'll expose the faith to such a reckless act. If he's a messenger from God I'll want a bloody sight better sign than a magical fog or the word of that bastard Bosco.' But among the faithful, desperate for a saviour, there was too much fervour for either of them to do nothing.

'Well then,' said Gant at last, 'let the dog see the rabbit.'

Within an hour a Pontifical messenger and eight armed guards arrived at Bosco's quarters and demanded that Cale come at once to an audience. Bosco, alarmed at the suddenness of this, attempted to go with him but was ordered with some obvious fear on the part of the messenger to stay where he was. 'I have received orders directly, Redeemer,' he apologized. 'You are not to come.'

And so unable to brief Cale on what to say and do, or not to say and do, he was obliged to watch him head off for what he knew would be some sort of trap.

Cale was brought to an antechamber and told to wait in the hope that he would have enough time to work himself up into a panic before the audience. At the far end of the room lit by candles and hazed with smoke from four incense burners was a statue of the first of all the Redeemer martyrs, St Joseph, being stoned to death. It was an event notable for one other incident: it was perhaps the last time someone tried to intervene out of compassion on a Redeemer's side. As the men of the town had gathered to take part in St Joseph's execution for dishonouring their own One True Faith, a wandering, though much respected, preacher tried to prevent the killing by calling out, 'Anyone of you who is without sin, let him cast the first stone.' Unfortunately for the compassionate preacher and even more unfortunately for St Joseph, one man, unabashed, rushed over to him carrying a large rock over his head and cried out confidently, 'I'm without sin!' and brought the rock crashing down on the shin of the Redeemer breaking his leg with a hideous crack!

The statue was of the moment when the sinless executioner had raised another large rock above his head and was about to cast it down on the agonized St

Joseph. Cale was used to seeing gesso-painted wooden statues of terrible martyrdoms – flatly painted in simple colours, crude or merely competent carvings produced by the thousand for the benefit of the faithful in every Redeemer church. The statues of Chartres, and there were many of them, were like nothing he had ever seen. They were more real than the real itself, the carving not just beautifully done but full of life. The carved hands of the executioner were not just beautifully carved but beautifully observed: they were the hands of a working man. There were small cuts healed and almost healed on nearly every finger. There was dirt under every fingernail but one. The expression on his face was more than just a snarl of malice; it also caught the delight in cruelty, the pleasure, and beneath the animated face a bass note of despair. The teeth made of the finest ivory had been carefully discoloured, two were chipped, one seemed to be dead. As for St Joseph, he would have drawn pity from the hardest heart: his left leg had not just been broken by the first stone but smashed, the bone protruding from his shin, jagged, bloody, agonizing – the glistening marrow leaking from the break was made of glass. His mouth was open in a cry of pain – no holy resignation to his fate but fear and anguish expressed in every line and fold. His hand was raised to stop the second blow, the arm thin, an old man's arm with liver spots, it seemed impossibly to shake with pain and fear. But Cale's eye was drawn back to the man who in, the Redeemer at his side touched his arm as if to prevent him leaping over the thickly corded barrier.

The great choir reached its nerve-shredding climax and there was a moment as the final note seemed to fill the air with something celestial, huge, capable of wiping away all sense of self and anything but the will for God. There was a long pause as the Pontiff, lion-headed, strong, God-appointed, looked at the boy in front of him exposing his soul to the wisdom of the rock of God.

'In whose name do you come to trouble the anointed of the . . .'

'You're not him,' said Cale, matter of fact. There was a gasp and the majestic face of the man on the throne dwindled in stature as if the air had been let out of a Memphis child's balloon.

'What do you mean by . . .'

'You're not him.'

'Who is then?' The voice of the man was now very far from that of holy majesty – it was querulous, miffed, clearly annoyed at having been rumbled with such ease.

Cale stared insolently into the eyes of the counterfeit Pontiff and without looking raised his right hand to point at a frail old man standing about midway in one of the lines of forty Redeemers leading to the throne. There was another ripple of astonishment, very satisfying indeed to Cale. Slowly, portentously, he turned to face in the direction of the man he was pointing at. He

# 17

Cale had rarely seen Bosco in a good humour but back in his company after the audience his old master was positively gleeful.

'Hah! How did you guess that pompous fool Waller was a fake? I'll bet he looked the part.'

'It was his shoes,' said Cale, a little bemused by Bosco's extreme joviality and admiration. There was a moment as Bosco considered what he meant and then it clicked. His face lit up with even greater delight.

'Wonderful! Wonderful!'

'What do you mean?' said Vague Henri from the other side of the room.

It was not easy for Cale to reply because he was not used to referring to the Redeemer in front of him when talking to Vague Henri as anything but 'that shit-bag Bosco'.

'For some reason, years ago when I was small, I remember – I remember the Redeemer here telling me about the Pope's shoes, that they were specially made for him in red silk and no one but the Vicar of the Hanged Redeemer could wear shoes of that colour or of silk. I don't know why I remembered that but when

I got into the chapel I could see them right off. Everyone else's shoes were black leather. They might just as well have hung a sign around his neck.'

'Nonsense,' said Bosco cheerfully. 'I never saw the hand of God so clear in anything. You were inspired.'

As it happens it is to be doubted whether this peculiar charade made much or any difference to Cale being appointed to lead the Eighth Army. Already there were preachers at the street corners in Chartres hailing Cale as the incarnation of the Wrath of God and only some of them were obedient subordinates of Bosco. If ever a group of men were readier and riper for a saviour than at that moment history does not record it.

Reports of the Laconics' inexplicable failure to advance either on or around the Golan had already reached Chartres but the about-to-be head of the Redeemer Eighth Army was not thinking about tardy mercenaries or startling plans of attack. He was, soft-hearted dog, weeping for his lost love. These were not, however, as the conventions of popular romances require, tears of loss and regret, though in the great commingled salmagundi of his feelings for Arbell Swan-Neck they were certainly present. These were mostly tears of anger and humiliation, particularly humiliation, and centred on a particular occasion that he hated to think about but was drawn back to in the bitter sleepless night like a poking tongue to a decaying tooth.

It had been the happiest night of his life. To be sure

the competition for this honour was not great but, unlike the popular romances already mentioned, real life has no consideration for the careful working up of a final climax that must be, after suitable loss and suffering, the high point of the story and come striding confidently at the end. How many men and women, how many children even, have only slowly realized that the high point of their lives is far behind? A melancholy thought whose only comfort is that you never know – things may look up, something may happen to save the day, the beautiful stranger, the successful child, the sudden recognition, the chance meeting, the happy return, all these are possible. The great and lasting comfort is that you never know. Cale, however, was not that night much in the mood for the consolations of philosophy. He was back in Arbell's bed remembering what seemed to him like centuries ago. She was asleep and lying next to him, breathing gently and making the occasional delightful sound. For some reason that night he could not sleep, with easier times the talent for dropping in and out of sleep at will had deserted him. There were several candles burning at the other end of the room and in the dim warm light he got up and went to get himself a drink. As he did so, leaning his back against the wall, he looked at her sleeping face. He hated the sleeping face of men, the noise they made, the smell, the everything about them as they dreamt around him in the shed. The candlelight did her face no harm – the sleep easier to come by that night, she might have stayed asleep herself and all would have been well and all manner of things.

Eventually to the gentle sound of the small bells that rang the quarter-hours at Chartres he fell asleep. At six he was woken by Vague Henri and there was no time for anything but war and matters of life and death.

Redeemer General Bosco would very much have liked to be equally single-minded. But he had a visitor. At first there were too many instructions to be given and information to be taken in but finally the scrawny Redeemer was so insistent he be heard that he stopped for a moment, attentive only so that this nuisance would go away.

'Who are you?' said Bosco.

The man sighed, clearly unhappy about his treatment. He was a man who expected to be taken seriously.

'I am Redeemer Yes, from the Office of the Holy Spirit.'

'Never heard of them.'

'We used to be the Office of Celibacy.'

'Oh, I've heard of *them*.'

'So you can see that this is no trivial matter.'

'What is it you want?'

'To help you, Redeemer.'

'I'm trying to fight a war, you can help by going away.'

'The church has a duty in love to help its bishops.'

'I'm not a bishop.'

'Its bishops and equally senior prelates to disable our celibate prelates from straying. As an act of love we of my office wish to be present with the prelate at all times to prevent any private or secretive lives. How can we ask of you, Redeemer, that all your actions as father of the church be pure and not give you the help required?'

'Help?'

'Constant attendance by a member of the office.'

'In my bedroom, constant attendance?'

'Especially your bedroom, Redeemer. But your helper will be blindfolded during the hours of darkness. And you will be provided as a further act of love with a pair of night gloves. Night gloves are. . .'

'Yes, I understand,' interrupted Bosco. His face softened. 'I understand your concerns, of course, Redeemer. Yes. You are right to say there can be no intrusion into the privacy of someone who has no private life.' He smiled, as if regretfully. 'But you see I must deal with . . . not a greater threat, perhaps, but a more pressing one.'

Redeemer Yes did not look as if he agreed that offences against the Holy Spirit were any more pressing than questions of survival. 'I will be back soon, one way or another – if I am spared – and then we can give this matter the attention it deserves.'

Redeemer Yes was not entirely at ease with this. It was a matter of deep regret to him that bishops were not more welcoming to him and his office. He was obviously only trying to help but you would hardly think so. With some reluctance he agreed to return the following week and then left. As soon as he had done so Bosco called Gil over to him. 'That Redeemer Yes. Put him on the list.'

The issue of being watched was also on the mind of others.

'How are we going to get away now you've been made the Lord bloody God Almighty of Everything?'

'What was I supposed to do – refuse? I'm all ears if you can come up with something.'

'Oh, I can see you're heartbroken.' Vague Henri looked at him as unfriendly as you like. 'You want this, don't you?'

'What I'd say is that as usual I can either like it or lump it. So what? I'm doing something I'm good at and it's not as if I had a choice anyway.'

'Lose.'

'What?'

'Lose!'

'Why don't you say it louder? I don't think they'll have heard you on the other side of the city.'

'All right. Pretend I said it softly.'

'I never heard anything so bloody daft in all my life.'

'Why? Let the Laconics through and you said yourself they could start rolling up the trenches all the way to Tripoli. Chartres will be lost in a week and then no one to stand in their way for three thousand miles. Why are we trying to stop them?'

'Because they're going to roll us up with them. You know what they do, the Laconics, don't you, to little boys? Or they would if they took prisoners. I killed Folk Antagonists by the thousand on the veldt. You think they haven't heard all about Bosco's Angel of Death. The Antagonists used to have twelve cards with a description of all the most unclean Redeemers who were to be killed on sight. Now there are thirteen.'

'And I bet you were delighted when you heard: Thomas Cale, the big "I am".'

'What's that supposed to mean?'

'You know damn well.'

'I never asked you to come after me. What are you *doing* here?' It was a question delivered with as much bile as he was capable of. And it stung.

'I keep asking myself the same question.'

'Well, it's a pity you didn't ask it in Memphis. Or anywhere else but here. For God's sake, as if I didn't have enough to worry about.'

'I didn't notice you complaining when I kept you alive while you played at being Fritigern the Frightful on the steps of old Materazzi's palace. And when you charged down the hill at Silbury like the bloody stupid berk you are over that treacherous beezle Arbell bloody Swan-Neck I saved your life a dozen times while you were thrashing about like a fish on a slab.'

There was a poisonous stay. And it was Cale who spoke first.

'I think you'll find that at Silbury Hill you didn't save my life above half a dozen times. But it's good to know you were counting.'

'I think you'll find I had a better view of what happened there than you did.'

'I'm not a stupid berk,' said Cale.

'Yes, you are,' replied Vague Henri. 'We need to think about how to get away and now.'

'Now you're the one being a berk. There's nowhere to get away *to*. In case you've gone deaf: we're surrounded by murderous bastards on all three sides. When we were in Memphis I didn't notice anyone there had a good word to say for the Antagonists. Just because they're not Redeemers doesn't mean it's all cigarette trees and a lie-in on Sundays.'

'They can't be worse than the Redeemers.'

'Yes they can. And even if they're not – as far as they're concerned we're Redeemers and me in particular. Who do you think I was fighting on the veldt – old Mother Hubbard?'

There was a knock on the door, which was instantly opened by the guard outside. It was Bosco. He was a lot less cheerful than the last time they'd seen him.

'The Pope has confirmed your appointment, temporarily. You must sign these.' He laid out two documents on the table.

'What are they?'

'Warrants.'

'What sort of warrant?'

'This one is for the execution of the Maid of Blackbird Leys.'

'She's just a girl.'

'Clearly not. Sign.'

'No.'

'Why?'

'I told you – she's just a girl.'

'You know she nailed placards on the doors of churches in the eight towns criticizing the Pope's burning of heretics as being contrary to the merciful teachings of the Hanged Redeemer. How could you do such a thing and expect to live?'

'And do the stars still shine?'

'You're being ridiculous. You know very well she must not live but die.'

And indeed he did know. It was surprising she had not caught fire spontaneously so great were the number of her inflammatory crimes. 'Let me list them for you,' said Bosco. 'Written words on a church door. Death. She criticized the Pope. Death. She showed consideration for the lives of heretics. Death. And she offered an opinion about the human quality of the Hanged Redeemer. Death. And had been a woman while she did so. Whipping. And all of this while dressed as a man so that she could manage to reach the door during the night. Death.' He gestured to the warrant. 'Sign if you please. Sign if you don't please. But sign.'

'Why does it need my signature?'

'Because the Pope is merciful he may not sign death warrants. They must be signed by the commander of the military wing of the Redeemers in Chartres. And that, as of this morning, is you.'

'As I'm the commander I've decided to think about it.'

'Oddly enough, it's not quite that simple. When you leave here, which should be by this afternoon, the next most senior military cleric in the city, which is to say me, becomes commander of the garrison. And I *will* sign.'

'Then there's no problem.'

'Yes there is. Signing this warrant is a great honour, as is attending the execution of that warrant. If you don't sign it will mean that your first act as a direct appointee of the Pontiff is to insult the One True Faith. Egregiously. You will be removed from office and then you'll be good for neither man nor beast. She's dead whatever you do. Sign.'

Cale looked at him, sullen and deflated.

'Van Owen,' he said, at last, 'Van Owen is the next most senior military cleric in the city.'

'Not,' said Bosco, quietly, 'when you sign the second warrant.'

*

As you will know if you've ever attended two of them, one execution is very much like another: the crowd, the wait, the arrival, the shouts, the screaming, the long or short death, the blood or ashes on the ground.

It was a feature of the Redeemers' dealings with one another that they were as obsequious and fawning as they were disdainful and arbitrary towards anyone who was not. Outside of the occasional reign of terror concerning Antagonist conspiracy or fiddling with boys, Redeemers were indulgent when it came to each other's sins. Even when it came to the grave matter of boys it was something that had to be witnessed mid-fiddle by an ordained Redeemer if the charge were to stick. As the consequences of bringing a false accusation – which is to say a true accusation that failed – the results for the accuser were hideous. The Redeemers were able to congratulate themselves that such filthiness was rare by ensuring that only the most desperate victims made a fuss. Most of these victims soon came to regret it.

Usually very cautious about punishing one of their own, the decision to blame Van Owen for the defeat in front of the Golan was unprecedented. Van Owen, therefore, was to be charged with treachery not incompetence. It was, after all, improbable that a general who had always fought well in the past should suddenly lead his men so badly. It was obvious therefore that this was an example of something that was often used to explain great Redeemer defeats: 'The stab in the back.' The Battle of

Eight Martyrs had been a stab in the back because it was as plain as the nose on your face that Van Owen was a secret Antagonist traitor and had conspired to create a defeat out of certain victory.

Van Owen was tried in his absence to ensure he did not use the occasion to spread any filthy Antagonist lies and this was what brought him to the Square of Emancipation mid-afternoon only three days after he had been condemned. However, even the Redeemer Bishop of Verona, head of the Sodality of the Black Cordelias who had suffered such terrible losses, had not objected when Van Owen's sentence was passed along with the not inconsiderable privilege of being hanged before he was burned. While personally he would have liked to disembowel Van Owen with a blunt shovel for causing the near annihilation of the Black Cordelias, even he was unwilling to break that precedent. One never knew after all.

The Notable Redeemers, led by a sulky looking Cale, sat on a platform overlooking the Square of Emancipation and two scaffolds. The Pope was not there and neither was Vague Henri. There was a good crowd, though, waiting with a seething good humour for someone to take the blame.

When he appeared between four guards there was a ripple of excitement from the crowd, some wild applause, a few indecent gibes and a fierce joy which, as the historian Solerine said later, 'made them resemble rather wild beasts than men'. Despite the many guards, the crowd pushed further towards the scaffold so they could get a better look. As was the custom the Dominican Overseer Novella ordered Van Owen to be stripped of his robe. Although he remained wearing a woollen tunic there was loudly muttered disapproval from the back of the Redeemer platform.

'Is this really necessary?'

But it was too late to intervene and Van Owen had removed his robe as obediently as if he were a child about to be punished. Knowing this was coming he had intended to say something pious at this point about how much he had dearly loved to wear that holy gown but fear had dried his mouth and the words stuck. Then an increasingly white-faced Overseer Novella led him over to the ladder. Van Owen asked for water and so distracted was the Overseer by the horror of performing something which, when it was an idea in a courtroom, he had most enthusiastically set out to accomplish, that he forgot himself enough to give him his own hip-flask. Van Owen wanted to wet his throat so he could speak but the executioner, more used to the reality of these occasions than Novella, realized what Van Owen was up to and had no intention of permitting any heroism to spoil the punishment.

'Abandon the idea of gabbing about your lack of guilt. Follow the example of our Holy Redeemer on the gallows and keep your mouth shut.' Then he was roughly pushed up the ladder. Halfway up, the executioner, cheered on by the ogling crowd, started playing the buffoon by giving a bow and nearly slipped and fell off. This disgraceful behaviour acted like salts under the nose of Novella and he furiously shouted at the executioner. This rattled him so much that by the time they had reached the top of the ladder all his swagger had been replaced by alarm. Van Owen began to say his last words.

'Into thy hands, O Lord, I commend my spirit and hope that I will today light such a candle as will never be pu—'

This carefully rehearsed farewell was interrupted by such a premature and hefty shove that he not only fell in the halter around his neck and had it instantly broken but was pushed so ineptly and so hard that he also began swinging back and forth like the pendulum on a clock. Rather than using his good sense to climb on the firewood and steady the already dead man, the Redeemer charged with setting the fire anxiously fired it with a torch at once. The wood was seasoned and soaked in oil and went up magnificently. Unfortunately as the corpse swung back and forth through the fire, like a child on a swing, as if by devilment a strong wind rose up and blew the flames away from it. The crowd gasped in fear at this. 'A miracle! A miracle!' But in a minute the wind dropped and the swinging slowed and soon the crowd pressed forward again to get a better look.

After a few minutes with the crowd gawping on in horror and fascination the fire completely burnt away the rope binding Van Owen's arms. So intense was the heat that it caused his right hand to move slowly upwards and as it did so it seemed to point accusingly at the crowd. Later it was put about by the Office for the Propagation of the Faith that this was not the sign of a curse by Van Owen on the faithful for having wished the death of an innocent man but his bestowal of a blessing as a sign of repentance.

The Redeemers on the platform were heartily sick of the whole process by now and some had the grace to be guilty and ashamed for what they had done. However it was not over yet. It was the task of the Arrabiate to humiliate the corpses of heretics and ten of them duly marched out dragging a heavy bag of the stones of repentance and remorse. In a line in front of the now much-burnt body, they immediately set about pelting the corpse with their fist-sized rocks so that from time to time fragments of the half-consumed body fell down in the fire. 'It rained,' wrote Solerine, 'blood and entrails.'

Few people outside the hegemon of the Redeemers or Antagonists will have seen a live burning. In the popular imagination of those who live in the four quarters, their experience is shaped by the vast pyres of winter festivals where the dummy of Guy Fawkes or General Curly Wurly is set on fire on top of a mountain of wood. The reality is more mundane and so by many degrees more horrible. Imagine if you would the bonfire at the bottom of the garden of a moderately well-off merchant. Then imagine burning alive an adult pig on such a modest pile.

You will understand why then I will not speak of the fifteen minutes it took the Maid of Blackbird Leys to die, of the screams beyond a pitch and sound you could ever expect to hear from a human throat, and the smell and, good God, the time it took. And throughout Cale watched and watched and did not look away, not once. And, after all, even the most dreadful martyrdom must run its course.

'What was it like?' asked Vague Henri.

'If you wanted to know you should have come.'

'Tell me it was quick.'

'It was very far from quick.'

'It wasn't your fault.'

'But you blame me anyway.'

'No.'

'Yes. You think I should have used my power to magic her away to somewhere safe – wherever that would be. If I knew a place of safety I'd go there myself. Perhaps you think I should have leapt from the platform of the Blessed and cut her hands and sprouted wings and flown away.'

'I didn't say that.'

'I rescued an innocent maiden in peril of her life

twice before and look at how many thousands died as a result of me sticking my big nose into things I had no business trying to change.'

'I know it's not your fault. I feel bad, that's all.'

'Not bad enough to come and watch with her.'

Vague Henri said nothing. And after all what was there to say?

Within a few hours they were out of Chartres and approaching the swiftly emerging camp of the quickly formed Eighth Army, already protected by ditches, banks and wooden palisades. Within minutes of his arrival he was examining the new Laconic swords that had caused such devastation to the ranks of the Black Cordelias. He tried its curved angle on several Redeemer helmets stuck on some wooden heads. All but one split open with the first blow. He went back to his tent and had a think for twenty minutes and then turned to Vague Henri.

'I want you to take thirty wagons over to the dump where they're keeping the Materazzi armour and bring me all the helmets you can find. Take fifty men, order more if you need them. Send a rider back as soon as you get there with half a dozen so I can test them.'

'Too late to go now.'

'Then go tomorrow. I want to see Gil.' Gil was there within five minutes.

'I want you to get me a dozen dead dogs,' said Cale.

'Where am I going to get dead dogs out here?'

'They don't have to be dogs and there don't have to be twelve. Twenty-four dead cats will do. Understand?'

'Yes.'

'I don't want you cutting the throats of some peasant's family pet. I need them rotten. I need them falling off the bone.'

'Redeemer Bosco would like to see you.'

Cale smiled.

'Always. Show him in.'

They talked around the houses for a few minutes and Cale went to every polite length he could not to raise the subject on both their minds so that his old mentor would be forced to raise the subject first.

'So,' said Bosco, at last. 'May I see your plans?'

'I don't have any plans. Not written down, as such.'

'And, as such, what do you have?'

'I'm still thinking.'

'And will you share your thoughts?'

'I need a day or two.'

'One or two?'

'Two. Probably.'

'And what if they attack before then?'

'It will be Plan B I suppose.'

'Which is?'

'Don't know, Redeemer. Don't even have a Plan A yet.'

'Taunting me is childish.'

317

'If I was taunting you, it would be. You have questions. But I don't have answers.'

'I understand these would be approximate.'

'No. You say you understand but you won't understand when I tell you.'

'I will.'

'No, you won't. You just think you will.'

'So the answer is, "No".'

'The answer is yes – but not yet.'

Five minutes later, as Cale knew he would be, Gil was in Bosco's tent and reporting to his master.

'He wants two thousand rusty helmets and twelve dead dogs.'

# 18

Within two weeks, by means of a traveller in medicines whose drugs were, if you were lucky, completely useless, Kleist and his heavily pregnant wife had news of the great events in the Golan.

There had been a great battle between the Redeemers and the Laconics – terrible slaughter had been done and the army of the Redeemers had been destroyed almost to the last man. Needless to say this delighted Kleist, although not for long. He nearly swallowed his tongue when he heard the story, much embroidered for the mountain yokels, of how the day had been rescued by a mere boy, and that this boy, Cale, was now being hailed as the Angel of Death capable of raising his own spirit a mile high.

'So this friend of yours,' said Daisy later when they were lying in bed as she rested her aching back and terrible piles and tried to untangle the garbled news they'd heard.

'He's not my friend . . .'

'This friend of yours, he is not the Angel of Death capable of raising his spirit a mile high?'

'Oh, he's the Angel of Death all right – wherever

Cale goes a funeral follows. He's got funerals in his brain.'

'But he can't conjure spirits?'

'No.'

'Pity – a friend who could conjure spirits a mile high would be pretty useful.'

'Well, he can't. And I told you, wherever he goes a lot of screaming goes with him. That's why I was trying to put as much distance between him and me as I could. If I hadn't met you I'd be on the far side of the moon if I knew how to get there.'

'Oh,' she sighed, full of sorrow. 'My poor arsehole.'

She said nothing further until the pain had subsided then handed him a jar with the cream the medicaster had sold her. 'Put it on for me.'

'What?'

'Put it on for me.'

He looked at her.

'You do it.'

'I'm too fat. I can't reach that far. It's easier for you to do it.'

'Can't you get your sister?'

'Don't be disgusting. Get on with it.'

He knew well enough by now when she was not to be argued with. It was not that he lacked medical skill. The Redeemers were famously good at tending injuries on account of the fact that people were always trying to kill them. Treating piles was not an injury as set out in the *Manifesto Catholico*, their medical handbook, but at least being gentle with injuries was not unknown to him. Still there was a sharp intake of breath from the unfortunate girl.

'Sorry.'

'It's all right.'

After a few more seconds he was finished and the pain in Daisy's bottom began to subside.

'Thank you.'

'You're welcome.'

'Liar. I'll bet you didn't think you'd be doing this a year ago.' Now Daisy just throbbed and she breathed a long sigh of relief. 'Lie down with me.' She waited as he did as he was told. 'There's something I want to talk to you about.'

'What?'

'Promise you won't sulk?'

'Why don't you just get on with it?'

'You're going on too many robberies. It's too danger-ous.'

'Believe me I know what risk is – and I don't take them. I never get within five hundred yards of anything sharp.'

'I *do* believe you – about you staying safe. But we're going on twice as many raids as we used to because of you.'

'And?'

'The Musselmen aren't going to just let that go on.

There are Musselmen mercenaries who know how to fight better than we do.'

'Anyone can fight better than you do. Dropping a rock on someone's head when they're not looking only gets you so far.'

'There you are then. Everyone's got greedy. It can't last.'

'Your father – he'll have a stroke if I refuse to go. And I'll be as popular as a case of piles if I refuse to help.'

'You understand what I mean, though?'

'Yes.'

'I'll talk to my father. I just wanted to talk to you first.'

'And if I'd said you couldn't?'

She looked at him, more astonished than annoyed.

'Don't be ridiculous.'

It was said of the tragically unfortunate Sharon of Tunis that she was doomed always to tell the truth but never to be believed. The Klephts may not have been hostile to women who showed a will of their own but they were no more enthusiastic about opinions they did not care to hear than people generally are. At first her father's irritation was solely directed at Daisy, who was angrily told to keep her big nose out of matters that had nothing to do with her. Affronted by his father-in-law's abrupt manner of speaking to his wife, Kleist defended her reasons and so brought on the general accusation that this was his idea all along and that he was using his wife as a shield for opinions that were really his, a strategy so common among the Klephts it was known as turning the cat in the pan. He was accused of laziness, cowardice and ingratitude, normally qualities that the Klephts positively admired when they were the source of them. No one except Daisy's sister and a few of her friends would speak to them and it was made clear that if Kleist refused to help there would be trouble in the shape of a vote – foregone – to ostracize them both.

The pair were faced with either leaving in the cold weather, with Daisy heavily pregnant and nowhere to go, or staying and doing as they were told. If there was a choice Kleist didn't know what it was. It wasn't giving in that bothered him. Daisy burnt with indignation and let her father know it but Kleist was more used to a lifetime of hostile but silent obedience. Still, it was a glum pair who backed down.

More news about Cale also made him uneasy. It was only partly that it stirred up unwelcome feelings of guilt – not about Cale but about Vague Henri – but also that it raised the ghost of something buried even deeper, so much so that he had never quite faced it directly. While Vague Henri had never once taken seriously the idea that there might be something unhuman about Cale's talent for killing, the garbled rumours that had made it to the Quantocks, however ridiculous he would normally have held them to be, stretched a nerve in Kleist's soul. From a distance the idea of Cale as a kind of living ghost going around the place causing supernatural

## 19

'Why aren't they advancing?' Bosco both wanted to hear what Cale had to say about the incomprehensible inaction of the Laconics and also to reassure himself that Cale realized just how incomprehensible it was.

Cale did not look up at Bosco as he asked this but kept on examining the half-dozen Materazzi helmets strapped to their wooden heads.

'Do you expect to find out?' he said to Bosco, still not looking up.

'I do not.'

'Then why worry about it?'

'You've turned very insolent.'

This time Cale did look at Bosco.

'Am I wrong?'

Bosco smiled, still never a pretty sight.

'No. You are not wrong.'

The master blacksmith he'd been waiting for arrived and Cale showed him a spare helmet.

'What do you think?' asked Cale.

'Good workmanship and good steel but the rust is too bad on this one I'd say. I wouldn't want it protecting my head. Can I look at the others?'

'When I've finished. Stand back.'

And with that he gave each of the six Materrazi helmets a ferocious set of blows with one of the curved Laconic swords. 'Help me take them off,' he said to the blacksmith when he'd finished. Three had held up well, one was damaged, two had been broken through.

'By tomorrow we should have a couple of thousand of these delivered.'

'In the same condition?'

'Probably. Not sure.' He gestured at the helmets that he'd pierced.

'Can you repair them – weld an iron plate to the top?'

The blacksmith examined them carefully for a full minute.

'Master, I think I could do something to strengthen them. How long do I have?'

'I don't know. A couple of days, at least, maybe longer. Do them as quickly as you can. Order in as many smiths as you can get here. The first batch will be here this afternoon. The Quartermaster has been told to give you everything you need. Come direct to me if there are problems. You're not to go through anyone else. Understand?'

The blacksmith looked at Bosco. Cale thought about making a point and decided against it. Bosco nodded.

'Yes, master.'

After he'd left Bosco could not stop himself from asking: 'Why do you need the dogs?'

'When I was in the veldt the Folk always left a dead animal in the water tanks to make life awkward. If there was a well they'd leave one there too.'

'I see.'

'No, you don't see,' said Cale. 'With standing water you can't hide the fact it's poisoned because of the smell. The Laconics are taking their water from the stream that runs past their camp. The dogs are going in upstream where the Laconics won't be able to smell anything.'

'If it's running water the poison will be diluted.'

'Yes.'

'The Redeemers at Silbury Hill all had the squits and they still won.'

'Yes.'

'You know that poisoning water is a mortal sin?'

'Then it's lucky for me I have no soul.'

The twelve dead dogs turned into eight dead pigs and a box of pigeons all suitably rancid and carefully placed by Vague Henri and twenty Purgators as close to the Laconic camp as they dared. In the middle of the night in freezing water and handling large amounts of putrid animal it was as pleasant a task as you might imagine.

Four days had passed and still there was no movement from the Laconics. The state of the helmets brought by Vague Henri could have been better, could have been worse and the smiths were well on the way to Cale's lowest target of two thousand strengthened helmets.

'Will you discuss your tactics with me now?' Cale was thrown a little by Bosco's cool but respectful tone. He considered stalling not because his tactics were unready but simply in order to be awkward. On the other hand much as he hated Bosco he was, besides Vague Henri, the only person who could properly appreciate his brilliance. Besides, he wanted to test it out against his old master and Princeps. It had been Princeps who had won the actual victory of mud and violence at Silbury even if the campaign had been planned by Cale. He was sure that his plans to destroy the Materazzi at Silbury would have worked no matter who was in command but after they'd made such a ballsucking tooze out of the whole battle how could you tell for sure? Granted he had made mistakes on the veldt but nobody was perfect and he'd learnt from them and the Folk were now banged up on their miserable prairie and not a squeak out of them in two months. Still, he could not afford a mistake against the Laconics. He needed to test his ideas but only against people he respected. And with the exception of Vague Henri the people he respected he also hated.

So it was that, sensitive to criticism and also pleased with himself, Cale set out the map of his plans to defeat the strongest army the Laconics had ever put into the field at one time and whose record of loss under such circumstances was unrecorded, presumably because it had never happened.

'The Laconics move more easily and quickly than any soldiers I've ever seen or read about. From the bluff I could see they only strengthened the right wing of their attack two minutes before they struck – that's where they break their opponents. They have their best men on the right and in a moment they move men out of the middle and are suddenly twice as strong where they're already strongest.'

'And so?' said Bosco.

'We must double the strength on the left.'

'Simple as that?' said Princeps.

'Not so simple.' He didn't mind this, Cale, a good question he had an answer to. 'Make them this deep without preparation and they just become a crowd – pushing and shoving and falling over each other. I've had them practising twelve hours a day to do it this deep. The more the Laconics delay an attack the better we get.'

'And the helmets.'

'There are only enough to go four deep on the right and two deep on the rest of the line.'

'Isn't there any chance to get more?'

'No. Most of them rusted out in the open. The ones we saved were buried deep in the pile. It was a great waste leaving them there.'

There was a silence enjoyed by Cale but not by Bosco or Princeps, though it was hardly their fault. 'In any case, if the Laconics break through further than four deep on the right I don't think we'd have much chance anyway. We lost so easily at Eight Martyrs because the late Van Owen, God rest his soul, was kind enough to plan to their every advantage.'

'And you won't?' said Princeps.

'No. If they do come on and avoid attacking the Heights then there's a point here where I'll try to fight.' He placed a finger on the map.

'It looks as flat as Eight Martyrs,' said Princeps.

'But it isn't. I noticed when I went through here and I've ridden over it half a dozen times since. The rise here in the middle of the plain, it's really gradual but it deceives. It's much more like a hill than it looks and it cuts the plain in two. You couldn't advance an army in a line down here like at Eight Martyrs – you've got to go one way or the other. I'm building a stockade on this rise for bowmen – the Laconics won't make it to the clashing point without taking twice the dead and wounded they did before. And I think I can make it worse. Over here is the slope of the Golan – too steep and far away for archers. I need to show you.'

It was half an hour later on the plain in front of the camp and the light was beginning to go. Hooke was, of course, missing his hideous red beard and his head was completely shaved but Bosco recognized him immediately.

'This is Chesney Fancher,' said Cale.

'Master Fancher.' A nod from Bosco, a silent nod from Princeps.

The problem in trying to introduce new ideas to a Redeemer (and what is a good weapon but a good idea made murderous flesh?) was that they disapproved so much of them. Ideas came out of thinking and thinking was something human beings were extremely bad at doing. But as St Augustine of Hippo, the nearest thing to a philosopher the Redeemers possessed, once said: 'The human mind is poorly formed for thinking. Like amputation, it should be performed only by the highly trained, and then rarely.' Even Bosco and Princeps, dangerously independent thinkers in their way, were not going to be easily convinced. In the callous way of youth Cale had wanted to use live pigs in his demonstration of the use of Hooke's adapted mortars. Hooke had persuaded him that, aside from his own squeamishness, the impossibility of strapping armour designed for a man on to inevitably recalcitrant pigs would be asking for trouble. Reluctantly Cale agreed. But not for the second demonstration. For this Cale insisted on live animals. At least, Hooke comforted himself, however hideous the second demonstration would be quick.

Cale gave the two Redeemers a tour of the two sites to the suspicious bewilderment of both. The first was a line of sixteen dead pigs, two deep, with bits of Materazzi armour strapped to the carcasses where they could be made to fit. The second, fifty yards away, was a pen with a dozen live pigs grunting happily next to three large wooden boxes tightly bound with rope.

Having retired behind a five-foot-high wall of thick logs about a hundred yards from the dead pigs and with Hooke having taken hold of a large red flag on the end of a pole, the Redeemers watched as Cale signalled him to begin. Hooke waved the large flag energetically in the air. Nothing had happened for about thirty seconds when the two expectant Redeemers saw a dense cloud appear in the air high up over the pigs and then land all at once with a series of light and heavy thwacking noises. Cale led the two priests back to the line of pigs and invited them to inspect the damage. Within an area of forty square yards the ground was thickly covered in the eight-inch-long bolts from the two dozen mortars positioned about eight hundred yards away on the Golan. Of those bolts that had hit the pigs not much more than an inch was sticking out of their flesh. But even the bolts that had struck armour had penetrated the flesh beneath to a depth of three or four inches.

'We can put fifty of these mortars on ledges halfway up the Golan. From that high up we can reach more than a mile into the valley. As long as I can force the Laconics to come up the left channel we can reach their right flank at least and probably deeper.' They asked questions but not many. It was hard not to be impressed. From fifty yards away the live pigs grunted at them as if in persuasive agreement.

'We'll need to go back,' Cale said to the two men. But this time a nervous-looking Hooke did not go with them but walked over to the pig pen, where one of Cale's Purgators was waiting with a lighted torch. Behind the wall of logs Cale, nervous himself but hiding it better than Hooke, signalled him to begin. He walked away from the pen along with the Purgator but the latter stopped about thirty yards from the pen while Hooke continued and suddenly disappeared into a large trench. There was a shout from Hooke, then the Purgator dropped his torch on the ground and, specially chosen for his speed, legged it over the field like a man pursued by Hummity and vanished into the trench beside Hooke. About five seconds later the gates of hell opened in the pig pen and a vast pit of fire erupted around the animals with a bang! like the end of the world.

Even Cale, who knew what to expect, nearly split his skin but Bosco and Princeps had been so shocked and startled they had fallen to the ground, driven not only by fear but by an irresistible physical convulsion away from such hideous power. In his heart Cale enjoyed their humiliation almost as much as the successful carnage he could see had taken place in the pig pen. He gave them five minutes to recover themselves and then led the appalled men over to Hooke and the Purgator, who were standing by the pig pen, and what was left of the pigs who once occupied it, waiting for their inspection. It had, as Hooke as Fancher hoped, been quick but the damage was beyond anything either of the two priests could easily grasp. The grisly process and effect of executions was something they had witnessed frequently – but these judicial deaths had been slow and laboured – that, after all, had been the point. What they saw in front of them, these bigger-than-human bodies scoured of internal organs, legs and heads was the mark of a power that was terrible but not human. This was the violence of another world and it was ungraspable to them. They could not have been more shocked if the devil himself had flown here and torn the pigs apart with his bare hands.

Nevertheless, Cale and Hooke were still astonished when an hour later, and still white with horror, Bosco refused to let Cale use this abominable engine against the Laconic mercenaries.

'Do you realize,' he said, 'what the Curia will do when they find out about these eruptions? They'll make such a bonfire out of every one of us they'll be able to warm their buttocks on it in Memphis. Do you and this loon have no idea what you've let loose today?'

'What we've let loose, Lord Redeemer,' shouted back a furious Cale, 'is the one sure way to defeat an army who've already wiped the floor with you. And if they do it again they can march all the way to the throne of the Hanged Redeemer in Chartres without anyone to so much as piss on them.'

This extravagant but substantially true claim seemed to startle them both into silence. Princeps and Hooke as Fancher looked on in amazement at this fishwife exchange between the great prelate and the boy who was not a boy but the indignation-of-God-made-flesh. In control of himself now it was Cale who spoke again first.

'If I lose there will be no second chance. This is what you wanted from me.'

'The time is not yet right to move against the Curia.'

'What other time will there be?'

It was not possible to disagree and once Bosco realized that everything he had worked towards for thirty years had come to the great pinch of action he said little more. If it was not now it would be never.

'We must go now if we are to prepare events in Chartres. If you have a victory, send news, surely and quickly. If not the Laconics will bring the news for you.'

And that was that. He left the tent without saying anything more but returned almost immediately with a letter in his hand. 'I meant to pass this on several days ago. It's from your replacement on the veldt. Thought you'd be interested.' With great show Cale put it in one of his ostentatiously numerous pockets – ostentatious because acolytes were forbidden to have pockets, which stood in the Redeemer faith for all that was secretive and hidden in the human soul. 'Pocket' was a nickname for the devil himself.

Twenty minutes later Bosco and Princeps were on their way to Chartres and Cale was finishing telling Vague Henri what had happened while he was outside the tent trying to listen in. They sat in silence for some time.

'Now might be a chance to slip away – if you wanted to try,' said Cale.

'I thought you said it was too risky.'

'Could be wrong. And now Bosco has to trust me whether he wants to or not. No one will be coming after you. It's risky if you stay – fifty-fifty.'

'I can't go.'

It was clear Vague Henri had something else in mind. 'Why?'

'I can't leave the girls.'

Cale groaned in disbelief. 'There's nothing you can do for them.'

'So I should walk away?'

'If there's nothing you can do, why not?'

'What if you win? What will you do about them?'

'What I can – which is probably not much. Or anything. I don't know what to do about myself – or you.'

'But you know how to beat the greatest army ever put into a war.'

'Possibly.'

'How can that be right?'

'Because beating the Laconics is possible but flying into and out of the Sanctuary on the wings of angels isn't.'

'You want to fight them, don't you?'

'Because I'd rather take my chances doing what I'm good at than running away, which I'm obviously not.'

'It's not just that – you want to fight them. You like this.'

'Tell me what choice I have.'

'Run away.'

'I told you. No. A worse choice isn't a choice.'

'But it's all right for me?'

'I didn't say that. Why are you trying to pick a fight?'

'Look who's talking. Picking a fight is just what you do. It's what you are. You could pick a fight with a one-eyed sloth.'

'That doesn't even make sense. What's a sloth?'

'They have them in the zoo in Memphis.'

'Amiable?'

'Very.'

'If you go up with Hooke on the Golan you should be as safe as anywhere.'

'Right.'

'So – you're not going to insist on staying with me in the thick of battle?'

'No.'

'Showing some sense at last.'

'Are you going to be in the thick of battle?'

'Not if I can help it.'

'You thought that at Eight Martyrs.'

'I'll try to learn from my mistakes.'

'You better not make any this time.'

'No.'

'We can't leave them.'

'We can. Bosco won't kill the girls just for the sake of it.'

'You didn't always think so well of him.'

'I don't. I just know him better. What he thinks I can do matters more to him than his own life. It matters a lot more than the girls in the Sanctuary.'

'And what do *you* think you can do?'

'What's that supposed to mean?'

'Not sure. Maybe it means that you're beginning to like the idea of being a God.'

'You're the one who thinks I can pluck girls out of thin air, not me. All I'm trying to do is stay alive – and, for reasons I can't put my finger on, do the same for you.'

'Tell me you aren't looking forward to tomorrow.'

'I'm not looking forward to tomorrow.'

'I don't believe you.'

'I don't care what you believe.' There was a silence while they both tried to think of something nastier to say. Oddly, it was Cale who backed down.

'He won't kill the girls even if we run,' said Cale.

'Why not?'

'Because if he keeps them they might be useful.'

'You don't know that.'

'No – but it's what I think.'

'It's what you think I want to hear, that's what you think.'

'That, too. But it's true all the same. Everything he

does is for a reason. I used to think he hit me because he was a shit. But it's more complicated than that.'

'You *like* him?'

'I admire him.'

'You like him.'

'He's as mad as a sack of cats – but he thinks every-thing through. I admire that. I *like* that. It's a quality that will save me – save *us* – if I can get him right.'

'If you end up understanding Bosco, you better watch out.'

'Blab! Blab! Blab! Are you talking or is it just the sound of the wind exhafflating from your backside?'

'There's no such word.'

'Prove it.'

## 20

'How can I help you, IdrisPukke? Or to put it another way, what have you got to offer that I could possibly want?'

The man talking was Señor Bose Ikard sitting across from IdrisPukke on the other side of a desk as large as a king's mattress. His expression was one of self-satisfied and cynical certainty – a look that said *I've-got-your-number-and-don't-think-I-haven't.* He was renowned throughout the four quarters as a lawyer, a natural philosopher (he had invented a method of preserving chicken in snow) and, most famously of all, an advisor of great men, particulary King Zog of Switzerland, a man famous as much for his learning as for his stupidity and unsavoury personal habits. It was not a matter of great doubt in the world at large that Switzerland would have lost its renowned ability to stay out of any sort of war for the last five hundred years had it not been for Bose Ikard – but there was considerable doubt as to whether in the widely predicted coming storm even a man so clever and unprincipled would continue to be able to do so. This explained his hostility to the presence of IdrisPukke, a man who had brought that

storm right into the heart of Spanish Leeds and Switzerland.

It had been more than ten years since IdrisPukke and
Señor Bose Ikard had spoken and even then it was not a
conversation in the normal sense, unless you count the
latter passing a sentence of death on the former and
asking him if he had anything to say before he did so.
Ikard knew perfectly well that IdrisPukke was not guilty
of the charge of murder for the simple reason that he
had himself ordered the killing for which IdrisPukke
was in the dock. There were no particular hard feelings
between them because the verdict was itself a way
merely of putting pressure on the Gauleiters who then
employed IdrisPukke. At the time the Gauleiters valued
him highly enough to hand over one of Bose Ikard's
political opponents who had taken refuge, as he thought,
with them on the grounds that they were sympathetic to
his cause (a complicated one, passionately avowed, few
could now be found to give any kind of coherent
account of it). In fact the Gauleiters actually were sympathetic to his cause – but not enough to prevent them
agreeing to the swap of IdrisPukke for the exile who on
his enforced return was summarily executed.

These days Ikard was in a more or less continuous
state of political irritation. For himself in everyday matters he was a pleasant enough fellow and would continue
to be pleasant even as his henchpeople were shoving
your remains into an isolated hole along with half a bag

of quick lime. He was, as Vipond described him, 'almost your standard political villain but much more sly. His greatest weakness is he thinks that everyone who will not admit to seeing the world as he does is a hypocrite.'

It was Vipond's presence in Spanish Leeds, the largest of Switzerland's border cities, that was the cause of Ikard's concern. Admittedly it was not Vipond as such who was the problem but the spavined but still substantial remains of the Materazzi who had fled there. They had, in Ikard's opinion, disgracefully easily lost their empire only to descend on his determinedly neutral country and become a serious bloody nuisance, and were threatening to be something worse. He had tried to pursue his standard policy when it came to allies who were no longer useful – offer them all aid short of help. Unfortunately King Zog of Switzerland was a sentimental snob and insisted on providing shelter and financial assistance to fellow royalty in distress. Ikard regarded this as both ruinously expensive in itself and fertile ground for God knew what unforeseeable problems. It was trying to work out what these problems might be that had made him decide to talk to IdrisPukke, having made the ostentatious point of refusing to do the same for his half-brother on the grounds that the most sensible course was 'to encourage the old bastard to feel as unwelcome as possible'.

'So,' he said to IdrisPukke. 'What can you do for me?'

'Your honesty is, as always, refreshing, Señor.'

'I'm sorry you think so.'

'As it happens, I *can* be of use.'

'Yes?'

'I am in the way of being able to arrange a defection that will be, in my view, of enormous advantage to you.'

'The last time I heard someone beat about the bush so they were trying to sell me shares in an expedition to Eldorado.'

'It's a Redeemer soldier, very young, so valuable to them that he alone was the cause of their attack on the Materazzi. You haven't heard of him?'

'No.'

'Then your intelligencers are very much less competent than they used to be.'

'All right. Thomas Cale.'

'What do you know?'

'What do *you* know?'

'Considerably more than you.'

'I am very willing to listen.'

And that's what he did. It was certainly most interesting and certainly most peculiar.

'Is that all?'

'Of course not. Have the Redeemers made contact with you?'

'Ye-ees.'

'You don't seem sure.'

'No. I distinctly remember. Absolutely frightful pair. One of them had teeth that were positively green.'

'And they wanted?'

'To express their disapproval of our help to the Materazzi.'

'Such as it is.'

'That merely sounds ungrateful. I think, all things considered, that we've treated them rather better than old man Materazzi would have done, peace be upon him, had the positions been reversed.'

'It suits you to think so.'

'True – but it's still what I think.'

'And what did you tell them?'

'The Redeemers? I told them to fuck off.'

'How very gratifying.'

'This monstrous prodigy of yours. What does he want and why should I give it to him?'

'He wants safe passage over the borders.'

'I can't think it would be a good idea to bring in a fellow when the Redeemers are ready to risk so much to get him back. Quite how the Materazzi managed to collapse so pathetically I'll never understand but I'd say that on the basis of the evidence it was unwise to go anywhere near him.'

'That depends.'

'On?'

'Whether you want this monstrous prodigy – a good term for him by the way – on their territory pissing into yours or on your territory pissing into theirs.'

'He seems a very troublesome young person.'

'He's coming here anyway.'

'How so?'

'Because they'll use him to destroy the Antagonists and when they've finished with them they'll come for you. And leading them will be a not at all happy Thomas Cale, very displeased that you told him to fuck off when he only offered you the hand of friendship. The Redeemers absolutely will not stop. Whether you're a heretic or a non-believer it's all one to them.'

'Why would they go on a crusade now? They haven't bothered in six hundred years.'

'Because they're changing. And if you don't buck your ideas up you're going to go the way of the Materazzi.'

'Why should I believe you?'

'You know something, I'm almost offended. Help me to bring Cale in.'

'I'll have to consider all this.'

'I wouldn't take too long if I were you.'

Señor Bose Ikard was certainly very much more alarmed after IdrisPukke had left than before he arrived. He fancied he could tell when he was bluffing but today he sounded altogether too convincing. On the other hand he knew, as IdrisPukke did not, that the Laconics had finally agreed to march on the Golan. Once the Redeemers and their adolescent monstrosity had been in a real fight with those murderous pederasts from Laconia he'd decide whether they were a threat or not.

Till then IdrisPukke could go and whistle 'Paddington Polly' – and his murderous brat along with him.

Go into any corner bibliothèque and you will find a hundred books on the flight of the Materazzi after the fall of Memphis: books fantastical, magical, mystical, historical, rough and ready, elegant mythical, hard-boiled tragical, plain and to the point, blackly embroidered, red with blood and suffering – somewhere in all of it will be the truth. To tell a tenth of it would be dull beyond enduring, in that one tale of horror and pain in such a time of bitter cold and scantiness becomes much like another. It's dreadful to say but there it is. A hard time they had of it before the four thousand escapees made it in half that number to Spanish Leeds, where their welcome had not been much warmer than their journey there.

'Well?' said Vipond when IdrisPukke wandered back to the recently vacated Jewish ghetto, the Chief Rabbi having decided that the Redeemers being in the ascendant it was time to put as great a distance between them and his congregation as was humanly possibly – which was to say so far that any further and they would be on their way back.

IdrisPukke gave his half-brother a summary.

'Will he see me?'

'No.'

'To be fair, neither would I in his position.'

'You men of the world,' mocked IdrisPukke. 'So shocking.'

'Will he see you again perhaps?'

'It depends. You know his type – always want you to know they've got a finger up your arse.'

'So to speak.'

'He's uncertain what to do next, for all his vanity. But he wants you off his municipality as soon as he can. Depending on that old bastard Zog's kindness isn't much of a guarantee.'

'No.' There was a long silence.

'What do you think Cale will do?'

'What can he do but wait? Ikard has put most of his troops to the margins. Cale and Vague Henri are facing six hundred miles of Antagonist trenches and a two-hundred-mile line of twitchy Swiss border troops. He'll be staying put, I'd say.'

There was a knock on the door which was instantly opened from outside. The guard, all reverence and solicitude, showed Arbell Materazzi into the room. She might well be the last ruler of the Materazzi, a rump now so diminished as to be barely thought of as being ruled, but at least she looked like the almost queen she was. Older, more beautiful, suffering having given her a kind of grey power to her looks. Everything had changed in only a few months, her world destroyed, her father dead, now first among the remaining Materazzi, married to her cousin, Conn, and heavily pregnant.

## 21

It was another four days before the Laconics began to move, as Cale had hoped, around the back of the Golan and directly to take Chartres. Whatever the losses they had taken of their profoundly precious soldiers during the victory on the Machair these deaths had to be balanced against their need for Antagonist silver. Their only alternative to the money gained from hiring out military power was the wealth provided by the vast number of Helot serfs who lived in Laconia and the enslaved countries that surrounded it on nearly all sides. They could terrorize the Helots and purge their leaders but doing so only decreased the Laconics' income – a dead slave was a dead slave – and ensured that the Helots repeatedly threatened to rebel because the Laconics killed them in large numbers whether they did so or not. Every cull of a few thousand Helots made them smug in the short term but more suspicious in the long. Unafraid of death, they were nevertheless terrified of annihilation. This was what drove the Laconics back to the battlefield and the attack on Chartres.

Cale's immediate concern was that the Laconics might have worked out that the Redeemers were going to try and stop them with the wall of the Golan on one side and, admittedly, only a slight rise on the other. The rise did little more than inhibit their level of sight of a much bigger field of battle, but for all its apparent unimportance it was almost as good as a great stone wall in that it would serve to funnel them into a much narrower space than anything before or after it. Once Cale could engage them not even the Laconics would be able to rearrange themselves mid-battle.

Unfortunately for Cale the newly elected Laconic King, Jeremy Stuart-Clarke, had indeed seen the problem but his choices were limited: he could move on Chartres via the Golan and risk the dangers of a bottleneck or he could stay where he was and wait, using up the valuable supplies he had only just received and bringing his men not only to a physical halt but also a mental one. However well disciplined, no soldier was ever a patient man. Soldiers went off the boil and having prepared themselves for a final push after a drearily long wait, stopping dead again was not something King Stuart-Clarke would do without good reason. He did not have one. Moving further south to attack Chartres from the flatter rear would take at least a week and give the Redeemers even more time to prepare – and they had been given enough of that. He knew the Antagonists were about to put extra pressure on them by attacking the trenches that extended west from the Golan – a manoeuvre he could not delay now and which would be completely pointless if he did not press on directly.

He weighed one set of risks against another and given he had already slaughtered one Redeemer army he thought it sensible to continue. Besides, the entire camp had been afflicted with an unpleasant stomach ailment which, while not as bad by a long way as dysentery, had left almost everyone with terrible runs and unpleasant stomach pains. All risks balanced, it made by far the most sense to take the shortest route to Chartres.

It was with a mixture of delight and sudden fear that Cale watched the Laconics, after a pause of nearly three hours, move into his only advantageous defensive battlefield for a hundred miles in any direction. But now it occurred to him that in his two previous experiences of a major battle he had been watching from a place of safety, a dismissive onlooker full of opinions as to what was being wrongly done. Now standing facing this most terrible of armies he was forced to recognize the difference between knowing something and feeling it. Now he felt the difference. For some reason it was a different fear from the one that had left him motionless with terror in the fight with Solomon Solomon in the Red Opera. This time it was his knees that seemed to suffer from terror. They were actually shaking. In the Red Opera it had been a terrible palsy in his chest.

He had ordered a tower built to the rear of his last line of men so that he could see the battle unfold but now he was worried that he would not be able to climb the thin ladder of the lightweight structure. He looked at his knees as if to rebuke them. Stop shaking. Stop. And on came the Laconics in their lazy squares. For a moment everything seemed hopeless, his soldiers weak, his ideas for defence and attack laughable in the face of the great device for killing moving slowly towards them. Then it was one foot on the ladder and another, slowly, a pause, another step. He wanted to be somewhere else, for there to be a rescuer for him, to take him away and keep him safe. Then another step and another. And then like a baby seabird reaching the shore after an over-ambitious swim in a rough sea he eased over onto the platform of the tower and was helped to his feet by the two guards already up there with their oversized shields to shelter him from arrows, bolts and spears. Staring out at the Laconics he calmed himself that it would be all right as long as nothing went wrong with the exploding Villainous Saltpetre.

Which it duly did. It started to rain. Villainous Saltpetre, as Hooke was later to explain, did not like water – or rather it liked water too much. It absorbed the slightest damp the way the desert sand loved rain. Within two minutes of the clouds opening the Villainous Saltpetre was as flammable as a marsh. Knowing this weakness, Hooke had been extremely careful to avoid demonstrating his invention whenever it was wet, not out of a desire to hide its vulnerability but simply because it would not work. His only experience of war-fare had been on the veldt during a time of year when it never rained. In hindsight it seemed obvious that he should have mentioned it but it had simply never occurred to him, at least not until it started raining: the life of the experimenter was quite naturally a life that involved creating the best possible circumstances for his experiment.

Unaware of his damp nemesis, Cale watched the Laconic advance from his tower protected by the two Purgators and waited in high tension to give the signal to set fire to the oil-soaked fuses. It was an ecstatic and agonizing wait, then his signal came and the trumpets blew, harsh as crows. At the first note the front line of the Redeemers stepped back behind the yew stakes driven into the ground and then teams of two waiting hammered in more stakes into the gap so that while it was not a fence, as such, it was impossible for a man to slip between the gap, not least because all the stakes had sharpened meat hooks screwed into the stake itself at ten-inch intervals. Cale had had two teams of two prac-tise their speed for twelve hours a day during the last two weeks and before the lit fuses reached the casks another layer of staggered hooked stakes had been hammered into the ground.

Meanwhile, halfway up the Golan, Cale's plan of bat-tle was disintegrating even further. Even though the rain was already easing off, the strength of the brief downpour was such that not only had it deliquesced the Villainous Saltpetre but it had wet the ropes of the mortars and reduced the power with which they could eject the unusually heavy bolts. Hooke had quickly covered them up but in order to reach the right wing of the advancing Laconics the mortars were operating at the extreme edge of their range. Now the ropes were slightly wet that range was reduced by a quarter, a distance that rendered them useless.

A desperate Hooke had a flag to signal that he was unable to fire and it was duly noted by an alarmed Cale on his rickety tower. He could also see lots of other makeshift flags waving from the Golan. They had not arranged a sign about the Villainous Saltpetre because there had been no good reason to do so. Now the Laconics were approaching the casks, as were the excellently timed burning ends of the fuses.

Another signal from Cale and another ear-cracking blast from the horns beneath him. This time the entire Redeemer front line ducked down and faced away from the caskets, each one curled up into a protective ball. The Laconics kept advancing, breaking into a run just as they had at Eight Martyrs. The fuses burnt as calculated, the Laconics arrived as hoped for and nothing happened. Many stepped on the lightly earth-covered container but though they could feel the ground change beneath them they were in no position to stop. Then one of the boxes exploded, the last but one on the

Laconic right. It had been designed to explode forwards but wood is unreliable stuff and the force of the blast shot out to front and back, killing almost as many Redeemers behind as it did their advancing enemies.

What this single explosion managed to do was bring the Laconic line to an astonished halt. None of them had ever seen such violence, the earth itself blown into the sky and the ear-blasting sound worse than thunder. The ranks shuddered and stopped and staggered back as if a single startled creature. Carnage delivered by the human hand is one thing, horrible in its close and personal gash and mangle of flesh and bone. Think, though, what it was like to witness for the first time the calamity of such a flash of power and smoke. For a moment after the roar of armies striving to come to grips, there was a great and sudden silence as if the hand swipe of some bilious god had lashed the ground between them. Used to delivering the hideous blow or cut, none of them had seen a man ruptured, pulverized and torn in less time than it took to blink.

Slack-jawed and stupefied at the failure of the casks, panic and fear ran riot in Cale. But he was not the only one – King Stuart-Clarke had been thrown from his horse as it reared from its terror at the explosion as had half a dozen of the messengers with him. Frightened horses were bolting everywhere and the attack, the worst of nightmares, had completely stalled and all the vital momentum along a line of a thousand yards was lost. All the commanders had been unseated like the king or were trying to control their mounts. Cale, horrified by the failure of the casks, had a few moments to collect his shattered wits.

He was short of archers but had held them back in any case to pick off the Laconics after they had been hit by all twenty casks, guessing that some were bound to fail. Now he was down the tower and onto his waiting horse and shouting at the four hundred archers in front of him to let loose their first volley and sending a messenger to the four hundred hiding on the rise to wait until the Laconics tried to come around his right. Then as the Laconics began to sort themselves to renew the attack he waved Gil to take the reserves as planned to reinforce his already much stronger left. The reserves, mostly the surviving Black Cordelias, began a slow run towards their left-hand flank and Cale stopped and realized that in the pause between altering his plans and the re-start of the fight he had no idea what to do. *Wait and see, wait and see.* But the horror of inaction, the panic induced by the sense that he should stay where he was or go back to the tower and wait, was simply too great to stop. He raced up and down the rear for perhaps twenty seconds – an age on an age – like some lost and desperate child before he came to grips with himself and stopped. Now, as he used to do during his terrible panics during the long and bitter nights as a child, he bit deep into his hand below the thumb and felt the rush of pain begin to calm him down. He stopped, breathing deeply, a few seconds, and then turned the horse back to the tower and in a few moments was in control of himself, watching the battle collect itself and the Laconics begin the attack again.

There was no running attack this time; the Laconics simply advanced and expected to close. This was what happened with their strongest forces facing Cale's now massively reinforced left. But he did not have the men to offer such a depth of soldiers to resist the Laconics' strongest wing and also have a line six or eight deep in the middle and the right. Hence the yew stakes and the hooks. This would slow the Laconics down and protect this so much weaker line. Then once the Laconics were through he had trained the Redeemers here to fall back slowly as they fought and refuse to make a stand. Then four hundred archers on the rise would hit the Laconics from the rear where they would either have to turn to defend their unarmoured backs and take the pressure off the attack or be picked off by ten volleys every minute by the best archers in all the four quarters.

There were no such measures to his left. The Laconic right wing was twenty deep of their strongest and most experienced but now the Redeemers opposing them were nearly fifty deep. As long as the helmets protected them from the crushing blows of the Laconic swords, and the dreadful push and shove of so many men did not lead to a collapsing crush, then he hoped to reverse

to fight in heavy armour for a day. And, credit where credit was due, the insane courage and self-sacrificing skill of the Redeemers. Throughout the day he was back and forth with his ten Purgators who were aching to die for him. He was on top of the tower one minute, scrambling down and heading to a section along the front threatening to decay and shouting at those who could not see where they were needed to rush here or withdraw from there. Along to his right he rode repeatedly, Purgators terrified on his behalf and shielding him as if their eternal life itself depended on it as he tried to get the line first to hold the Laconics along the razor wall of the spikes of yew and when they were through to pull back in steady order so that they were kept penned in where the archers on the rise could hurt them most. Then it was back to the great scrum on the left where the battle would be won or lost, urging on the deadly push and shove, picking up men who fell, shouting for others where the lines of force had eased to move around the other side and add their weight. Now the fear had gone and he was so busy in the fight he had no time to worry that he was in his element, that for once he was neither angry or sad but exhilarated beyond all reckoning and only now and again a still small voice calling to him to show some sense. All day throughout the fight he was like some fly or wasp at a window buzzing back and forth as if he were trying to find a weakness in the glass. Lead from the front: always, sometimes, never. It was the last he always promised to himself but today it was impossible. Sometimes he had to lay into the Laconics as they cut a hole into the Redeemer line, sealing it up, lashing his enemy like the calmest madman in the asylum, cutting and blocking like the machine he had been brought up to be, his Purgators and the men he most hated in the world running in to die next to him as if they had no other destiny but this. And then the Purgators would form a ring around him and he'd withdraw and back onto his horse and up his spindly tower like God in his heaven surveying the chaos of his own creation. Then the glass impossibly bowed to the wasp and bulged and broke. The right flank of the Laconics warped and twisted and then not so much broke as burst. In such a beast as this it was the collective power that went, collapsing like a long-exhausted animal, at once falling under its own weight as much as that of its enemy. It was a collective death and not a matter of bravery or even strength, and once it was down it was finished as a battle. But not as an individual slaughter – now the creature was breaking into its parts, disassembled into each man, alone and weak and easy to kill where he could not re-form himself into a smaller beast to run away.

With the battle won, the slaughter against the Laconics was as dreadful as they had inflicted against the Redeemers only a few weeks before. What is to be said? The terror, the horror, the downward stab, the blood upon the ground. He could not have stopped them even if he had wanted to. He left it to the centenars to stop it as they could. By the time they did there were only five hundred prisoners and the few thousand who managed to get away completely. Cale himself had two pressing tasks. One was to inform the waiting Bosco of the victory, the other was to shrivel the hairs on Guido Hooke's arse by means of a bollocking so desperate in its vituperativeness that it became almost as much a legend as the battle itself.

What Cale did not realize was that his victory had replaced one mortal danger to him with another, this time one over which he would have no control. Bosco's reluctance to take decisive action in Chartres was not born out of indecision but the complexities of the problems that he faced. He must not only destroy his enemies, and do so quickly above all, but also destroy a great many of his friends. He knew perfectly well that many of his allies were allies of disaffection. They were not passionate supporters of Bosco's dream of a completely cleansed world for the simple reason that they did not know what it was he believed and would have been appalled if they had. He had put together an ugly rainbow coalition of theological disaffections, many of them utterly incompatible, personal grudges, religious grudges and self-seving malcontents clear that change was in the air but wary of being caught on the wrong side. Most dangerous of all were those as committed as

Bosco to a vision of a pure new world, who considered themselves just as vital to the scouring that must precede it. Chief among these dangerous partners was Redeemer Paul Moseby, long the keeper of the money that supported this collection of visionaries and fellow travellers. Distributor of favours and influence, he was owed much by many and expected to be paid. A year before, Moseby had gained even greater power in Chartres by arresting with great speed a cadre of Antagonist plotters who had burnt down the Basilica of Mercy and Compassion in the very heart of the old city, second in importance and holiness only to the vast Dome of Learning. Moseby, having grown impatient of a real conspiracy, had set the fire himself, or arranged for it, and arrested four previously designated brothers with a history of mind disease helped along in their incoherence by the careful administration of soporific drugs. They had been swiftly executed and as a reward Moseby had been put in charge of administering an 'enabling' Act, so called because it enabled him to imprison anyone for up to forty days without bringing charges. He rarely required the allotted time to find something to justify any arrest he made. Some were released both because it looked fair-minded to do so but also because their card had been duly marked and a lesson learnt as to what would happen if they did not co-operate in future.

But Moseby started to enjoy the increase in power he

now began to experience in its almost purest form. He arrested and threatened Redeemers that Bosco did not want arrested or threatened. He started to argue with Bosco about his own ideas concerning the renewed Redeemer faith. More, he disagreed in meetings, and not in private, where he could show his importance compared to Bosco and that he was not a retainer to be taken by the new faithful for an obedient servant. Worse, it had come to Bosco's attention that he had questioned Cale's divine origins. It had, in fact, been only a joke to the effect that while he might indeed be the anger of the Lord made flesh he did not look like it. A casual sneer had the same effect on Bosco as it so often does in life of causing as much, or more, damage than a carefully reasoned argument. From that point it might be said that the fate of Moseby, and that of his familiars, was decided. It was by no means sealed, however. Bosco was about to take on two powerful factions at the same time, neither of whom he could be sure of destroying separately let alone together in a few hours. He had one great advantage: the complete unexpectedness and shocking originality of what he was about to try and do.

Few battles are truly decisive. Even the one fought at Golan Heights which seemed to define that term depended for any lasting significance on the events that took place in Chartres immediately following the victory over the Laconics. Bosco had first convened a

Congress of the Sodalities of Perpetual Adoration with the intention, avowedly, of praying for the deliverance of Redeemers from the Laconics. If Cale lost they could pray away for all the good it would do them. If he won what would happen was very much the opposite of prayer.

Once Bosco had heard of the defeat of the Laconics he had his own battle to fight. The members of the congress, which included most of Bosco's supporters, reliable or otherwise, were sealed into the meeting house by his religious sentinel, Redeemer Francis Haldera. A senior member of the Sodalities, he had been of considerable use during Bosco's years of trying to build support in Chartres from his distant power base in the Sanctuary. He was an endlessly biddable fixer and easer of things, smooth as butter to those who needed flattery, ruthless to those for whom blackmail was the most useful approach. The time was coming, one way or another, when these qualities would no longer be required and his essential lack of belief or courage was to be made a central part of Bosco's delicately balanced plan. Haldera had been taken aside and isolated in a private room before the beginning of prayers and reassured with certain lies. Once news of Cale's victory had been received he was confronted with evidence that he had pugnated four acolytes and burglarized another, which was true, and conspired with the Antagonist heresy along with numerous others, which was not. It was made clear to him he would be slowly grilled alive for the crimes he had committed, real and false, but that if he confessed and co-operated he would merely be exiled. It was unsurprising, therefore, that he agreed to denounce both himself and anyone else he was told to. He was given a document to read out and twenty minutes to rehearse it, while the unsuspecting Sodalities prayed on for a victory that had already been won.

At the same time as Bosco was revenging himself against his friends, a group he could easily gather together in one place, he had also to commence eliminating his enemies, dispersed as they were over the entire city, and to achieve all of this at approximately the same time. It was vital to keep news of Cale's victory out of the city for as long as possible. News of such an epic deliverance would lead to great celebratory chaos and any chance of destroying his opponents depended on most of them being where they were supposed to be.

As a terrified and bewildered Haldera ascended one of the two great stone-staired lecterns at the congress eyed by a watchful Bosco already waiting thirty yards away in the other, the first assassinations were about to take place at the Bequinage. Redeemer Low and two of his confreres who merely had the misfortune to be in his company were approached as they prayed for victory by four of Gil's assassins and were stabbed some six or seven times. Others could not be approached so easily. The Gonfalonier of the Hasselt, as he emerged into the street from a thirty-minute silence, was struck by a bolt from a nearby window the force of which was said to be so great that it passed through his body and wounded a monk standing guard behind him. This unlikely story was, in fact, true because the weapon of preference of Gil's assassins was the over-strung Fell crossbow, so called because it was almost always fatal to its victims. It had one disadvantage, as its name suggests, that so powerfully tensioned was it that on occasions when the trigger was released the whole device disintegrated as explosively as if it had been filled, successfully, with Villainous Saltpetre. This was how Redeemer Breda, head of the Papal Bodyguard, the Beghards, survived. More attuned to the experience of assassination than most of the other intended victims, he realized the significance of the hideous 'Twang!' that resulted from the crossbow's disintegration as it was fired by his would-be murderer and instantly made off down the nearest exit. There his luck and good judgement deserted him. The nearest escape route was called the Impasse Jean Roux and his ignorance of the local dialect cost him his life. As soon as he realized it was a dead end, he quickly made his way back to the main road but found the way barred by his assassin, bleeding heavily from a deep wound to the forehead caused by the exploding crossbow. He was so mortified by his failure that he was prepared to sacrifice his life to them did the better job depends on your preference for ingenuity and quick thinking or enormous skill in the handling of weapons and leaving nothing to chance.

The problem with murdering Gant and Parsi was not that they treated the world with suspicion (Bosco's murderous plan was unthinkable, after all) but that their grandiosity and self-importance completely isolated them from any casual contact. They went from the Holy Palace to basilica to shrine and back to palace again only in carriages entered into and exited from out of sight of the ordinary people and common Redeemers as a conscious way of elevating their status. That they were unapproachable by virtue of vanity and not fear was neither here nor there when you were trying to kill them.

Brigade had worked out his plan – but like a true artist who had produced a good work but not a great one, he knew it was inferior. He loved simplicity, sparseness, few moving parts – mostly because there was less to go wrong but also because it suited his taste for plainness. Bosco's one sympathizer in the Holy Peculiar, Gant's palace, ensured that he had been able to find a corridor used by Gant to enter his chapel to pray at noon during the canonical hour of sext. The entrance to the corridor had a door only five feet high, the irksome invention of a humbler predecessor, deliberately designed to force all who entered to bow meekly before they entered the chapel. Once Gant was through Brigade planned to shut the door, bar it, kill Gant and escape. It seemed simple but was not. Gant did not always attend sext here – prone to late-morning headaches he would sometimes, if infrequently, retire to his darkened rooms to recover. It took no great worrier to reckon that on a day of such great tension he might easily succumb to the migraine. There was also the difficulty of escape – the chapel was right in the middle of the gargantuan complex that made up the Holy Peculiar. The final weakness was that Brigade would have to trust the calmness and reliability of a traitor to get him in and out. So uneasy had he become that he decided on a hardly less dangerous strategy of walking the palace and looking for another opportunity. Changing plans at the last minute was something he had never countenanced before but he could not shake off the sense of unease. His original plan was plausible but he smelt disaster. After ten years as a holy assassin Brigade had learnt to dismiss instinct. Now after twenty-five he had learnt to value it once more. Perhaps, he thought, he was just getting old.

Meanwhile at the gathering of the Congress of the Sodalities those collected there were if not uneasy then certainly mystified at the size of the assembly. Bosco had worked hard over the years to build this group but just as hard to keep its size, and many of its members, secret. There were many present who were by no means natural allies or who believed themselves to be part of a quite different conspiracy or none at all. These differences had to be reconciled – but not by agreement. Both mild-mannered reformists who would have been horrified by Bosco's larger plan and disagreeable zealots who had other ambitions for salvation would alike have to be dealt with and dealt with this afternoon.

Standing at one of the great lecterns at the Congress Haldera looked across at Bosco like a little boy who has angered his mother terribly. Although he was not shaking he seemed to be so, his face so white and shocked. And like a mother, a terrible and unforgiving one who no longer loved and protected the child across from her, Bosco impatiently signalled Haldera to get on with it. The dreadful unease spread at once through the assembly the way laughter does through an audience gathered to be entertained by a conjurer and his amusing dog. Haldera confessed to his terrible sins on behalf of the Antagonist heresy, the words emerging as pale as the man himself, and that he had, to his heartbreaking shame, conspired with others. ('Don't mention the numbers,' Bosco had instructed. 'I want everyone on their toes – I want them to feel the wind from the wings of the Angel of Death as he passes over them. Or not.')

One by one, with many fearful glances at Bosco, who looked now deeply saddened, betrayed and even tearful, Haldera went through the stumbling list of names of those whose breaths in life could now be counted:

excited by the inspiration of his new plan as any author wracked by a failure in his art who finds the sudden revelation or the clue that sets it right and leads him out of the confusing maze of the not quite good enough. The son of a master builder, Brigade could not help noticing with disapproval scaffolding three storeys high loaded with bricks for work the builders had been told to stop so that they could go and pray for victory. Having spent hours loading the bricks upon the scaffold the labourers had been faced with a problem: spend another hour or more lowering them back to store them on the ground and miss the call to prayer or take a minor risk and leave them where they were. And they were right to judge the bricks were safe, the scaffold would hold – why would they take into account the possibility that up-to-no-good Jonathon Brigade would happen by? How could they have guessed that such a malign presence would know how to weaken the reverts holding the scaffolding together and at which point to tie a rope to them so that when Gant and five of his holy brethren passed, as they must in order to enter the chapel, a hefty pull would cause more than a ton of bricks to collapse on top of them? It was simple and it was not far from an external wall where additions to the kitchen would make it easy for Brigade to escape. Perfect, except for the return of the builders, whose foreman had seen them leaving and demanded they return and move the stone blocks from the scaffolding back to the extremities. It was impossible to get in a killing shot from the tower, in other words. But Parsi walked at an almost constant speed, a monotonously rhythmic rolling gait, and Gil knew that out of his sight in the tower but at the other end of the garden he was in the open for perhaps as long as twenty seconds. He was not in his eagle's nest to take a shot himself but to measure the walk and calculate when Parsi was in the open but out of his sight, then signal to a group of forty archers in a courtyard three hundred yards away to fire their arrows over the wall of their own yard, arch over two streets then down into the end of the cloisters where Parsi was in the open praying to be punished for his sins – concerning which Gil, with enormous contrivance, was hoping to oblige him.

There was a witness, as it turned out, to what happened next, saved from execution by Gil because he was curious about the precise details of what happened to Parsi.

Gil gasped himself as the archers loosened their sharps, the terrible and beautiful curve flocking towards the unseen mumbling prelate on the ground, the graceful whoosh as they passed towards their mark and then the mixing of the thwack and ping and thud as they struck wall and earth and man. Gil, as it turned out, got the numbers right but only just. Parsi was hit by three arrows but only from the extreme edge of the cloud; one in the foot, another in the groin, a third in the belly.

The shocked cry and the scream of agony reached Gil in his tower just as he made to leave. But such pain can come from any wound. He was not satisfied for sure until he saved the witness, a novice who had been sitting down in the cloisters while his master said his prayers, more than four hours later.

Four hundred yards away an irritable Moseby, unused to being kept in the dark and ready to give Bosco a bad-tempered reminder of who he was dealing with, waited in the nearest room that Bosco had to an oubliette. It was small with a window high up so that no one could see out, and as far away from the arrests and slaughter as was possible. Moseby politely asked a servant for a drink (he regarded it as a sign of inadequacy to be rude to servants) and Brzica came in with a jug to see it done, moving behind him and tinkering with a mug and cup and pouring the requested water. Then someone with a resemblance to Bosco entered and Moseby looked up. 'I must –' but what he must was lost in eternity as Brzica took him by the hair and cut his throat.

Meanwhile Jonathon Brigade was beginning to feel that he must stop looking for some ideal site for his murder and yet he was sure that if he only looked on a little further there it would be. All the time a voice, not his conscience to be sure, nagged at him to revert to his first plan however unsatisfactory and risky it was. *Something is better than nothing. This is going to get you killed. Stop.* But he could not – always he felt that just a little further on would be the answer. And then a door opened in front of him and he was face to face with Redeemer Gant and behind him half a dozen priests. They stared at each other as Gant tried to place him and failed. Brigade's mind went blank for a second but every cell of his body was that of the instinctive murderer. He stepped forward gently so that Gant was forced to stay in the doorway blocking the priests behind. Then an idea – a truth that's told with bad intent beats all the lies you can invent.

'My Lord Redeemer,' said Brigade, 'an assassin has been sent to kill you. Come with me.' He took him gently by the arm and smiled at the priests. 'Please wait here until Redeemer Gant sends for you. Protect this doorway with your life.' He then shut the door and gripping Gant by the arm pulled him swiftly down the stairs, building up speed as they reached a spacious landing on which he grasped Gant by the shoulders and, pushing the protesting Redeemer at ever greater speed, launched him out of a large window which splintered into a thousand pieces as the great prelate fell screaming to his death on the cobbles fifty feet below. A brief look and Brigade was on his way to find his escape, haring down the stairs and shouting: 'Fire! Fire!'

This was the famous First Defenestration of the Holy Peculiar. The second is another story.

What a day!

Momentous, spiteful, terrible, tragic, cruel – no word

or list could capture its horrors and its brutal drama of lives lost and empires won. There were, perhaps, fewer than fifteen hundred Redeemers that required executing but it had to be done quickly and this was awkward even for a man as experienced as Brzica and as reluctantly determined as Gil. High-quality executioners are as rare as high-quality cooks or armourers or stonemasons – and mass executions were, in fact, extremely rare. After all, except to demoralize one's opponents, as in the massacre at Mount Nugent that sent such a clear message to the Materazzi or the peculiar circumstances of the death of Bosco's so carefully chosen Redeemers in the House of Special Purpose what was the need? The real point of an execution was either to dispose of an individual permanently in private or to do so extravagantly in public to make an example of them. If the former then you could take your time; if the latter, it was necessary to produce something spectacular and highly individual. Killing fifteen hundred men not weakened by hunger and months of darkness and cold was a difficult matter. He did not have the assistants for this number of killings because normally he didn't need them. So this was a damned difficult job for Brzica and Gil.

'You ever cut the throat of a pig?' said the former to the latter.

'No.'

'When I was a boy on my father's farm,' Brzica pointed out gloomily to Gil, 'he used to reckon it took two years to train someone to slaughter a pig. It's a lot harder to kill a man.'

'I've brought you experienced men. They know why this is necessary.'

Brzica grunted with the impatience of a man who was used to having his great talents diminished.

'It ain't nothing like ... *nothing* like killing a man in battle or running away from battle – it has its own rhymes and reasons, its own knacks and techniques. Few're cut out to kill in cold blood constantly – and specially not kill their own kind. But I don't suppose you believe me.'

'You're more convincing than you give yourself credit for, Redeemer,' replied Gil. 'But I'm sure with your guidance we'll manage.'

'Are you now?'

Manage they did, grim though it was. First Gil reassured the prisoners, collected in half a dozen halls of up to three hundred – that they had nothing to fear unless they were guilty of involvement in that day's Antagonist uprising of fifth columnists. It was regretfully necessary to question them all to find the few believed to be involved. But it was, as they would themselves understand, necessary for them to be questioned before the overwhelming majority could be released. They would also, he was sure, understand that they would need to be bound hand and foot but that it would be done with respect due to the great number of the innocent among them. He asked for their co-operation at a time of great crisis for the faith. To demonstrate his sincerity Gil allowed himself to have his hands tied loosely behind his back and – again loosely – from ankle to ankle. He then shuffled meekly out of the room. Reassured the arrested Redeemers allowed themselves to be bound and led out in groups of ten. The first groups were led into the nearest courtyard where Brzica and his four assistants forced them to their knees and cut their throats as a demonstration for Gil's watching chosen men.

Initially Brzica's baleful predictions proved accurate and only the fact that Gil had so skilfully prepared the victims and the fact of their being carefully bound prevented a fiasco as the inexperienced executioners found that cutting a throat fatally required more accuracy and precision than they were used to displaying on the battlefield. Brzica saved the day with a simple improvisation – he used a piece of charcoal to mark a line along the throats of the victims just before they were led out so that the increasingly nervous and jumpy executioners had something to follow. It remained an ugly business even for men very used to ugliness. But, as Brzica quoted, smug as well as grim, after it was over (and who would know better than him?): even the most dreadful martyrdom must run its course.

By evening the plot, like some brutal harvest, was gathered in and for all the errors and stupidities Bosco's great gamble was closing in his favour; even this calm madman was astonished that it was done. But there was a twist of sorts to come. With the city secure, many more successes than failures, a few escapes and some regrettable errors of identity, the news of Cale's great victory was released to a fearful and mystified population wound up to breaking point by the dreadful events of the day. News of victory gave wings to the claims that Antagonists, deep sleepers in the city's life, had risen up and been defeated at a terrible cost in famous men and Holy Fathers of the church. It all made sense and any other explanations would have been far less plausible: a coup? A revolution? Here in Chartres? There were, besides, few left willing to contradict it. In less than thirty-six hours the Redeemers had themselves been redeemed and in Bosco's mind the world had turned towards its greatest and most final purge.

In the late evening Pope Bento had retired to sleep knowing as much of the real nature of the day's events as the nuns in the doorless convents of the outskirts of the city. Bosco finally had the chance to pause and eat in the palace itself, joined by Gil. Both were exhausted, worn out in ways neither of them would have thought possible, and neither spoke much.

'You've done a man's job,' said Bosco at last. 'And God's great work, too.'

'And might do more,' replied Gil, but very softly as if he hardly had the strength to speak.

'And how's that?'

Gil looked at him as if he had some enormity on his mind that might be better left unsaid.

'I want to speak freely.'

'You can always speak freely to me. Now more than ever.'

'I want to speak of something that can't be spoken about.'

'It must be infandous indeed if you need to beat about the bush so much.'

'Very well. I've done horrible things in your service. Today I've walked knee-deep in the blood of good men. I'll sleep differently now for as long as I breathe.'

'No one would deny that you have risked your soul in our business.'

'Yes, that's right. My soul. But having risked it to the door of hell itself I do not want to have taken such a dreadful chance and let it be for nothing.'

'I've taken the same risk.'

'Have you?'

'Meaning?'

'You are, if you dare, able to be the voice of God on earth. Whatever you loose on earth would be loosed in heaven. Yet his current proxy sleeps a dozen rooms from here, babbling into his pillow and dreaming of rainbows and warm milk.'

'What of it? He is the Pontiff.'

'This feeble-minded creature is in the palm of your hand. Let me close it for you.'

Who knows what thoughts hammered away in Bosco's extraordinary mind, the delicate and the gross together mixed. He did not say anything for some time.

'You should have just done it,' he said to Gil at last, 'and said nothing. I am sorry that you blabbed and gave away an act that being done unasked I should have found it afterwards well done. I must sleep.'

He left the room, closing the door softly behind him. Gil helped himself to a large glass of sweet sherry.

'And found myself no doubt,' he said loudly to no one, 'rewarded with a command in the forefront of the hottest battle like Uriah the Hittite.' He took a deep swig of the hideous wine and sang softly.

'Everyone knows it, even a dunce,
Opportunity knocks once.'

But, as we all know, there is never an end to garboils.

## 22

At the Golan Heights the victorious Redeemers cele-
brated even more grimly than was their custom. It had
been hard, shoving, hacking, killing work and they were
exhausted. Tired as he was, Cale could not sleep and he
called a pair of guards to bring a captive he had noticed
being brought into the camp, the jovial scout he had
met out on the plains three weeks, but what felt like a
thousand years, before. He left his hands tied in front
of him and his feet tied to the chair then told the guards
to leave completely – he didn't want any earwigging to
what he was about to say.

'What about loosening my hands?' said Fanshawe.
'It's not very relaxing talking to someone with your
hands tied.'

'I don't care whether you're relaxed or not. I want to
make an indent with you.'

'Sorry?'

'A deal – an agreement.'

'About?'

'We have five hundred prisoners. Their outlook is
gloomy. I want to let you take two hundred and fifty out
of here and try to escape and make your way home.'

'Sounds like a trap.'

'I suppose so. It isn't.'

'Why should I trust you?'

'What you can trust, Fanshawe, is that by midday tomorrow there'll be two types of Laconic prisoners: the dead ones and the ones going to die.'

He let Fanshawe consider this.

'Some people would say it's as well to die facing up to it as it is acting the goat in some game.'

'It's not a game.'

'How do I know that?'

'Do I seem playful to you?'

'Not really.'

'I have my reasons you don't need to know anything about. How long will it take to get to the border?'

'Four days, unopposed.'

'You won't be opposed because I'll be following you – a few miles behind.'

'Why?'

'There you go again.'

'You have to admit it sounds pretty fishy.'

'It sounds pretty fishy.'

Fanshawe sat back and sighed.

'No.'

'What?' For the first time in their conversation Cale was on the back foot.

'They won't leave half their number behind.'

'Let me persuade you to change your mind. You will

be executed tomorrow and I can't stop it. You should already be dead.'

'Me?' said Fanshawe, smiling. 'I was convinced when you mentioned the word execution. But the other Laconics won't see it like that. It's not in their nature – and if I try to persuade them to betray each other I won't be making it as far as tomorrow. You don't have something to drink, do you?'

Cale poured a mug of water and held it to Fanshawe's lips. 'Another would be *luverly.*' Again Cale did as asked.

'How do I know I can trust you to keep going and not to try to make a fight of it once you're free of the camp?'

'We haven't been paid to take on a guerrilla war,' said Fanshawe. 'As long as we can leave honourably, which is to say not one half leaving the other half in the lurch, we're duty-bound to return home as quickly as possible. We are possessions of the state, and very expensive ones.'

He said nothing for a moment.

'How many of us died today?'

Cale considered lying.

'Eight thousand. Roughly.'

This seemed to shock even Fanshawe. He went pale and did not speak for a while.

'I'll be straight with you.'

Cale laughed.

'No, I will.'

'We cannot replace so many in twenty years. We need

this five hundred, every one of them, back home. There won't be any revenge attacks.'

'I couldn't care less what you do once you're over the border and arrange to bring me and up to two hundred of my men with you. That's what we're agreeing. I release all of the prisoners. You make sure we get safely across the border.'

'If my hands were free I'd shake on it.'

'Not a chance.'

'I agree,' lied Fanshawe.

'I agree,' lied Cale, in return. They discussed the details and within an hour Fanshawe was back with the other Laconics.

Cale went through the deal with Vague Henri and left him to stand down the Purgators guarding the Laconics, tied hand and foot in a small stockade built for no more than fifty captives – prisoners not normally being a problem for the Redeemers. The Purgators were replaced with an assortment of cooks, clerks and other highly unsuitable persons and the same was done with the soldiers guarding the horses the Laconics would need to make their escape; Cale announced a celebration to be held as far from the stockade as was feasible and supplied it with enough sweet sherry as could be got.

The escape itself was as undramatic as could be hoped except for the poor cooks and bottle-washers about whose fate no more sadly needs to be said. Vague

Henri met Fanshawe as he came over the wall of the stockade with the five hundred-odd Laconics he had released from the ropes that bound them using the knife Cale had given him. As silently as an exaltation of swans they made their way to the hapless guardians of the horses and in ten minutes were leading their stolen mounts away from the Redeemer camp and on their way towards the Golan Heights and through the site of their recent so disastrous defeat.

By virtue of a deliberate failure to make it clear who was responsible for taking over the following watch of the stockade and the horses, it was daylight before the escape was discovered. On being informed, Cale pretended to threaten every kind of death and torture for those responsible before ordering instant preparations for pursuit of the Laconics by the Purgators, led by himself swearing to undo this blot on his reputation personally. If there were awkward questions to be asked no one asked them and by nine o'clock Cale, Vague Henri and some two hundred or so Purgators were off in pursuit weighed down with what might in other circumstances be considered a suspiciously excessive quantity of supplies for a chase of this kind.

Gil or Bosco would also have asked why Cale was taking along Hooke, someone who could be of no possible value in such circumstances. Just before he left, a message arrived from Bosco congratulating him on his victory, setting out briefly the events in Chartres and ordering him to return immediately if the victory permitted. He handed the letter to Vague Henri.

'Odd. I wonder what's going on.'

'Let's hope we never get the chance to find out.'

'Will you reply?'

'Best.'

Instructing the messenger not to leave until the following day, Cale wrote a quick response lying, as was his usual habit, with as much of the truth as possible – that a number of Laconics had escaped and he feared that they might meet up with those who had fled the battle and possibly make a counter-attack. With this in mind he had ordered trenches dug for a major defence and decided to pursue the escaped either to destroy them or at least be sure that they were returning to the border and not planning further attacks on Chartres. With luck it would be several days before Bosco worked out what was happening and he, Vague Henri and Hooke would be well clear. There remained two problems: the danger of pursuing twice their number of troops and ones with a powerful reason to turn on them if they learnt the truth; and what he would say to the Purgators once they realized they had, instead of being welcomed back into the fold of the Redeemers, become outcasts again?

On the second night of the chase Cale had demanded that Fanshawe light a small beacon so that he could check on his position without coming too close by daylight, something which would involve some tricky explanations to the Purgators if he did not attack. He sent Vague Henri ahead to spot the fire and on his return was surprised to discover that Fanshawe had done as he agreed.

'I didn't think he'd stick to his bargain.'

'He did and he didn't. The beacon wasn't in their camp – it was just two Laconics on their own.'

'He could be miles away.'

'Could be, but isn't. I arrived as they were changing guards and followed the watchmen. Fanshawe and the rest of them are about four miles away.'

'Murderous arse-bandits who keep their word. Odd bunch.'

'When are you going to tell the Purgators?'

'Tomorrow. If they don't kill us we'll have the whole day.'

'Rather you than me.'

'Now I think about it, you'd better keep your distance. See how it goes. Badly and you can take off – have the 'scope.'

'That's very generous.'

'I'm a generous person.'

They both laughed but Vague Henri didn't say yes or no.

The next morning after most of the Purgators had eaten a breakfast of porridge mixed with dried fruit, pot-walloped by Cale as an alternative to the dead men's feet that some of the Purgators still preferred, he called them together. Ten minutes earlier he had watched as Vague Henri had ridden out of camp, both nodding goodbye to each other as he did so. Just as he leapt up onto a rock to talk to the Purgators Vague Henri came wandering back into camp and dismounted. With another nod Cale simply stared at him for a few moments. But now he had other things on his mind. He began to regret not just legging it with Vague Henri during the night. On the other hand, the chances of two people making it across such heavily guarded borders didn't look any better. Was this the least worst of two bad choices?

'You, my Lord Redeemers, know me as well as I know every one of you. On all occasions,' he lied, 'I have told you everything it was possible to tell you straight and plain.' There was a general murmur of agreement that this indeed was true.

'Two days ago I lied to you.'

Another murmur. 'Pretty good,' thought Vague Henri from his perch at the back and with the safety catch of his crossbow loose and lying out of sight behind him on the grass.

'But it was a lie I made only to save your lives.' He waved the paper not unlike the one he had received from Bosco in the air. 'This is a letter, more poisonous than a toad, from Bosco – a man I trusted more than my life itself and on whose word I risked your lives and lost so many who were dear to us, men who had suffered next to you in war and in the House of Special Purpose. This letter attempts to draw us together in a plot against the Pontiff that we love, to kill those dear to him and turn the One True Faith into who knows what toxic lies Bosco is ashamed even in the presence of these other treacheries to write.'

The letter was not the one from Bosco but a fake that Cale had bodged together with Vague Henri. The truth of Bosco's betrayal might have been just as corrosive to his reputation among the Purgators but the real letter implicated Cale as much. The Purgators were silent now, many had gone white. Cale detailed the names of the newly dead in Chartres – all true enough, it should be said, and watched eyes on every face as the Purgators to a man stood still as stumps asking themselves whether to believe the unbelievable.

'I brought you here, a two-day ride, so that you can make a choice, and not be chained to the wheel with me as I make mine never to accept this disgrace. Each one of you must choose: return or leave with me. I promise now that he who has no stomach for this flight, let him depart. His parole and passport freeing him I'll sign myself. Ten dollars in his purse that man will have, for in this dreadful division of our faith I would not want it on my mind to die in that man's company who in his conscience would not die with us. Read this letter,' he said, waving it towards them. 'If it does not turn your blood to stone and make your choice. I saved you once and every one of you has paid me back a dozen times. The man who comes with me will be my brother – the man who leaves shall in his leaving still for ever be my friend. I'll stand aside and let you read but make it quick – our flight is noted and the dogs are up.' With that he jumped down, handed the letter to the nearest Purgator, and walked over to Vague Henri and sat down.

'What will you do,' asked Vague Henri, 'if some of them decide to leave?'

'Why not all?'

'And make it through the rancorous priests, the dogs, all for a chance to knock on the door of the slaughter-house of Chartres?'

'They have the letter.'

'And it's almost true.'

They watched as the Purgators talked and read and talked and read.

'Good speech,' said Vague Henri.

'Thank you.'

'Not yours.'

'I read it in a book in Bosco's library.'

'Do you remember the name?'

'Not of the maker, no. I remember the book,' he paused. 'Tip of my tongue.'

'Not very grateful . . .'

'*Death to the French*,' Cale interrupted with satisfaction. 'That's what it was called.'

In the end Vague Henri turned out to be wrong.

About twenty of the Purgators, to the great hostility of the remainder, decided to return. Cale stopped a row that could have turned ugly and took some pleasure in keeping his promises of parole and money. His reputation for integrity among the Purgators was one he valued. Besides, being seen to be honest in these matters would ensure that everyone who came with him would do so willingly. And indeed, seeing him prove his honesty, three more Purgators chose to leave. In five minutes they had collected their gear and were gone. Another five minutes and Cale, still with slightly more than a hundred and sixty men, was heading in the opposite direction having ensured that Vague Henri had let slip to one of the ringleaders of the departed the direction in which they were heading.

'I'm amazed,' said Hooke, as he left riding between Vague Henri and Cale, 'that even a Purgator could let himself be fooled by such a palpable device.'

'Keep your mouth shut,' said Vague Henri.

'What about me?' said Hooke.

'What about you?' replied Vague Henri.

'You may keep your ten dollars but I want a passport and a parole the same as you offered them.'

'You?' said Cale. 'I own you from snout to whistle. You're going nowhere.'

'If I'm so grossly incapable I wonder it wouldn't be a relief to see the back of me.'

'I'm sure,' said Cale, softly smiling and all the more

menacing for it, 'you can learn to see the world more like I do.'

'What do you mean?'

'I mean that the next time I use one of your devices in a brew – you're going to be two steps in front of me when it all kicks off.'

After two more days heading in the direction he'd asked Vague Henri to spill to the returning Purgators, Cale realized that those who remained would have been getting suspicious as to why they kept following the Laconics but not engaging them.

'I am calling off this chase. With our band of brothers shaved by more than twenty, we are outnumbered three to one. The Antagonist border is close and with it Laconic reinforcements might be anywhere and lying in wait for us. We will head to Spanish Leeds.'

'They are allies to the Antagonists,' called out a Purgator.

'Only in good weather. The Swiss are neutral in their nature – even when they offer help it never comes. Even so you must remove your cassocks before we cross – it's no easy feat in any case – impossible if you're dressed like this.'

'You ask a great deal, Captain, to deny our faith.'

'Keeping your mouth shut isn't a denial of anything – just common sense.'

'I thought we were brothers, Captain.'

'And so we are. Just as I'm the eldest. Take your

money and your pass and go. My promise is entente even now.'

'I want to stay, Captain.'

'No.'

'I want to stay. I talk too much.'

'I don't. Leave.'

The rest of the Purgators, Cale could see, were shocked at the insolence shown to Cale and pleased by his arbitrary exercise of power. They were not used to the first and comforted by the second.

Realizing the entire mood of the Purgators was against him the man left quickly.

'Should I follow him?' said Vague Henri.

'Follow him?' replied Cale pretending not to understand.

'You know what I mean.'

Cale shook his head.

'You've grown very bloodthirsty in your old age.'

'He's just a Redeemer – the loyalty the pig farmer owes to the pig – right?'

Cale smiled. 'You've been talking to Hooke. He's a bad influence that man, as well as useless. As to the other, leave him alone. He's too far from Chartres to do us any harm – even if he gets there. Which I doubt. I want you to take five men and let Fanshawe get a good look at you.' He drew a few lines in the dust. 'Then double back and we'll wait for you here.'

first and worthy of blessing your good fortune but in reality nothing but trouble and a drain on your time, patience, blood and treasure. Steal!'

It was such a squabble of the endless kind Merk predicts that brought five hundred bad-tempered Redeemers marching into the foothills of the Quantocks to deal with an increase in the number of raids by mountain bandits on the local Musselman communities. It was cold and it was wet and there was little enough to eat because so much had been stolen from the Musselmen. The Redeemers could not see why they should be enduring these deprivations, not to say risking their lives, coming to the aid of people who were not even heretics. They worshipped false gods, not even the right God wrongly like the Antagonists. It was not a habit of the new Redeemer Governor of Memphis to explain his actions to his men and nor did he, but the reasons were simple enough: Memphis must eat and the Musselmen provided the city with a significant proportion of its food. The actions of these mountain crooks were a fairly serious nuisance and an advertisement that Redeemer rules could be flouted and flamboyantly so. The expedition was not intended to restore order but to demonstrate to anyone watching what could be expected if Redeemer authority was challenged in any way. The Redeemers arrived as punishers not policemen.

While the notion of having nothing to do was certainly an agreeable one among the Klephts there was a deep antipathy to being obliged to have nothing to do and fulfilling that obligation in a prescribed place. Guard duty was therefore regarded with special loathing and while everyone under the age of forty was supposed to take their turn it was a custom, as Mary, Countess of Pembroke, used to say, 'more honoured in the breach than the observance'. Those who had the means paid others to take their place, generally those too lazy, useless and stupid to earn a living any other way. Now with so many of the daring and intelligent earning so much from the increased number of raids on Musselman territory there was more money around for more people to bribe the least competent of their fellows to stand on a hillside during winter in the extreme cold with nothing happening and nothing much likely to happen.

There were strict guidelines about the use of fires by the guards – only at night, small, in the recesses of light-smothering rocks and with the driest wood. It was not easy in the cold and rain to conform to these sensible but uncomfortable rules. There was also the sheer unlikeliness of an attack by the Musselmen in winter and at night. Blundering around on the steeps in the dark and in the ice or rain, possibly both, was as good a way to get yourself killed as any. Lying there in the cold or wet the temptation to take a tiny risk, probably not even that, and build up the fire a bit and use the damper wood because keeping anything dry up there was a mare, you could see how things would slip. And so the

'There aren't any Materazzi any more.'

'Not official maybe. But there must be any number of trained men needing to earn a bob.'

'They're not Materazzi for hire or anything else,' said Kleist.

He explained and for some time there was silence.

'When the Materazzi came we just upped sticks and hid in the mountains. We wait them out, they burn the villages – a pity – but they can't stay here for ever.'

There was considerable protest at this: their recent increase in wealth had started not just the richest to build themselves new houses more fit for their improved circumstances. Many were half finished and there was much resentment at the idea of abandoning them to be destroyed. This squabble continued for some time.

'For God's sake!' said Kleist when he couldn't bear it any longer. 'They haven't come here to make a point – not to you anyway because there won't be one of you left alive to learn any lesson they're bringing with them. They're not going to burn a few houses to teach you not to be so greedy. They're going to wipe you off the face of the earth. They'll kill the old men, the young, the girls, the children. They'll pass over nothing that lives. And they'll do all this in front of you so that it's the last thing you see before they put you under with saws and harrows of iron and the axe and the rope. Then they'll pass all of you through the brick kiln. Then they'll pour the ashes into the rivers and the streams so that they run black and all that will be remembered of you is cinders, all that will remain of you is a byword for ruin.'

There was, as you will have guessed, a dreadful silence, broken by Dick Tarleton, well known for his refusal to take anyone or anything seriously.

'That bad,' he said.

'Wait here for two days, fool, and you'll be laughing on the other side of your face.'

'Are you suggesting we fight?'

'You'll lose.'

'What then?'

'Leave.'

'And go where?'

'Where's the nearest border?'

'Upper Silesia.'

'Then go to Upper Silesia.'

'Hundreds of the old and young over the mountains in winter. It's a fantasy.'

'Well, you better find a way because, if you stay, within a week there'll be one kind of Klepht – dead ones.'

And indeed what Kleist was saying was unthinkable and full of terrible possibilities. For hours they argued as Kleist delivered one story of Redeemer cruelty after another.

'You're exaggerating to get your way.'

Exhausted and afraid and frustrated Kleist lost his

temper and punched this sceptic to the ground and had to be dragged away, though not before he had managed a kick to his ribs so hard he broke two of them. This outburst seemed to help convince the shocked onlookers that Kleist was, even if wrong, completely sincere. When he calmed down he could see the mood had changed.

It was time for some boasting. The problem with the Klephts, however, was that they not only tolerated exaggeration concerning one's former achievements, it was positively admired. To have created a reputation for something without having earned it was an accomplishment often more highly regarded than an actual accomplishment itself. This was no place for diffidence or modesty.

'You know me,' Kleist began. 'The new houses you are so willing to die to protect are being built because of me. My skill has made you rich – nothing else. There isn't one of you who could beat me in a fair fight or an unfair one. If I didn't choose to kill you from half a mile away I could do it face to face – not that there'd be much of it left after I'd bitten your nose off and thumbed out one of your eyes.' He might have enjoyed these flourishes if the lives of his wife and unborn child were not at stake.

'And where do you think I got these talents from? Under a stone? I got them from the men who are less than a day from here. And remember that I'm just a footboy, a novice in killing and cruelty compared to the

Redeemers coming here – they have no more pity than a millstone, iron is straw to them, arrows are stubble. You must take the women and children now and the bulk of the men will come with me. We will try and draw them away from the march as best we can. This is my last word. If you don't agree I'm gone and my wife with me.'

'Your wife, Kleist, is about to drop.'

'So you know I mean what I say. She has more chance, both of them, giving birth in a ditch by the road than staying here.'

This was not quite good enough for the assembled Klephts, but they had to have Daisy called out to confirm what Kleist had said – young as she was, Daisy was regarded with a certain respect. Bluster was one thing, and to be admired, but taking a wife nearly nine months gone out into the wilderness during winter was a dire thing to do if it were true and all too horribly convincing.

Daisy turned up and, now enormous, waddled into the meeting house with an aching back and an aching arse. She was not much in the mood for persuasion and gave the sum of things to them straight.

'I thought we admired a man who knew when and how to be afraid. We've always had the brains and thought ourselves better than anyone else because we delighted in the usefulness of a savvy coward. I know you suspect my husband of courage but you should trust him all the more if he's ready to take me now, like this, rather than face the Redeemers. Show some sense – live and don't die.' And with that she left and went back to her home to lie down and be terrified.

There was another hour of wrangling and some of course refused to put themselves at such a risk – and it was a dreadful one – on the say-so of a boy, however useful. But it would be fair to say of the Klephts that once they had decided to run away they did not do so by halves – and running away was something they knew how to do. Desperate as he was to be gone, Kleist realized that nothing could happen in the way of a start until the next day, when the Redeemers might be no more than twelve hours away. They must be deployed and quickly if there was to be any chance of the train making it out of the mountains and to the borders.

'I will have Megan Macksey with me as midwife,' said Daisy, trying to be reassuring in a way she did not feel.

'But how good is she in a fix like this?'

'I suppose we're going to find out.'

He smiled. 'You're very brave all of a sudden.'

'Take that back. I never felt more of a coward than I do now. And I want you to be a coward too.'

'Trust me.'

'I don't trust you. You love me and it makes people stupid that kind of thing.'

'You want me to love you less?'

'I want you to love me enough to stay alive.'

'You have to take risks if you want to stay alive. The

403

trouble with the Klephts is that they don't mind killing but they don't want to die in the process.'

'All the more reason not to sacrifice yourself for their sake.'

'I've as much intention of dying for the sake of the Klephts as they have of dying for me. I'm not doing this for anyone but you and that creature.'

'Good. And you'll remember that.'

'I'll remember. You're an odd girl, aren't you?'

'What do *you* know about girls?'

There was not much sleep for either of them that night and when they went to the first of the staging posts the next morning it was in a terrible silence. Kleist felt like a child being abandoned and a father deserting his children all in one. He had known a good deal of misery in his life but nothing as sharp and deep as this. When they arrived, however, these dreadful emotions were smothered by sheer fury. It was clear that the Klephts had decided that because what was left behind would be lost they would not leave anything behind. Kleist would not have believed so few people could own so much and be able to fit it on what looked like every horse, ass and donkey in the known world. He needed little enough provocation given how he felt and he flew into a bitter rage, cutting ropes, belts, left, right and centre, screaming at the women and threatening the men until in less than an hour a mountain of stolen pots, pans, hideous knick-knacks, silk, boxes, and carpets and bolts of cloth lay in a vast pile of the plunder of fifty years. He took the five commanders who were to lead the hundred men set aside to guard the train and swore he'd disembowel them personally if they didn't strip every caravan they collected on their way out of the mountains in the same way. This delayed their leaving even longer and there was no time to say goodbye to Daisy. He kissed her, helped her onto the small but stocky mountain horse with great difficulty, and held her hand as if he couldn't bear to let her go.

'Be careful,' he said, at last. But she couldn't speak as he took his hand away and she then tried to snatch it back. And then she found her voice – wrenched out of her with a fearful sob. 'I'll never hold it again.'

'You will. I know how to stay alive. Believe me.'

And then she was moving away looking back at him all the time, although it hurt her neck and back as if they were in a splint. She did not take her eyes off him once until she had turned out of the village and was lost to sight.

Daisy's father walked over to him.

'Let's hope you're right.' He almost said it aloud but what he was really hoping was that he was wrong.

Redeemer Rhodri Galgan was ten back from the front of two lines that trailed more than five hundred Redeemers down the pass at Simmon's Yat. It was a steep climb and he was carrying nearly half his own weight in materiel. To keep his mind off his exertions he was praying to St Anthony.

'Dearest Saint,' he whispered under his breath, 'for whom the fish rose out of the water to hear him preach, to whom a mule knelt down as you passed him by with a reliquary of the true gibbet and who restored the leg of a young man who cut it off in remorse for having kicked his mother, have mercy on a poor sinner: forgive my audacity, my lust and my cupidity, my pride and my gluttony, anger and fultony, envy and sloth, forgive me for both.' Looking up for a moment from his supplications he noticed a small black object in the sky about sixty yards away. The very first tingling of fear had begun on the nape of his neck when the object moving faster than a falling stone struck him in the chest. All around him a dozen others fell but the dreadful pain and burning in his ears distracted him in the very few seconds he had left to live.

The Redeemers had barely grasped what had happened before fifty or so Klephts led by Kleist were already running away back up the Yat hoping to vanish before the Redeemers pulled themselves together and caught up with them. They would only be surprised once and Kleist waited just a little longer than the Klephts to see what the damage was. Perhaps a dozen, he thought, but not enough or anything like it. The trouble was that the passes were easy to ambush but were also wide enough to provide plenty of cover among the great boulders that had fallen down the sheer sides.

As he expected, the Redeemers shed most of the weight of their rucksacks and left them to be guarded by fifty men and moved on, but now in groups of ten moving up and on in spurts overtaking each other, taking cover and then being overtaken in turn. The first attack had slowed them but it was not enough.

'You must take more risks,' he said to the Klephts, 'or they'll catch the column.'

If he was surprised by their response it was because he had not entirely grasped their way of thinking. However much Kleist hated the notions of martyrdom and self-sacrifice he had been brought up to regard as the very essence of what it meant to be a worthy human being, they had nevertheless left their mark on his way of seeing war. The fact was that the Klephts would not die for an *idea* of freedom or honour (a notion they found not so much ridiculous as incomprehensible – what good were freedom or honour if you were dead?). On the other hand, they were still cautiously ready to do so for the lives of their families. The word for hero in the ancient language of the Klephts was synonymous with the word for buffoon – but they were not dead to the idea of reluctant courage of a kind only to be demonstrated when absolutely necessary, a kind of bravery known as brass. There are few men, after all, who do not draw a line somewhere with regard to the importance of their own lives, and now convinced that Kleist was not taking them for fools – the Klephts being obsessed with not having the wool pulled over their eyes – they began to knuckle under.

Kleist was impressed by the change in them but he found it hard to see how much practical difference it would make. They were now determined but not being men of great martial skill against Redeemers who had nothing else, this determination was of limited value. So the Klephts heaved rocks at the Redeemers from the tops of the high passes, they slowed them down with their inferior skills at archery and they occasionally put themselves in a position where they were forced to stand toe to toe and slug it out. They always lost, and badly. So much so that Kleist found himself telling them to stop being so rash – a speech it can certainly be said that was never given to a Klepht before.

But even the most honour-fixated society, the most prone to martyrdom and high-minded principle, has its share of traitors. The Redeemers had the legendary apostate Harwood, the Materazzi had Oliver Plunkett. Even the Laconics, obedience as much a part of them as their spines, had Burdett-Harris. For the Klephts at this time of their greatest hazard it was Burgrave Selo. Of all the Klephts he had the most to lose, being the wealthiest of them by far. He was a wheeler and a dealer, moneylender, a time-serving slippery coquette, a charmer, a black-leg and a trimmer. He could go into a twelve-inch gap behind you and come out in front. In short, Burgrave Selo, an ancient title to which he, of course, had no right at all, thought he could outmanoeuvre everyone. And it is to be said in his defence that he always *had* outmanoeuvred everyone and so why shouldn't he have regarded Kleist as a child and an alarmist who did not know how to tergiversate and come to an agreement that suited everyone – especially Burgrave Selo. He did not, reasonably enough, believe in Kleist, but he did with good reason believe in himself. So, genuine in so far as genuineness was a quality he possessed at all, Selo believed that what was good for him would in the end, once you took the long view, be good for the Klephts. He took, it should also be fairly said, many hours to square his conscience but after what was for him a great and terrible struggle he did what he thought was best all round. He approached the Redeemers almost personally – at considerable risk – by sending his most trusted brother to shout out at them in the dark that he wanted to talk. The Redeemer captain in charge, a man trained by one of Cale's Purgators, was suspicious but cautious of missing a chance and promised Selo's brother safe passage (broken promises made to worshippers of false gods were said to make the Hanged Redeemer smile with pleasure. Not that the Klephts really had a god in the sense that a Redeemer would have understood). A meaningless deal was struck in which the captain guaranteed the lives of Selo's family and his possessions and position and executions were to

into a trap or on a frolic of his own to take them in the wrong direction but Santos Hall calculated that Selo was entirely sincere in his duplicity and the attacking Klephts were clearly trying to slow them for a reason. Sending their women away even under such risky circumstances was exactly what they should be doing given what was in store for them.

So as Santos Hall pushed ahead through the Yat and up into the steeper Lydon Gorge, half of his men were slowly moving over Mount Simon towards the Klepht train making its slow progress out of the mountains altogether and onto the plains that led to the border five days away. Hall was now taking fewer risks as they fought up the Lydon Gorge and he allowed progress to slow both to protect his men and to give the impression that the Klepht tactics were working. Santos Hall now knew about Kleist from Selo and though he did not know the name or the connection to Thomas Cale – Santos Hall was now a devoted follower – it did explain the terrible accuracy of some of the sharps coming from the Klephts. If this Kleist was once a Redeemer acolyte he would be in no doubt what was coming to him if they caught him, something Santos Hall was confident they would. Once the other half of his cohort was over the mountain they'd be with the train and then turn back to take the Klephts, fighting them in the mountains from the rear.

With the Redeemers so cautious the Klephts were

elated; with every hour that passed the train, however slowly, moved an hour further from disaster. They had, they thought, inflicted so many casualties on the supermen of the Redeemers that this was what had slowed them to a crawl. It was not, perhaps, entirely unforgivable that some began to question whether Kleist was right in his estimation of their abilities and if so in his assessment of the dangers that had cost them so grievously. Others wanted to hang on to the idea that the Redeemers were monsters of military excellence – it made them, and who can't understand such an impulse, all the more impressed with their own bravery. And it was considerable. Klephts died in what was for them great numbers. They were few after all, and no one shirked. But now, even as they inflicted fewer deaths themselves, they also suffered fewer losses.

Given that Kleist had feared the worst you may perhaps blame him for not questioning the lack of aggression of his old masters. He did. But hope is a great obstacle to clear judgement. He knew nothing about Burgrave Selo and had barely even talked to him. No one had brought the path over Mount Simon to his attention – there being no shortage of them and their being so treacherous to the unguided. In addition he excelled himself in murderous accuracy – there were no inhibitions about killing when it came to the priests. Any movement and he would let loose and, to his own grim delight and the noisy joy of the Klephts, he would find his target far more often than not. Redeemer Santos Hall was forced to sit behind various rocks devising ever more hideous punishments for the little shit causing him and his men so much grief. And, besides, Kleist had never fought in any battle other than at Silbury Hill and that was of no useful comparison here. So he puzzled over the comparative ease of his success but lacking anything solid to challenge it had little choice but to accept it as it stood. So as the Klephts and Redeemers fought in the gorges and died in small numbers, two hundred and fifty men crawled over the freezing top of Mount Simon making their way after the nine hundred women and children now easing their way onto the Mulberry Downs and making better progress than anyone had a right to expect.

It was late on the second day of the slow Klepht withdrawal up the gorges that Kleist realized it was profoundly wrong to kill the Redeemers. It made much more sense to wound them instead. Whatever their belief in the value of suffering for others they took their own pain less patiently and this applied at every level: they were insanely touchy about criticism of any kind and regarded the slightest resistance to their freedom of action, no matter how brutal, as evidence of outrageous persecution. In the white heat of battle they would sacrifice themselves and their fellows in great numbers without a second thought, but subsequently treated their wounded in a manner that would have

413

been touching if it were not for their brutality towards those of their enemies. The Redeemers were the superior of all in their treatment of wounds and had a great willingness, one extended to no other field of learning, to try any new method of healing. From that time on, where it was possible, Kleist shot to the arm or the leg or the stomach knowing that in slow ambush warfare of this kind they would be hard pressed not to stop to treat the injured. The result was a satisfying increase in weeping and gnashing of teeth from his old tormentors and an even greater slowing of their progress.

But now the other Redeemers were off Mount Simon and moving down quickly to the Mulberry Downs. When they caught up with the train they were still more than two days from safety.

What is to be said about what happened next? The great Neechy held it to be true that even the most courageous must reserve the right to look away.

By sunset, some five hours after they caught the train, the Redeemers were riding away back to the mountains to attack the Klephts who were now utterly bereft of wives, children and parents. They left behind them ten hangmen's scaffolds and piled around each a heap of ashes.

# 24

For two days Vague Henri had been searching up and down the Swiss border to find the crossing where IdrisPukke had promised, if he survived, to try and arrange safe passage. But he had warned Vague Henri to be careful and his plan had not included bringing with him slightly more than a hundred and sixty Purgators, whose presence would be likely to put off even the most heavily bribed guard. As it happened, when he recognized the Rudlow crossing IdrisPukke had described and shouted out the password 'IdrisPukke' all he got in reply some twenty seconds later was a volley of arrows and crossbow bolts.

Returning, Vague Henri brought the bad news to Cale. He was sitting by a small fire on his own, as he always did when Vague Henri was away. His loathing for the Purgators and refusal to have anything to do with them unless he was obliged to was interpreted by them as a sign of his splendid isolation – a mark of holiness not hostility. He was reading the letter Bosco had given him before the second battle of the Golan and which he'd put in one of his many pockets then forgotten about in the face of more pressing business.

'What's that?' asked Vague Henri as Cale looked up from his reading and quickly put the letter away.

'Nothing.'

'Why so anxious to hide nothing?'

'What I meant when I said it was nothing is that it's none of your bloody business.'

The conversation that followed about what Vague Henri had found on his expedition was predictably bad-tempered. When they had finished Vague Henri went off and built his own bonfire.

They left at dawn and probed further up the border for nearly two days looking for a likely weak spot where a silent entry might be made. But it was clear from the ditches, fences and other obstructions being built that the Swiss were becoming nervous and preparing for something unpleasant.

In the end they decided to find the nearest and least guarded crossing close to Spanish Leeds and make a dash for it. Insomniac, twitchy Switzers might have been expecting something but they were not expecting it *now*, tonight. In any case, the guards on the Wanderley crossing were inexperienced and the sudden emergence of a hundred and sixty soldiers out of the dark at three in the morning took them completely by surprise. They surrendered immediately and were tied up in their guard block. All except one, who hid in the nearby forest and as the Purgators left let loose a defiant arrow which took Vague Henri full in the face as he

416

looked back to check everyone had passed through safely.

Redeemer Gil stood silently in the Vamian Room watching Bosco staring out of the window at the great Chapel of Tears, where the surviving princes of the church had been locked up and told that they would not be allowed out until they came to a wise verdict in harmony with the manifest will of God. This wise verdict in harmony with the manifest will of God was the election of Bosco as Pontiff to replace Pope Bento, who had died of a stroke after he had been told during a brief bout of clarity of the great victory at the Golan Heights. He was also informed that Gant and Parsi had been plotting to kill him but were now dead along with a great many of their treacherous Antagonist followers. The mixture of elation followed by horror proved too much for the frail constitution of the old man.

And so for Bosco the last great problem in pursuit of his goal to become the supreme representative of God on earth had dispersed like the early morning mists in Vallombrosa. It was as if he was standing at the top of an impossible mountain and having, against every obstacle of rock and ice and precipice, arrived at the top only to look down and see truly the sickening horror of what had been attempted. But it was not his life that had been at risk from the terrible fall and the smashing of bones but his immortal soul. Staring at the

Chapel of Tears he began to shake – not that even the watchful Gil noticed anything but the usual thoughtful calm. But Bosco's soul vibrated like the aftermath of the great bronze bell of St Gerard's struck only on the occasion of the election of a Pope of the Universal Church of the Hanged Redeemer. It was said that if you held a tuning fork to it even a week after it had been struck it would make the fork resonate from the still-vibrating bell. But for Bosco the blow from the horror he had set loose would stay with him until the day he died. The most terrible ideal, after all, lay still in front of him: the purifying death of everything. He almost fainted from the enormity of what he'd done and what was still to do. The strange atmosphere in the room made Gil uneasy, however little he understood its origins. At last he could no longer endure it.

'The ritual of the Argentum Pango has been performed on the late Pontiff and he has been taken to the mortuary for the funeral preparations.'

The Argentum Pango was a test, its origin long lost in the fog of Redeemer tradition, that involved the striking of three blows to the forehead of the Pontiff with a silver hammer in order to be quite sure he was dead. The Redeemer who struck the first of the three blows had never performed the ritual before, it having been so long since the death of the preceding Pope, and hit the forehead of the corpse with such vigour that it left a dent. A bad-tempered Gil pointed out that he was supposed to wake him up not make sure he was dead, and taking the hammer from him finished the job with two light taps.

He also confirmed, since he wrongly thought that Bosco seemed unusually calm, the more important information that Cale had indeed used his pursuit of the Laconics as a means of escape and that he was thought already to be in Spanish Leeds with his Purgators.

There had been a distinct cooling between Gil and Bosco after the former's suggestion that he be allowed to hurry along the death of the late Pope. Gil still felt deeply aggrieved at the refusal, even though the situation had resolved itself so conveniently without the need to take such a dangerous step. *Just luck*, was what Gil thought, *I was in the right*. Bosco had not in any way tried to imply his greater wisdom or judgement in the matter because he also felt he had been fortunate. But then it is in the nature of such resentments that he didn't have to. Bosco looked out at the smokeless chimney of the Chapel of Tears used to signal the election of a new Pontiff. 'Any longer,' he said, 'and I'll give them something to cry about.'

But what was really on their minds was not the Pontifical election, about which there could be no doubt, but Thomas Cale. Only a few days before, Gil would have offered to follow the treacherous little shit to the bottom of the fourth quarter and beyond and have taken great satisfaction in wiping the sweat from his forehead with the impious ingrate's still-beating heart.

Now apparently his old master had grown too proud to listen to what he had to say. Still, he could not refuse the chance to pour salt in Bosco's wounds.

'What do you want done about Cale?'

Without looking at Gil, Bosco spoke softly.

'Nothing. Leave him to heaven. Our Father has caught him with an unseen hook and an invisible line which is long enough to let him wander to the ends of the world and still to bring him back with a twitch upon the thread.'

*That's what you think*, Redeemer Gil wanted to say. In his opinion neither of them would see Cale again, not this side of the grave, not if they all lived to the age of Metushelach. Or not unless it was to bring disaster.

There was a loud banging on the door as if whoever was on the other side was desperate to escape the pursuit of some soul-hungry devil. 'Redeemer Bosco! Redeemer Bosco! Open the door! Open the door!'

It was not so easy to alarm Bosco but even through the six inches of wood the confusion and fright of whoever was on the other side were clear. Bosco signalled to Gil who, so alarmed by the terror in the voice, opened the door with one hand and held his other on the butt of his knife. He pulled it open swiftly and stood back.

At first he barely recognized the man, so distorted was his expression by astonishment and fear.

'What on earth's the matter? Hardy, isn't it?'

'Yes, Lord,' said the distressed Redeemer.

'Calm down.' Gil turned to Bosco. 'This is the Redeemer in charge of funeral rites for the Pontiff.'

'My Lord,' began Burdett. It was all clearly too much for him. He began to gasp so noisily they were like the sobs of a terrified child.

'Control yourself, Redeemer,' said Bosco softly. 'We'll wait for you.'

Burdett stared at him, wide-eyed, utterly shattered. 'You must come, Lord.'

Seeing that they would get nothing more out of the deeply distracted Redeemer, Bosco told him to lead the way and they followed in silence, but they, too, now feeling as if hammers, and not silver ones, were beating them on the head. The silence was interrupted only by the still frenzied gasps of the Redeemer leading them deep into the cellars of the great cathedral. In no more than five minutes they were down in a part of the complex they had never imagined existed, ugly and drab and brown with endless streets of corridors leading off the dimly lit route and into the vasty dark beyond.

After a few minutes Hardy stopped in front of a purple door and opened it wide without knocking, holding the door open for the two men whose presence seemed to terrify him more with each passing moment. Both of them were used to the fear of others in their presence but there was something deeply unsettling about this man, dread rather than fear.

Bosco first, they entered suspicious and apprehensive, utterly clueless as to what disaster waited, though they could sense disaster it was. The room was windowless but well lit with the best candles, including one almost the thickness of a man's waist just next to something that looked like a bed but was not. On the embalming table covered up to his neck in a linen sheet was the late Pope. Either side of him, it was clear from their aprons and gloves, were two embalmers, faces the yellowy white of old ivory, with expressions that gave off the same exquisite anxiety. Burdett shut the door behind them but still said nothing.

'Enough now,' said Bosco. 'What's this about?'

Burdett looked at the two embalmers as if he could barely stop himself from being sick and nodded. The embalmers reached for the linen sheet that covered the Pope's body and quickly rolled it down to his feet and removed it without drama. The body of the late Pope was naked, thin, pasty pale, wrinkled and saggingly ancient. His legs though were unusually parted, slightly more than you would expect when displaying the naked body of a Pope. There was a most terrible silence, perhaps one unlike any other in the history of silence. It was Gil who spoke first.

'My God, they've stolen the Pope's cock!'

# 25

'Don't be an idiot!' said Bosco, cold and angry. 'It's a woman.'

This was harsh. It was not Gil's fault that he was completely ignorant of the anatomy of women. How could he be otherwise? If the conclusion he leapt to seemed outlandish it was surely nothing like as monstrous as the truth: that the rock on which the Holy Church of the Hanged Redeemer had been built for the last twenty years was a creature regarded by many moderate theologians as possibly not having a soul at all. Before the stroke had ruined the Pontiff's mind it was one much admired by Bosco for its clarity and ruthlessness. Even in the fog of a broken brain this Pope had sought with passion and great enthusiasm the terrible death of the Maid of Blackbird Leys. Gil was almost too stunned, but not quite, to be insulted.

'Give me the keys to the room,' said Bosco to Burdett. There was a considerable jangling as Burdett loosened the key of the cremulatory from his vast collection. 'Have you said anything about this to anyone else?'

'No, Lord,' said Burdett.

Bosco looked at the first embalmer.

'Have you said anything to anyone else?'

'No, Lord.'

He looked at the second.

'Have you said anything about this to anyone else?'

The man shook his head, horror-dumb.

'Stay here until I send Redeemer Gil for you. And cover up that monstrosity.' He ushered Gil out and locked the door behind him.

It was half an hour, having twice lost their way in the under-streets of Chartres, before Bosco and Gil were back in the Vamian Room. Even then it was ten minutes before either of them spoke – the earthquake still shaking in their souls.

'How could this have happened?' asked Gil.

'It hasn't. You will arrange for the body to be displayed as normal. In fact everything will proceed as normal. Because nothing that is not normal has happened.'

'What if there are others?'

'Then the threat to the One True Faith is deadly. You will prepare an investigation into that possibility but do so in the greatest possible secrecy. You will also prepare an encyclical statement that it is a mortal sin punishable by eternal damnation in the fires of hell to raise the woman question.'

'The woman question?'

'Of course.'

There was a beat.

'What *is* the woman question?'

Bosco looked at him but it was unclear if he was joking or not.

'You don't know?'

'I require guidance.'

Bosco looked at him for a moment. 'The woman question concerns what kind of sin it is to enter into any discussion of the ordination of women. The answer is that it is a sin crying out to heaven for vengeance.'

Gil was puzzled. '*Is* anyone discussing it?'

Bosco looked at him. 'You can ask me – with that hideous gynocoid lying in the basement?' There was no obvious answer to this.

'And the three Redeemers in the mortuary. What shall I do about them?'

Bosco sighed. 'Do you remember the story of Uriah the Hittite?'

'Yes.'

'Reassure yourself that they'll say nothing. I don't want any more innocent blood on my hands but you must be sure of them. Say nothing. Allow nothing to be said. Do not allow anyone to say anything.'

Something out of the window caught Redeemer Gil's eye – from the great chimney of the Chapel of Tears white smoke oozed droopily into the damp air.

'We have a Pope,' he said to Bosco. 'Congratulations, Your Holiness.'

# 26

Chancellor Vipond hurried into his rooms followed by IdrisPukke. If this sounds grand for someone who was no longer the Chancellor of anything but the rump of an idea there were only two of these rooms, neither of them very large. The heavy, if grubby, curtains were pulled even though it was the middle of the day and he had already opened them himself that morning. IdrisPukke by nature more alert to small oddities was about to stop him but his half-brother was too quick and whisked the curtains open with great and sudden briskness.

'Good God!' shouted Vipond. IdrisPukke had put his hand to his sword as soon as the curtain started to open and it was out and raised by the time Vipond stepped back in such great alarm. Both looked on astonished at the sight of Cale sitting in the thick window ledge with a knife on his lap and staring at them.

'You want to be careful with that,' he said, looking at IdrisPukke. 'You'll have someone's eye out.'

'What in God's name are you playing at?' shouted Vipond.

Cale stepped down from the ledge and put away the knife.

'I'd have got the butler to announce me properly but I didn't like the look of him. His eyes were too close together.'

'You did that deliberately,' said Vipond and sat down. Cale did not reply.

'You know, Cale, the Ghurkhas swear a vow that they'll never sheath their sword until it's tasted blood.'

'Lucky for you you're not a Ghurkha then.'

'Where's Vague Henri?'

'He's hurt – bad. He took an arrow in the face at the border. Can't get it out. We need a surgeon.'

'There are two, I think, with us here. I'll see . . .'

'Not a Materazzi surgeon. No offence.'

'I'll see what I can do. Where is he?'

'He's with three of my men in a farm about ten miles away.'

'So it's not just you and him?'

'Not exactly.'

He explained about the Purgators.

'You're telling me,' said Vipond, 'you've brought a hundred and sixty Redeemers here.'

'They're not really Redeemers.'

'And what do you expect me to do with these hundred and sixty non-Redeemers?'

'Well, I won't tell anyone who they are if you don't. Have you ever seen a Khazak mercenary?'

'No,' said Vipond.

Cale looked at IdrisPukke.

'No,' he said at last.

'Then they're Khazak mercenaries. Who's going to know different?'

'It's a bit thin,' said IdrisPukke.

'It'll have to do. I'll worry about it later. Vague Henri is the point.'

'He must be in great pain.'

'Not really.'

'Every philosopher can stand the toothache except the one who has it, right?'

'No. You've seen that kit I have for stitching wounds and that.'

'I remember.'

'It's got a small cake of opium in it.'

'You never said.'

'Why would I?'

'Sounds a bit indulgent for Redeemers,' said Idris-Pukke.

'They can be very generous when it comes to themselves. Nobody likes the idea of dying in agony if they don't have to. Anyway, with a hundred and sixty of us we can keep him toked until the cows come home. We got the shaft out but it snapped off and the head is stuck real deep.'

In the end IdrisPukke persuaded Cale to bring Vague Henri into Spanish Leeds while he sorted out the surgeon. Cale took two days of rations for the Purgators in one of two wagons and sent it on to a wood twenty miles away with the two Purgators who'd been guarding Vague Henri. Then along with Hooke, who fancied himself as a bit of a doctor, he made his way back to Spanish Leeds with the nearly unconscious Vague Henri lying in the back of the other wagon. As long as they could keep him from his occasional fits of shouting they'd have a good chance of getting into the city. The borders might be jumpy but Spanish Leeds was a merchant town and the men who'd made it rich didn't see that it was necessary yet to start annoying customers or encouraging the authorities to begin sticking their noses into things that didn't concern them. So Hooke gave Vague Henri an extra half-cake of opium to keep him quiet and shoved a pile of blankets over him. They passed into the city without a problem and soon Vague Henri was snoring away back to a lighter state of unconsciousness in Vipond's bedroom being examined by the uneasy surgeon, a John Bradmore, who IdrisPukke had managed to bribe to come and offer his opinion.

The surgeon spent twenty minutes examining Vague Henri and dictating to a secretary.

'The arrowhead has entered the patient's face just under the eye.' He felt along the side of Vague Henri's neck. A groan. 'Fortunately it is, I think, a narrow bodkin type, head – five or six inches perhaps. Um . . . no question of pushing it through the wound – we'd take half his brain with it.' He sniffed and grimaced. 'Close to the jugular. Tricky.' For a further three or four minutes he touched and squeezed, apparently indifferent to the continuing smothered cries of poor Vague Henri. He dictated a few more notes and then turned to IdrisPukke.

'What did Painter tell you?'

'I'm sorry?' evaded IdrisPukke.

'I know you consulted him. Besides, you needn't tell me, I already know. He said the wound should be left for up to fourteen days until it becomes loosened by pus. No?'

IdrisPukke shrugged.

'That'll work – once the wound has filled with rot the arrow will be easy enough to remove. Mind you, he'll die – slowly of blood poisoning or pretty quickly as the withdrawal bursts his putrefied jugular vein on the way out.' Bradmore sighed. 'It's very difficult, you see. The head of the arrow is jammed in against the bone. It's a question of getting a grip on the head but it's in too deep and stuck so far. That's why Painter wants to let it decay its way out.'

'What do you suggest?'

'Not that anyway. The wound must be cleansed and deeply – an infection has started already. It must be stopped while I work out some way to grip the arrow-head.'

There was a short silence broken by Hooke, who had crept in unnoticed and hidden himself at the back of the room.

'I think I can help.'

There was another muffled groan from Vague Henri. It was not a cry of pain but of protest. Unfortunately the wound and the opium meant that no one could understand a word he said.

# 27

While Vague Henri was unwillingly having his life put in
the hands of a man in whom he had absolutely no confidence, Kleist was also fighting to stay alive in the
mountains along with fewer than a hundred Klephts.

The Redeemers who had murdered the old, the
women and the children in the escaping Klepht train
had returned to the mountains and attacked the men in
Lydon Gorge from the rear. Unable to go forward or
back they began to take casualties in far greater numbers. The Redeemers were now in no hurry, picking off
the Klephts with bolts or arrows and by heavily
armoured forays that lasted only a few minutes but
inflicted heavy casualties. In two more days they would
have finished the job with barely any harm to their own
number, but the Redeemers from the massacre made
the mistake of shouting out at night what they had
done to the Klepht women and children only three days
before. To bring a man to despair is a very desirable
thing if hope, or freedom, safety, a return to a loving
family, is what keeps him fighting. It was in their attitude to sacrifice, or, to be more precise, self-sacrifice,
that the Klephts differed so greatly from almost all

other men. Now in the terrible jeers of the Redeemers the priests unwittingly released the Klephts of that high hope that came above everything. Despair robbed them of their greatest weakness as soldiers: a willingness to kill but not to die in the process.

Kleist was in a dreadful moil himself, but knowing the Redeemers and their willingness to use lies against an enemy, he was still tormented by the hope that his wife and unborn were still alive. Now was not the time to give the Klephts hope. Only their belief that there was nothing left living for would do. He stopped them from rushing the Redeemers and persuaded them to wait till dawn and attack at his direction in such a way that they would exact the heaviest price. Meanwhile the taunts and gibes from the surrounding Redeemers in the dark were like a noble speech to honourable men as far as making the Klephts determined to die bringing as much mayhem with them as possible. Kleist knew the Klephts were lost but he had done his best and did not intend to lose himself along with them. He had done what he could but he had every intention of using the attack to push through on his own and find out whether or not his wife was indeed dead. It would not end for him here on this mountain in the back of beyond.

Kleist gathered the ninety or so survivors and drew a map in the gravelly dust. Their situation was simple enough: they were trapped in a pass about a hundred yards wide with sheer sides and with the remaining Redeemers split equally between their front and rear.

'We attack the Redeemers who've come up from the plain. Those are the ones we want, yes?'

There were nods all round.

'In my view we attack the line here in two wedges either side then try to break through and join up behind them. We'll almost certainly fail to do even that but it will surprise them and you'll kill more of them. If we can join up then we'll have all the Redeemers in front of us. It'll be a bloody sight harder for them if we can do that.' His plan was probably hopeless – it certainly sounded pretty thin when he said it aloud – but with speed and surprise and the new desperation of the Klephts he might make the space to get away. He owed these people something but not his life – and they would have taken the same view about him. They wouldn't have agonized about it either.

*This is the best I can do*, he thought. *Mea culpa. Mea culpa. Mea maxima culpa. I can't save them but I can save myself. That's all there is.*

He nearly broke as he went through the plan again but not quite – the still, small voice of survival screaming in his soul got him through.

When he finished he divided the group into two with a few swaps for family reasons and placed himself on the right wing because he judged that group to have the better fighters.

He did not want any shouting or noise of any kind to signal the attack and undermine the surprise so they led out a line of pack twine between the two groups. Kleist would give it a hefty pull when he thought it was just light enough for an attack. Kleist's one concession to the finger-wag of his nobility was to tell them to head to a flagpost he'd place behind the Redeemers to show them where to regroup. He regretted making this promise as soon as he'd spoken but it meant he had a good reason to outstrip the others. Once he'd planted it they were on their own.

It would have been too much to have expected the Redeemers to be unprepared but the circumstances were ideal for the Klephts given that revenge had made them careless of their own lives for once. They were quick and this was their ground. It was hard to judge what you could see and not see in the early light and the Klephts were nearly on top of the Redeemer lookouts before the shout of warning went up – each took a Klepht or two with them but the rest of the attackers did as they were told and silently rushed on to the camp, itself already stirring but still surprised. Kleist, bamboo pole in hand, was already ahead and running into and through the camp and shouting 'Retreat! Retreat!' as if he were one of the Redeemers running away in panic. 'Shut your mouth!' shouted one centenar and pulled at his arm as he went past – but it never occurred to him that Kleist was anything but a scared young Redeemer.

He pulled away and ran like hell. Just as he was about to clear the compound another Redeemer stepped in his way and knocked him over.

'Show some –'

But what he was supposed to show was unspoken as Kleist stood up and knifed him in the chest in one movement, picked up his flag and was over the wall of rocks the Redeemers had raised to cover their rear, never expecting it would be used. It would make an excellent wall of defence for the Klephts. Kleist loosened the large red cloth of silk and stuck it into a crevice where anyone who made it through would see it easily. Then he hared off up the mountain, fast and agile as a goat and never looked back.

A day later he was off the mountain. Another day after that he stood in front of the ten gallows of the Redeemers and the piles of ash and dry bones underneath them. He stood for a while then sat down with his head in his hands and cried. He was still there a day later when, in threes and fours, the twenty-one Klephts who had survived the fight in the mountains walked up and sat down next to him. Had he known the Klephts better he would have realized that it had never occurred to any of them that he would stay.

They could not bury the women and children because the Redeemers were surely following. They left, promising to return, and went on as best they could.

## 28

Unusually for medicine men, who generally suspected each other of stealing their cures, Hooke and Bradmore got on like brothers, no doubt because the lines between their skills were so plain. It was clear that the wound must be correctly enlarged to make Hooke's idea possible. He intended to build a set of hollow tongs in reverse and the width of the arrow. This would then be inserted into the wound and inside the hollow metal head of the arrow. Then by means of a screw the tip of the device already divided in two would slowly be forced apart inside the arrow shaft which it would grip tightly. The arrowhead could then be pulled out the way it had gone in. While Hooke went off to the foundry to make this subtle and tiny device, Bradmore set about enlarging the wound so that it could be introduced. First he made a set of probes from elder wood also the thickness of an arrow shaft, dried them and covered them in linen soaked in rose honey to prevent infection. The shortest probe first, he inserted them into Vague Henri's wound and then progressively introduced longer probes until he was satisfied he had made a clear run to the bottom of the wound. This took three days and by the end of this hideously painful process, Hooke, through great trial and error, arrived with a device that he was satisfied would do the job. Coming to Vague Henri's face he presented the mechanism at the same angle the arrowhead had first entered and, placing the tip of the mechanism in the centre of the wound, slowly pushed it the six inches inside necessary for the tip of the tongs to fit inside the socket of the arrowhead. They were obliged to move it about backwards and forwards a good deal. Then Hooke turned the screw at the top of the device hoping it would open at the far tip, grip the head and stay firm enough for them to extract it.

They again began moving the device back and forth tugging firmly and, little by little, finally pulled the offending arrow out of Vague Henri's face. Of the agony the poor boy endured it need only be said that the opium has not been grown that could dull the pain of that exercise.

His suffering was not over anyway. The danger of such a wound was the terrible risk of infection, something concerning which Bradmore was a great genius. Once the arrowhead was out – and big enough it was once it was lying on a plate – Bradmore took a squirtillo and filled it with white wine and flushed it into the wound. Then he placed in new probes made of wads of flax soaked in finely sieved bread, turpentine and honey. He left this for a day and then replaced the flax wads with shorter wads and so on for another twenty days. Afterwards he covered the wound in a dark ointment called Unguetum Fuscum and concerning which he was very secretive. After this treatment had stopped hell no longer held quite the terror it used to have for Vague Henri.

Bradmore had been appalled by the amount of opium Cale had been feeding Vague Henri and demanded he hand it over before he killed him, not least by causing him to explode – a terrible constipation having afflicted him as a result. He spent as much time as he could sitting with his friend, who was often in too much pain to reply or hallucinating even on the much more limited supply of opium Bradmore was prepared to give him. He instructed Cale to go into the market, almost as famous as that formerly of Memphis, and buy various types of food that he had never heard of and nearly all of which was extremely expensive.

'You've bunged him up, you sort him out.'

The trouble was that no one had any money – the question of Bradmore's fee having been carefully avoided. Bradmore had assumed that the Materazzi had escaped with at least some of their renowned wealth. This was not the case, as Cale well knew, and what they did have was not going to be spent on ruinous medical fees for some boy. They had troubles enough of their own. Vipond agreed to create the impression to Bradmore that money was no object when it came to the treatment of Vague Henri but paying was going to be Cale's problem. Cale's one option was to sell a small ruby he had stolen from the diadem of a statue of the Redeemer's Mother in the anteroom at Chartres. At least he hoped it was a ruby, or at least valuable.

It was not his only financial problem. He had the Purgators as well as Vague Henri's future to pay for. Part of him wished they just vanish but he knew this wasn't going to happen. Not only were they devoted to him but he knew that having control of a hundred and sixty experienced fighting men would give him a good deal of heft in what was to come. But they had to be paid for and kept out of sight. If any of the Materazzi found out who they were there would be trouble.

So the day after Bradmore's removal of the arrow, Cale went off on his own to buy food to treat Vague Henri's terrible constipation but also to see if he could get something for his ruby. While he was making his way among the numerous stalls and the incomprehensible cries of the sellers ('Bompos! Bompos! Bompos! Tufradoluh! Chiliwillis luvilanascarleta! Mushrumps cheap enough, luvli, to cook for someone yu don even like!'), he noticed three shops together opposite a stall of carrots and parsnips and cauliflowers artfully composed in the shape of a face. In each shop was a woman at a table stitching clothes. He watched the first two for a couple of minutes but lingered at the last of the three, partly because the woman was much younger than the others but also because she was working at such an astonishing rate. He watched for several more minutes now, fascinated not so much by her speed as the almost magical skill with which she was stitching a collar to a jacket. He liked watching skilled people work. She looked up a couple of times at Cale – there was no glass in the window – and finally spoke.

'Want a suit?'

'No.'

'Then bugger off.'

It was not his way these days to let anyone have the last word, even a girl in a shop, but he felt tired and ill. Coming down with something, he thought, best get on. He left and she did not look up from her work. After a ten-minute walk that would usually have taken five he made it to Wallbow Gardens. Unlike the usual commercial squares of Spanish Leeds there were half a dozen extravagantly liveried guards wandering about to warn off criminals from the twenty or so gold and jewellery shops that made up the square and which had now replaced Memphis as the centre of trade in the four quarters for dealings in precious metals.

The first jeweller told him it was only semi-precious and worth about fifty dollars. This pleased Cale because it was clear the jeweller was lying and this must mean it was worth considerably more. When he told him he wanted it back the jeweller offered more but Cale thought it best to move on. The next claimed it was glass. The one after that again claimed it was only semi-precious and offered him a hundred and fifty dollars.

Finally, and somewhat dispirited because he knew it was worth something but not how much, he went into Carcaterra's House of Precious Metals. The man behind the counter was perhaps in his mid-thirties and probably a Jew thought Cale because the only people he had seen before wearing skull caps were Jews.

'Can I help you,' said the man, a little warily. Cale put the ruby or whatever it was down on the table. The man picked it up, interested, and held it over a candle, examining the light refracted through it with the quiet care of someone who knew what he was doing. After a minute he looked at Cale.

'You don't look well, young man. Would you care to sit down?'

'I just want to know what it's worth. I know already, mind, I just want to know whether or not you're going to try and steal from me.'

'I can try and steal from you just as easily if you're sitting down as if you're standing up.'

As it happened Cale was feeling not just tired but exhausted. The black circles around his eyes were as bad as those belonging to the tragopan in the Memphis Zoo. There was a bench behind him and as he sat his legs almost gave way.

'Would you care for a cup of tea?'

'I want to know what it's worth.'

'I can tell you what it's worth and give you a cup of tea.'

Cale felt too shattered to be awkward. 'Thanks.'

'David!' called out the jeweller. 'Would you be kind enough to bring me a cup of tea – builder's tea if you please.'

There was a shout of acknowledgement and the jeweller went back to looking at the gemstone. Eventually David, Cale presumed, brought in a cup and saucer and was waved over to Cale by the jeweller. All three noticed that as he took it the cup and saucer began to jangle as if it was being held by an old man. David, puzzled, left them to it.

'Do you know what this is?' said the jeweller.

'I know it's worth a lot.'

'That depends on your idea of worth, I suppose. It's a type of gemstone called Red Beryl. It's from the Beskidy Mountains and I know this not only because I am very well informed when it comes to gemstones but because that's the only place they can be found. Do you agree?'

'If you say so.'

'I do. And the thing is, the very interesting thing is, that time out of mind the Beskidy Mountains have been in control of the One True Faith of the Hanged Redeemer. Did you know that?'

'I can honestly say that I didn't.'

'So this must either be very old – I've only seen two

before today – or it's been taken off the statue of the Mother of the Hanged Redeemer for whom this particular gem is, I understand, solely reserved.'

'Sounds about right.' Cale was too exhausted to try and invent anything and was impressed by the man's knowledge and skill.

'I'm afraid I don't deal in looted religious artefacts.'

Cale finished his tea and, still jangling, put it down on the bench beside him.

'I don't suppose you know anyone who does?'

'I'm not a fence, young man.'

'Sorry.'

Cale stood up feeling not so much exhausted now as unutterably weary and walked over to the jeweller, who handed the gemstone back to him.

'I didn't steal it.' He paused. 'All right, I *did* steal it. But no one ever earnt something they stole more than me and Red Beryl here.'

He walked over to the door. As he left the jeweller called out: 'Try not to sell it for less than six hundred.' And with that Cale shut the door behind him and was off into the square wondering if he had the energy to make it to his room.

'You Cale?' asked a pleasant voice.

Cale ignored it and walked on not looking up.

He tried to keep moving but the way was blocked by two hard-looking types he would have been wary of at the best of times. This was not the best of times.

'And there are another three of us as well,' said the pleasant voice.

Cale looked at the man.

'You're the bloke from Silbury Hill.'

'How gratifying you remember,' said Cadbury.

'Not dead then?'

'Me? I was just passing by. IdrisPukke?'

'Still alive.'

'So it is true – only the good die young.'

'And your owner – Hagfish Harry?'

'It's a coincidence – remarkable really – that you should ask. Kitty the Hare would like a word.'

'I have a butler now. He'll give you an appointment.'

'That's enough cheek, now, sonny. My owner doesn't like being kept waiting. Besides, you look as if you could do with a sit down. You've disimproved since we last met. If Kitty the Hare meant any harm to you we wouldn't be talking now.' Cadbury gestured the way and Cale went as gracefully as he knew how.

Fortunately they didn't have to go far. In a few turns they moved on to the rich houses of the canal district with their huge windows open to let the light in and along with it the envy of the passers-by. They stopped at one of the swankiest and were let in as if expected momentarily. Cadbury motioned him further into the house and into a large and airy room overlooking an elegant garden of box-tree mazes, espaliered fruit trees in vertical and horizontal cordons, cut knee and navel, nipple and nose.

'Sit down before you fall down,' said Cadbury, pulling up a chair.

'Is someone cooking onions?' asked Cale.

'No.'

The door opened and a servant came in and lit several candles. Then he pulled the curtains shut but with some effort because they were so thick and tall, more like those for a stage than a house. Shortly after, the door opened and Kitty the Hare passed into the room. No other word would do. The hood he wore was deep enough to cover his face in that poor light and the gown like a small boy's too large dressing gown. There was, however, nothing of the priest about him. His smell was different too. The Redeemers had the body odour of too little washing and something indefinably sour; Kitty the Hare smelt of something not unpleasant exactly and not just odd but oddly odd. Cadbury held a chair for him all the while carefully watching Cale to see how he reacted to this unsettling creature. No one said anything and no one moved. There was only the different rhythm of Kitty's breathing, something like a dog panting only not.

'You wanted . . .' began Cale.

'Move into the light so I can see you well,' interrupted Kitty. The non-look of him, the great performance of his arrival in the almost dark made Cale expect a voice fit for all this portent – doom-filled, dark and menacing. But it was the cooing and the lisping, the almost but not at all feminine liquid tone that raised the hair on his arms, damp as they were from sweat. 'Please do as I ask,' said Kitty.

Shaken and poorly, Cale shuffled forward, not by much. He was cautious now because he felt so weak but it also left him feeling a certain freedom. He was in no state for any swashbuckling – he could barely walk to the door let alone dash for it. In his present state he would have had trouble wrestling a kitten to its knees.

'So. This is what the wrath of God looks like,' said Kitty. 'Original. Don't you think so, Cadbury?'

'Yes, Kitty.'

'But it makes sense, the more you think about it, to have a child represent the anger of the almighty – given what so many of his innocents must endure. You are not well, I think.'

'Just a cold.'

'Well, don't give it to us, eh, Cadbury?'

It may have been jovial – it was impossible for Cale to tell.

'I have heard a great deal about you, mister. Is half of it true?'

'More.'

'He's vain, Cadbury, how I like that in a god.'

'What do you want?' The strange sweet smell that at first had not bothered Cale was becoming more and more unpleasant and was beginning to make him feel even worse.

'You have information?'

'About?'

'A great many things no doubt but I won't insult you by trying to buy news about your friends – curious though I am to know where Vipond and his brother are sticking their snouts, I want information that is valuable to me and which I think you will quite happily share.'

'About?'

'The Redeemers. Bosco. Now that he is Pope . . .'

Had he been feeling less dreadful Cale might have hidden his surprise better.

'You didn't know.' Kitty was clearly amused.

'I left in a hurry while I had the chance. So you see I'm not worth what you thought.'

'Not at all. News I can always get easily enough. Intelligence – that's something else. You were more than close to Bosco, you can tell me about his plans for you and for his faith now that he is the rock on which it is built. These things are valuable to me. There will be war but a new kind, I think. If so, I need to know what it is.' He leant back in his chair. 'You will be well paid but just as useful is that you will have influence through me in a world that doesn't as yet have very much time for you. Influence more precious than rubies. As for your Purgators – find an excuse for their presence pretty soon.' He stood up as Cadbury quickly moved to pull away his chair. 'In a couple of days when you're feeling better we'll talk at greater length. Cadbury will

448

give you tea. Mint might give you a lift.' With that he was moving to the door, which was opened from the outside by someone who must have been remarkable of hearing, and then Kitty the Hare was gone. The same servant as before came in, opened the curtains and to Cale's intense relief, because he thought the smell would make him sick, also opened the window to clear the air. Cadbury ordered tea and Cale went to the casement, drawing in the sweet air as if he had been at the bottom of a dirty pond for the last ten minutes.

'What you expected?' said Cadbury.

Cale did not reply. Cadbury handed Cale a small jar whose label announced in grand lettering: MRS NOLTE'S CHRISM. 'It'll help if you stick it up your nose next time you come. Just don't leave a trace round your nostrils. Kitty takes offence.'

When Cale got back to his room feeling stronger for his black, not mint, tea and two cream slices he fell asleep, making fourteen hours over the last twenty-four – this for someone who usually got by on six or seven. When he woke up he noticed a large envelope had been pushed under the door. It was an invitation to a dinner in the Great Hall of Spanish Leeds Castle. He had barely finished reading it for the third time when there was a knock on the door.

'IdrisPukke.'

Cale opened it, invitation in his other hand. It was so pompously ornate and grand it could not be overlooked and IdrisPukke was not, in any case, an overlooking sort of person. 'May I?' he said, pulling the invitation out of Cale's hand.

'Help yourself.' Cale was curious to know what this great dinner was about and why he was invited but before he had a chance to pump IdrisPukke for information he was offered some unequivocal advice.

'You can't go.'

'Why?'

'It's a trap.'

'It's a dinner.'

'For everyone else. For you it's a trap.'

'I'm all ears.'

'The invitation is from Bose Ikard.'

'It says the Lord Mayor.'

'He wants there to be trouble so that he can persuade the King that it's dangerous to have the remnants of an embittered empire filling his second-largest city and hoping for a war to get their broken fortunes back.'

'He has a point.'

'Indeed he has.'

'What's it got to do with me?'

'Your reputation goes before you.'

'Meaning?'

'That wherever you go disaster follows you like a spaniel.' Cale was not easily lost for the last word but even he was startled by this. 'He wants to see a quarrel with you and the Materazzi and he has a pretty good idea how to start one. You'll find yourself sitting opposite Arbell and her husband.'

This brought about a silence of an altogether different kind. 'Does Vipond know about this?'

'Vipond sent me.'

'So he expects me to do as I'm told.'

'Do you ever do as you're told? These days we all know you're a god and not a bad-tempered hooligan with a big fist.'

'I'm the *anger* of God not *a* god. I explained that.'

'Vipond is warning you not to do what someone who wishes you harm wants you to do. Show some sense.' He paused. 'Please.'

Cale had been excited by the idea of a grand dinner but he could see IdrisPukke was right. But he could no more stay away than he could have prevented himself from falling to earth after he had launched himself from the tallest tower in Spanish Leeds.

# 29

Great the magnified cumulus of incense, pure the sopranos, sonorous the bass notes in the cathedral in the heart of Chartres where the new Pope, Bosco XVI, was crowned on the old rock on which the One True Faith was built. And the celebratory vestments of gold and green, orange and yellow and blue. Truncated rainbows of holiness. Except, of course, for the twenty nuns who were allowed to participate dressed all in black and just a little white around the face. But what faces! As they looked up at their Holy Father, hands tied behind backs to prevent them reaching out for the disgusting touch, smiles of ecstasy and so intense it seemed another holy expiration might take place to add to that of the Blessed Imelda Lambertini who died of ecstasy at her holy communion at the spiritually precious age of eleven.

But great the excitement of the prelates, bishops and cardinals, nuncio, mandrates and gonfaloniers. Many were newly enobled, their predecessors gone to the fires, or the oubliettes and ditches out in the desert, fodder for foxes. This was their Pope, their chance, their time to be personally responsible for bringing about the end time and the great renewal.

The new Pope Bosco ascended the calumnion step by step, obliged to stop for obeisance and holy grovelling at each so that it took half an hour of renunciation for Bosco to make it to the top and to the great cantilevered lectern that jutted out over the vast space of the Sistine Chapel and which made it look as if he was about to leap into the upturned congregation waiting to hear of a new life and a new purpose. They knew well enough what was coming; they had been primed for years on the new beliefs. They knew that God had lost his patience yet again and that where once they had been sacrificed to rain and water there would now be fire and a sword delivered by the hand of a boy who was not a boy but the manifestation of God's exasperation. And there would be no ark offering a reprieve this time. First the Antagonists, then everyone else and then the Redeemer faith itself would wither away. All this was delivered to an audience that could barely contain its joyful anticipation of God's momentum concerning the ruin of his most blighted creation.

'The wind of change is blowing through our world,' said the new Pope. 'Nothing can stop a blessed idea whose time has come. So we must come to the woman question.'

There was a certain heart murmur of surprise among the priests and monks. *What woman question?* And the same if understandably even more more trepidatious question amongst the nuns. *What woman question?*

There was always something slightly oily about the tone of voice of a Redeemer when he spoke well of women, not by any means so rare an occurrence as the casual follower of the faith might imagine. The nervous nuns were about to get a full dose of unction. When you flatter, lay it on with a trowel.

'Blessed is the woman whose words can cheer but not influence. How can we not respect their strength in obedience, admire the doggedness of their submissiveness that God – and his likeness man – commands from the femininity? Redeemers are distinguished by unusual respect for the female sex that supplements and aids the labour of men and priests by her unwearied collaboration. But the great Abbess Kuhne is now more correct than ever when she says that virginity is the true emancipation and proper state of women. In anticipation of the life to come no more will the Redeemer faithful give or take in marriage. Both men and women from this day will be virgins. I have set aside days on which the marriage debt, which most resembles the union of the beast in us, may not be paid between man and wife.

'All Thursdays in memory of the arrest of the Hanged Redeemer (fifty-two days a year).

'All Fridays in memory of the death of the Hanged Redeemer (another fifty-two days).

'All Saturdays in honour of the Hanged Redeemer's Virgin Mother (another fifty-two days).

'All Sundays in honour of the resurrection (fifty-two more days).

'And all Mondays to remember the departed souls (fifty-two days).'

In addition to banning marital intercourse on two hundred and sixty of the three hundred and sixty-five days of the year, Bosco went on to forbid physical contact of any kind for varying periods before and after half a dozen particularly sacred holydays.

It took Gil, no mean calculator, several minutes to work out that in the first year it would be possible for married couples to dench on only five days.

'Do you think it's too many?' said a concerned Bosco. 'By the third year all that will be behind us.'

'More than enough,' said Gil. 'But where are our soldiers to come from?'

'We have enough to wipe the world clean with a sponge as we are. You and I must be here to see the Redeemers wither away so that God can begin again with a creature more deserving of his gifts.'

The other question, the Cale question, had been dealt with by the invocation of a great secret prophecy concerning his return. The prophecy was now locked away in the vaults of the Holy City of Chartres having been given credence by a group of nuns he had talked to when they visited the Golan Heights. He had then mysteriously disappeared from amongst them although no one had actually seen him disappear. In this way the useful belief arose that he would return to fulfil his eschatological duties but only if the Redeemers faced great peril in their attempt to wipe evil man and his dreadful nature from the face of the earth.

'What if they find out the truth?'

'We don't know the truth.'

'He betrayed us, the ungrateful shit-bag.'

'You keep talking about him as if he is a person. He is not. When he realizes and when others realize he'll return, because if he is not part of the coming deluge there's no point to him. At the right time a twitch on the thread will do it.'

Gil had wondered if Cale's disappearance would damage the cause. What was the point of an absent saviour? God had revealed his hand when it was needed but then withdrawn it with a clear demand that the Redeemers themselves must act. Otherwise what was the point of them? However much destruction must be delivered to the world, including their own, God did not need them to achieve this. By sending Cale to intervene so miraculously he had made this obvious. By withdrawing Cale, God had shown them that he had not deserted the Redeemers and that if they followed his will by destroying all apostates and unbelievers he would not forget them when the time came to destroy themselves. Their annihilation would surely be a door to the next world. It was in mulling over his mistake that Gil, still a profound believer in the end of mankind, began to see that, whatever Bosco might think, Cale had now outlived his usefulness. A permanently absent Cale would do no harm at all. Quite the contrary. A live one, on the other hand, could and probably would become a serious threat. Something must be done.

To bring his great speech to a climax Bosco warned against a dangerous new kind of woman he knew was emerging, not the naughty beauties of the Materazzi with the stretched-forth necks and mincing walk and big hair that the Lord would smite with scabs at a point of his own choosing, nor the wantons of Spanish Leeds who made a tinkling with their feet because soon instead of a girdle about their womb there would be a rent. But there was a new threat from women who wanted to be the spiritual equals of men, to show off their strictness and persecute anyone insufficiently pious and even burn other women as a warning by showing that they too could be as generously harsh in the ways of orthodoxy and righteousness. The congregation nodded but did not understand that his wrath was aimed at his predecessor and his fear that there might be more like her. Perhaps many more. Perhaps they were everywhere. There were rumours out there, though, digging in like slugs for the winter, emerging in gossip and drunken talks among friends late in the night, but nothing at all like the truth that a woman, no better or worse than her male predecessors, had ruled the Redeemers for twenty years.

'Consider the last four things as you go back to your diocese,' finished Bosco. 'And prepare for the extremity to come.'

After he had left the celebration that followed Bosco's inaugural speech Gil went back to his enormous apartments, where his new secretary, Monsignor Chadwick, who had not been invited, was desperately hoping that Gil would be in the mood to let fall some news of who had been there and what had happened and how the new Holy Father was. There was only disappointment to be had.

'Find me the Two Trevors,' said an ill-tempered Gil. Hope on Chadwick's face was replaced by instant dismay.

'Ah,' said Chadwick followed by a long pause. 'Would you know by any chance where they might be at all?'

'No,' replied Gil. 'Now get on with it.' As Chadwick shut the door as mournfully as a door can be shut Gil knew perfectly well how very unreasonable he was being. The Two Trevors were not a pair it was at all easy, or even possible, to find no matter who you were.

'More light?' asked Cale.

'I can see well enough,' said the seamstress from the vegetable market. 'The question is: what'm I lookin' at?'

'Old lady who spidered a fly,' sang Vague Henri.

'What's he saying?'

'He's singing a song – he's well off his track. Don't

458

worry about it. I want you to stitch his face. He won't feel anything – or much anyway.'

'You're crazy. I just stitch clothes. You're crazy. I don't know anything about stuff like that.'

'But I do. I've stitched people a hundred times.'

'Then *you* do it. I'll get into trouble.'

'You won't get into trouble. I'm a very important person.'

'You don't look like anyone important.'

'How would you know? You just stitch clothes for a living.'

'You want me to do somethin' like this an' you insult me? I'm goin'.' She made for the door.

'Fifty dollars!' She stopped and looked at him. 'He's my friend. Help him.'

'Let me see it – the money.'

Because of Kitty the Hare's generosity, a wallet with three hundred dollars had been delivered the day after their meeting; he was able to count it out on the table there and then. The girl thought for a moment. 'A hun'red dollars.'

'He's not that much of a friend.'

They settled on sixty-five.

As she went back to examining the mess of Vague Henri's face he started singing about goats. 'He won't feel a thing while you work and I'll take you through it. I know what needs to be done but it'll take a fine touch if his face is to be saved. Think of it like you were sewing

459

a collar to a jacket. Just make the neatest job you can.' He remembered to flatter her. 'Without you he'll look like a horse's arse. I saw how good you were. You have talent – anyone with brains can see that. Forget it's someone's face and think of him as a suit or something.' Softened up by the compliments and understandably tempted by such a large amount of money she began looking at Vague Henri as a professional problem.

'He'll need a fillit.'

'What's a fillit?'

'I thought you knew all about stitching.'

'If that was true I wouldn't be needing you. What's a fillit?'

'There's a finger-sized hole in his face. I can't just stitch over a hole even in cloth let alone skin. I'll need to fill it with something.'

'What?'

'How would I know? In a suit or something we'd use felt.'

'We can't do that. I've seen what happens to wounds with even a bit of cloth left in them.'

'If we're reparing an old suit we use a bit of material from somewhere you can't see. That way it's the same an' don't pull away when it gets wet.'

'Are you saying we should cut a bit off him from somewhere else and stuff it in the hole in his face?'

She had just been thinking aloud but now she caught fright.

'No, I wasn't saying that, I was just thinking that's all. *Like with like* is what we say. I was just thinking.'

'Why not? It makes sense.'

'You could make things worse.'

'You can always make things worse.'

'If he's your friend – praps you could cut a finger piece from yourself.'

'Don't,' said Cale gently, 'be bloody stupid.'

'Greater love hath no man than he lay down his life for his friend.'

'What idiot told you that?'

She was greatly put out by this disrespect but by now she had her heart set on the money and, also, the challenge. She was no shirker when it came to getting on in the world.

And so the ingenious operation born of luck, wit, skill and ignorance began and proved a wonderful success. Cale, reassuring the seamstress that he knew what he was doing when it came to knives, cut an exquisite round sliver of flesh from Vague Henri's buttocks where he felt he would miss it least and the seamstress duly filled the deep hole in his face. With a skill that made Cale's heart warm to witness she carefully cut and stitched, Tailor of Gloucester perfect, Vague Henri's sorely battered face. Throughout, Vague Henri accompanied her with more songs concerning spiders, old ladies, cats and goats. When she had finished they stood back to admire what she had done and it was worth admiration. Red-raw as it was, anyone could see the skill with which a ragged hole had been transformed into something that simply looked right. Cale knew that it might become infected or the sliver of flesh he had taken might die and then God knows what. But for now it *looked* right.

And indeed it was. For two days it looked worryingly angry for all the neatness and then on the third morning it began to pinkify and grow calm and was obviously on the mend. Vague Henri had only one complaint: 'Why is my arse so sore?'

As for their great co-operation and the good fortune in happening upon this ingenious process it was rarely thought of by either Cale or the seamstress and was utterly lost to mankind.

# 30

It was the night of the banquet and IdrisPukke and his half-brother, Vipond, were in particularly good form. The former had teased the women concerning their beauty and bantered with the men about their failure to live up to the women, and Vipond, a more restrained humorist when he felt like it, created storms of laughter with a dryly amusing story about the vanity of the Bishop of Colchester and a misadventure involving an Aylesbury duck that concluded with the observation that 'Whatever discoveries have been made in the land of self-delusion, many undiscovered regions remain to be explored.'

Not to be outdone, IdrisPukke smoothly passed into one of his aphoristic moods and was giving those around him the benefit of his many years' experience of mankind's idiocy, absurdity and wickedness, including, it must be said, his own.

'Never argue with anyone about anything. No, not even Vipond, though he's possibly the wisest man who ever lived.' Vipond, just across the table and enjoying his half-brother's performance and the double flattery involved in the mockery, laughed along with the others and the banging of approval of half a dozen now tipsy Materazzi.

'When it comes to self-delusion my brother is completely right. You could talk to Vipond for a thousand years and barely touch on the number of absurd things he believes.'

Then Vipond's face fell and for a brief moment IdrisPukke wondered if he had gone too far. But it was something he had seen not heard that alarmed the Chancellor. IdrisPukke followed the apprehensive look to the top of the room. Though the chatter and laughter of the rest of the vast room carried on, the table around the half-brothers went very quiet.

At the top of the stairway leading down into the hall stood Cale, dressed neck to foot in a black suit not unlike an unusually elegant cassock then very much the style among the rich young men of Spanish Leeds and which he'd had specially made by his seamstress and paid for again with Kitty the Hare's money.

He looked like a nail and didn't care who knew it. But, unsurprisingly, the greatest shock among the few dozen there who knew him by sight was that felt by Arbell Materazzi, sitting next to her husband and eight months pregnant. If a woman can be white as a ghost and blooming at the same time then so she was, the blue veins of her eyelids like the thready filaments in Sophia marble.

IdrisPukke, heart sliding out of humour, watched as

Cale walked slowly down the aisle like the wicked witch in a fairy tale, his eyes in their black circles to match his clothes fixed on the beautiful pregnant girl in front of him. He should have realized, thought IdrisPukke, he really should. The chair next to him, meant for Cale's non-arrival, was eased back by a servant as Cale, full of himself at the satisfying catastrophe his presence was causing, came up, gave a gentle nod to Vipond and then fixed his murderous scowl on Arbell Swan-Neck. There was no word sufficiently strong to describe the look on Conn's face but no one had much difficulty imagining what was going on inside his soul. The question of whether or not he knew often crossed IdrisPukke's mind afterwards. It was hard to believe that if he did know the evening would end well. Bose Ikard must have hoped for trouble given what he must have known about Conn and Thomas Cale. But he had stumbled on something much worse than a glorified squabble between precocious boys.

There are many words for the different kinds of silence that exist between people who hate. IdrisPukke considered that if he was ever in prison again with a year or two weighing on his hands he might be able to arrive at a suitable list. But whatever kind of silence it was, it was ended by a guest of Vipond's, Señor Eddie Gray, an ambassador of sorts for the Norwegians trying to get a handle like many others on what, if anything, the Materazzi would do next and how it might affect them. Provocative and supercilious by nature, Gray looked Cale up and down ostentatiously.

'You're the right colour for an Angel of Death, Mr Cale. But a little short.'

There was the unheard sound of souls drawing breath. There was hardly a pause from Cale as he took his eyes for the first time from Arbell and looked at Gray.

'It's as you say. But if I was to cut off your head and put it under my feet I'd become taller.'

The cordon of silence of those who realized something was up had now extended either side of the Materazzi, including and not by accident Bose Ikard. Alerted by the contempt in Gray's tone and the odd appearance of the young man in black they had caught both Gray's dismissal and the devastating reply and burst into laughter.

Filled with a noxious mixture of hatred, adoration, love and considerable smugness at the sharpness of his own wit, Cale allowed the chair to be eased under him and turned his gaze at once ludicrous and terrifying to the hapless Swan-Neck. No bullock in a perfumier's maddened by wasps could have let loose such an ungovernable mix as the clouds of desires, resentments, betrayals and disappointed lusts that mingled and fumed within that stupendous hall. It was no wonder that the baby in its mother's womb began to kick and squirm like a piglet in a sack. It was a monument to

buns to a bear. He knew how to deal with aggression, verbal or physical. Arbell simply looked down at her soup bowl as if she hoped the contents would part like the Reed Sea and swallow her whole. Conn just glared at him. For all her misery she looked utterly and heart-breakingly beautiful. Her lips, usually somewhat pale brown, were a deep red and the white teeth just show-ing beneath them made him lyrical in his hatred and he thought of roses with snow between the scarlet petals. He had spent so much time thinking about her over the last hideous months that, now she stood only a few feet away, it seemed incomprehensible for all the hatred that she would not laugh with delight, as she used to when he closed the door of her rooms behind him, and squeeze him tightly in her arms and smother his face with kisses as if she could never get enough of the touch and taste of him. How was it possible that she had tired of him? How was it possible that she could prefer the creature sitting next to her, have let him . . . ? But that thought was too near madness and he was already too close. It had not even for a moment – you must excuse his utter ignorance in these things – occurred to him that he might be the father of the leaping bastard folded in its mother's womb. Nor had it occurred to him that in the eyes of any objective person the obviousness of Arbell Materazzi preferring a tall and beautiful youth of her own kind and breeding, the great hope for the future of all the Materazzi, over a dark-haired, shortish, harsh-souled murderer with a grudge against the world was a matter anyone would have even thought of questioning. It was true that she owed her life to him, and in an extraordinary way the life of her younger brother, but gratitude is an awkward emotion at the best of times, even or especially towards those you once adored. It is particularly difficult for beautiful princesses because they are, in a manner of speaking, born to be given things and even a normal capacity for gratitude would weigh more heavily on them than human nature is generally able to bear.

'Are you well?' said Cale at last. At no time in all the history of the world has such a question been asked as if it were a threat.

She briefly looked up, her natural boldness getting the better of her confusion.

'Very well.'

'I am glad to hear it. For myself times have been hard since we last met.'

'We've all suffered.'

'Speaking personally I've caused more suffering than I've endured.'

'Isn't that always your way?'

'You have a short memory – and worse since you were so many times in my debt.'

'Mind your manners,' said Conn, who would have stood and thrown his chair back with a dramatic flour-ish were it not for the fact that Vipond had gripped his thigh and squeezed with a strength surprising in a man of his age and profession.

'How's your leg?' replied Cale. He was, after all, in many ways still young.

'For God's sake,' whispered IdrisPukke. By now the wave of attentive silence had spread down one half of the hall. But having come with the intention of torment-ing Arbell at length Cale realized that the control that would have made this at least plausible had deserted him – a reservoir of loss and anger had opened up far deeper than he had realized he felt – and he had certainly known that it was deep. 'You're not wanted here,' said Conn, 'why don't you stop embarrassing yourself and leave.' Either of these would have done. Like some hypocaust bellows – fed by a frenetic bedlamite – Cale was fired up beyond control. He stood up and was reaching for his belt when a weak hand curled around his wrist.

'Hello, Tom,' said Vague Henri gently. 'I've brought someone to see you.' Like cool water his voice poured over the expectant silence of the lookers-on. Cale stared for a moment at the white skin and the still striking mark along his face and then the two standing next to him: Simon Materazzi and the always reluctant Koolhaus.

'Simon Materazzi says hello, Cale,' said Koolhaus. Then the deaf and dumb young man folded him in his arms and would not let him go until they were out of the hall and having a smoke in the damp cold air of Spanish Leeds.

It was two hours later before IdrisPukke tracked them down by the simple expedient of waiting in Cale's room until he returned.

'Take Henri and Simon back to bed before they fall down,' he told Koolhaus, who very gladly did as he was told. Cale sat down on his bed not looking at IdrisPukke.

'I hope you're pleased with yourself. Your reputation is no longer that of being God's wrath, more his village idiot.'

This stung enough at least to get Cale to look at him, although he still said nothing, miserable as a limp drum.

'Do you think you can bully the world?'

'I've done all right so far.'

'So far I suppose you have. But that isn't all that far considering you're so very young and there's such a lot of the world to go.'

Neither of them said anything for a full minute.

'I want her to suffer. She deserves it.' He spoke so softly and with such sadness IdrisPukke hardly knew what to say.

'I know how hard it is to give up a great love.'

'I saved her life.'

'Yes.'

'Did I do something wrong?'

'No.'

'Why then?'

'Nobody knows the answer to that. You can't say to someone love this woman or love that man.'

'But she used to.'

'What lovers say to one another is written in the wind and the water. Some poet or other said that but it's true all the same.'

'She gave me away to Bosco. It's not right to let that go.'

IdrisPukke might, in the interests of balance and fairness, have pointed out that Arbell had been in something of a difficult position at the time. But it had been years since he was foolish enough to have said so.

'Unfortunately we live in interesting times. You can have a great say in them, perhaps the greatest – so, young as you are and however much this is a pain to you, in matters of love and politics and war small things in life must give way to greater.'

Cale looked at him.

'Not if the small come first.'

Another long silence. Not even IdrisPukke could think of a reply. He changed the subject.

'I don't know what the Redeemers and their Pope are going to do about you. I wouldn't bank on it being nothing. You make enemies the way other people breathe. To speak angrily the way you do, to show your hatred by what you say or by the way you look, is an unnecessary proceeding: dangerous, foolish, ridiculous and vulgar – though I suppose vulgarity is the least of your problems. You must either learn more discretion or start running now.'

Cale said nothing while IdrisPukke sat on the bed feeling sorry for the strange boy next to him. After a few minutes IdrisPukke began to worry that in his silence Cale was drifting too far.

'Did you look up at the night sky while you were out?'

Cale laughed, softly and oddly, thought IdrisPukke – but it was better than the silence before.

'No,' said Cale. 'Do the stars still shine?'

'You have been the Master of Ceremonies,' said Vipond to IdrisPukke later that night, 'to a great many disasters but this must be one of your finest.'

'Not at all. I've been involved in many worse things than a squabble between two lovers.'

'You know it's a good deal worse than that. Bose Ikard wants us expelled and you can be very sure a report about a brawl between the Materazzi heirs and your friend Nogbad the Bad will be on its way to the King of Switzerland as we speak, and a carefully embroidered one at that.'

'King Zog may be an old woman but he's not going to throw us out over a squabble like this – however much Ikard stirs it up.'

'He will if he tells him that there is some question over the paternity of Arbell's child.'

'What do you think?'

'What do *you* think?'

'It's possible.'

'There's no arguing with that. The point is that the rumours are leaking under every doorway in Spanish Leeds. King Zog takes a very dim view of promiscuous behaviour and particularly between an aristocrat and some yob who carries the coal into her bedroom.'

'He's a great deal more than that.'

'Not to King Zog of Switzerland. God never created a greater snob. His only reading is to spend hours sighing with pleasure and delight over his ancestry in the *Almanach de Gotha*.'

'In case you hadn't noticed, brother'– IdrisPukke never called him this unless he was particularly annoyed with him – 'the Materazzi have descended into a kind of nothing. Without Cale to stop them the Redeemers are ready to roll up the Antagonists, the Laconics, Switzerland and everyone else like an old carpet. And they'll piss on King Zog as they go by.'

'Conn Materazzi is a prospect, given time.'

'Cale plotted our destruction and that of the Laconics. Not bad for a coal-carrying yob. If you think Conn Materazzi has that in him you must be the old fool that there's no fool like.'

'We only have his word for the defeat of the Laconics.'

'We were there at Silbury to witness what Cale's plans did to us.'

'All excuses aside, that was as much luck as judgement.'

'What isn't?'

'You can't control him.'

'No.'

'He can't control himself.'

'He wouldn't be the first. He's young, he'll get over it.'

'You're wrong about that. I heard him threaten her when he left Memphis and again tonight. He'll never be free of her. People talk about children as if they're in some way different from adults. But there isn't any difference, not really. Just souls crazy for love. The lover and the killer are in him like linsey-woolsey – never to be singled out.'

'Then get Arbell out of Spanish Leeds and Conn with her. Out of sight, out of mind. Then we use Cale to come up with a plan to deal with the Redeemers.'

'Why should he help us?'

'He hates Arbell because he loved her and saved her and still she gave him up to them.'

'We all did that.'

'Speak for yourself. And he didn't worship the ground you walked on. It's in his interests to strike a deal with us because there isn't anywhere else he can go. With Cale directing a Swiss army there's at least a chance for us and a chance for him. He'll see that. Arbell or no Arbell, he's always had survival on his mind.'

'Isn't he just a danger to everyone?'

'Then we must help him focus his attention where he can do most damage.'

'It's not much of a plan.'

'It is when you don't have a better one.'

'Did you know he's been talking to Kitty the Hare?'

'Yes.'

'You liar!' As if they were young boys again no offence was intended or taken.

'Do you tell anyone else all your comings and goings?' said IdrisPukke.

'I'm renowned for my candid nature.'

'Exactly so. If he's going to save the rest of us from the Redeemers I hope to God he has his thumbs on as many scales as there are sea shells on the shore.'

'Another threat to Arbell from the Redeemers would be useful – good excuse to encourage Arbell's absence.'

'Would Conn go with her?'

'Too much to hope for. Besides, Zog won't have a guttersnipe leading an army he's paying for, whatever you think.'

'Then he's a fool.'

'No one has ever argued otherwise.'

'Can you control Conn?'

'Yes,' replied Vipond.

'Enough to let himself become a front for someone who might be the father of his first child?'

'Not an approach I was thinking of trying. Besides, we have an advantage.'

'Which is?'

'He doesn't want to believe it. We must encourage that natural desire as much as possible.'

But their plan had an unforeseen flaw – though this was not in itself something that would have surprised either of them.

Part of Bose Ikard's way of making the Materazzi feel unwelcome was to ensure the inadequacy of their accommodation. When it came to Arbell this involved a message delivered by putting her in rooms designed two hundred years earlier as living space for the then King's new bride, the Infanta Pilar. The Infanta never grew above two and a half cubits (a cubit being the distance between the elbow and the fingers of an outstretched hand). Adored for her good nature, wit and generosity to the poor, she inspired numerous buildings in the resultant craze for all things Spanish that had given what was then mere Leeds its unusual additional name. Once a byword for all that was dismal ('You look like Leeds' was an ancient joke at the expense of the unhappy – and the expense of Leeds), the desire to please the tiny Infanta led to an explosion of exotic public and private houses in the Spanish style. The Infanta's personal apartments were built by her doting husband to her scale rather than that of the giants who surrounded her. The result for Arbell was that while her apartments were certainly fit for a queen they were fit for a very small queen

477

forty-two inches high. To the Infanta the ceiling was lofty, to Arbell there were many parts of her rooms where she had to bow her beautiful neck just ever-so-slightly.

It was the night after the dreadful banquet and Conn and Arbell were sitting down in her apartments. Given they were both tall this gave the proportions of the room a comic aspect as if they were sat in a place somewhere between a ship's cabin and a large doll's house.

Arbell was looking down at her breasts and stomach. 'I feel,' she said ruefully to Conn, 'as if I'd swallowed the heads of three bald men. Big-headed bald men. God, how much longer?'

'You look very beautiful.'

'I made you say that.'

Conn smiled.

'It's true you did make me say it. But it's true anyway.'

'You lie so sweetly it's almost a pleasure to be deceived by you.'

'Have it your own way,' he said, taking her hand.

'Promise me you'll stay away from Thomas Cale,' she said.

'I wondered how long before you brought him up.'

'Now you know. Promise me.'

'You forget that he saved my life. It's not so easy to kill someone you owe so much to. He saved yours as well and that makes it harder still. So I promise – even if he was so rude to you.'

'I'll live. But I want to ask you something much harder.'

'What?'

'He is not so gracious. I want you to promise to walk away if he comes looking for you.'

'And my pride?'

'It's nothing. It'll pass. Pride is nothing.'

'You say that because you're a woman.'

'And so I don't have any pride?'

'What makes you proud is different – so what's possible or impossible is different.'

'Will you take pride in giving Cale what he wants? He's not stupid enough to provoke you when you're in full armour. He knows that you'd have the advantage.' Some flattery, probably true, was needed here. She had pushed him too far already.

'And what am I supposed to do if he dares me?'

'My God, you sound like a schoolboy!'

'If you choose not to understand.' He was annoyed at being spoken to like this but allowances must be made for women and especially women in the late stages of pregnancy. 'If I walk away from him then my reputation, the thing that I am, walks away from me at the same time. You tell me that you will continue to respect me – but will you?'

'Of course I will.'

'That's what you say now. But I won't have the respect of anyone else.'

She sighed and said nothing for a while.

'I know what you are – you are courageous and skilful and daring.' More necessary flattery – and also true. 'But he's not,' she looked hard for the right word and failed, 'he's not normal. He doesn't bring catastrophe, he *is* a catastrophe. His friend, Kleist – the one who never liked him – he said he had funerals in his brain. Well, it's true.'

'How is anyone to live without respect? What's the point?'

She sighed again and moved her stiff neck from side to side and groaned. *Look at yourself*, she thought, *as fat as gluttony*. 'When will it ever end?' she said aloud and looked at her husband sideways. 'You owe him your life.'

'Yes.'

'Then how can you honourably kill him? Let it be more widely known that he behaved bravely – more, praise his courage so that people will admire you more than they admire him. Make it clear that you are inevitably in his debt and everyone will praise you for walking away if he provokes you. What courage! What true honour that Conn Materazzi could so easily fight and yet risks that honour in order to be honourable. It's true after all, you said so yourself.'

'Won't that mean he gains a reputation . . .' He had to think about this: was it an honourable objection to make in the circumstances? '. . . a name for courage?'

'Don't worry about that,' replied Arbell. 'He'll soon spoil the good opinion anyone has of him. He thinks it's beneath him to be admired by people he despises – and he despises everyone.'

'You're very clever.'

'Yes I am.' She squeezed his hand. 'Now go away and let me sleep.'

He stood up and cracked his head on the ceiling.

'Ow!'

She winced along with him but could see he was not hurt. She made to get up to kiss it better – no mean feat. 'Stay where you are,' he said.

She needed no encouragement. 'I will if you don't mind.' He bent down and kissed her lightly on the mouth. Then with exaggerated comic carefulness he made his way to the door and was gone. She eased herself further back onto the sofa, twisting from side to side to stretch her aching back and decided to wait for another ten minutes before making the effort to go to bed. She closed her eyes, enjoying the peace and quiet.

And then from the shadows at the back of the room a low voice said softly:

'I do haunt you still.'

Some say the world will end in ice. If so, it was something of that terminal cold that froze the hairs on the neck of the young mother-to-be. She moved quick as you like for all the aching back and enormous bulge and turned in horror as Cale emerged into the candlelight.

'In case you were wondering,' he said, putting his finger precisely on the fear uppermost in her mind, 'I heard everything you said. Not very nice.'

'I'll scream.'

'I wouldn't. Things would be grim for anyone who came through the door when you did.'

'You expect me to die without a word?'

'God no. I wouldn't expect you to comb your own hair without complaining.' This was not fair. She was by no means a trivial person. 'Whine all you like, your majesty, but do it quietly.'

'Are you going to kill me?'

'I'm *thinking* of killing you.'

'I know you believe I've offended you but how has my baby offended?'

'That's why I'm thinking about it.'

'It's yours.'

'You would say that.'

'It's true.'

'It's true that I saved your life twice and you said you loved me more deeply than . . .' He smiled, not pleasantly. '. . . you know I can't remember but I seem to recall it was a thing of great depth. Perhaps you can help me.'

'It *is* true,' she said, almost impossible to hear.

'The rumour in the vegetable market is that you're a slut – and betting is even as to who the father is: either the Memphis village idiot or the prole who carried the coals into your bedroom.'

'You know that isn't true.'

'I don't know. You sold me to men who for all you knew were going to take me to a place of execution, hang me and then cut me down alive, gut me . . . while I watched . . . fry those guts . . . while I watched . . . cut off my cock and balls . . . while I watched. Well, you see. It looks bad.'

'They promised me they wouldn't hurt you.'

'And what made you think a promise meant more to them than it meant to you. You were tired of me, and wanted to see the back of me, and didn't care how.'

'That's not true.' She was crying now but barely audibly.

'It may not be the whole truth but it's true enough. Anyway I'm sick of listening to you.'

'They didn't do any of those things to you. He promised to make you a great man. Aren't you? Didn't he keep his promise?'

This was too much. In a few strides he was over to her as she backed away to the wall holding her hands out in terror to protect her child. He reached behind her head and grabbed her golden pony tail and dragged her over to the sofa, pushing her to her knees.

'I'll show you how he kept his promise, you lying bitch.' He kept tight hold of her hair with one hand and pulled the lamp on the table next to the sofa so that it cast a better light. Then with his free hand he reached into a back pocket and took out the letter given to him by Bosco and over which he had squabbled with Vague Henri. He unfolded it on the sofa rug, violently pushing her head down so that her face was almost touching it.

'Read!' he said.

'You're hurting me.'

He twisted her hair sharply. She called out.

'Scream quietly,' he whispered. 'Someone might be unlucky enough to hear. Now read who it's from.' Another encouraging tug.

'From Redeemer General Archer, Commander Forces of the Veldt, to Redeemer General Bosco.'

'You can skip the first five lines.'

Arbell continued with some difficulty – his grip was fierce and she was too close to the script.

'Before he left Thomas Cale ordered us to sweep up every village on the Veldt within fifty miles of our camps and bring in all the women and children, their animals to be used to feed the three thousand souls we managed to intern. Some sort of rinderpest killed most of their cattle and reduced very much the milk of those that survived. Often lacking sufficient rations ourselves there were none to spare. Given their weakness many have succumbed to starvation, measles and the squits, in all about two and a half thousand. I was not informed until very late and when I inspected the camp I saw such wretchedness any heart would have rued the sight . . .'

'Don't worry about the next bit,' said Cale, pointing further down the letter, 'start again there.'

'Out of every corner of the place they came creeping on their hands and knees because their legs could not bear them; they looked like the very anatomy of death and spoke whispers like ghosts crying out of their graves. It was told to me that they were happy to eat moss where they could and then finally in desperation to scrape the carcasses out of their graves also. I know you to be a person of clemency but though I describe pitiable things, and ones easier to read about than to witness, there is no hope that these Antagonists will amend and it is a dire necessity that they be cut off. This judgement of the heavens that makes us tremble touches us not with pity.'

'That's enough,' he said, letting her hair go and bouncing her head off the soft bolster of the sofa – not the cruellest violence he had offered the world it must be said.

Slowly she pulled herself up and eased into a sitting position.

'I don't understand,' she said at last. 'What has this got to do with me? Or even you? This dreadful thing wasn't what you intended, was it?'

'Haven't you heard? The road to hell is paved with good intentions. My *intention* is to be left alone with a decent bed and some decent food to go with it. But what I *do* is just what you said. Catastrophe follows me everywhere. I sat in the shadows back there listening to your chinless wonder whining about his reputation –'

'He's not chinless!'

'Be quiet. My *reputation* is that I'm a bloody child who cares no more for the lives of people than he cares for the life of a dog. My reputation is that I consume everything I touch. *You* put me there back with them. The blood of everyone I've wasted since then is on your hands as well as mine.'

'Why don't you just stop killing people instead of blaming everyone else?'

She said this more violently than was perhaps wise given the circumstances. But she did not lack courage.

'And tell me how am I supposed to do that? The Redeemers won't stop, not for anything. They intend to wrap this world in a blanket, pour on the pitch, and then set fire to it like a match. There's no *stopping*.' He stood back glaring like the Troll of Gissinghurst. To be fair, she glared back giving as good as she got. 'Now I'm going to leave by the door – not how I got in, just in case you were wondering. I want you to think about that in the nights to come. You're not going to call anyone because I'll kill them if you do and even if I'm caught I'll be sure to mention to your chinless wonder of a husband that you claimed I was the father of his child.'

'He won't believe you.'

'He will a little bit.'

And with that he walked to the door and was gone.

He moved quickly down the almost empty corridors – where the only guards were the young and inexperienced

huge wall carved into the granite that topped the city. It had been cut flat and into it, and thickly carved were the great figures of the Antagonist Reformation who had taken refuge in Spanish Leeds during the initial persecution and before they had moved on to found the Antagonist city at Salt Lake. Here were thirty-foot-high reliefs of men who had fought against the Redeemers to the point of hideous death and yet he had never heard of them: Butzer, Hus and Philip Melanchthon, Menno Simons, Zwingli, Hutt and the unhappy-looking Mosarghu Brothers. Who were these giants in front of him and what in the name of God did they believe? It was almost impossible to grasp that the rejection of the Redeemers had such heft to it. Then he moved on across the park feeling ever more distant and removed from the flow of ordinary human happiness taking in the sun and each other as they would do a week today and all spring and summer long. And now he had to get away, out of the great ornate cast-iron gates of the north end of the park and round the side heading for his room. But he was so tired now, utterly weary, exhausted in a way that was completely new to him. He walked ever slower down the street as if each step was ageing him by a year, but it was so much worse than ordinary fatigue. He felt he had been on the move for a thousand years and nowhere to sit down, no rest, no peace, nothing but fighting and fear of the next blow. His heart was so heavy in his chest he felt it dragging him to a halt. How was it possible to feel like this and live? By now he was at the West Gate and he stopped and rested his head, pouring sweat against the sandstone.

'Are you all right, son?' But he did not have the strength to reply. Afterwards he could not remember how he made it back to his room, not even unlocking the door, only his lying on the bed gasping like a fish drowning on dry land. And then it came for him – the earthquake in his guts, a shaking and an avalanche of collapse and burst. His inside world gave way of flesh and soul together, hideous pain of tears and eruption. He rushed towards the jakes and retched and retched and nothing came but so violent it was as if his soul was trying to leave his bowels and belly while he was still alive. And so it went on for hour after hour. And then he went back to bed and wept but not like any child or man and nothing to do with release, and then when he thought, whatever thinking was, that bellowing in tear-less pain would never stop, that was when he began to laugh over and over and for hours on end. And laughing was how Vague Henri found him just before dawn, still laughing, weeping and retching.

For a week they kept him in his room but he did not improve. He would sleep for twelve hours or more but wake more exhausted and black-eyed and white-lipped with weariness than when he went to sleep. There would be a pause for three hours during which he would lie on his side, knees bent, and then the retching would begin – a hideous sound more like some great animal trying to expel some poisonous thing it had eaten. After a few days the terrible laughter stopped – no relief to Cale, only to those who had to listen to it. Cale kept retching and such tears as he wept clearly gave him no ease or peace. Soon the tears stopped too. But he kept on retching though never being sick and even though he ate and hungrily enough. After that week it settled into a dreadful pattern: hours of sleep that gave no rest, eating hungrily, then the spasms lasting for an hour, then rest in silence, another attack, more food and then an exhausted sleep. Then the cycle would begin again.

They brought doctors who prescribed noxious substances at enormous cost that Cale refused to take. Then finally, in desperation, they brought in John Bradmore at Vague Henri's suggestion.

He sat with Cale for an hour or two and tried him with some honey mixed with wine and opium, which seemed to make him calmer until, for the first time, he threw the lot up in one great spew all over the bedroom floor.

Later IdrisPukke, Vipond and Vague Henri talked with Bradmore outside.

'Other than to point out he's horribly sick I can find nothing wrong. From what you say he gets neither worse nor better. If you can pay him I would try and fetch Robert of Salerno.'

'Salerno is five hundred miles away.'

'But the money is here. He treats the mad girls of the aristocracy and merchants of Spanish Leeds, God knows there are enough of them.'

'He's not a girl.'

'Neither is he sick in any way that I can treat. Robert of Salerno is an irritation and a pest, full of himself, but he's had good results with people who are sick in the head.'

'Bradmore is right,' said Robert of Salerno, the next day standing in the same corridor. 'This is well outside his understanding. There'll be no ingenious devices here.'

'Thank you. The point?'

Robert of Salerno with a hundred dollars of Kitty the Hare's money in his pocket was not as easy to insult as was normally the case – normally it was very easy indeed.

'Do you know where you can find the best picture of the human soul?'

'I am sure you'll tell me.'

'For a hundred dollars I would tell anyone. The best picture of the human soul, Mr IdrisPukke, is the human body. The soul has its kidneys and its liver, its stomach, its arms and legs. And it has disease of every limb and organ too: there are different fevers of the soul as there are scarlet fevers of the body, yellow fevers; for every rash that degrades the skin there is one for the will, the soul has its hard abscesses and its weeping ones; there are many ulcers of the mind, cancers of the passions.'

'We understand,' said Vipond. 'The boy?'

'You know, I think, as well as I do what's wrong with him. According to this young man' – he gestured at Vague Henri – 'you are familiar with his history. He's been treated like a dog all his life, moiled, beaten, fed bad food by wicked men. He has seen and done horrible things.'

'Why hasn't it happened to me?' said Vague Henri.

'Who's to say it won't. I've been in cities where bubonic plague has carried away three quarters of the population and left the rest untouched. Who knows the answer to these things?'

'A hundred dollars in pocket says that you should.'

'As my old nurse used to say: "The doctor who can mend this boy isn't born and his mother's dead." Your boy is like one of those mountain trees that's grown up in the teeth of the wind. This is his shape and you can't unbend him into another.'

'So what are we to do now? Nothing?'

Robert of Salerno sighed. 'Treat him kindly and don't allow anyone to give him any painful treatments. There are plenty who will offer to make him better by harsh means. Don't allow it. They will open holes in his skull, keep him in vats of freezing water for a day or feed him drugs that would kill a horse. You would better show your love for him by drowning him in a bucket. I will write a letter to the Sisters of Mercy in Cyprus. People will tell you they are very strange, and they are, but they are good-natured. They help the mad by talk and kindness. They won't make him any worse.'

'How long do you think it will be before he gets better?' said Vague Henri.

Robert of Salerno looked at him and did not reply to the question. 'Do you want me to make the arrangements?'

'Yes,' said Vipond.

Robert of Salerno bowed very slightly and was gone.

At the same time some two hundred miles away in Upper Silesia, Kleist along with twenty-one men between the ages of eighteen and forty-two entered the coal town of Bytom, as grim a dump as any they had ever seen.

'If this is Upper Silesia,' said Tarleton, 'what in God's

name is it like in Lower Silesia?' No one said anything, let alone laughed. They were too full of hopeless hatred. They wanted revenge it was true, but they were crippled by shame and despair at what they had allowed to happen to their wives and children.

They bought a week's worth of supplies with the money they had left and stood in the damp main square and talked about what to do next. After half an hour they decided. Four of them wanted to go north and get as far from the Redeemers as the earth would carry them. The remaining twenty-two and Kleist decided to head for Spanish Leeds, where they'd heard, wrongly, an army was being assembled to fight the Redeemers. The four going north took their share of the supplies, shook hands and left. The twenty-two and Kleist went east.

Two days after they'd left Bytom the widow Kleist, heavily pregnant and thinking herself to be the last survivor of an obscure clan from the Quantock Mountains, made her way though the same square heading for Spanish Leeds, where she hoped her child would be born a citizen of that town and country, where it was said widows were paid a pension by the state and that there was free milk for babies under three years of age.

It had taken Redeemer Gil some time to learn to take pleasure in his new power, even if he disapproved of himself for enjoying the vast desk with its ornate carvings

494

of the various atrocities commited on the bodies of the faithful, or the speed and obsequiousness of the answer to his bell as he summoned and dismissed men who were often of great substance in Chartres but now demonstrated so obviously the necessity of pleasing him. There were pangs of guilt now and again as there always must be for a Redeemer, but they were less and less frequent, or if not less frequent then less and less sharp. Only a very few months ago Redeemer Warren, the man opposite him listening so gravely and so attentively, would have regarded him as an uncouth member of the Militant, not to be treated with contempt but certainly condescended to. Now he was staring at Gil and horribly thrilled at the responsibility involved in what he was being instructed to undertake.

'You're to bring only the most reticent and trusted into your confidence and few of them, but you are to say nothing of the true identity of the impostor who stole the papacy. They're only to know that they're searching out vile women we have reason to suspect might have disguised themselves as clergy. They are to root out the truth of this one way or the other. If it is not the case I must know it. As to the means by which that abomination made her way to Pope, I want you to get to the bottom of how it was done. Was it a conspiracy or was this creature acting alone?'

There was a knock at the door and Monsignor Chadwick entered and with a deferential nod to Warren walked over to Gil and whispered in his ear, 'The Two Trevors.' Gil said nothing but Chadwick left, sliding out of the room as if he were on wheels.

'You must excuse me, Redeemer,' Gil said to Warren. 'You have questions but there are few answers. Consider what I've said and give me your thoughts in a day or two. You're to say nothing of what you've heard until we talk again.'

Warren stood up, walked to the door in a state of shock and was gone. A minute later there was another knock from a small door on the left of the room. Again it opened and again it was Chadwick. This time he stood aside to allow in two men. One looked like a whippet, the other not just handsome but engaging, his expression warm and good-humoured. Gil gestured them to come forward and for Chadwick to leave.

'Thank you for coming. Sit down.'

The eel-faced Trevor Lugavoy stretched out his legs in an insolent manner as if to make it clear that he did not mind if he was here or somewhere else. It was the engaging Trevor Kovtun who spoke.

'You want us to bring someone to Death's attention?' It was more playful but just as impudent as his companion's outstretched legs.

'In order to bring about certain prophecies in holy writ it's necessary for you to martyr someone.'

They seemed distinctly put out by the idea, although not because of the crime involved.

'We don't chastise people before we kill them,' said Trevor Kovtun.

'Yes, we're not common torturers,' added Trevor Lugavoy.

Gil was not about to take any nonsense no matter what their reputation. 'Fortunately for your fine sensibilities no chastising is necessary. You'll be very well paid but let me remind you that you've had refuge at my say so on Redeemer territory for a good few years.' The point did not need labouring.

'Who then?' asked Trevor Lugavoy.

'Thomas Cale.'

That got their attention – the swagger of the outstretched legs, the insolence of their violent profession diminished satisfyingly enough.

'And for the avoidance of doubt, I don't want you to bring him to Death's attention, whatever that means. I want him dead.'

# Acknowledgements

My thanks to my editor Alex Clarke and his insightful and clever notes on the original manuscript.

'Tradition is not the worship of ashes,
but the preservation of fire'

Gustav Mahler

There are many acts of righteous larceny throughout these three books, from *Paradise Lost* to a shampoo ad from the sixties, from Francis Bacon to a Millwall Football Club chant. Two of Bosco's speeches in *The Last Four Things*, on the essential worthlessness of mankind and the lonely greatness of the hangman, are based on essays from the Catholic philosopher Joseph de Maistre.

There are a number of scenes indebted to the long-forgotten Mary Herbert, particularly *Death To The French* and *The Unhappy Prince*. Arthur Schopenhauer and La Rochefoucauld take their usual bow in the observations of IdrisPukke and Vipond. Much of the tactics and the idea behind the episode at Duffer's Drift come from E. D. Swinton's imaginative training manual of the Boer

War, *The Defence of Duffer's Drift* (out of print but available on the web). Lines and half-lines from the King James Bible are everywhere, the beautiful and the ugly. The practical usefulness to me of the *Iliad* and its descriptions of violence is straightforward. The web in general and YouTube in particular made it possible to use the shouts and cries of men in the middle of battle in Iraq and Afghanistan. It also enabled me to find footage of Saddam Hussein's denunciations of his soon-to-be-dead rivals during the Ba'ath Party Assembly in 1979, here used during Bosco's similar strategy at the Congress in Chartres.

The idea for the Klephts came from John Keegan's brief but incisive discussion of these impressively unheroic Greek bandits on page ten of *A History of Warfare*. The details of the operation on Vague Henri follow closely the account by surgeon John Bradmore of his successful attempt to remove an arrow from the face of the fifteen-year-old Prince Henry (later Henry V) in 1403. Anyone who doubts the potential physical strength or tactical ability of adolescents should read an account of Henry's youthful military campaigns and note that he took this hideous wound in the face early on in the Battle of Shrewsbury, fought 'hand-to-hand' for the rest of the day and then led a cavalry charge in the evening which had a major effect on the outcome.

The harrowing description of the starvation of the Folk that Cale forces Arbell to read aloud comes from

*A View of the Present State of Ireland* by Edmund Spenser, author of *The Faerie Queene*. Spenser is not just responsible for the terrible brilliance of the description of famine, a brilliance that might be expected from someone generally considered to be one of the greatest of all English poets, but also for the view that a policy of genocide through starvation was the only solution to the problem of Ireland. Anyone who believes that it is not possible to write hideous ideas beautifully might like to read the full text. The assumption that someone as noxious as Hitler, a deeply talentless painter, could never by definition be a great artist has to confront this little-known work.

Cale's idea for a concentration camp to isolate his opponents from the support of the native population was first carried out during the Boer War with the same, admittedly unintended, consequences.

Also thanks to Nick Lowndes of Penguin and Mark Handsley for their work on the preparation of the text. As always, Alexandra Hoffman and my agent, Anthony Goff. Anna Swan read the manuscript with the sharpest of eyes. I remain deeply grateful to Kate Burton (née Brotherhood) for placing this book in so many languages.

'Your joy is all in laying
waste to things – blight and
desolation is what makes
your soul glad.'

Read on for an extract from The Beating of His Wings,
the final instalment in the Left Hand of God trilogy.

# I

**A brief report on Thomas Cale, Lunatic. Three conversations at the Priory on the Island of Cyprus.**

*(NB This appraisal took place after Mother Superior Allbright's stroke. The notes she filed have been mislaid along with Cale's admission details. This report needs to be read in the light of this absence and so I will not be held liable for any of my conclusions.)*

PHYSICAL CHARACTERISTICS
Medium stature, unusually pale. Middle finger of his left hand missing. Depression fracture to the right side of his skull. Severe keloid scar tissue in wound in left shoulder. Patient says he experiences intermittent pain from all injuries.

SYMPTOMS
Severe retching, usually in mid-afternoon. Exhaustion. Suffers insomnia and bad dreams when able to sleep. Loss of weight.

HISTORY
Thomas Cale suffers no hysterical delusions or uncontrolled behaviour beyond that of his sour nature. His mid-afternoon retching leaves him speechless with exhaustion, after which he sleeps. By late evening he is able to talk, although he is the most sarcastic and wounding of persons. He claims to have been bought for sixpence from parents he does not remember by a priest of the Order of the Hanged Redeemer.

Thomas Cale is droll, not his least irritating affectation, and always tries either to make his interlocutor unsure as to whether he is mocking them or, by unpleasant contrast, to make it abundantly clear that he is. He tells the story of his upbringing in the Sanctuary as if daring me to disbelieve the daily cruelties he endured. Recovering from an injury which caused the dent in his head he claims – again it is not possible to tell with what degree of seriousness – that his already great prowess (he seems boastful in hindsight, but not at the time) was greatly increased as a result of the injury and that since this recovery he is always able to anticipate in advance any opponent's movements. This sounds unlikely; I declined his offer of a demonstration. The rest of his story is as improbable as the most far-fetched children's story of derring-do and swashbuckling. He is the worst liar I have ever come across.

His story briefly. His life of deprivation and military training at the Sanctuary came to a dramatic end one night after he accidentally came upon a high-ranking Redeemer in the middle of performing a live dissection upon two young girls, some kind of holy experiment to discover a means to neuter the power of women over mankind. Killing that Redeemer in the ensuing struggle, he escaped from the Sanctuary with the surviving young woman and two of his friends, with more Redeemers in vengeful pursuit. Evading their pursuers, the quartet ended up in Memphis where, plausibly, Thomas Cale made many enemies and (rather less plausibly) a number of powerful allies, including the notorious IdrisPukke and his half-brother, Chancellor Vipond (as he then was). Despite these advantages his violent nature asserted itself in a brutal but unusually non-fatal altercation with (so he says) half a dozen of the youths of Memphis in which (of course) he emerged triumphant but bound for prison. Nevertheless, Lord Vipond again mysteriously intervened on his behalf and he was sent into the countryside with IdrisPukke. The peace of the Materazzi hunting lodge where they were staying was interrupted shortly after he arrived by a woman who attempted to assassinate him, for reasons he was unable to clarify. His murder was prevented not by his own wonderful abilities – he was swimming naked at the time of the attack – but by a mysterious, unseen and insolent stranger who killed his would-be assassin by means of an arrow in the back. His saviour then vanished without explanation or trace.

By now the priests of the Sanctuary had discovered his general whereabouts and attempted to flush him out (he claims) by kidnapping Arbell Materazzi, daughter of the Doge of Memphis. When I asked him why the Redeemers would risk a ruinous war with the greatest of all temporal powers for his sake, he laughed in my face and told me he would reveal his magnificent importance to me in due course. The inflated mad, in my experience, take their importance most seriously but it is a feature of Thomas Cale that his demented state only becomes apparent a few hours after a conversation with him comes to an end. While you are in his company even the most implausible stories he tells cause you to suspend disbelief until several hours later, when a most irritating sensation creeps over you, as if you had been tricked by a marketplace quack into parting with ready money for a bottle of universal remedy. I've seen this before in a lunatic, though rarely, in that some are so powerfully deluded and in such a strange way that their delusions run away with even the most cautious of anomists.

Of course, Thomas Cale rescues the beautiful princess from the wicked Redeemers but, it must be said, not by means of the fair and noble fight against overwhelming odds but by stabbing most of his opponents in their sleep. This is another unusual feature of his delusion – that each one of his endless triumphs is not generally achieved by heroism and noble audacity but through brutal trickery and conscienceless pragmatism. Usually such madmen present themselves as gallant and chivalrous, but Thomas Cale freely admits to poisoning his enemies' water with rotting animals and killing his opponents in their sleep. It's worth recording briefly one of our exchanges in this regard.

ME
Is it a matter of course with you that you always kill unarmed prisoners?

PATIENT
It's easier than killing armed ones.

ME
So you believe the lives of others are a matter for sarcasm?

PATIENT
(NO REPLY)

ME
You never consider showing mercy?

PATIENT
No, I never did.

ME
Why?

PATIENT
They wouldn't have shown it to me. Besides, what would I do but let them go only to find I'd have to

fight them again. Then I might become their prisoner
– and be killed myself.

ME
What about women and children?

PATIENT
I never killed them deliberately.

ME
But you've killed them?

PATIENT
Yes. I've killed them.

He claimed to have built a camp to sequester the wives and
children of the Folk insurrection and that because of his
having been removed elsewhere almost the entire cantonment
of five thousand souls died through famine and disease.
When I asked him what he felt about this he replied: 'What
should I feel?'

To return to his story. After his brutal rescue of the beautiful
Arbell Materazzi (are there any merely plain princesses in the
world of the delusional?) he was promoted, along with his
two friends, to guard the young woman towards whom he
maintained throughout our three long conversations a deeply
held resentment as to her ingratitude and disdain for him.
This bitterness seems to hold a great sway over him because
of his belief that when Memphis later fell to the Redeemers,
it did so because the Materazzi failed to execute his plan to
defeat them. (He is, by the way, very insistent that his skill in
generalship is greater even than his talent for personal
savagery.)

Usually sarcastic and matter-of-fact as he boasts of his great
rise to power – again, his droll tone makes it seem not like

boasting until one reflects upon his claims in tranquillity – he became most indignant as he recounted the way in which he was caught by the Redeemers after the Battle of Silbury Hill (certainly a disaster for us all whether or not Thomas Cale was involved). It is possible he was caught up in the battle in a minor way; his description of the events there has the note of real experience. Like all skilled romancers he can use his actual events to make the imagined ones truly plausible. For example, he frequently expresses repentance for any noble or generous actions he has performed. He says that he risked his life to save a Materazzi youth who had bullied and tormented him – an act of sanctity which he says he now bitterly regrets. When I asked whether it was always bad to act generously towards others he said that in his experience it might not be bad but it was always a 'bloody catastrophe'. People thought so well of doing good, he said, that in the end they always decided it should be done at the end of a sword. The Redeemers thought so highly of goodness they wanted to kill everyone including themselves and start again. It turns out that this was the reason his former mentor, Redeemer Bosco, wanted him back at any price. Thomas Cale is (of course) no ordinary boy but the manifestation of God's wrath and destined to wipe his greatest mistake (you and me, for the avoidance of doubt) off the face of the earth. I have treated shopkeepers who thought they were great generals and men who could barely write who thought they were poets of unparalleled genius but I have never encountered an inflation of such magnitude before – let alone in a child. When I asked him how long he'd had such feelings of importance he began to backtrack and – with very bad temper – said that this was what Bosco thought, not what he, Thomas Cale, thought. More circumspectly, I asked him if he believed Redeemer Bosco was mad and he replied he had never met a Redeemer who wasn't and that in his experience a great many people who seemed to be right in the head, once you got to see them 'put under grief', were 'completely barking' – an expression I have not encountered before though its meaning was clear enough.

He is clever, then, at avoiding the implications of his delusions of grandeur: in the opinion of great and powerful men he is mighty enough to destroy all the world but this delusion is not his but theirs. When I asked him if he *would* do such a thing his reply was extremely foul-mouthed but to the effect that he would not. When I asked whether he had the *ability* to do such a thing he smiled – not pleasantly – and said he had been responsible for the deaths of ten thousand men killed in a single day, so it was only a question of how many thousands and how many days.

After his recapture by the Redeemer Bosco, his role of Angel of Death to the world was explained to him in detail and he was put to work by his former mentor. This 'Bosco' (the new Pope is called Bosco but Thomas Cale clearly likes a big lie) is much hated by Cale although, since buying him for sixpence, training him and then elevating him to the power almost of a god, Bosco is paradoxically the source of all his excellence. When I pointed this out he claimed to know this already, though I could see I had scored a hit to his vanity (which is very great).

He then detailed an endless series of battles, which all sounded the same to me, and in which he was, of course, always victorious. When I asked if, during all these successes, he had not suffered even a few setbacks he looked at me as if he would like to cut my throat and then laughed – but very oddly, more like a single bark, as if he could not contain something very far from high spirits or even mockery.

These numerous triumphs led in turn to his being less watched over by Bosco than formerly. And after yet another great battle, in which he overcame the greatest of all opponents, he slipped away in the resulting chaos and ended up in Spanish Leeds, where he suffered the first of the brain attacks that brought him here. I witnessed one of these seizures and they are alarming to watch and clearly distressing to endure – his entire body is wracked by convulsions, as if he is trying to vomit but is unable to do so. He insists he has been sent here by friends of some power and influence in Spanish Leeds. Needless to say, of these important benefactors there is no sign. When I asked why they had not been to see him he explained – as if I were an idiot – that he had only just arrived in Cyprus and that the distance was too great for them to travel to see him regularly. This great distance was a deliberate choice in order to keep him safe. 'From what?' I asked. 'From all those who want me dead,' he replied.

He told me that he had arrived with an attendant doctor and a letter for Mother Superior Allbright. Pressed, he told me that the doctor had returned to Spanish Leeds the next day but that he had spent several hours with the Mother Superior before his departure. Clearly Thomas Cale must have come from somewhere, and there might indeed have been some sort of attendant who arrived with him bearing a letter and who spoke with the Mother Superior prior to her stroke. The loss, as it were, of both letter and Mother Superior leaves this case somewhat in the Limbo in which unbaptized infants are said to wait out eternity. Given the violent nature of his imaginings (though not, to be fair, his behaviour) it seems wisest to place him in the protective ward until the letter can be found or the Mother Superior recovers enough to tell us more about him. As it stands, there is no one to whom I can even write to make enquiries about him. This is an unsatisfactory state of affairs and it is not the first time by a long chalk that records have gone missing. I will discuss the alleviation of his symptoms when the herbalist comes the day after tomorrow. As to his delusions of grandeur – in my opinion, treating those is the work of many years.

Anna Calkins, Anomist

For weeks Cale lay in bed, retching and sleeping, retching and sleeping. He became aware after a few days that the door at the end of the twenty-bed ward was locked at all times, but this was both something he was used to and, in the circumstances, hardly mattered: he was not in a fit state to go anywhere. The food was adequate, the care kindly enough. He did not like sleeping in the same room as other men once again but there were only nineteen of them and they all seemed to live in their own nightmares and were not concerned with him. He was able to stay quiet and endure.

# 2

The Two Trevors, Lugavoy and Kovtun, had spent a frustrating week in Spanish Leeds trying to discover a way of getting to Thomas Cale. They had been thwarted by the cautious nature of the enquiries forced on them in Kitty the Hare's city (as it had now become). It didn't do to upset Kitty and they didn't want him to know what they were up to. Kitty liked a bung, and the amount of money he'd expect for allowing them to operate in his dominion was not something they were keen to pay: this was to be their last job and they had no intention of sharing the rewards with Kitty the Hare. Questions had to be discreet, which is not easy when fear is usually what you do, when threats are your legal tender. The two were considering more brutal methods when discretion finally paid off. They heard of a young seamstress in the town who had been encouraging a better class of client to come to her by boasting, truthfully, that she had made the elegant suit worn by Thomas Cale at his notoriously bad-tempered appearance at the royal banquet held in honour of Arbell Materazzi and her husband, Conn.

Who knows what helpful information Cale might have let slip while he was having his inside leg measured? Tailors were almost as good a source of information as priests, and easier to manipulate – the tailors' immortal souls were not at risk for blabbing a bit of dropped gossip; there was no such thing as the silence of the changing room. But the young seamstress was not as easily menaced as they'd hoped.

'I don't know anything about Thomas Cale, and I wouldn't tell you if I did. Go away.'

This response meant that one of two things was going to happen. Trevor Kovtun had by now resigned himself to committing an atrocity of some kind, Kitty the Hare or not. He locked the shop door and brought down the shutter on the open window. The seamstress didn't waste her time telling them to stop. They lowered their voices as they worked.

'I'm fed up with what we have to do to this girl,' said Trevor Lugavoy. This was both true and a way of frightening her. 'I really do want this to be our last job.'

'Don't say that. If you say it's our last then something will go wrong.'

'You mean,' said Lugavoy, 'some supernatural power is listening and will thwart our presumption?'

'It doesn't do any harm to act as if there were a God sometimes. Don't tempt providence.'

Trevor Kovtun walked over to the seamstress, who had by now realized something dreadful had come into her life.

'You seem to be a clever little thing – your own shop, a sharp tongue in your head.'

'I'll call the Badiel.'

'Too late for that now, my dear. There are no Badiels in the world we're about to take you to – no defenders or preservers, no one at all to watch over you. Here in the city you believed you were safe, by and large – but being an intelligent girl you must have known there were horrible things out there.'

'We *are* those horrible things.'

'Yes, we are. We are bad news.'

'Very bad news.'

'Will you hurt him?' she said – looking for a way out.

'We will kill him,' said Trevor Kovtun. 'But we've given our word to do it as quickly as we can. There will be no cruelty, just the death. You must make a decision about yourself – live or die.'

But what decision was there?

Later, on leaving the shop, Kovtun pointed out that even a year earlier they would have killed the girl in such an unspeakably vile way that any question of resistance to their investigations would have evaporated like the summer drizzle on the great salt flats of Utah.

'But that was a year ago,' said Trevor Lugavoy. 'Besides, I've a feeling we're running out of deaths. Best be thrifty. Cale should be our last ticket.'

'You've been saying we should stop almost since we started twenty years ago.'

'Now I mean it.'

'Well, you shouldn't have said anything to me about finishing until we were done – then we could just have finished. Now that you've made a thing about this being our last job you've turned it into an event, so. If you want to get God's attention, tell him your plans.'

'If there was a God who was interested in sticking his nose in, don't you think he'd have put a stop to us by now? Either God intervenes in the lives of men or he doesn't. There's no halfway.'

'How do you know? His ends might be mysterious.'

They were experienced men and used to difficulties and they were not especially surprised to discover that Cale had gone somewhere else for reasons the girl was unclear about. But they had the name of Vague Henri, a good description of a boy with a scar on his face, and a convincing assurance that he'd know exactly where Cale had gone. Three days of hanging about followed, asking their unsuspicious questions and trying not to be conspicuous. In the end, patience was all that was required.

Vague Henri liked people but not the kind of people who lived in palaces. It wasn't that he hadn't made an effort. At one banquet at which he'd accompanied IdrisPukke he'd been asked, with a polite lack of attention, how he'd come to be there. Thinking they were interested in his extraordinary experiences he told them, starting with his life in the Sanctuary. But the details of the strange privations of the place did not fascinate, they repelled. Only IdrisPukke overheard the chinless wonder who said, 'My God, the people they're letting in these days.' But the next remark was heard by Vague Henri as well. He'd mentioned something about working in the kitchens in Memphis and some exquisite, intending to be overheard, drawled: '*How banal!*' Vague Henri caught the tone of contempt but couldn't be sure – he didn't know what it meant, perhaps it was an expression of sympathy and he'd misunderstood. Deciding it was time to leave, IdrisPukke claimed he was feeling unwell.

'What does barn owl mean?' asked Vague Henri on the way home. IdrisPukke was reluctant to hurt his feelings but the boy needed to know what the score was with these people.

'It means commonplace – beneath the interest of a cultured person. He was a drawler: it's pronounced *ban-al.*'

'He wasn't being nice, then?'

'No.'

He didn't say anything for a minute.

'I prefer barn owl,' he said at last. But it stung.

Most of the time IdrisPukke was away on business for his brother and so Vague Henri was lonely. He now realized he wasn't acceptable to Spanish Leeds society, not even its lower rungs (who were, if anything, even more snobbish than their betters), so several times a week he took a walk to the local beer cellars and sat in a corner, sometimes striking up a conversation but mostly just eating and drinking and listening to other people enjoying themselves. He was too used to wearing a cassock to be comfortable in anything else and, like Cale, had got the seamstress to run him up a couple in blue birdseye: twelve ounce, peaked lapel and felted pockets, straight, no bezel. He was quite the dandy. But in Spanish Leeds, a fifteen-year-old in a cassock with a fresh scar on his cheek was hard to miss. The Two Trevors watched Vague Henri from the other side of the snug as he enjoyed a pint of Mad Dog, a beer he marginally preferred to Go-By-The-Wall or Lift Leg.

For the next two hours, to the irritation of the Two Trevors, he chatted away to various locals and was cornered for half an hour by an amiable drunk.

'D'yew liked metalled cheese?'

'Sorry?'

'D'yew like metalled cheese?'

'Oh,' said Vague Henri, after a pause. 'Do I like melted cheese?'

'Shwat I shed.'

But he didn't mind. There was something miraculous to him still about the talk, buzz and laughter, the ordinary good times being had by almost everyone except the occasional maudlin boozer or angry bladdered toper. At chucking-out he left with the others, the inebriated and the sober. The Two Trevors followed at a cautious distance.

These experienced men were never careless, they were as prepared for the unexpected event as if one took place daily on the backs of their hands, but their position as they closed on Vague Henri was a little more hazardous than even these careful murderers had reckoned.

Cale's reputation as an epic desperado had not so much overshadowed Vague Henri's as caught it in a general eclipse. To the Two Trevors he was dangerous, no doubt – they knew his background as a Redeemer acolyte and that you would have to be unusually hard-wearing to make it to the age of fifteen – but they were not, in truth, expecting a nasty surprise, even though nasty surprises were something they were used to.

Be clear, two against one is hideous odds, particularly when it's night and the Trevors are the two who want a word with you. But Vague Henri had already improved his chances: he knew he was being followed. They soon realized their mistake and stepped back into the shadows and called out to him.

'Vague Henri, is it?' said Trevor Lugavoy.

Vague Henri turned, letting them see the knife in his right hand and that he was easing a heartless-looking knuckle-duster onto his left.

'Never heard of him. Buzz off.'

'We just want a word.'

Vague Henri opened his mouth as if in joyous surprise and welcome. 'Thank God,' he said, 'you've come with news of my brother, Jonathan.' He moved forward. Had Lugavoy, who was ten yards in front of Kovtun, not been an assassin of a very superior kind he would have had Vague Henri's knife buried in his chest. Unluckily for Vague Henri, Lugavoy instantly backed away, alarmed by the boy's oddness as he stepped forward and struck out. The trick that had earned Vague Henri his nickname, the sudden incomprehensible question or answer intended to distract, had failed, if only just. Now they were alert and the balance in their favour once again.

'We want to talk to Thomas Cale.'

'Never heard of him, either.'

Vague Henri backed away. The Two Trevors moved apart and then forward – Lugavoy would make the first jab, Kovtun the second. There would be no more than four.

'Where is he, your friend?'

'No idea what you're talking about, mate.'

'Just tell us and we're on our way.'

'Come a bit closer and I'll whisper it in your ear.'

They wouldn't have killed him right away, of course. The knife driven in three inches deep just above the lowest rib would have taken the fight out of the boy long enough to get some answers. Never before in his life and only once afterwards was Vague Henri rescued – but tonight he was. In the almost silence of the trio's scuffling manoeuvres there was a loud CLICK! from behind the two advancing men. All three knew the sound of the latch of an overstrung crossbow.

'Hello, Trevors,' said a cheerful voice from somewhere in the dark.

There was a moment's silence.

'That you, Cadbury?'

'Oh, indeed it is, Trevor.'

'You wouldn't shoot a man in the back.'

'Oh, indeed I would.'

But this wasn't quite the rescue in the nick of time so loved by magsmen and yarn-spinners and their gullible audiences. In fact, Cadbury had no idea who the young person in the peculiar clothes was. For all he knew, he might entirely deserve the fate the Two Trevors were about to hand out to him – the people they were paid to murder usually did. He had not been watching over him but, only in a manner of speaking, the Two Trevors.

They'd had a change of heart about Kitty after talking to

the seamstress; it was no longer plausible to imagine he wouldn't become aware of their presence. So they'd observed the proper form by paying him a visit and, while declining to say what their business was in Spanish Leeds, assured Kitty that it would not conflict with his own. As he pointed out to Cadbury later, who were these pair of murderers to know what did or did not conflict with Kitty the Hare's multitude of concerns? Kitty invited them to stay as long as they wished. The Two Trevors replied that they would almost certainly be gone by the following Monday. The result was that, at considerable expense and some difficulty, Cadbury had been keeping tabs on them, not the easiest of things to do. The reason he was here in person was that his watchful intelligencers had lost them for several hours and Cadbury had become nervous.

'What now?' said Trevor Lugavoy.

'Now? Now you buzz off like the young man said. And I mean out of Spanish Leeds. Go on a pilgrimage to beg forgiveness for your shitload of sins. I hear Lourdes is particularly horrible at this time of year.'

And that was that. The Two Trevors moved to the wall opposite Vague Henri, but before they merged with the dark, Lugavoy nodded towards him. 'See you.'

'Lucky for you, old man,' said Vague Henri, 'that he came when he did.' Then they were gone.

'This way,' said Cadbury. As Vague Henri stepped behind him he let go of the overstrung bow and with an enormous TWANG! the bolt shot into the blackness, bouncing between the narrow walls in a criss-cross series of pings. As Vague Henri and his not-exactly rescuer put on some speed down the road, a mildly offended distant voice called out to them, 'You want to be careful, Cadbury, you could've had someone's eye out.'

It was unfortunate that Cadbury and Vague Henri met under such circumstances. The latter was no fool and was getting less foolish all the time – but if someone saves your life only the most disciplined could fail to be grateful. And he was, after all, still just a boy.

Cadbury's offer to stay with him for the evening was well taken and Vague Henri very much needed the several drinks he was offered on top of the ones he'd had already. No surprise then that he told Cadbury a great deal more than he should have. Cadbury was, when not murdering or carrying out doubtful business on behalf of Kitty the Hare, an amiable and entertaining presence, and as capable and desiring of affection and friendship as anyone else. In short, he quickly developed a fondness for Vague Henri, and not one like that of IdrisPukke's for Cale that was particularly difficult to understand. It even had the mark of true friendship, if by that one means the willingness of friends to put aside their own interests for the other's. Cadbury decided it might be better if Vague Henri were not drawn to Kitty the Hare's attention in any more distinctive way than he already had been (as an unimportant familiar of Thomas Cale). Kitty was skilled at not letting you become aware of what he knew or did not know.

'They are *hoi oligoi* of assassins,' Cadbury replied to Vague Henri's questions. 'The Two Trevors cut down William the Silent in broad daylight, surrounded by a hundred bodyguards; they poisoned the lampreys of Cleopatra even though she had three tasters. When he heard what they'd done to her, the Great Snopes was so afraid that he ate nothing he hadn't picked himself – but one night they smeared all the apples in his orchard using a strange device they made themselves. They leave no survivors. Whoever it is that Cale has upset, they have money and a great deal of it.'

'I'd better disappear.'

'Well, if you can vanish into thin air then by all means do so. But if you can't evaporate you're better off where you are. Not even the Two Trevors will ignore Kitty the Hare's instruction to stay away from Spanish Leeds.'

'I thought they could get to anyone?'

'So they can. But Kitty isn't just anyone. Besides, no one has paid them for such a risk. They'll look for another way. Just stay out of sight for the next week, until I can say for certain that they've gone.'

# 3

It was mid-morning and Cale was waiting to go mad again. It was a sensation something like the uneasy feeling before a chunder heaves out the poisons of a toxic meal; the sense of a horrible, almost living creature gaining strength in the bowels. It must come but it will take its time, not yours, and the waiting is worse than the spewing up. A juggernaut was on its way, passengered by devils: Legion, Pyro, Martini, Leonard, Nanny Powler and Burnt Jarl, all of them gibbering and shrieking in Cale's poor tum.

Face to the wall, knees to his chest, waiting for it to be over with, he felt a hefty shove in the back. He turned.

'You're in my bed.'

The speaker was a tall young man who looked as if his clothes were filled not by flesh but large ill-shapen potatoes. For all his lumpiness there was real power here.

'What?'

'You're in my bed. Get out.'

'This is my bed. I've had it for weeks.'

'But I want it. So now it's mine. Understand?'

Indeed, Cale did understand. The days of invincibility were over for the foreseeable future. He picked up his few possessions, put them in his sack, went over to a free corner and had his attack of the conniptions as quietly as he could.

In Spanish Leeds, Vague Henri was on his way back to his room in the castle, protected as far as the gate by four of Cadbury's stooges, and with a promise of financial help from his new friend in the matter of the Purgators. Vague Henri detested all one hundred and fifty of these former Redeemers who Cale had saved from Brzca's knife – for the simple reason that they were still Redeemers as far as he was concerned. But they were valuable because they would now follow Cale anywhere, under the entirely mistaken belief that he was their great leader and as devoted to them as they were to him. Cale had used them to fight his way across the Swiss border, intending to desert them as soon as he and Vague Henri were safe. But Cale soon realized that controlling so many trained soldiers willing to die for him would be extremely useful in the violent times ahead, however much he loathed their presence. There was one weakness in Cale's plan: how to pay the ruinous amount of money it cost to keep so many in idleness until the expected war started – which, of course, it might not. With Cale gone, Vague Henri desperately needed money for himself and for the keep of the Purgators. He also needed a friend and he had found both in Cadbury, who thought it useful to have someone indebted to him who could draw on such a resource in these uncertain times. It was clear that Vague Henri was unwilling to discuss Cale's whereabouts and would only say that he was ill but would be back in a few months. Cadbury was too smart to raise Vague Henri's suspicions by pressing him. Instead of asking questions he offered help – a winning strategy in all circumstances.

Now Kitty had an influence over someone who knew and understood the Purgators and who possessed information about the whereabouts of Thomas Cale. This information might become important in due course and now he knew where to get it should this prove necessary. Kitty the Hare was a person of intelligence but also considerable instinct. When it came to Cale, he shared Bosco's belief in his remarkable possibilities, if not their supernatural origin; but news of Cale's illness, however vague, meant that Kitty's plans for him might have to be revised. On the other hand, they might not. It would depend on what kind of sickness was at issue. Desperate and dangerous times were coming and Kitty the Hare needed to prepare for them. The potential usefulness of Thomas Cale was too great to let the question of his current ill-health entirely diminish Kitty's interest in what became of him.

A thumb on every scale and a finger in every pie was Kitty's reputation, but these days most of his concentration was on what was being weighed and cooked in Leeds Castle, the great keep that scraped the skies above the city. Its fame for not having required a defence in over four hundred years was now threatened, and King Zog of Switzerland and Albania had arrived to discuss its defence with his chancellor, Bose Ikard, a man he disliked (his great-grandfather had been in trade) but knew he could not do without. It was said of Zog that he was wise about everything except anything of importance – a worse insult than it appeared, in that his wisdom was confined to skill at setting his favourites against one another, reneging on promises and a talent for taking bribes through his minions. If they were caught, however, he made such a show of punishing them and expressing complete outrage at their crimes that he was generally more renowned for his honesty than otherwise.

All the posh with power, the who whom, the nobs who had gathered in Leeds Castle to discuss the possibility of staying out of the coming war were anxious to become favourites, if they were not already, and to stay that way if they were. Nevertheless, there were many who disliked Zog on a matter of principle. They were particularly agitated at the great gathering because on his way to Leeds he had stuck his royal nose into a village council inquiry (he was a relentless busybody in minor affairs of state) regarding an accusation that a recently arrived refugee from the war was, in fact, a Redeemer spy. Convinced of the man's guilt, Zog had stopped the proceedings and ordered his execution. This upset many of the great and good because it brought home to them the fragile nature of the laws that protected them: if, as one of them said, a man can be hanged before he has been tried, how long before a man can be hanged before he has offended? Besides, even if he were guilty it was obviously foolish to upset the Redeemers by hanging one of them while there was still, they hoped, a chance of peace. His actions were both illegal and thoughtlessly provocative.

Zog was of a fearful disposition and the news from his informers that a notorious pair of assassins had been seen in the city had unnerved him to the extent that he had come into the great meeting hall wearing a jacket reinforced with a leather lining as protection against a knife attack. It was said that his fear of knives came from the fact that his mother's lover had been stabbed in her presence while she was pregnant with Zog, which was also the reason for his bandy legs. This particular weakness also caused him to lean on the shoulders of his chief favourite, at that time the much despised Lord Harwood.

There were perhaps fifty *hoi oligoi* of Swiss society present, most of them beaming with witless subservience as is the way of people in the presence of royalty. The remainder looked at their monarch with much loathing and distrust as he shuffled down the aisle of the great hall, leaning on Harwood, with his left hand fiddling around near his favourite's groin, a habit that increased in intensity whenever he was nervous. Zog's tongue was too large for his mouth, which made him an appallingly messy eater according to IdrisPukke, who had in better times dined with him often. Careless of changing his clothes, you could tell what meals he had golloped in the previous seven days, said IdrisPukke, from looking closely at the front of his shirt.

After much royal faffing about, Bose Ikard began a forty-minute address in which he set out the present situation regarding the intentions of the Redeemers, concluding that while the possibility of war was not to be discounted, there were strong reasons to believe that Swiss neutrality could be maintained. Then, like a magician producing not merely a rabbit but a giraffe out of a hat, he took a piece of paper from his inside pocket and waved it before the meeting. 'Two days ago I met with Pope Bosco himself, just ten miles from our border, and here is a paper which bears his name upon it as well as mine.' There was a gasp and even a single cheer of anticipation. But on the faces of Vipond and IdrisPukke there was only dismay. 'I would like to read it to you. "We, the Pontiff of the true faithful, and Chancellor of all the Swiss by consent of the King of Switzerland, are agreed in recognizing that peace between us is of the first importance."' There was a loud burst of applause, some of it spontaneous. '"And . . ."' more applause, '"and that we are agreed never to go to war with one another again."'

Cheers of high relief rang up to the roof and echoed back. 'Hear, hear!' someone shouted. 'Hear, hear!'

'"We are resolved that discussion and dialogue will be the means we shall use to deal with any outstanding questions that concern our two countries and to resolve all possible sources of difference in order to maintain the peace."'

There were hip hip hoorays for Chancellor Ikard and a chorus of 'For He's a Jolly Good Fellow' all round.

During the commotion, IdrisPukke was able to mutter in Vipond's ear. 'You must say something.'

'Now is not the time,' replied Vipond.

'There won't be another. Stall it.'

Vipond stood up.

'I am prepared to say without any hesitation or doubt that Pope Bosco has another paper,' said Vipond. 'And in this paper he sets out the general scheme for the attack on Switzerland and the destruction of its king.'

There was the distinctive murmur of people who had heard something they didn't care for.

'We are negotiating acceptable peace terms,' said Bose Ikard, 'with an enemy we know to be violent and well prepared. It would be astonishing only if Pope Bosco did not have such a plan.'

The murmur was now one of sophisticated approval: it was reassuring to have a man negotiating for peace who was such a cool realist. Such a man would not have his pocket picked by wishful thinking. Later, as the meeting came to an end and the conference filed out, mulling over what they'd heard, King Zog turned to his chancellor. Ikard was hoping, with good reason, to be complimented for dealing so skilfully with an opponent like Lord Vipond.

'Who,' said Zog, tongue aflutter in his mouth, 'was that striking young man standing behind Vipond?'

'Oh.' A pause. 'That was Conn Materazzi, husband of the Duchess Arbell.'

'Really?' said Zog, breathless. 'And what kind of Materazzi is he?' By this he meant was he one of the clan in general or of the direct line of descent from William Materazzi, known as the Conqueror or the Bastard, depending on whether he had taken your property or given it to you.

'He is a direct descendent, I believe.'

There was a wet sigh of satisfaction from Zog. From Lord Harwood there was a thunderous look of resentment. The royal favourite, who signed his letters to the King as 'Davy, Your Majesty's most humble slave and dog', now had a rival.

An equerry, somewhat hesitant, sidled up to the King. 'Your Majesty, the people are raising a clamour to see you at the great balcony.' This impressive platform, known as El Balcon de los Sicofantes, had been built two hundred years before to show off King Henry 11's much adored Spanish bride. It looked out over a vast mall on which more than two hundred thousand could gather to praise the monarch.

Zog sighed. 'The people will never be satisfied until I take down my trousers and show them my arse.'

He walked off towards the great window and the balcony beyond, calling out to Bose Ikard casually, 'Tell the young Materazzi to come and see me.'

'It would send a wrong signal to many, including Pope Bosco, if you were to see Duchess Arbell personally.'

King Zog of Switzerland and Albania stopped and turned to his chancellor. 'Indeed it would be a mistake. But you are not to teach me to suck eggs, my little dog. Who said anything about seeing Arbell Materazzi?'

Conn had barely returned to his wife's apartments when Zog's most important flunky, Lord Keeper St John Fawsley, arrived to command him to attend the King in two days' time at three o'clock in the afternoon. The Lord Keeper was known to the older princes and princesses as Lord Creepsley On All Fawsley – like royalty everywhere, they demanded servility and also despised it. It was said that on hearing his nickname Lord St John was beside himself with delight at the attention.

'What was that about?' wondered a baffled Conn after

he'd left. 'The King kept looking in my direction and rolling his eyes at me with such distaste I almost got up to leave. Now he wants to have an audience with me on my own. I'll refuse unless he invites Arbell.'

'No, you won't,' said Vipond. 'You'll go and you'll like it. See what he wants.'

'I'd have thought that was obvious. Did you see him fidgeting about in Harwood's groin? I could barely bring myself to look.'

'Don't fash yourself, my Lord,' said IdrisPukke. 'The King was badly frightened in the womb and as a result he is a very singular prince. But if he's mad about you then it's the best news we've had in a long time.'

'What do you mean – mad about me?'

'You know,' taunted IdrisPukke, 'if he looks on you with extreme favour.'

'Don't listen to him,' said Vipond. 'The King is eccentric, or at any rate, given that he is a king, we've all agreed to call it nothing more. Except for a certain over-familiarity with your person you've nothing to worry about. You'll just have to put up with his strangeness for the reasons my brother has referred to.'

'I thought I wasn't supposed to listen to IdrisPukke?'

'Then listen to me. This is a chance for you to do all of us a great deal of good. God knows we need it.'

Arbell, still plump but pale after the birth of her son, reached up from her couch and took Conn's hand. 'See what he wants, my dear, and I know you'll use your good judgement.'

*'"Where have you come from boy?"*
*He looked at her again.*
*"From hell, to take you away in the night and eat you."'*

Paul Hoffman's Left Hand of God trilogy reaches into the darkest recesses of mankind, to the Sanctuary of the Redeemers, where Thomas Cale is groomed to kill, outwit, save or betray those who cross his path. He is the Left Hand of God – the Angel of Death – and he is put in charge of an army to bring about the last four things.

## DEATH    JUDGEMENT    HEAVEN    HELL

Until one day, the opening of a door shows him an act so terrible he must leave, and now he is running from his destiny and the truth of his making. Hunted by the very man who made him the Angel of Death, his final judgement is coming.

'Breathless chases, duels, ambushes, kidnap and damsels in distress. It has tremendous momentum' *Daily Telegraph*

'A dark and wildly imaginative story, well told and packed with hair-raising twists' *The Times*

'Brilliant. Funny, violent and intriguing' Charlie Higson

'Gripped me from the first chapter and dropped me days later, dazed and grinning' Conn Iggulden

'A cult classic' *Daily Express*

# He just wanted a decent book to read ...

Not too much to ask, is it? It was in 1935 when Allen Lane, Managing Director of Bodley Head Publishers, stood on a platform at Exeter railway station looking for something good to read on his journey back to London. His choice was limited to popular magazines and poor-quality paperbacks – the same choice faced every day by the vast majority of readers, few of whom could afford hardbacks. Lane's disappointment and subsequent anger at the range of books generally available led him to found a company – and change the world.

*'We believed in the existence in this country of a vast reading public for intelligent books at a low price, and staked everything on it'*
**Sir Allen Lane, 1902–1970, founder of Penguin Books**

The quality paperback had arrived – and not just in bookshops. Lane was adamant that his Penguins should appear in chain stores and tobacconists, and should cost no more than a packet of cigarettes.

Reading habits (and cigarette prices) have changed since 1935, but Penguin still believes in publishing the best books for everybody to enjoy. We still believe that good design costs no more than bad design, and we still believe that quality books published passionately and responsibly make the world a better place.

So wherever you see the little bird – whether it's on a piece of prize-winning literary fiction or a celebrity autobiography, political tour de force or historical masterpiece, a serial-killer thriller, reference book, world classic or a piece of pure escapism – you can bet that it represents the very best that the genre has to offer.

**Whatever you like to read – trust Penguin.**

read more
www.penguin.co.uk